Z-ROD

Part 1: Chosen Wanderers

A Celtic saga of warriors and saints

Martin C. Haworth

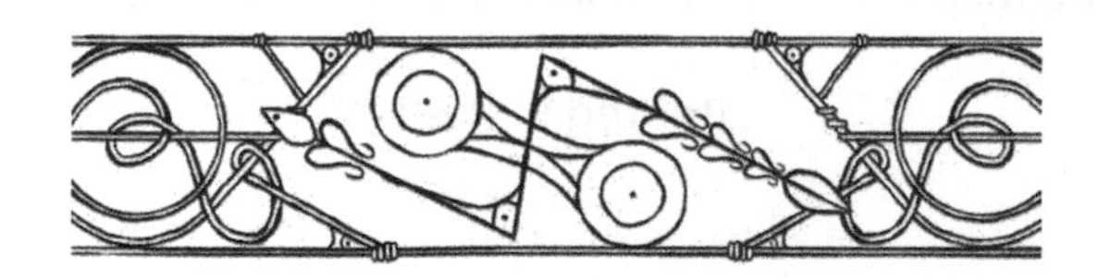

malcolm down

PUBLISHING

25 24 23 22 21 7 6 5 4 3 2 1

First published 2021 by Malcolm Down Publishing Ltd.

www.malcolmdown.co.uk

British Library Cataloguing in Publication Data
A catalogue record for this book is available from the British Library.

ISBN 978-1-912863-71-6

Cover design and Celtic geometrical designs by Meg Daniels:
https://www.bergamotbrown.com/

The map and Pictish images are drawn by the author.

Printed in the UK

Endorsements

"The Bible shows the power of wrapping the most profound truths in a story. Martin, through that technique, has provided us with a historical novel that reminds us what can happen when Christians marry the words of their message with the demonstration of the power of the Holy Spirit, in lives marked by hospitable, servant-hearted love. Perhaps it will help you, as it helped me, to reconsider how we can shine like stars in our own dark and confusing times, bearing witness to the Light of the World."

Rev. Kenny Borthwick, Church of Scotland Minister and former leader of "C.L.A.N. Gathering" and "New Wine, Scotland"

"This is an interesting read; vivid, engaging and compelling. I found I engaged with some of the characters and felt it was relevant and thought-provoking with a surprising ring of truth and immediacy."

Andy Raine, Northumbria Community

Contents

Map of 'Scotland' in the mid-6th century AD

Some historians suggest around 7 Pictish tribal groupings but are not always in agreement with the location of their territories with regard to the Fortriu, Fotla and Fidach groups. I have avoided delineating boundaries, opting instead to suggest that the borders these early people probably recognised, followed significant topographical features like rivers, firths, hills and glens. For example, the Rivers Spey, Dee and Tay, the Firth of Forth, and the 'Great Glen' probably defined boundaries. Mountainous barriers formed a buffer between peoples, like the 'Druim Alban' separated Dal Riata from Strath Clud, and the Pictish tribes of the Fotla and the Fortriu. Another mountainous region, 'The Mounth', provided a natural barrier between the Pictish tribes in the central part of the Highlands.

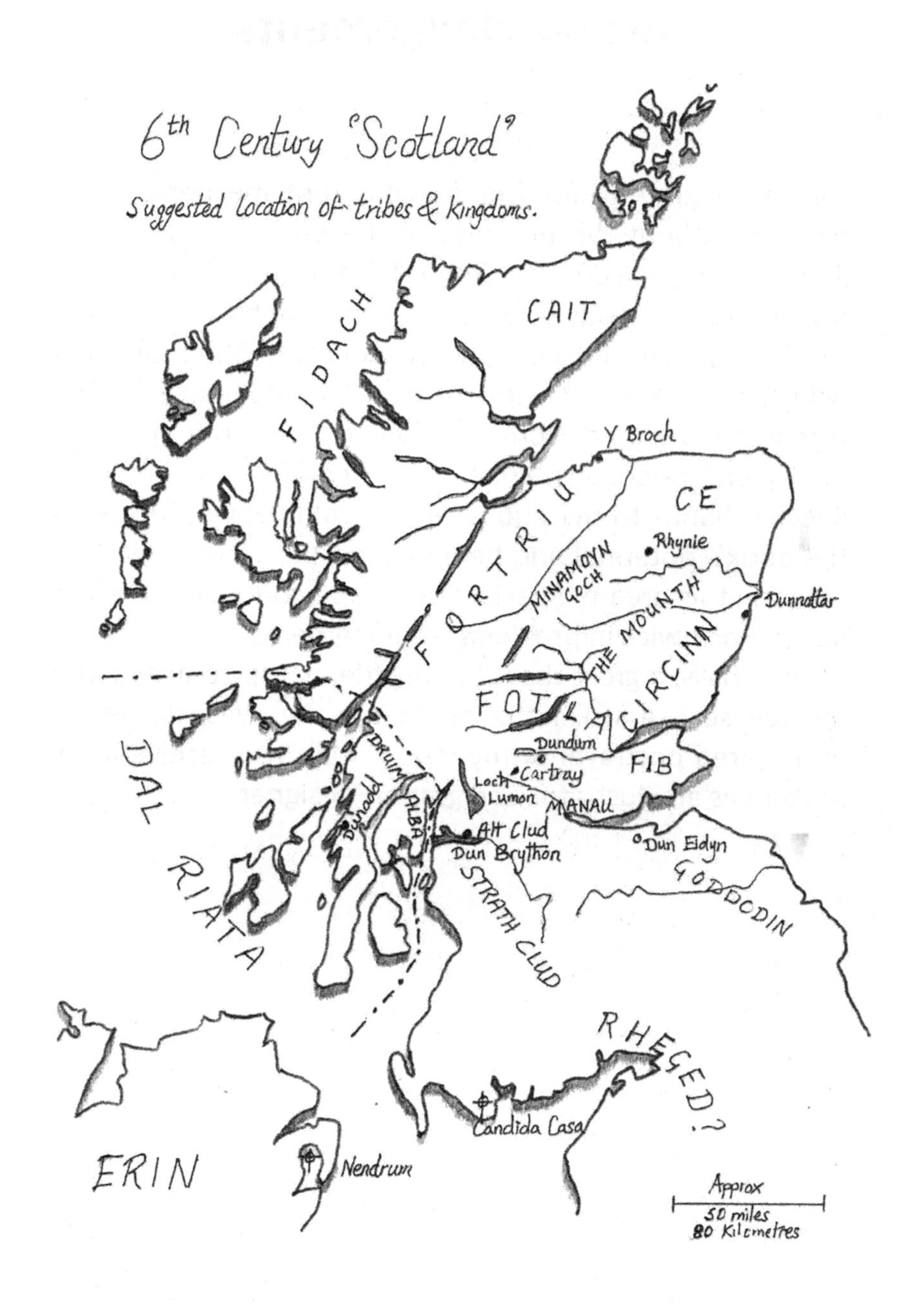
6th Century 'Scotland'
Suggested location of tribes & kingdoms.
CAIT
FIDACH
Y Broch
FORTRIU
CE
Rhynie
MINAMOYN GOCH
THE MOUNTH
Dunnottar
CIRCINN
FOTLA
Dundurn
Cartray
FIB
Loch Lumon
MANAU
Alt Clud
Dun Brython
Dun Eidyn
GODODIN
STRATH CLUD
DRUIM ALBA
Dunadd
DAL RIATA
RHEGED?
Candida Casa
ERIN
Nendrum
Approx
50 miles
80 Kilometres

Acknowledgements

I am very grateful for friends who kept me persevering by asking about the progress of the book on its lengthy journey to publication, who did not lose faith when my confidence waivered. I am also indebted to Laurie Korchinsky, Ailie Rosie, Ailsa Hanson and Alexandra, my wife, who interacted with the text to help shape it. The text has benefitted from the constructive criticism from publishers' rejections which led to crafting a finer book. Special thanks to my publisher, Malcolm Down, in seeing the book's potential and being a pleasure to work with in realising this dream. Special thanks also to Andy Raine and Kenny Borthwick in providing endorsements.

And finally, a great thanks to my friend, Meg Daniels, who created such a striking cover before my eyes, delivering an inspired portrayal of my vision. May you receive early acclaim as an illustrator and graphic designer.

Dedication

To our grandchildren who started making their appearance into the world over the course of the five years whilst writing this saga. May you each embrace the adventurous spirit and conviction described in this book.

Also dedicated to my constant companion, Spartikades Keristophanes, (otherwise known as 'Sparkie') the inspiration for Garn in the story. Together, we made most of the adventures described in this story and in the following book, memorably the multi-day trek through the 'Minamoyn Goch' (The Cairngorms).

Introduction

In the sixth century AD, Scotland as a nation was not formed. The Picts occupied the lands north of the Forth and Clyde rivers, comprising of the Highlands, and particularly populated the eastern coastal fringes and fertile straths and glens further inland. They were divided by tribal loyalties into seven suggested groupings. In the time our drama is set, the Gaels of Dal Riata (corresponding roughly to modern day Argyll) populated the coastline from Kintyre in the south, to Ardnamurchan in the north, including the Inner Hebrides within this geographical delineation. From the Forth-Clyde line, south to Hadrian's Wall, were the kingdoms of Celtic Britons: Strath Clud (Strathclyde) in the west and Goddodin to the east, with possibly Rheged occupying parts in the far south. All were warrior-led societies whose ambitions produced conflicting interests and mistrust between tribes and kingdoms.

Into these pagan cultures came the Christian faith, introduced primarily by Ninian, probably around 400 AD, and then later by rugged, Irish saints who lived close to nature, aflame with a love for their King. They undertook perilous journeys to establish muintirs, Christian communities sometimes referred to as 'Colonies of Heaven', to welcome the God-fearing and those seeking refuge or healing. The historical saints, Kessog and Fillan, featured in this drama, were contemporaries, both from Cashel in Ireland. The extremely scant documented evidence does not state the two worked together, but it is a reasonable assumption that they did, at least initially, in their pioneering role among the Picts in the early 6th century. Kessog is clearly linked with Luss on Loch Lomond, which provides an excellent springboard to extend Christian influence to the Pictish communities of Callander and Auchterarder to the northeast; foundations attributed to Kessog. Fillan is identified with the high status Pictish fort at Dundurn, near the eastern end of Loch Earn. Dundurn is close to what is now named St Fillans. The town's Gaelic name is 'Dun Fhaolain', meaning 'Fillan's fort'. Their faith, lived out on the wild edges, communicates afresh into today's neo-pagan culture, of God made manifest through the splendour of his creation. They conveyed an image of God as the 'High King of Heaven' who offers sanctuary amidst the upheavals of brutal times and provides a new identity transcending the enmities of linguistic, political and ethnic prejudices. This joyful and holistic faith did not separate religious expression from life; for heaven was tangible upon earth. Spiritual intuition accompanied theological knowledge, which delivered them from 'airy-fairy mysticism or spirit-numbing rationality'. [1]

This story attempts to capture the spirit of these times, deliberately keeping within the bounds of academic research and received tradition. The flesh I have added to the bare bones of the historical record, is normally more by way of educated conjecture rather than fictional fantasy. I have been keen to also reflect the practices and mindset of the Celtic saints as gleaned from accounts concerning them. The best-documented saint's life is that of Columba, written by Adomnan. Its account is so full of the miraculous that not only do most historians discount much of it,

1. *Quote from 'The Forgotten Faith' – Anthony Duncan*

but contemporary Christians feel alienated from what is described. But to strip away all supernatural occurrences would be a disservice, as we would fail to understand how Christianity appealed to, and made a profound impact on, the spiritual mindset of the Picts led by druids known for their supernatural powers. This book is an honest attempt to be true to the challenge facing those early Christian pioneers, and of how they were perceived by the druids, warlords and the rest of pagan society. I have intentionally avoided daubing all pagan belief as dark, for within it there are honest strivings and expressions that without Christian illumination, attempted to make sense of their world, recognising a dependence upon higher powers to be venerated. Neither did these Christian pioneers ignore indigenous beliefs, but sensitively recognised right spiritual aspirations, made helpful connections with their prophectic expectations, and were committed to liberating them from their fears and evil forces.

Ask yourselves, how did a proud, warrior people reject the old traditions and embrace a new religion, if it were not for the signs and wonders accompanying the Christian message? The book of Acts testifies to the same phenomena of proclamation and the miraculous going hand in hand, persuading people to find faith in Christ. Are not similar accounts reported from the mission frontiers in our own age, when the Kingdom of God impacts a pagan world peopled by fickle deities and evil spirits? This will challenge the theological understanding of those who say the acts of the Holy Spirit ceased with the first apostles.

Some may feel affronted by the pagan practices recorded in such detail in this drama. These are to highlight both the challenge and the opportunity facing the Christian pioneers. Pagan beliefs were not avoided by the early

Christians out of fear of the dark side, for they believed implicitly in the supremacy of Christ disarming satanic powers; nor did they condemn such beliefs as irrelevant or foolish folk superstitions, for they witnessed the suffering of those held under such capricious powers. My intention is to give credit to their largely unknown and unsung example of courage and steadfastness under the threat of brutality and wizardry, who are deserving of our curiosity, understanding and respect.

Regarding the enigmatic Pictish symbols found on standing stones, which feature large in this story. There are many theories about what these symbols may represent, from a coded form of language to personal insignia, denoting marker boundaries of land ownership. These rather facile contemporary views more reflect our own society's rejection of formalised religion than give credence to the spiritual beliefs held by ancient societies. I believe the clue to the likely significance of these symbols is the fact that the Christian cross is frequently depicted on the reverse side of these symbol stones. Does that not suggest that the stones were meeting places where people gathered to observe rites led by their druids? We also know that early Christians took over the places used in pagan worship, presenting Christ as their liberator and fulfillment. I have used artistic licence in attributing the Z-rod symbol as a power sign reserved exclusively for the warlord. However, in explaining the significance of other symbols, I have plausibly connected some with features known from their folk tales and beliefs and reasoned out their spiritual significance as might have been expounded by learned druids.

A brief word about the Pictish language. Pictish only survives in some placenames and people's names in a few surviving medieval chronicles. Scholars debate whether

Pictish was allied to Brittonic (Old Welsh), Irish Gaelic, or a non-Indo-European language. Based on the evidence of some place names, I have opted for the Brittonic link. So, for the sake of authenticity, I have attempted to use a phonetic rendering of Welsh for proper nouns to refer to pre-Gaelic placenames and deities. Please see the appendix for individual explanations of these.

The appendix will assist with the understanding of unfamiliar terms, pagan deities and festivals as well as locating ancient placenames. In the aim to be authentic to a pre-Gaelic speech, it will also explain why some spellings will sometimes look unfamiliar.

Royal Line of the Ce

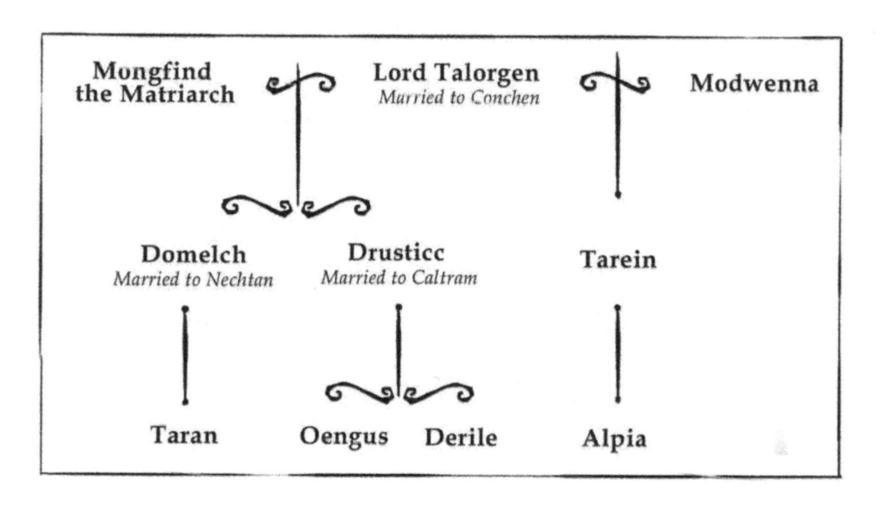

The Ossian Prophecy

Make great haste when you leave. Be cunning, be brave, be humble. Your surrender will be in the south; your transformation in the isles of the west; your fulfilment coincides with the anticipation of the learned ones far to the north, before you return east with great peace. Before that peace blossoms, there will come much strife, like a blight threatening to consume. Heartache and anguish lie before you. Many a journey awaits, full of ordeals that you consider will be your undoing, though these are in truth, rites of passage for your own preparation. You will be the doer of mighty deeds and the acts will be the making of the man. Take heart, my son, through one you will overcome the world.

Chapter One

Coming of Age

555 AD Rhynie

"Brave warriors, noble women and their kin, let us all be upstanding for our warlord . . ." continued a burly man in his mid-thirties. He strode briskly along the dais where the eminent ones were seated, more out of nervous agitation than from being energetic.

Although irked by this flabby fellow elaborating his part to its most tedious degree, Alpia had longed for this day. How dull life had been in Rhynie, which although the royal seat of the Ce tribe, still felt like a stagnant backwater in the foothills of their country. Since she was six, all her male peers of noble birth had been taken and placed with foster parents in distant places, to be trained in matters of war. She reckoned it had been twelve years since they had left; today, they were returning.

Her great aunt Conchen had requested her to wait upon her and her lord. "Although the tasks are those of a servant," she had explained, "we desire one from our close family upon whom we can depend on so special an occasion. After all, Lord Talorgen would not want some peasant girl making a muddle of proceedings!"

Was she not the envy of her friends! She would have the inside view of this important homecoming and hear what was said about the two notable cousins, whom the court referred to as 'princes'.

". . . Let us demonstrate our esteemed respect for our honourable warlord, the most resplendent Lord Talorgen!" the round-faced fellow announced.

Talorgen entered through a door leading from his private quarters. Alpia observed her great uncle's wearied air, which expressed a similar disdain that she shared for the extended protocol. His long hair was thin and silver, in contrast to his long moustaches, which were luxuriantly bushy and white. About his sagging neck, he wore a thick, golden torc, finely embellished with intricate swirls and a pair of boars' heads depicted on their terminals. After briefly surveying his audience, he sat down with a sigh that was audible to Alpia.

The rotund fellow resumed. "Noble people of the Ce – are we not men to be reckoned with, able to defend our fine ancestral lands from the envy of our Circinnian neighbours? Are we not united under the wise leadership of our most excellent Lord Talorgen for thirty-two years . . . ?"

Alpia observed that the hall, which had been astir with mutterings, was now beginning to calm.

". . . In the Lord Talorgen, we see a man who observes the times well, knowing when it is right to talk, and when it is appropriate to take decisive action." Pausing for longer than expected, the spokesman shifted his weight to his other leg. Wiping his brow, he continued. "Thrice, the Circinnians have recently crossed the border of the running Dee, to plunder our cattle and spoil crops. Brothers – are we going to stand aside and let this continue?"

Three disgruntled voices raised a small commotion, making oaths of bravado.

"Quite, quite!" interjected her uncle, visibly impatient. "Do be brief and conclude."

"Which brings us to this occasion – the return of our noble youth. A happy day indeed, to welcome back those who left soft-cheeked, now returning as veritable men, our heroes of tomorrow."

This provided the cue for strong applause as the homecoming young men were ushered into the hall at the far end. Framed by the bright portal behind them, Alpia could see they were enjoying a good deal of backslapping from those close by, but was frustrated by seeing only silhouettes, unable to identify who was who.

"We especially welcome the princes: Oengus and Taran. This is a timely return to take your place in the affairs of mankind," the announcer hastily concluded. "And without further ado, I invite our most illustrious, Lord Talorgen, to address us all."

Further applause followed, which Lord Talorgen ended with a peremptory raise of his hand. He rose, tired of the protocol that other men relished, who needed to assert their importance.

"Brothers, sisters, friends – let me be brief." After the rousing tones of the announcer, Talorgen's words sounded flat, clipped with an economy. "We all know why we are here: to start the process of who will be my successor, who will put these troublesome Circinnians in their place. The coming weeks will test and find the one who is to be chosen."

A casual hand gesture indicated the youthful returnees to proceed to the dais. Alpia began to recognise features that bore some resemblance to the boys she had known years before. Knowing their parents also helped in identifying a few. All were now young men, sporting various growths of beards or moustaches, according to their ability. She craned her neck over her aunt's shoulder, searching for the princes, wondering how the cousins would present themselves. She recalled how Taran had pulled her hair once and how she had soundly kicked him. With a smile, she recollected that Taran had not pursued her.

"Oengus and Taran, come on over to me," beckoned her aunt.

The two stepped forward. Taran was the taller, with a shock of light brown hair that fell with a wave over his forehead, which lent him a carefree manner. Except for fair, wispy moustaches, he was clean-shaven. Oengus had sandy hair and wore a red beard, closely cropped. He had a bull-like girth more commonly found in men ten years his senior.

"Come here and embrace your grandmother," entreated Conchen, who beckoned them to an elderly woman sitting beside her, immobilised by palsy.

How sad, she thought, that the one who determined the legitimate bloodline for the selection of the next warlord should have been rendered speechless and teetering on the brink of extinction. Her Aunt Conchen acted as the matriarch's spokesperson.

"My, oh my, you have both grown into fine young warriors!" Conchen exclaimed, after the cousins awkwardly embraced their grandmother, who barely managed half a smile. "Come and sit beside us – we have much to talk about."

Her aunt's grey blue eyes shone with an exceptional animation. How beautiful she must have looked as a young woman, Alpia considered, standing out from her peers, most assuredly catching the eye of a young Talorgen. Her graciousness, that sets beauty apart, was a most appealing quality.

"Fine young men indeed!" remarked Talorgen, "but as for warriors, we have yet to see!" Diverted by the group of some twenty young men standing before the table, Talorgen gestured them with slight impatience. "Be seated along the step of the dais."

Illuminated by the firelight that swelled and shrank in the gloom of the timber hall, Alpia studied her uncle's features. His brow was criss-crossed by wrinkles that rarely expressed any animation these days. His profile presented what she deemed a resolute air. He was still someone to be reckoned with, certainly to fear as an adversary.

Alpia could detect the princes' admiration and respect for an old hero. Judging by the many pelts lining the floor, her uncle undoubtedly could regale them with many a hunting escapade. As for his military exploits, had these not long since reached proverbial acclaim and had become the stuff of legend? Talorgen briefly re-arranged his clothing and took up a more comfortable posture. Alpia noted the cousins' slight surprise over his slightly laboured movements.

She wondered which of these two would be their uncle's successor? Taran looked the more flamboyant, the man of charisma who could inspire others to follow by force of personality. He had a carefree, heroic aura, jauntily displayed by the way he held his jaw high. He was handsome too – not that this was a matter of consequence, she corrected herself. Oengus was intense, probably impatient of anyone he considered lesser than himself. He struck her as being ambitious, not one to be outdone. He had lively eyes that sized up people and situations.

What was it like for them, she wondered, to be returning to the wellspring of their origins? Did things appear familiar? Was life more interesting where they had come from? How fortunate, she wistfully thought, to be born a male – at least a male of noble birth, destined for a life of adventure.

Talorgen moved behind his nephews, looking upon the other youth seated before him. The hall went quiet. "It is time for all you young men to prove yourselves worthy of bearing the title of warriors of the proud Ce." Placing his hands upon his nephew's shoulders, he added, "Especially you two. The choice is not just made by man, but is determined by the gods too, and so all the usual rituals will be followed."

Perhaps due to the smoky hall, the old man coughed in a frail manner that caused evident discomfort, followed by a lengthy pause to recover his breath. Conchen gestured Alpia to fetch the drinking horn hanging from a peg on the wall. She promptly placed this in her uncle's hand. Taking a draught, he wiped his long, bushy moustaches with relish and faintly smiled, with brightening eyes, upon his two nephews to whom he passed the drinking horn. She received an empty horn from Oengus, who held her with a lingering gaze; the look of one who knew what he wanted. She felt self-conscious as she withdrew.

Conchen made a furtive gesture to fetch the fine Roman glassware. Handling these exquisitely crafted objects for the first time was a pleasure. The glass felt fragile and cold in her hands. She held one to the light, briefly admiring the fine engraving of ferns and grapes that adorned the chalice. She contemplated the sophistication of the society which made such objects and could only wonder. Into these she poured a ruby wine. She observed how Oengus and Taran seemed dazzled too by their finery. So, they were not as worldly-wise as she had thought.

"This fine glassware," explained Talorgen to the young warriors, keen not to miss this opportunity, "had been gifted me by the king of Dal Riata!" The treasures we craft, considered Alpia, are made from more robust bronze, silver and gold. Her people valued stone too, hulks of hewn stone, quarried from afar, dragged on logs and set up as vast monoliths, which they adorned with incised symbols. These artefacts would endure forever, unlike the brittle finery of cut glass that the transient Romans had introduced.

"You young men," Talorgen continued, "are to prepare a raid on our troublesome neighbours, the Circinn. This is your opportunity to exhibit what you have learned these past years. Taran and Oengus will lead you. Some of the elders, seasoned warriors that they are, will observe how you plan and execute your charge. You are to lift cattle, recovering at least as many as we have lost!

"But now, let the feasting commence!"

A spirited applause erupted from the hall.

Talorgen sat down decisively, turning his attention from the near crowd to those at his table. Alpia noted how the two cousins glanced briefly at one another, looks that conveyed a sense of excitement mixed with a little trepidation. The stakes were high. A raid to decide who was the worthier to succeed their illustrious uncle! She was in no doubt that they had longed for this day, to be reckoned as grown men to prove their war-like ability.

Food was served. The majority gathered their portions from outside the hall, where two spits of boar were ready roasted, then returned to speak noisily in small groups. Once this had been consumed with relish, people dispersed, occasioning Talorgen's intimate group to leave the table and be seated upon fur pelts around the fire in Talorgen's private quarters.

"You have come of age and certain rites need to be performed." Talorgen now lent back in deference to his wife, casting a nod towards his sister, the matriarch of the tribe, in recognition that if she could speak, this would have been her moment.

Conchen made a place for herself between the two young men on a bearskin, where she sat cross-legged, her own knees touching theirs. “We need to prepare you both for your initiation. Beltane is just two weeks away.” She placed a hand briefly on Oengus’ knee. “You are to go through the rites with Maelchon. He is the most learned in druid lore and will do things properly so that all your endeavours will be blessed. I have been most impressed by Maelchon’s assistant . . . Oh! What is the young man’s name?”

“Gest,” volunteered Alpia.

“Yes, Gest. What artistic ability! He is quite the master, and so young too! Maelchon will instruct him on what is to be tattooed on you both. Tomorrow, at first light, you are to present yourselves to Maelchon. Drink nothing stronger than water tonight, for your body to be pure at the time of its bleeding. Carry out the required oblations; mind the milk is fresh from the cow, not yesterday’s leftovers, so that Brigantia, our goddess of spring, will look with favour.”

She drew each nephew to herself in turn, hugging tenderly, chuckling with slightly audible laughter.

“So, young men,” Talorgen spoke more brightly. “What did you learn these past twelve years?”

“We have been taught to combat with swords, mounted on horse, as well as on foot,” began Oengus, keen to impart the extent of their training.

“And what about combat with spear?” interrupted Talorgen.

“Aye, that too; both the long lance as well as the shorter one that is good for wheeling round and thrusting with!” Oengus rose to his feet to demonstrate some of the actions with deftness and aggression.

“We know how to shoot skilfully with bow,” Taran took up.

"And do you know how to craft arrows and to mount feather flights?"

Hearing the joint assent of his nephews seemed to give Talorgen satisfaction that the old skills were not being overlooked to streamline their training.

There was a pause. Talorgen smiled good-humouredly.

Oengus asked, "Uncle, what was tattooed on you when you came of age?"

Talorgen sat motionless for a moment, looking slightly taken aback by the question. Then he briefly chuckled and slipped off a woven plaid wrapped about him and, removing an arm from his sheepskin waistcoat, pulled up his grey smock shirt. He turned about somewhat awkwardly, presenting his back to the young men. Oengus carefully raised the smock shirt to his uncle's shoulders and gently angled the warlord's back towards the firelight to better illumine the artistry of the tattoo designs.

An upright rectangle was tattooed between his shoulder blades, with notches and a corridor. Intersecting this at a diagonal was a large Z-rod, drawn vertically up each shoulder blade. One terminal was adorned with leaves with a flower-like motif of open petals. The other terminal depicted an unopened bud. Further down his back was a deer head looking upon a spiral. The colours had faded, and their shapes were splayed, producing a smudged effect.

"Were all these tattoos executed at the same time?" asked Oengus.

"Those on my lower back were first, at the time of my initiation. The spiral represents autumn, suggesting the disturbed waters in which the Bulàch's garment is washed; once it is white, it is hung to dry over the hills.[2] The deer represents spring, when the herd rear their young in the

2. Bulàch is the mother earth goddess.

woods and the old winter hag is resurrected as the young Brigantia. These are symbols of birth and transformation, appropriate for coming of age."

Some of the weariness had disappeared from Talorgen's tone.

"And the Z-rod crossing through the notched rectangle?" enquired Taran with keen curiosity.

"Ah! Well, that came later," Talorgen smacked his lips. "Tattooed when I was instated as warlord." Talorgen paused thoughtfully, before adding, "The meaning is hidden to you for now."

Alpia perceived a stern glint in her uncle's eye; a look that conveyed he was guardian of dark mysteries.

"But know this: these are symbols of power and authority. One of you shall bear the Z-rod once your time comes."

Alpia fetched a bowl of cheese curds and some freshly griddled oatcakes arranged on a platter, which she placed in the centre of the group. Intent to be discreet, she kept her gaze downcast. Again, she became aware of both young men watching her. Could they recognise the girl they had known twelve years previously? She had drastically changed too. Her once fair hair had considerably darkened to a copper colour, which now she wore long and braided, quite unlike her dishevelled appearance as a child. She was no longer the skinny girl who could outrun many of the lads. She had become conscious of her power to turn heads and despaired when only this was noticed concerning her person. Could she not outwit most young men with her knowledge and insight?

Bulàch is the mother earth goddess.

Despite intentions, her eye briefly met Taran's and she could not restrain a slight smile. He was the gentler of the two, ironically, for he had been the hair-puller. Conchen gestured her nephews to eat, and it was not long before only crumbs were left on the platter.

"Before you go, I have something for each of you." Talorgen rose, pulling the plaid about him. The lameness in his knees was apparent in his first steps towards the wall. By the time he reached a large woven basket that hung from a peg, he had become fully upright, regaining his noble air. He rummaged and, finding what he was searching for, produced two daggers with deer horn handles.

"Take one each. Your grandmother had these made," he looked across at his sister to acknowledge that she would be speaking now had she been able. "These were crafted by the blacksmith when the two of you were born within days of one another. They have never been used." He extracted one dagger from its scabbard and turned it admiringly in his hand. "They are good blades! The skill of the former blacksmith was considerable. Blades like these are not made anymore; the art has died with their maker. I have, of course, cleaned and oiled them, just as you would a blade you use daily." He stooped forward to exhibit the fine swirls and knots that embellished the blades.

"Some murmured whether it was wise to have such blades fashioned when you were both only days old. They questioned, what if one, or both of you, did not make it through your first year? Was it not being presumptuous?"

He clicked his tongue noisily against the roof of his mouth. "People invent all sorts of nonsense, as though your grandmother was tempting fate! Bah – that is not right thinking! Be intentional, my lads, act with purpose. But," he paused, raising a finger in the air, "we need also to respect the gods. However, I tell you though, and mark my words: the gods are most likely to respect the one who aims to be a hero."

The old man winked and slapping his thigh suddenly, exclaimed, "The gods like a hero – at least for a time!"

Conchen interjected. "Know that our times are not in our hands, but with the Bulàch. Offer her due veneration, present your sacrifices, as your grandmother made to her when you two were born. She asked for her favour, to give you health, to enable you to grow strong in limb and wise in thinking. Well, the Bulàch has answered the first request – you are both fine men. Time will tell whether she has given you the double blessing of wisdom as well!"

At this, Talorgen laughed and patted Oengus and Taran heartily as a parting farewell. The two cousins left the hall, chatting together, petting somewhat warily the hounds that rose to see them off. Their lively banter could be heard for a second outside, before it was lost in the general hubbub of townsfolk going about their daily business.

Chapter Two

An Initiation

555 AD Rhynie

Taran had been woken in the night by a goat complaining outside their hut. He had arisen reluctantly to disengage it from a thicket. His resentment turned to gladness on seeing the heavens laid bare, shining with such splendour that he could trace the opaque trail of the Milky Way from one end to the other. Now emerging from the hut at the start of a new day, he noted the night sky had turned a deep blue, and the morning star alone was all that remained of the once brilliant, star-studded night. A light ground frost gave a ghostly pallour to the village, presenting it like a faded recollection of a place he had once known well. Oengus appeared from the neighbouring hut to gather firewood from underneath the thatch.

"Are you almost ready?" enquired Oengus.

"Of course – I am waiting for you!" replied Taran curtly.

Neither had eaten, nor had their mothers returned from milking the cows.

The oatmeal, which had been left soaking night long beside the dying embers of the previous evening's fire, soon came to full form under the rekindled flame. Taran ate without appetite but, not knowing when he would next eat, he finished a large bowl. When his mother returned, she offered him a comb and a polished metal mirror, saying, "Make yourself presentable. You will be before those who are greater than kings."

He took care to train his forelocks to curl in a wave over his brow.

"You will need this!" His father handed him the dagger that Uncle Talorgen had gifted the previous day.

He looked at his father quizzically.

"Just take it – you will find out what it is for."

At the threshold, his mother gave him a bowl of milk. Taking a couple of paces outside, he turned to the north to face a bold and steep hill standing particularly clear under the solid white of a hard frost. He knew the hill was sacred, having been formed, as the old people said, by the Bulàch herself: the shaper of the landscape. It strongly resembled a recumbent woman, with its high rounded top known as the 'Pap of the Bulàch'. Raising the wooden bowl in a reverential gesture, he muttered a supplication, before cupping three fingers to scoop some milk onto the ground. He drank the remainder.

"For fruitfulness and good pasture," his mother reminded him, although it was perhaps said by way of a blessing.

The two cousins made for the portal of the wooden palisade that encircled their village and from there took the path down the brae to the home of Maelchon beside the ford.

The druid was at his door and greeted them with a perceptible nod. Adjusting a rabbit skin cap on his bald head, he disappeared briefly indoors, and re-emerged with a smouldering brazier suspended from a short pole over one shoulder, counter-balanced by a woven basket at the other end.

"Good morning to you sir!" Taran greeted the druid.

Maelchon merely grunted, avoiding eye contact.

Oengus passed him a meaningful look, noting the druid's taciturn nature. They followed him upstream to Gest's home, Maelchon's celebrated assistant and wondrous worker of tattoos. Gest raised his head in a warm-hearted gesture. Lifting the lid to a woven basket, he made a final check that he had what was required. Slinging the basket over his left shoulder was taken by Maelchon as the sign to start for the hill.

Gest was of an age with himself and was talkative. "My home is a good day's ride from this place, where the Deveron River spills out into the sea. Do you know it? Oh, it is a wonderful place for a bairn to find his feet and enjoy the world."

"We carried out a military exercise near to the Deveron once," replied Oengus, which encouraged Gest to talk more about home.

"There are all manner of creatures that swim the seas! Take dolphins. They are almost as large as a man, but can move with great speed and agility. They like our company, perhaps recognising that we humans can be playful too. Why, they have even been known to save drowning men!" He stopped to note their reaction.

Taran noticed that their smiles were received with evident relish.

"Then there are the seals . . ." he continued expansively, looking at them wide-eyed, and to Taran's amusement, he often paused for dramatic effect. On finishing his lengthy monologue, he ran his fingers through his thick curly hair, consciously changing the subject. "It is an honour though to have been called here." He paused circumspectly. "It was under your aunt's instigation – she admires artistry."

By now, they were climbing towards the summit of a lower hill to the east of their village.

"Think upon it!" Gest resumed. "There I was, a young artist, an apprentice to another druid, when suddenly I am summoned by the warlord!" He cast a meaningful glance. "Who knows, but just maybe, it was in anticipation of this very day!"

As they neared the hilltop, Taran felt the keenness of a chill wind, blown from where the sky blossomed into a warm peach hue. They emerged from woods, whose young, delicate leaves, he noted, looked shrivelled by frost and arrived at a stone circle on the hill's crown. The sun was close to emerging over the horizon.

Placing the portable brazier on the ground beside a standing stone, Maelchon blew repeatedly on the barely smouldering charcoals. The mass of ash blossomed orange. From his basket, he placed two dried sprigs of juniper on the coals, whose withered foliage soon ignited, filling the air with a bittersweet, pungent smoke.

"Strip yourselves to the waist," Maelchon ordered the two young men.

Oengus stood beside him with his burly chest braced against the chill of the wind, looking immoveable. Being of leaner build, he felt the chill of the air. They faced the heavily frosted, sacred peak and waited.

Maelchon muttered an incantation low on his voice. Taran could make out some words, but others were archaic or unintelligible, said with speed and clipped by custom. Taking hold of a flaming juniper sprig in each hand, Maelchon wafted them gently before the sacred hill, extinguishing their fire in the process. He then passed the smouldering sprays about their heads and, with long slow sweeps, traced the outlines of their upper bodies. A litany of words ensued. Noting the medicinal scent of the smoke, Taran considered that it had a cleansing effect.

The druid's gaze seemed to pass through him, a penetrating look into his soul, determining the very stuff he was made of. It felt unsettling. Maelchon did the same with Oengus.

The druid concluded his petitions with a solemn bow to the sacred hill, before turning to Gest. Taran observed him whispering instructions, which the young apprentice seemed bemused by, even to the point of wanting to question. Probably it was on account of being the novice, he thought, that Gest decided not to say anything and obediently set his woven satchel down to make the preparations.

Maelchon returned to them. "We revere that which was erected in a bygone age by our illustrious ancestors who perhaps better knew the secrets of the gods. This stone circle has eight stones and perhaps represents the eight-fold cycle of the year." Taking up his brazier, Maelchon gestured the two young men towards a stone larger than the others.

Finding Maelchon's grimness somewhat disconcerting, he felt misgivings over the kind of initiation that awaited them. Could any good portent come from such a man?

"This stone marks Yule, aligned with the place of the sun's earliest setting." Maelchon fixed them with an unsmiling gaze, perhaps trusting that solemnity forced them to listen well. "It is on the solstice when we druids keep vigil all night till sunrise, waiting to be born again, searching our souls for all that is dark or is spent; for all that is inert and impotent. It is the time to throw off anything that holds us back."

Maelchon looked Taran searchingly in the eye. "To be a leader, you would do well to do likewise. Cast off anything that impedes."

Taran noted Oengus nodding with approval. Surely, he ought to be more disciplined himself. His foster father often remarked that talent needed to be honed if it were to be best used.

"At Yule, we do not kindle from an existing fire, but from a flint, marking the fresh start. It is the point when the sun ceases to die and begins his ascendancy."

The symbolism was not lost on him as he considered the close to their uncle's rule and the new beginnings.

They moved on to the next stone, marking Imbolc, the first glimmer of spring, then to Ostara, the spring equinox. The sun lifted above the horizon with warming rays that he welcomed.

Maelchon smiled perceptibly on reaching the next stone. "This marks Beltane, celebrating fertility. This festival is almost upon us, auspicious for you both this year marking your spiritual coming of age."

They continued, completing a single revolution of the stone circle. "Our lives are a wheel moving gradually onwards. Nothing remains static: old things pass away. Living things perish, making way for the new."

The druid called Gest to join them. Turning to Oengus, he ordered, "Take hold of the stone and offer your back. Taran, wait over at the Beltane stone opposite."

Maelchon sounded a little weary, or was he slightly perturbed? As he crossed the stone circle, he could just hear the murmur of Maelchon's voice speaking with gravity. Was there a note of perplexity in his tone?

Why had his cousin been chosen first? Was it significant that Oengus held on to the Yule stone, the ending of the old and the coming of the new? Was he not worthy himself? Had he not the same birthright, had undergone the same preparation? All their youth they had done everything together, striving as much as other lads for supremacy. Playing runner up was never an option for either. If Oengus were to be the next warlord, where would that lead him? And if reversed, what would become of Oengus? These considerations unsettled him.

Perhaps, though, it was not altogether insignificant that he was to wait at the Beltane stone. The festival, marking their coming of age, surely indicated a significant transition. Beltane was about spring fertility, looking forward to summer abundance. Perceived in spiritual terms, Beltane represented the complete transformation of the Bulàch, the old hag, reborn as Brigantia, the young maiden, impregnated with the seed of Beli Mawr, the sun-god. Was that not a portentous omen?

He noted Oengus was still clasping the stone as Gest continued with his iron point and deep dyes on the exposed back. Maelchon then stooped close to Oengus and spoke a lengthy monologue. Surely, this was a prophecy or a prayer.

Exhausting his imagination at the conceivable things being prophesied, he found his mind wandering. Alpia was exquisite, so unlike the disagreeable girl known at the time of his leaving home. It was not just her beauty and comely body that made him take special note, but her slightly haughty manner, hinting of noble origins, made her beguiling. He recalled how catching her eye momentarily, she had looked at him with a hint of warmth, followed by a smile that inspired hope. Unable to rid his mind of her image, he considered how he might gain her favour.

Maelchon and Gest crossed the stone circle. Taran's skin had turned quite red, despite the warming rays of the rising sun dissolving the frost about his feet into a dew.

"You, Taran, are to have the Z-rod with viper tattooed!" The words seemed to choke in his throat. The news thrilled him, although this astounding pronouncement felt mingled with a hint of foreboding.

"I have to confess that I am perplexed!" continued Maelchon. "This symbol is always reserved for the warlord. It is unprecedented that two living in the same tribe should bear that symbol concurrently except by the warlord's consent." He scratched the back of his neck. "But I cannot oppose what the Bulàch has decreed!" He pushed his rabbit skin cap back and muttered under his breath, "Who are we to question or to oppose?"

Taran longed to speak, but knew to hold his tongue, especially with the stern Maelchon.

The druid pondered, seemingly disquietened by what had been revealed. Eventually, he spoke.

"The Z-rod means power from on high. The symbol is like lightning – instrument of Beli Mawr – who hurls his bolt onto the earth to the fear and dismay of man. At auspicious times, the lightning produces a harvest of mistletoe, most revered of all fruits, upon the oaks, the most sacred of trees. His great power bestows fruitfulness in the womb of the goddess of the earth."

Maelchon bit off a broken end of fingernail, and turning aside, spat it onto the ground. "Upon you is bestowed the means to bless and to hold authority, but . . ." Maelchon paused, pushing his rabbit skin hat even further back so that it hung precariously from the crown of his head. "I doubt that it conveys all that we would have it mean in our earthbound understanding. There is mystery here, into which even I cannot fathom or have been granted to know."

"And what is the significance of the viper?" Taran surprised himself by his forwardness in questioning the druid.

"The Z-rod is always combined with one of three symbols. We are in the season when vipers re-emerge from the earth, soon to shed their old skins. Like the old Bulàch herself, they are seen to be reborn after the winter. They are a mystery symbol of resurrection!"

Maelchon looked down into the valley, to the course of the winding stream that moved serpent-like, silvery in the sun. "Acquiring the symbol of ultimate authority, before time, is indeed a riddle, and . . ." His voice tailed off, seeming fearful to reveal more.

Taran watched him delve deep into these perplexities as he took a few slow paces to one side. Gest proceeded with the task of tattooing the symbol, something that the numbing cold enabled Taran to more easily tolerate. Maybe that had been the reason to have stripped early? Before long, though, his body started to convulse with uncontrollable shivers. Gest wiped the pinpricks of fresh blood budding on his back and took a step back to appraise the work. The artist then vigorously rubbed the exposed flesh, slapping it to stimulate the blood flow.

"You are still shivering!" remarked Gest. "You should move about vigorously before I continue."

He executed some of the warmup exercises taught prior to armed combat.

Able to proceed again, Gest set about the more intricate work of the embellishments to the ends of the Z-rod horizontals: its leaves and flowers, one set furled, the other open in full bloom.

His mind was reeling over the revelation of the Z-rod, grappling with questions to which he had no answers. Would the ambitious Oengus be humble enough to serve under his rule? All the longed-for anticipation of this day seemed now overshadowed by forebodings.

Once Gest's work was finally complete and Taran had dressed, Oengus was hailed over. The cousins exchanged enquiring looks. He observed that Oengus was looking pleased with himself. What could that mean? Maelchon's sternness, though, prevented any communication.

"Now we proceed to the centre, to the hub of this wheel," spoke Maelchon. Standing at the axis, he explained, "Take the blades you were gifted by Lord Talorgen and cut a thumb to shed blood in this place."

The cousins dripped their blood onto the sacred hub of the stone circle.

Maelchon proceeded with a prayer. "Receive the homage of blood, fresh from the vein, an offering to be united with the Mother of the Earth. Keep them from ill favour and look not on their shortcomings, but rather on their potential. May their allegiance to the one who raises up and has the power to bring down be proved strong and faithful. Encircle them with your protective favour, as this stone circle encompasses us about. May it be a covenant as steadfast and changeless as stone."

The sacred entreaty and the binding of great oaths left him feeling sick in the pit of his stomach. He looked at Oengus, whose demeanour suggested he was taking things more in his stride.

They followed the druid and Gest down the hill, crossing the water downstream from the main part of the village. Maelchon led them up a steep brae to a raised burial cairn, where he petitioned the favour of their ancestors in the things that were to come. Beyond that, Taran could not determine, for whenever Maelchon spoke words of some significance, he lowered his voice or quickened his speech, slipping back into the ancient tongue. Perhaps it is not my role to question the outworkings of fate, just to accept. Again, a deep-seated concern gnawed away.

Proceeding uphill, they arrived at the wooden palisade about their village. He felt brighter to be near home, anticipating these strange rituals to be at a close. They halted at the portal, before a standing stone, and noted for the first time how it was aligned with the burial cairn and two standing stones far off in a field beyond. The two engravings on the stone, of a salmon and a beast, were familiar objects, known from his childhood.

"Tell me the story of the salmon?" Maelchon questioned flatly.

"The salmon is perhaps one of the immortals called Fintan," began Oengus, "who swam in the well of knowledge, over which nine hazelnut trees grew. Nine hazelnuts fell into the well, which Fintan ate, and he became the wisest being in the whole world."

"And what became of the salmon?" asked Maelchon testingly.

"Well the bard, Finn Eces, spent seven years to catch the wise salmon. He gave it to his servant, Fionn, to cook, with strict instructions not to eat any of its flesh. Whilst testing whether the salmon was cooked, Fionn burnt himself, and sucking his scorched thumb, he tasted of the salmon. When he served the fish, the bard noticed the young man's eyes shining with a wisdom unseen before. Fionn became the great leader of the Fianna – the heroes of old. Whenever he needed special knowledge to lead his heroic band, he only needed to suck his thumb!"

"You remember correctly," Maelchon smiled faintly. "The salmon of knowledge reminds us of our need for the wisdom of the immortals. In venerating Fintan, such special knowledge and foresight might be granted to the warlord."

Maelchon smacked his lips audibly with a degree of satisfaction, before turning to Taran.

"So, what can you tell me about the beast?"

"The beast lives in the depths of the water, master over

everything. All other swimming things acknowledge his dominion over them. It is feared not only beneath the depths, for at times, it emerges to seize prey that walks the shore – even men! It is said to inhabit a loch in the territory of the Fortriu and is greatly feared."

Maelchon slowly nodded his head in a judicial manner. "It also represents the fears that lie beneath the surface," elaborated the druid. "Fears that can rise up and overwhelm us. Wisdom is required if we are to overcome the fear that the beast incites; hence the salmon of knowledge is pictured over the beast. When wisdom, and not fear, is our master, we shall be master indeed."

Expecting to be dismissed following this lesson, Maelchon unexpectedly led them away from the village, westward, across open ground. They ascended a low but steep hill, where two significant stones, part of another stone circle, formed a portal, framing the hill of the Pap of the Bulàch. Again, they were instructed in the ways of wisdom, preparing them for future responsibilities. They continued in a northerly direction down into a valley and, crossing its stream, climbed the flank of the Pap of the Bulàch. The slope was steep, which sapped the druid's strength. Part way up, they veered off to a spring.

"This is Brigantia's source," spoke Maelchon out of breath. He removed his rabbit skin, revealing a baldpate flush with perspiration. He fixed each in turn with an intense gaze and spoke staccato like, still recovering his breath. "Drink and be renewed . . . Be gladdened in your hearts . . . You are putting adolescence behind . . . and embracing manhood." Placing his hands upon his knees, Maelchon lent forward and remained in that posture until his breathing had regulated. Straightening himself, he said, "The former things are passing away, and now it is time to fulfil your destiny. At the end of winter, it is said that the Bulàch departs to the isle of youth and drinks from a spring. There she is transformed from an old hag, emerging as the youthful Brigantia who brings new life to the world. Through her will, the grass and leaves of spring flourish. Drink thoughtfully, as you imbibe upon this elixir, desiring that energy of transformation."

They descended to the north of Rhynie and reached two more upright stones, standing like a portal through which the hill of the Pap of the Bulàch could be partially framed. In the opposite direction, the stone circle upon the crown of the hill where they had been tattooed could also be sighted. As he had observed earlier, these two stones were also in alignment with the burial cairn and the salmon and beast stone.

"We have completed a circuit of your birthplace, where one of you is destined to rule. Pass through this portal and enter back into the community that has nurtured you. Forget not the wisdom imparted this day."

Half-turning to leave, the druid imparted a final word over his shoulder, "Tell no one about your tattoos, nor about the prophecies."

"But . . . people will ask?" objected Oengus.

"And family will see when we are undressed!"

The druid briefly considered their objections. "You would do well to keep them secret until one of you is chosen. And should anyone discover these symbols, swear them to secrecy."

Gest lingered a while after Maelchon had left. Was his verbosity an attempt to cover what Taran perceived as a certain awkwardness?

"This is all very strange!" remarked Oengus, once Gest had departed.

"I agree. What do you think – should we disclose the symbols with just one another?"

"I do not know," replied Oengus, chewing the side of his thumb. "Maybe we should first ponder, rather than be too hasty."

Chapter Three

New Arrivals

496-97 AD Erin to Dal Riata & Din Brython

Kessog looked over the muintir, reflecting on how their round cells now often contained six people, whereas when he had arrived here four years previously, sleeping four was considered ample. Had not the thirst for Christian knowledge become great throughout the land of Erin following Patrick's incandescent trail, he mused. Looking up, he saw the half-moon riding swiftly through the racing clouds, like an illustrious one executing some urgent business. Tomorrow he was to depart. The night air was damp, causing him to pull his woven plaid tightly about him. This shift of season, emerging from the lifeless winter, still felt hostile, full of unpredictable days ahead.

Nearing his hut, a voice greeted him. "Ah, Kessog, I desire to speak with you."

He recognised the Abbot Machaloi's voice, but in the darkness could only determine his shadowy features.

"I have come to bid you farewell and to pray." He paused. "I also have some letters. One is for Fergus Mac Erc, prince of men, or king – as he deigns to be addressed now – of the rising power of Dal Riata. He will make you welcome and provide quarters. The task is easier for your companions, for their tongue is the same as ours. He desires Christ's rule to be established in his kingdom."

The abbot fingered the coarse seam of his grey cloak. "But you, brother Kessog, have been set aside for a greater task – possibly an unenviable one. You are to face the stubbornness of the Men of the North." He inhaled noisily. "I have chosen the young Fillan to accompany you."

"The Fillan with the big eyes?" queried Kessog, unable to conceal his surprise.

"Aye, the eyes of an owl full of wonder!"

"But master, he is but a youth!"

"Indeed, he is barely a young man at only fourteen. Fillan will benefit from an older, steady head like yours. What he lacks in age is compensated by his years at the muintir. You know he was left as a baby by a young woman of obvious status at the entrance of the vallum over yonder. Rumour says he is an illegitimate child and his mother a princess. Anyway, that is of little importance, other than it might account for his capacity for knowledge. He is keen to go wandering for Christ, but has been held back until now on account of his age."

"This is an unusual choice for a task fraught with opposition!"

"Quite! I understand your misgivings. His life has been sheltered, knowing only the company of godly men and women. Despite his extreme youth, I sense that his time has come, that in the passing of the years, great things will eventually emanate from his dedication."

Trusting the abbot's judgement, he responded with acceptance.

"Furthermore . . ." The abbot drew out the syllables thoughtfully. "You are well into your middle years and when your heaven calling comes, it would be well to have a successor well used to the ways of the Britons. Like iron proved in the forge, Fillan will be ready to withstand the onslaught of pagandom and clasp firmly to the banner of faith."

The abbot's gaze searched him in the darkness. "I have encountered the stubbornness of the Britons of Strath Clud during my days at Lennox and it nearly had me head home on a number of occasions! Yet, young and old are called to hard places and who am I to withhold? Hardships focus our purpose, do they not? But in one so young, opposition can destroy. Look out for him; encourage him for what he can become in Christ."

"I will try with God's help. And that same counsel I shall apply to myself!"

Machaloi pulled out another short parchment roll from inside his cloak.

"This letter is for King Dyfnwal Hen of Strath Clud. His boats have plied our waters for the finery of our metalwork and jewellery – such frequent contact has made them curious about our keen faith. They would claim to be Christian," he continued with a raised pitch, "but their abominable piracy some years back would question this, shedding the blood of the newly baptised and taking the virgins of Christ away to be the slaves of barbarians." Machaloi shook his head with disgust, as though it was recent news. "Oh, some 35 years back I suppose, Patrick wrote strongly to their then king, Coroticus. Patrick showed me the letter himself and had me deliver it and it sent the king into a fit of rage. So, note well that I only said 'curious'. I do not detect the awakening that we see among our brothers in Dal Riata. However, King Dyfnwal Hen welcomes you both to become part of the court from whom you will learn their tongue."

Kessog swallowed heavily. He had grown restless of late, knowing his time at Nendrum was ending, but this information sobered his enthusiasm. "Master, there is a courage greater than my own that compels me on. I trust that it is not in blindness of spirit, but shall express itself with a valour that is ready to face hardship."

"You are a diligent disciple and have been well used to the ways of the court. I do recall your father – a most noble king – telling me about his being baptised by Patrick. He prophesied that one of his sons will lead others to Christ, and that like Patrick, would go into exile to take the light into the darkness."

Kessog warmed to this recollection. "Just before going into the river, Patrick accidentally caught my father's foot with his pastoral staff. The graze started to bleed. Thinking this was part of the baptismal rites, my father did not complain. Emerging from the river, he looked upon his bleeding foot and remarked, 'I believe I have one from my own blood, who will follow Christ across the seas.' So may it be."

"Ah yes, I do recall now your father sharing those details. You will not return defeated, I have no doubt of that."

Kessog found these affirmations comforting, especially from a veteran who had laboured in this very same kingdom.

"When you have mastered their tongue," continued Machaloi with great equanimity, "the king promises land to establish a muintir, where men may retreat from the business and allurements of this passing world and come to know the way of the true King. From this base, may God's light penetrate to other peoples, even to the godless Picts; for such is God's will that none should perish."

Kessog felt his mouth forming a faint grin. "I hear they are a proud warrior people, just like the men of Erin, but untouched, like our father's generation had once been, by the compassion of the Lord – until Patrick's coming, that is."

"I will send more brothers should this venture be blessed." The abbot nodded positively.

Kessog paused. Realising their interview was near its conclusion and that this occasion might be their last to say farewell, he cleared his throat. "I have benefitted much from your teaching, master, for you bring clarity and joy to learning where others easily make tedious. You have inspired us with your endeavours in Lennox, where faith was tested in the harsh world of political ambitions."

"It is true; the Britons did not stop short of putting even soldiers of Christ to the sword!"

"I am thankful, for I came here under a heaviness of soul, drawn like a moth to the light of Nendrum. Here, fugitives running from injustices and those of enquiring minds have found spiritual nourishment and sanctuary through your gentle, persuasive manner."

The abbot raised a hand, gesturing him to speak no more. Kessog could perceive a smile flicker briefly on Machaloi's lips, before they uttered a benediction.

Machaloi embraced him firmly. "Be strong through the challenges ahead. Do not despise anyone, but with charity, receive those Christ sends to your door. Our actions are stronger than our words. And when well received, give an answer to those who question the cause of your kindness."

Kessog bowed his head perceptibly.

Machaloi made the sign of the cross. "Now go in peace and know that the Lord is with you. It is his work; we are merely servants of his purposes. Your task is to remain faithful to God's will – that is the most and the least you are to do."

Kessog considered the few things required to prepare for his departure: mostly food provisions, a change of clothes, a razor, parchments on which he had copied some of the psalms, and a sealskin in which to wrap Machaloi's letters and the word of God. Stripping back to the bare basics had been liberating after his privileged upbringing. *'Simplicity brings genuine thankfulness for the essentials,'* had become something of his motto.

Many well-familiar faces gathered on the pier the following morning to see the pilgrims off. Fillan caught the eye of another youth, slightly older than himself, who expressed the same longing for adventure in his keen gaze as he knew in his own heart. As their boat heaved off through the turgid waters of the lough, a cheer rose from the shore, followed immediately by a psalm, started softly by a few but picked up with vigour by the many. The singing rang clear across the waters of Strangford Lough and settled on them like a benediction. The morning sunlight swept in brief intervals, eradicating the shadow from the tilled lands their boat was heading towards.

On reaching the mainland, they took a final, lingering look at the small island that had been their whole world. Their fellow monks had departed from the jetty.

Being the eldest and most eminent, Kessog brandished his staff. "Are we all ready?"

With a nodding of heads, the group moved as one, striking up a psalm, countering their unsettled emotions.

"Well, it is farewell!" spoke Fillan with a mixture of gratitude and longing to one of his peers.

"You are travelling light," remarked his companion with a twinkle in his eye. "I do not suppose you need to carry a razor like the rest of us!" He nudged him in his side.

"I know! I have the rosy complexion of an apple!" he retorted self-consciously. What could he do? His downy cheeks gave him an almost feminine look, were it not for the hair shaved from the front of his hairline and the wild manner of his long hair running halfway down his back. He dismissed the teasing, telling himself with some reassurance that he had been deemed suitable for the tougher of the two assignments. He felt ready to take on anything, an invincibility grounded in the conviction of the supremacy of his God and the energetic possibilities of his youth.

His eyes scanned the fields where the wholesome soil had been turned, harrowed and sown. Pastures abounded, all neatly walled in, where the land, from the edge of the shore to the heather on the higher ground, was utilised. Was not their tamed land a place of plenty? Marshes had been drained and now sprouted good grass to fatten cattle, gifting farmers with an abundance of milk and cheese, beef and mutton, tasting like produce no other land could possibly emulate.

He felt pangs of insecurity to be leaving his beloved land.

Much later that day, they came to a port where he was fascinated by the commerce of different worlds colliding in a noisy and greedy display. Lining the wharf, shipments awaited loading onto tethered vessels, where crates had been discharged by many hands in accordance with the foreman's shouted instructions. Merchants eyed their departing goods guardedly, giving final instructions to those entrusted with these precious cargoes.

He noted a group conversing with tall, blonde-haired strangers who, either not understanding or determining to get a higher price, pretended not to comprehend. How alien it felt to his upbringing; a stranger to the love of silver and the wheeling-dealing that accompanied it.

"It is all settled," Kessog said, returning to their group. "We are to divide into two groups and sail tomorrow at dawn. Most will sail in the wooden vessel from Gaul over there. They have enough space for nine passengers, having discharged half their cargo of wine. The remainder of us will sail in a much smaller currach."

Kessog pointed in its direction, but the craft was too small to be seen above the sides of the wharf.

"Father Kessog," asked Fillan later, when they were alone. "Why are we not taking the boat directly for Din Brython – it will save us time?"

"It is the abbot's instruction for us to go via Dal Riata." The older man leant knowingly towards him, saying in an undertone, "We might need allies to call upon in the future."

The next morning broke cloudy, with moisture on the wind.

"It is a steady north-westerly," remarked one of the sailors, curious to have a boatload of monks as passengers.

"Is that a good thing?" asked Fillan.

The sailor grimaced, looking undecided before answering, "It is not the usual prevailing wind!"

Fillan received this information with a smile. This was not a usual day for him and the rest of the pilgrims.

"It will cause us to tack to begin with," elaborated the sailor, "as we sail up the coast. However, once we change course for Dal Riata, the wind will be in our favour, promising a fast passage."

The pilgrims settled among the wine cargo of the Gaulish ship, whilst Kessog and Fillan were joined by one other in the large currach.

"Our currach looks frail alongside the sturdy ship from Gaul!" he observed, feeling the nervous anticipation mingled with an embracing sense of adventure.

"Indeed," assented Kessog. "By the will of God, we move through life and navigate its dangers."

"Sailing in the less predictable looking boat though," reflected Fillan aloud, "rightly places faith in God, does it not, rather than in a misplaced confidence in the sturdiness of a vessel?"

Kessog looked at him with a hint of surprise. Pursing his lips, he nodded in agreement. Fillan grinned broadly. The wonder of the adventure ahead, combined with the approval of this prince of priests he had been assigned to, made his future feel most agreeable.

Kessog gestured for him to share his bench in the currach and take up the heavy oar. Upon the order from the skipper, Fillan dipped the long, cumbersome oar into the sea and heaved with all his might. The currach seemed to resist their combined efforts before moving sluggishly. He beamed, considering himself a sailor now. His arms were soon complaining from the unfamiliar exercise as he worked up a sweat. Just when he felt he could pull no further, the skipper ordered the oars to be stowed and for the sail to be hoisted. He felt relieved and knew the excitement of the wind filling the sail; before long, their leather craft surged clumsily through the water, but at a speed far greater than had it been rowed. This was exhilarating and he did not even mind the dampening of the rain, which cooled him from his recent exertions. When the boat went about, waves splashed against the side of the bow that the wind caught up and hurled as spume. There was no shelter from this assault and before long he was drenched.

"Ready-about!" called the helmsman late morning. "This will be the last tack for a long while." The sail settled into a new position, billowing with a full belly on its new northeasterly course.

"Look how far ahead the others are," remarked Fillan, squinting into the disturbed greyness of the open sea. Kessog smiled indulgently.

"I do not feel well," remarked Fillan.

"Fix your eye on the horizon – that should help steady your stomach," advised Kessog.

Fillan looked at their low-lying homeland, consumed in the murkiness of poor weather. Anyone who had not been keeping their gaze so fixed on their shore would have been hard pressed to tell whether there was still land to be seen on the horizon. Fillan could just detect a thin smudge of his home coast. At this point of departure, he vomited over the side.

"Land ahead!" the skipper announced heartily, a little while later.

Fillan spun round to get his first glimpse of a thick grey line rising steeply out of the sea, ascending into dark, brooding clouds. The wild, mountainous shore of Kintyre came into growing relief, cliff girt, backed by dark, misty hills.

"What could thrive in such a waste?" questioned Fillan, somewhat unsettled. "What kind of people can endure so hostile an environment?"

The older man looked kindly upon him. "We have been called, like Abraham, to leave our country for a strange land. But consider this: do we not learn more about God through the grandeur of his creation?"

"Yes," he pronounced emphatically after a moment's reflection. He warmed to the older man, who did not seem to resent his youth but undertook his responsibilities seriously towards his novice charge. "This is truly a godly adventure," grinned Fillan, recognising the fulfilment of his dream, "leaving our homeland for the sake of Christ."

A low-lying island to their west appeared exceedingly green and fertile. He smiled approvingly at so fair an isle. Was it not like their own? Maybe God would lead them to such a place. Beyond, the mainland coast became riven with drowned valleys running so far inland into the hills that their loch heads were out of sight. Later, to their west, a great island reared out of the water like an enormous beast with three huge, grey heads.

The late afternoon light broke through the sky's mantle and, sweeping the coast, suddenly highlighted a fantastically bright and pristine beach of broken shells. The light was momentary; radiant footsteps suddenly swept aside by a sable curtain of storm. Eventually, they rounded a promontory and sailed into a broad bay backed by a plain of reeds. Lumpy, convoluted ridges ringed these marshlands.

"See that far hill – the lone one rising out of the plain and topped with huts?" gestured the pilot. "That is Dunadd."

The sun was setting as the monks swiftly followed the road that took an indirect way, skirting the marshes and watercourses, to the fortress. The lone hill grew distinct in the gathering dusk, with the sprouting of fires and flaming torches.

King Fergus Mac Erc stood tall. His very determined jaw, accentuated by being clean-shaven, made him look a man of ambition. His intense eyes exuded confidence, a man to whom the office of ruling came naturally. He received them with warmth, ordering the kitchen to lay extra places at the tables frequented by warriors and officials.

"Eat well, my friends, and we shall sup together. Tell me, how was your crossing?"

When he heard their replies, he added, "You will be tired." Nonetheless, he continued to ply them with many questions, keen to know the news from Erin.

"Our peoples are of one accord," continued the king as the monks came to the end of their meal. "Sharing the same tongue, we aspire to a common destiny. I am keen to have this realm as fully Christian as it is over in Erin. That will unite us more firmly."

"It will bring the peace of God's favour to your realm," added Kessog.

"Yes, and that too!" assented the king. "As Dal Riata is cut off from the east by impenetrable forests and rugged mountains, we are dependent on good links with Erin across our watery highway."

"We did notice that this seems a wild land!" smiled Fillan.

Ignoring his comment, the king proceeded enthusiastically. "I am delighted at your coming. I have already assigned my learned ones to help you better establish a church here in our capital. Our young people shall learn from you."

Kessog presented Machaloi's letter. Fergus Mac Erc had an older man read it aloud in a rather high-pitched voice that stumbled at times over the words.

"So, you are not to remain here with the others!" reflected the king, raising his dark brows with some disappointment. "Strath Clud is not like our government!" He uttered the name of their neighbouring kingdom with disdain, his mouth pulling a grimace as though this was necessary to pronounce its syllables accurately.

"Many of them are pirates – villains and swindlers. These Britons, I suppose," he waved his hand by way of a concession, "are a useful buffer, on some fronts, between us and the Picts who are of even worse reputation!"

Fillan shifted restlessly as the king elaborated his opinions. He did his best to stifle his yawns, resisting the overwhelming urge to sleep. His eyes burned with an itchy dryness and his mouth tasted stale.

Eventually, the king brought their audience to a close. "You are to remain here for some days so that we may be better acquainted. If good Machaloi has singled you two out for this tough mission, you must be made of special mettle!"

The king looked at him rather questioningly, he thought, no doubt on account of his extreme youth. He turned again to Kessog. "I would have you instruct me in the ways of Christ before you depart."

"That we will gladly do, most noble king."

Over the next three days, they found their time with the king frequently interrupted by messengers, making concentration on theological matters that much more taxing. Fergus Mac Erc never showed special interest in their teaching, eventually professing to have understood all that he needed to know. He arranged for them to be guided across the narrow isthmus from Dunadd upon the Atlantic, to a sea loch a half morning's walk away.

They sailed at high water, bound for Bute.

Fillan looked upon the expanse of hills to the north and east rising abruptly out of the briny waters, backed by mountains of far greater height. The long, hilly peninsula of Kintyre stretched south, like a long finger pointing to Erin, indicating to where its identity and allegiances lay.

"So, it is another adventure for us, Father Kessog," said Fillan with renewed excitement.

"I do not know about you, but I am keen to reach where we are destined for," replied the older man.

"Oh, I agree! But it sounds like we will not have such a warm welcome at Din Brython."

Kessog nodded. "If King Fergus Mac Erc is keen to be a Christian king, and yet found it difficult to concentrate, then how will King Dyfnwal Hen be with us? This warrants our prayers, Fillan."

Fillan thought on how he would surely learn the art of diplomacy and careful argument from this wise man. One day, once he had risen in stature, he would hold his own before kings and warlords. Would it not be like reclaiming his own birthright, since he was presumed the son of a princess? He wondered what his life might have been like had he not been rejected as a baby, something he idly speculated upon from time to time with a certain mournfulness. Then he acquiesced, for had he not been passed over by a royal family to then be brought up in a holy family? Was it not ironic that Kessog, the one-time prince trained to rule one day, had been called to be God's servant? Had not their noble origins been elevated from the politics and warfare of petty fiefdoms, to serve an everlasting kingdom? He would have it no other way.

Another boat took the pilgrims the next day up to the head of the firth. Shorelines became tamer with flatter ground broadening towards receding hills. The twin-domed rock of Din Brython presented its proud citadel encircled by extensive battlements, its finest fortification being its cliff-like nature and its sole entrance of a steep and narrow defile.

King Dyfnwal Hen was much older than Fergus Mac Erc, with a grey beard and a rather inscrutable face. To Fillan's surprise some of the guards started sniggering, whispering to one another. As soon as the formalities were over, the king explained, through an interpreter, "You amuse my soldiers, but do not take offence. We were expecting more of you, but it seems just a father with his son have been sent!"

"This is not my son," clarified Kessog, "although he is certainly of an age to be."

Both men stood self-consciously, though relieved to find the king in good humour.

"We are glad Erin sends us good things, not least its Christian instruction," continued Dyfnwal Hen. "Not that we are strangers to Christ's teaching. You will have heard of one of our own monks, from a long time back, Ninian by name. He laboured in the south, beyond the thrall of our kingdom, at a place he named Candida Casa."

"Indeed, we have," responded Kessog. "It was Ninian's mission who founded the monastery we have just come from, located . . ."

"Candida Casa is still there, of course," interrupted the king, not curious to have Kessog elucidate further on their monastic foundation. "It has existed for a hundred years and its monks have come north to us. We became a Christian people before Erin; even further back in history, it is said, before the Romans abandoned their wall."

"Excuse me lord," Kessog interrupted, "but why do you then send for monks from Erin, who do not speak your language, rather than receive men from Candida Casa?"

"That is a good question, and I will come to it in a moment. We were sometimes allies with the Romans, sharing a common enemy in the Picts. Mostly due to the efforts of Strath Clud, the Picts were contained, preventing them from rampaging through Rome's territories to the south."

Fillan was aware that the guards were vigilant of every new entrant to the hall, giving him the impression of a kingdom constantly looking over its shoulder. As though reading his thoughts, Dyfnwal Hen explained. "Dear friends, I must confess that Erin is currently among our best allies and this explains why we requested monks from Erin, and not from Candida Casa. The alliance between our nations is not new; rather, it is one that we desire to strengthen."

"Indeed, our abbot, Machaloi, had years ago laboured in your kingdom at Lennox," responded Kessog.

"Ah yes, Machaloi. I know him, which is why I requested him to send us monks. He had a rough time trying to establish a church in a place where two clans were at loggerheads!" The king shook his head judiciously. "That is a sorry task, even for a king with the force of sword, to unite a people."

The king looked at them with a brightness Fillan had not witnessed before. "But Erin! Regard how suddenly your kingdoms have become Christian. The zeal of Patrick swept like a wildfire through your island!" His arms splayed out wide either side of his simple throne chair and his jaw deliberately fell slack, conveying his wonderment. "Our realm is not so influenced. As I have grown old, I am thinking of what legacy I will leave my people."

The king gestured a servant to replenish the monk's drinking goblets.

"Now, tell me something about yourself," continued the king in a bright tone, looking at Kessog. "Who are your people? How were you brought up?" Hearing his reply, he remarked, "Ah, I thought I could detect a noble lineage."

"I had assumed that I was destined to follow my father, but that was not to be."

"How come?"

"My destiny was written long before I came into this world. The great Patrick came to Cashel when my father was just a young man and made such an impression upon him. My father prophesied that I would take Christ's light across the waters, but as is the nature with some prophecies, it took time to be fulfilled. Although I knew Christ, I took my place as a princely warrior in the court, needing time to be convinced of my calling. Only when I had reached my mid-thirties did I feel the strong call to be a monk. That is when I went to Nendrum and met Father Machaloi. Now I have turned forty!"

"So, you are an indirect prodigy of Patrick!" the king smiled approvingly. "Forty you say?" he grunted. "Not so young, but still time to leave your mark, as I believe there is time too for me to leave a Christian legacy."

He paused to smile. "As I was saying, Erin is an ally. The sea makes for a good border. All our other boundaries are land ones." He took a deep breath. "The Picts are to our north – their ill-reputation preceeds them, a by-word for all that is evil. Goddodin lies to our east – they are fellow Britons. Then to the south is Rheged – also a realm of Britons, wary of the Angles and Saxons coming across the sea to seize land and skirmish upon its borders. The times are evil, my friends, and we need to keep alert." The king concluded with a care-worn gesture of a hand.

"We come in peace, dear lord!" reminded Kessog. "Our message is one of consolation for all men, whoever they may be."

Fillan detected that the last statement made the king slightly uneasy, for he shifted his posture in his seat.

Kessog elaborated. "Our desire is to lead you and your people into the way of peace, that the favour of the Lord may rest with you."

The rock became their home for many months whilst studying the language and the ways of their hosts. It required patient application, the testing of words, discovering their different usages, diligently grappling to understand all the language's nuances and its grammatical peculiarities. Summer was anticipated, came and passed into ever shortening days as the sun lost its strength. When they began to pick up some of the idiomatic expressions and used these appropriately, they felt they had grasped the essentials of the language. Fillan was pleased to have understood the language well, better than his master.

One bright morning of frost, the king took them for a turn along the battlements.

"See that big mountain over there, the nearer one?" The monks followed the direction of his hand, indicating the domed summit of a considerable hill in the distance, all snow clad. "At the base of that peak is a large loch where different cultures converge. Upon the nearer shores, I am granting you land. Tomorrow we will journey to see it."

He stretched out a hand, placed it upon Fillan's shoulder and said in a fatherly tone, "There are several islands nearby that scatter the loch. Knowing you Christian Gaels are fond of making communities on islands, this will be an ideal place for you!"

Chapter Four

Over the Beltane Fires

555 AD Rhynie

On the eve of Beltane, the cousins set off with a dog apiece, taking a trail down into a glen at the base of the sacred hill. Leaving the trail, they went up into the woods, passing the ancient grandsire of an oak.

Taran stopped and exclaimed, "Is this not where once we ran as bairns and lost our way and were reprimanded for returning home after nightfall?"

"Aye, maybe. But it does seem different now."

"What, the trees look taller?" Taran asked rather oddly.

"Well yes, they'll have grown somewhat."

"I expect the trees look larger to you than they do to me, for I have grown taller than you!"

So that was what he was inferring. Oengus shoved Taran's shoulder before setting off at a determined pace. "Come on. If we position ourselves on top of that raised ground, we can lie quietly for deer to graze in this grassy glade."

They called the dogs to heel, climbed the slope and took up position behind bushy scrub. "Let us agree that should there be two or more deer, I shoot to the left and you to the right?"

"Agreed," Oengus said, fixing an arrow to his bowstring.

The day was overcast but without wind, ideal for not betraying their presence to the deer.

"This is our first opportunity to talk since the initiation!" remarked Taran.

Oengus pursed his lips. "Let me show you my tattoo," he said in an undertone, so as not to give away their presence. Devesting himself of his top, he turned to present his back towards Taran. The tattoo consisted of two circles, one within the other and closely aligned. Attached was a curved box shape.

"Well, what do you think?" asked Oengus feeling proud of his insignia.

"It is quite plain!" remarked Taran, unimpressed.

"It might look plain to you, but hear what the learned Maelchon said." Oengus pulled his top back down and faced his cousin. "The circles represent a broch as seen by a bird from above. The stone tower provides security for people, livestock and food stores; a place of refuge from the foe, and within its walls is provision and community. The box shape represents the tunnelled entrance that some brochs have, outside which, an assembly may gather. As warlord, I will preside over the court and hold authority over all who pass through; a man of strength, sustaining the community and providing refuge in times of strife."

Taran was quiet and his silence irritated him.

"How else can you interpret it other than me being chosen as warlord?" Oengus pursued.

"Well, I suppose the broch gives a certain status of rule," conceded Taran, but his concessionary tone was upset by a playful movement of his head. "It could be interpreted that you will be a significant member of the council, renowned for your war feats."

Looking pleased with himself, Taran pulled up his top and presented his tattoo.

Oengus fell silent, staggered. The words came thickly from his mouth with clear dismay. “The Z-rod with viper!”

“It is similar to what Uncle bears, is it not?” continued Taran confidently. “He told us himself, the Z-rod insignia is reserved for the warlord.”

Oengus was aghast by this revelation. What sense did his broch depiction have now compared with this conclusive evidence? His mind waded through a sea of turmoil.

He ordered his dog to sit in a stealthy tone, who sank disconsolately beside its mate. Recovering, he spoke in a tone keen to review the facts. “My tattoo was done at the Yule stone, the indicator of the end of the old and the beginning of the new! Is that not proof that the lordship is to be conferred upon me?”

“It is baffling having two conflicting interpretations! My tattoo was done at the Beltane stone – the new season of fertility, of promised harvest. Is that not also an indicator of a new era?!”

“That is no proof of you becoming warlord!” protested Oengus, feeling the flush of blood rise into his cheeks. He took a moment to be still and decided to make light of the situation. “It could equally be true that the significance of the Beltane stone is that you are soon to marry!”

Taran shrugged his shoulders, laughing briefly under his breath. They were quiet for a while.

Oengus broke the silence. “Well, even Maelchon was reluctant to be drawn into discussion and perhaps was perplexed.”

“Yes, but is that not just his way? He is one for keeping aloof.” Taran pulled a face.

"Perhaps we should both agree that the matter, thus far, is undecided?"

"Oengus, I agree – that is the first sensible thing you have uttered. Besides, we have yet to be tested with the cattle lifting. Uncle did say that would be the determining thing."

"Right enough. Neither of us should be presumptuous, then."

"Maybe we should agree not to talk about the matter further," suggested Taran.

Oengus agreed, but in the secrecy of his thoughts, he pondered all possible outcomes, some raising alarm and others appearing more flights of fanciful thinking. However hard he tried to forget the portents of these strange tattoos, the more his thoughts turned towards the evidence and plausible interpretations. He wondered whether Taran experienced the same internal struggle. His cousin could be slower to state his ambition at times, but he knew Taran to be a strong contender to whatever he put his hand.

"Have you considered what will become of the one who is not made warlord?" he voiced aloud.

"Aye, I have." Taran ruffled his long hair and flicked back some stray strands from his face. "Truly, it concerns me!"

"Me too!" He bit his lower lip.

"Do you think we could serve together, one as warlord and the other as a significant warrior and counsellor?" suggested Taran.

Oengus looked him thoughtfully over, determining if his cousin were sincere. He did appear in earnest, in keeping with his manner, which sometimes Oengus considered naïve.

Taran elaborated. "Rather like in the scenario I mentioned of me, with the Z-rod, as warlord, and you, with the motif of the broch, being raised to the most eminent status within the court?"

"Or vice-versa," he objected, letting loose his pent-up frustration.

A couple of deer they had not noticed were startled in the grove by the sound of his vehemence, vanishing in an instant into the denseness of the forest.

"Look what you have caused to happen, cousin!" The remonstration felt unwarranted the moment it left his mouth.

"Me?" Taran left his defence hanging in the air. He seemed to choose not to be riled by the accusation Oengus knew to be unfair. "Yes, or vice-versa," he conceded. "Have we not been as close as brothers all our lives? Our two households are almost joined physically, expressing the bond between our families. We have trained together all these years; it would seem a huge waste if one were to be cast off!"

"Well said. That is what I have been thinking, too." Oengus stalled here. He wanted to say more and speak of the very thing uppermost on his mind. It was a delicate matter that he could find no way of conveying subtly. Finally, he brought himself to pronounce it bluntly. "So, whichever one of us becomes warlord need not kill the other, eh?"

Taran looked at him shocked. It took him a few moments to respond. "Certainly not!"

At least they had reached this all-important decision. However, there was another matter that he could not bring himself to share with Taran. It concerned his father, Caltram, who was much more curious than he had anticipated, examining him about the initiation. Oengus had been driven to utter desperation. With his father's mounting resentment over his refusal to answer, Oengus told him everything. His father then conjectured about the outcome, naturally favouring his son as the obvious choice, giving voice to various scenarios: who would say what and how to overcome every conceivable obstacle. He could comprehend how a proud father would want the best for his son, but his father had exceeded that.

When Taran caught sight of Alpia at the Beltane feast, he forgot to turn his gaze away; such was her allurement to a young man who had been long devoted to military training. He felt his stomach heave in nervous anticipation of how he might renew a long-lapsed acquaintance. He considered her grey dress, embroidered with a simple floral motif along the neckline. Lacking elegance or refinement, he decided that he did not care for her attire, except that it had one redeeming quality: its plainness accentuated the beauty of its wearer. Looking upon her resplendent hair, he imagined it had been combed and combed to reach such an exquisite fineness to now shine like fiery bronze in the late afternoon sun. Her beauty was the more beguiling because she did not flaunt it.

"Her loveliness has no equal," remarked Taran.

"Indeed!" agreed Oengus. "She would make me a fine wife."

"Despair, my friend," he retorted. "Abandon any such hope! Unless I am very much mistaken, she has eyes only for me. What a lovely smile she gave me when she served the oatcakes and cheese curd at Uncle's."

"You are mistaken! She is just a smiley girl. She smiles at everyone, make no mistake about it!" Oengus dug him in the ribs with his elbow.

Although among a group of other fair girls, it was as though her companions just did not exist.

"Stop staring like a ravenous wolf with a tongue hanging out," Taran chastised. "Let us go on over. Look, there is the fair-haired Eithni too – she would suit you well."

"I was going to say the same to you!" retorted Oengus.

They gingerly approached, looking awkward and unsure how to begin. They stalled close by, truly lost for words. The girls laughed, casting glances over their shoulders to indicate they had noticed them.

"And what is it that amuses you?" ventured Oengus.

Taran noticed Oengus looked very pleased with himself for getting the first words in.

"That you have a tail wagging behind you!" blurted out Eithni with half a mouthful of pork. Oengus involuntarily checked his rear in case some prankster had indeed attached a tail. The girls burst out laughing, covering their mouths with a hand. He blushed to have been taken in and compared to a dog bounding on over to the girls.

He recovered quickly. "And what hound would not be pleased to greet so fair a pack?"

"What do you mean? Do you infer that we are a pack of bitches?" Eithni was in good form, keen to flirt by repressing his boldness in a ploy to goad him on. Oengus' blush was noted. The girls were finding this sport much to their liking.

"No, of course I did not mean that – at least not about you all."

Taran groaned at his cousin's clumsiness.

"Oh! And who among us is excluded from that comment," remarked another girl.

When Oengus turned to Alpia, words failed him.

"And what does Taran have to say?" asked the same girl.

"Taran has to distance himself from his cousin's remarks." He smoothed his wispy moustaches. "I say we start again. Good evening to you all who look so fair." His tone attempted to sound sober, but his keen remark had got the better of him. When fixing eyes on Alpia, his smile broadened. Alpia held his gaze for a moment before averting her eyes.

"Would you be happy for us to dance with you this evening?" ventured Taran.

"Well, depends on which of us you intend to dance with!" responded Eithni, giving him a flirtatious smile.

"Aye, we might! But which of you asks . . . and who is to be asked?" clarified another. Taran had eyes only for Alpia, so much so that he affronted Eithni. As if to show she did not care, Eithni started to talk with Oengus, who seemed relieved to have been given a second chance. This development pleased Taran, who stared at Alpia ardently.

She looked uncomfortable. "Here, would you like some?" She offered Taran some meat from her platter.

That was the reckoning over and he was able to talk to her in a relaxed manner. A couple of times, when looking over at Oengus, he caught a resentful look, even though Oengus seemed to be warmly engaged with Eithni.

A bard, singing to the accompaniment of his harp, concluded a lengthy ballad. Talorgen rose, clapping his hands for silence. A sound went up from someone to indicate both respect for their chief and to tell the unaware to be quiet.

"This is a special Beltane, and a fair evening it is too. There will not be many more springs that I will celebrate with you!"

At this, someone shouted, "Nonsense!"

"I mean it – this could be my last one, and I am glad to be here celebrating with you. I wish your crops may yield much grain and that your cattle will fatten and give you much cream." Raising his goblet aloft, he saluted the assembly. "May your cups overflow."

There were cheers and applause.

"Tonight is very special, for we have the most famous bard in the whole of the north. I want you to welcome Ossian. I invite him to come forward, for *'he who travels has stories to tell'.* Let us honour him, dear friends!"

A huge cheer, interspersed with whistles and raucous whoops, rose up as Ossian mounted a step and alighted upon a cart. Despite his age, he still had a full head of hair, which had largely turned grey. He swept it back from his forehead, giving prominence to his brown eyes that shone with a benevolent lustre.

"Before I sing and tell you tales, let me first bring you news," began Ossian, his head scanning the crowd. "Our overlord and esteemed cousin, King Galam of Fortriu, sends you greetings. I celebrated the spring equinox with him at Y Broch where he announced that Brude would reign with him this year and to then hand over power completely come Yuletide."

People exchanged words upon hearing this news.

"But you need not fear!" Ossian held up his hand with a calming gesture. "There will not be any internal rivalry that could drag you in to choose sides unwillingly. Brude will make a strong ruler." Ossian paused whilst a couple of cheers were made at length. "But watch out for Dal Riata! They are ambitious, acquiring more coast to settle and claim as their own."

"What can you expect of the Gaels?" a red-faced man shouted. "A land-grabbing lot!"

"If things get troublesome, then Brude might call upon your help, for he shares a border with Dal Riata." He nodded to lend weight to his prediction. "Although he has many fighting men who may well be able to contain the Gaels."

"And shall we not fight them, brothers?" blurted out the red-faced man again. "We will put a stop, once and for all, to the ambitions of the Gael! We will drive them into the sea and turn the tide red!"

Ossian paused, allowing the hubbub to die.

"As you know, the Britons to the south have for some time been dabbling with the new religion. Christians, they call themselves. They believe in a God who became man, who was then executed for some supposed rebellion. He then came back to life again and was taken up into heaven. Worshipping him alone, Christians will not tolerate other gods or goddesses."

This grabbed Taran's attention for some reason. A God who became a man! Well, there was nothing novel in that, for were not the gods always contriving to wheedle their way into the affairs of men in an unsuspecting manner by assuming human form. Did not the Bulàch appear before some as an old hag, or Brigantia as a beautiful young maiden? Deity could choose how to reveal themselves. However, what sort of god was he if he were powerless to prevent his own death? But then, on the other hand, being a god, he took his life back again. Perhaps all of that was plausible.

"This teaching is infiltrating the Picts in the south – the Fib and the Circinn – although not many are following. The mild-mannered Christian 'druids' have been granted permission to establish what they call muintirs, or 'Colonies of Heaven'."

Taran reflected further. The part that struck him as absurd was the declaration of only one God! What use was that? For, if finding yourself pitted against such a god, to what other god could you turn? Was it not narrow-minded to insist upon worshipping only one god? Why were some

Picts ready to believe, when the majority would not? The Bulàch was sure to have her revenge on those turning away from her.

"I remember King Dyfnwal Hen, when still alive, inviting two monks over from Erin. The king gave them land north of Din Brython on a loch shore. Again, few believed. They were so disheartened, it was said, that the younger of the two wanted to return to Erin!"

Oh well, thought Taran, these Christians do not seem to be much of a threat, especially if their leaders are so mild mannered.

"No one is going to tell us what to believe and who to worship," shouted a fat woman, waving a knife in the air.

"Well, my friends, that is the news, and on that note, I think it appropriate to sing you an ancient song about Mons Graupius, when we Picts turned the tide against the Romans." Taking up a small harp, he tuned it awhile with his grey head bent close to the strings. Approving the sound, he cleared his throat.

The red-faced man, who had a presence to make others heed his summons, bellowed, "Will you all just shut up!"

The gathering hushed, expectantly looking to the famed bard with the setting sun mellow upon his animated face.

"We the last of the free, the first among the brave,
The choice of all the men that will not fear the grave;
We the flower of the hills withstand the cruel bite,
The proud race of the north that never give respite.
We who run the secret glens to confound our foe,
Shall spring from the purple hills to bring them down low.
On the heights of Bennachie many breathed their last,
We Picts they couldna chase for our feet were o'er fast
And on that very day, the whole sad land grew grey

But Caledonia shall rise another day,
We Picts sent the Romans over their crumbling wall,
We the true, regained our honour, our land, our all
Our land, our honour, our fame, we regained once more."

A great cry erupted from the whole assembly. Men, ruddy faced, raised battle cries; the women, who were not ones for being outdone, whooped in a series of cheers, and a cauldron suspended from a beam was hit repeatedly with an axe. This was just the beginning of many more songs. Taran never left Alpia's side, nor did she find excuse to wander off, even when her friends, one by one, drifted away. Dancing followed. Taran only danced with one girl, and she seemed happy.

When the Beltane fires were lit, and the cattle held in the enclosure below were freed, the crowd herded the lowing throng between two bonfires of burning juniper. Once all cattle had passed, Oengus was the first to leap through the flames alone, flying with extraordinary height and agility, bellowing a great whoop that seemed had been long pent up.

I wonder what he wishes for, thought Taran, taking note.

Others followed. Young couples leapt through the flames wishing for fertility of family and livestock; men wishing to be fathers of heroes and women for helpmates around the hearth.

Taran turned to Alpia. She looked radiant with the spirited flames of the fire lighting her face. The fire glow washed over her body, giving it more vigour to one who was already allured. Alpia held his gaze with a faint smile puckering the corners of her mouth. There was a noble way in which she held her head, and at times, her eyes could look almost haughty.

The dying sky pulsed with the luminous deep sapphire of a summer's night, charged with the fleeting bright sparks flying from the bonfires, like the heady wishes, incandescent, on a night full of promise.

"Well, what do you think?" asked Taran, extending his hand to her.

She looked at him quizzically, unsure of his intention.

"Shall we leap through the flames together?"

She took the hand extended, hesitantly at first it seemed. No way was he going to let go of a hand that felt so enchanting, that brought him untold gladness. He trotted her playfully up the hill and she fell into step with him, following the others above the bonfires to gain a running start before the big leap.

"What do you hope for?" paused Taran on reaching the point at which people turned to start their run.

"What?" Alpia sounded puzzled.

"Well, I wish this night would never end. That, in all honesty, is what I most wish for!"

He looked into her eyes, awaiting her response. Hearing none, he tried to fathom what it might be that she most wished for. Her hand did not retract.

"So, you want this night never to end!" she said slowly, slightly mocking him with widening eyes.

At a loss for words, a confusion descended, disrupting his ability to think clearly.

"Well, of course it is not this night that is the object of my affection," he said, looking down at his shuffling feet. "When I first set eyes upon you, two weeks back, I was struck by your beauty, your whole person . . ." Taran looked up, hardly daring to see the response his declaration might be making.

"Go on," Alpia coaxed, although somewhat cautiously he noted.

Never having been in this situation before, proving his affections was seemingly a difficult thing to express, and she was not making the task easy. Then, her enigmatic smile and her gaze that appeared intrigued, encouraged him to speak things that he had never spoken before, sentiments that were intoxicating. He had been trained in all kinds of engagement, in combat and political diplomacy, but this was entirely unchartered territory.

"Alpia . . ." he paused involuntarily. "What beauty is in a name! I had never imagined that I could say a name with such feeling, for it to evoke so strong a reaction. Alpia belongs to you and it becomes you, the loveliest of names of all women. And I start with only the sound of these syllables upon my lips, without even attempting to describe the loveliness of the one bearing that name."

"You are poetic this night," teased Alpia. "You are making progress! You started in praise of the night, wishing it to never end, and now you find much to praise in the sound of my name. How opportune that my parents should have chosen to call me Alpia, it would seem, and not by some other name that sounded less interesting to your ear!"

"Come now, you are making this difficult!" He felt somewhat crestfallen, then raised his face as he thought of his retort. "You remind me of the proverb: *'There are three things that are difficult to understand; the mind of a woman, the work of bees and the coming and going of the tide'*. I think it is clear what I am trying to say!"

"That you like me." She tilted her head to the side, her mouth elongating in that enigmatic smile.

"Yes, and what about you? After all, I was the first to ask, 'What do you hope for as you leap through the Beltane flames?' Is it not time that you gave me some inkling as to how you feel?"

"You are alright," she replied. The teasing smile faded from her mouth and she frowned.

Taran tried to withdraw his hand only to find that she held it more firmly.

"Life in this place was dull and boring until you all came back home!"

Taran felt his face flush. "You mean it is not just this night that has dispersed your tedium, but my arriving in Rhynie?"

"And all the others." Her smile seemed to wither.

"That is a revelation! I had no idea." He chose to ignore 'and all the others' part of her reply and smiled with a good deal of satisfaction. "I noticed you from the very first day when you were sat behind Aunt Conchen. I thought to myself, who could that wonderful young woman be? Then I realised it was the one whose hair I pulled when I was just a stupid wee bairn."

"Oh, so you remember! You were not so very nice back then." She withdrew slightly from his side but kept hold of his hand. "I will admit, you have improved somewhat since then."

Alpia's smile was very rewarding.

"Well, you have not said what you would wish for! I shall speak first, since you have revealed that I have improved greatly from the days when I used to go around pulling girls' hair."

"Improved somewhat," she corrected.

Clearing his throat, he looked her straight in the eye. "I wish that you will be with me amidst all the good that promises to come my way this year. In fact, if I am to be the chosen successor and yet fail to win you, the triumph would no longer be there."

She was quiet for some moments, looking away over the valley. “And I would wish to be your friend, even if you are not the chosen heir!”

He wanted her to say more, noting how her response was measured and sober. Although her words assured no more than friendship, the hand that remained in his, however, promised more. Taran squeezed that hand and with a nod in the direction of the flames, led her in the heat of his conviction, heartened by her compliance.

Chapter Five

Cattle Lifting

555 AD River Dee

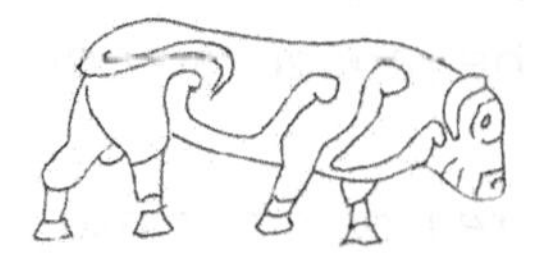

Ossian had thought much about Talorgen's plans of succession, which was quite unlike the smooth agreement among the Fortriu with the ageing Lord Galam choosing his successor. The situation among the Ce boded trouble. Although both young men seemed good contenders, the outcome required fast resolve, lest ambition should gain the upper hand and cause one to take matters into his own hands and possibly create a factional divide, taking hundreds of lives.

Ossian determined to speak with Maelchon and Gest privately. He gained nothing from Gest, who was sworn to secrecy and he respected that. The interview with Maelchon had not been an easy one. Knowing how taciturn the druid was, it took considerable skill to wheedle any information. He hoped that his status as a well-known outsider might make Maelchon confer in confidence. Perseverance was required to extract the desired information.

"You need to keep this to yourself," insisted Maelchon.

"Go on," said Ossian calmly, which the druid seemed to take for an assent.

"Well it is all quite a mystery – one might say a huge contradiction!" Maelchon rubbed his clammy hands together.

"I objected in my own head to what was being revealed. But who can oppose the Bulàch's will, especially when she is looking to do some great mischief? Both prophecies mark each to be the warlord. How could this be – unless they were to serve side by side with equality?"

"That seldom, if ever, happens as a lasting arrangement. They are warriors," he replied, smoothing his hair with the flat of his hand.

"But the cousins are close, as close as any brothers could be. Oengus has more drive, the mettle to bring people together under authority. The tattoo of the broch says as much. Taran is the more charismatic, the inspirer rather than a man of force."

"Well, they will not rule together," ruminated the bard, speaking as though he had foresight on the matter. "It is shambolic what is happening!"

Maelchon protested his innocence gruffly, accusing the old man of meddling and that such things were not the designs of men, nor even of druids, but born of the will of the Bulàch. This brought a swift close to their meeting.

Ossian left, anxious about the outcome, and observed the cousins from a distance. Skilled at discerning hidden things from the way men talked and comported themselves when no eyes were thought to be upon them, he surmised Taran to be in the first flush of love. Not that it took his seer's powers to discern, for Taran was not discreet, totally preoccupied by his infatuation. As for Oengus, he noted how that quiet determination burned with an inner intensity; a fire stoked by his father, Caltram, whom he perceived to be a particularly menacing threat.

He admired in Taran a particular noble quality: a sincerity to do what was right, to pursue his goals with a degree of purity of soul, rare in so young a warrior. Such men he considered vulnerable by their very naivety, for they put the best interpretation on the words and actions of others and failed to recognise guile until it was too late. Moral goodness could make fools of men, causing them to only look ahead and not see the enemy to the side. But adding love to this mix – Taran was oblivious of the dangers.

Taran was surprised to see Ossian setting a good pace towards him along the ridge, as though age had not sapped strength from limb. The two greeted and fell into casual conversation about the cattle, and where Ossian would be heading next and such like. Then, lowering his voice, Ossian caught his eye meaningfully with a piercing stare from beneath his bushy eyebrows. The bard spoke great mysteries in a low voice and with urgency.

"Make great haste when you leave. Be cunning, be brave, be humble. Your surrender will be in the south; your transformation in the isles of the west; your fulfilment coincides with the anticipation of the learned ones far to the north, before you return east with great peace. Before that peace blossoms, there will come much strife, like a blight threatening to consume. Heartache and anguish lie before you. Many a journey awaits, full of ordeals that you consider will be your undoing, though these are in truth, rites of passage for your own preparation. You will be the doer of mighty deeds and the acts will be the making of the man. Take heart, my son, through one you will overcome the world."

"What does this all mean?" asked Taran, astonished.

Ossian held up a hand, refusing to be drawn, not even by a single word of illumination. His manner returned to that of the gentle and jovial bard that everyone knew him to be.

But the old man did say one thing more before they parted on the hill. "Here's another secret that you are to tell no one." Ossian lent forward and whispered the words Oengus had uttered when he flew through the Beltane fires. 'I shall be warlord at any cost.'

How could he possibly know that? It was all too incredulous.

Ossian walked peacefully away as though nothing of import had passed. Taran remained on the hillside, trying to make sense of what he had heard, taken together with the conflicting insignia he and Oengus had received. He would not flee for his life; there was no logical threat right now. He reflected on the words to 'be cunning, be brave, be humble'. Cunning and bravery made sense, but to be humble? That was incomprehensible. Maybe the confusion was all the making of Ossian's mind.

This bewilderment added to the dismay felt following his talk with Alpia the day after Beltane. He had gone with a jaunty step after their evening together and she had left her chores to speak with him outside Conchen's hut.

"Alpia, I am overjoyed to set eyes upon you. I had little sleep last night," he declared.

Alpia appeared slightly taken aback and did not return his ardent smile. She looked as though she was about to say something, but maybe he was mistaken.

"Alpia – are you not pleased to see me?"

She looked steadily at him without smiling. Her eyes appeared calculating, and beyond a pause he found too long for comfort, she said, "I am your friend, Taran, but no more than that."

If words can wind a man, then this occasion was proof he thought. "But what about that sense of togetherness last night?" he appealed. "We talked, we danced; you appeared pleased!"

"As I said last night, I am pleased by the return of the warriors for it has broken the monotony of life in this place."

"But hand in hand we leapt through the flames!" he exclaimed, recalling his own commitment to her and that absolute sense of accord with another person.

"Ah! That was maybe a mistake!" She turned her head aside, looking searchingly to the horizon. Her face did not betray confusion or embarrassment; it was more like detachment. Her eyes then appeared to harden. "Taran, if I led you astray to hope, then I ask your forgiveness. I do not share your feelings."

"Then why spend the entire evening with me as though I was the only one who mattered?" The words came more forcibly from his lips than he had intended, from dismay rather than anger. He certainly felt piqued by this unexpected coolness.

"As I said, it was a mistake to have done so – that is clear in hindsight. I did not intend to mislead you, to give you false hope."

"Did you not feel any pleasure then from being in my company?" he protested mildly.

Again, her eyes met his without any suggestion of regret, or even pity for him. "Should I spare your feelings and pretend that we continue as a couple who had leapt together through the flames?"

"You confess then that we were a couple last night?" he appealed.

"Well, yes, it did appear so," she began in a concessionary tone, "but it was not my intention." For the first time, her brow knitted slightly, betraying a sense of confusion. "I was moved by the occasion, and I admit . . ." She paused thoughtfully. “I admit to having felt flattered and enjoying the attention of a noble, young man.”

“There!” he declared, feeling there was a semblance of proof for how she had felt. “Those feelings are nothing to be ashamed about.”

She swallowed and inhaled heavily. “Taran, I do not wish to mislead you. You are a fine man, but I do not know you! Not many days ago you did not even register in my thoughts.”

“But now I have returned and am here to stay. Opportunity presents itself to know one another.” At last, he felt common ground had been established to redefine a friendship. His mind felt frantic, keen not to lose this momentum. “Alpia!” He reached out and touched her upper arm gently, withdrawing it when she met his look, not that her expression withered hope, but rather he had determined to tame the expression of his feelings that clearly had alarmed her. “Let us be friends . . .”

“Friends we are,” she affirmed.

“So, would there be harm in my calling upon you so that we may come to know one another better?”

“No, I suppose there would be no wrong in that.”

They lingered a good while, talking easily about the people they knew in common.

“If Aunt Conchen is also your aunt,” Taran thought aloud, “does that not make us cousins?”

“It is not as simple as that.” She smiled with that half smile of hers that puckered the corners of her mouth, which he found most beguiling. “We share the same great-grandmother – the grand matriarch of the Ce.” She looked at him with some humour and ease. “So Taran, you are more than a friend, you are kin, a second cousin to me, and I should be glad to know my relative better.”

Oengus and Taran rode at the head of a warband of young warriors into the dawn. Spears of light splintered through the trees, evaporating pockets of mists rising from the damp vegetation. The River Dee ribboned the green fields of the borderlands to their right; the far bank, densely forested, marked the lands of the Circinn. The brilliance of the light upon the swift flowing river, combined with the smell of snow thaw, lifted their spirits. All morning they continued downstream, passing through the monotony of forest. Around noon, the cousins separated from the others, entrusting their horses to their care before reaching a community built on either side of a ferry point. It formed a frontier zone where the two tribes held cattle fairs. Small in size, it was big in reputation.

The two men crossed on the coracle and passed beyond view of the last of the huts on the Circinnian side.

"Let us leave the trail and take to the undergrowth to avoid detection," suggested Taran.

Oengus felt disinclined to respond.

"Come on – you are not going to sulk over my success with Alpia, are you?"

"Just shut up!" Oengus snapped as he left the path. His jealousy over Taran gaining Alpia's affections, and seemingly so easily too, fuelled his indignation. This was nothing, though, to the Z-rod, a clearer claim than his own was to the lordship. His father had spoken ominously about its significance, countering the negativity by sharing his big ambitions for Oengus.

"A druid's sign is one thing, but the cattle lifting is the test in which you need to seize the initiative to prove you are worthy as Uncle Talorgen's successor," he had said more than once. Being thwarted in love made Oengus determined to gain the upper hand with the succession.

He concentrated on their scouting to identify a suitable herd and to plot a course along which to spirit the cattle over the hill and across the Dee.

The following day, gathering opposite a river crossing where two islets eased the fording of the Dee, the cousins reported on all they had reconnoitred. After detailing their plans, Oengus announced, "Take a good rest, for the night will be long and tense."

Oengus found it easy to sleep in the new grass, wrapped in his plaid, lulled to rest by the gurgle of the river and the munching and contented breathing of the grazing horses.

Later, swords and knives were sharpened on a stone down at the water's edge, arrows in quivers were checked, and bows were strung then unstrung. All was done with that meticulous care when lives depended upon these instruments. Prayers were said, food was eaten and some even poured libations to the Bulàch.

The last of the sunlight swiftly climbed the hilltops, engulfing the valleys in dusk and deepening shadows. They crossed both the river and the pass above and stealthily descended to the deep shadow of the wood beside the pastures. Three huts dotted the clearing all with lamps burning. Weaponry was again checked, and bows were strung, waiting for the night to truly darken. A thick bank of cloud concealed the rising moon for a while, before its waning crescent emerged.

"These cattle are too close to the farmstead – their lowing will awaken the occupants," commented Taran. "But there is a herd of thirty or so further up the valley."

"We can drive the cattle straight into the forest from there and on up to the pass," remarked Oengus.

"Let us go that way," agreed Caltram.

They moved quietly in a broad line through the forest. When someone stumbled over a stone, or where the undergrowth lay thick with briers, the ground was cleared. They nicked the tree bark at head height; a long cut of clean wood that marked a trail to the forest edge.

"This is what we will do," proposed Taran. "We will post three men along the edge of the wood, standing guard with bows. Once the light in that hut over there has been extinguished a good while, the rest will spirit the cattle into the wood."

"I think five bows would be better, if an alarm is raised!" advised Oengus.

"Aye, five would better deal with whoever may come at us," added Caltram demonstratively. Others murmured approval.

"Let us keep our distance, for the time being, from the herd," his cousin countered assertively. "We do not want any unnecessary lowing before time."

Oengus smiled that Taran was feeling the pressure when his word was not readily heeded. If Taran showed that he felt ruffled whilst he held his calm, it would be noted by the elders and reported back to Talorgen.

They waited a long while; the moon rose higher, dimly illuminating the meadow. Still the firelight burned brightly through the half open door.

"Do you think they have fallen asleep with the door ajar?" someone remarked.

"Bah! It is way past their bedtime," another retorted, sounding like a disgruntled parent about a child staying up late.

"How much longer can we wait? We need as much cover of darkness to put a good distance from here!" Taran muttered.

"I could go on over to the farmstead," suggested Oengus. "See if I can hear voices or snoring."

As everyone found the interminable waiting all too much, they agreed.

"I will join you," spoke Taran.

There is the striving for posture again, identified Oengus. Was this not becoming somewhat irksome? Had it not been for this contest, these decisions would be natural and taken in solidarity.

Opposite the farmstead, Oengus and Taran swiftly crossed the open field. As they neared the dwelling, they proceeded more stealth-like. It was a conical hut, built on a stone base, with wattle and daub walls and a low thatch. They crept round to the door that strangely stood open, stopped and listened. All seemed quiet inside. Oengus stealthily peered in. A family group lay around a fire that had recently been stoked.

Taran suddenly lurched towards him with raised sword. What was he doing? He had been taken off-guard, astounded by his cousin raising a blade against him unprovoked. A clash of swords sounded instantly above his head as he instinctively stooped low and swirled round. He tripped over Taran and saw an assailant coming forcibly down again with his sword this time upon Taran. Oengus' unintentional contact with his cousin had spared Taran from the next blow that, executed with such force and missing its intended mark, unbalanced their mysterious assailant. Oengus could taste the iron-like blood from a lip pierced by a tooth. It worked like an energising potion, and he raised his sword to strike the man, but Taran had already deftly run his sword through the man's back, angled to pass between the rib bones. Penetrating with little resistance, the blade must have pierced the heart for the man made a brief and wretched cry before slumping forward, instantly dead.

Just then, a flaming firebrand emerged in the doorway. Oengus stepped forward with outstretched sword. A woman's startled voice rang out in surprise, followed immediately by a sickly cry. Taran joined him as he looked upon a woman slumped in the doorway. The horror of what was taking place began to dawn.

Oengus knelt to check if she was dead.

"Mummy? Mummy, where are you?" came the frightened voice of a child within.

Oengus arose and stepped into the home with his drawn sword. A boy of about eight stood before him, suddenly wide-eyed with terror.

"Oengus, no!" shouted Taran urgently. "He is just a child."

The boy backed away and stumbled over his sister, who awoke groggily.

"They'll raise the alarm!" reasoned Oengus.

"There has been enough bloodshed!" protested Taran. "Let us barricade the door, so they cannot escape and awaken the neighbours."

Oengus stood motionless, breathing heavily, weighing up the situation. The first flush of his murderous instincts subsided. They exited the house, dragging the door firmly into position. He brought over three stones that had formed a tripod of an outside cooking fire to wedge the door, making it impossible for children to slide the door to one side from inside. Not finding other suitably sized rocks, they took hold of the parents' bodies and propped them, side by side, heavily against the door. He thought they looked grotesque in their bloodied death, outrageously preventing their own children from escaping.

"Do not try to get out," threatened Oengus through the door to the children, panting through his words. "And do not shout or bang, otherwise I will come in and kill you both, that I will." The children said nothing.

"Do you understand? Tell me that you understand!" he rasped through his clenched teeth menacingly.

After some whimpering, a thin, petrified voice replied, which satisfied Oengus. With a sheen of sweat that animated his flushed face, Taran looked at him. Could Taran detect his lower lip quivering?

Hearing running feet fast approaching, they simultaneously turned, swords ready to take on three dark figures that were nearly upon them. Two men brandished raised swords and a third wielded a hefty battle axe. Oengus decided to launch himself at the figure on his left. A slashing blow would bring him to the ground and then he would swing round with a stab into the back of the middle one. He hoped Taran would take the man to their right.

"Stop! We are your fathers," came a suppressed shout.

Once they had regrouped, Oengus tried to understand what had just taken place.

"Our assailant must have gone outside to relieve himself."

"But why take a sword with you?" queried Taran.

"The remoteness of these borderlands perhaps requires that," reasoned Nechtan.

"But did any of us see him leave? Why was the door left ajar long into the night?" commented Caltram.

"We need to act hastily," urged Oengus. "Round up the cattle and let us be off."

As the Ce spirited away the cattle, the cows lowing seemed especially loud in the quiet of the night, as though alerting others of their location. Progress was fine through the waymarked woods but driving cows uphill, who felt none of the urgency their thieves felt, was slow.

They reached the pass with no one in pursuit. Had it not been for the unexpected deaths, they would have felt light-hearted.

Chapter Six

The Fiend

519 AD Loch Lumon to Cartray

Fillan was looking north up the long, grey loch of their island home. He noted how capriciously the spring behaved, with its warm sunshine promising the long-awaited passage out of the interminable days of cold and gloomy skies, only to be followed by winter whitening over the snowy ribs that traced the indentations of the dead hills. Spring would be well underway by now back in Erin, he thought.

How slow too was the pace of their work! What was there to show for twenty-two years, for their muintir remained relatively small. The island they settled, which previously had no name, had since become known as 'Inis y Mynachon', 'Isle of the Monks'. They had been left in peace, enjoying the protection of the king, and although glad of that sovereign shield on this volatile borderland, he had not come north just for this. He constantly felt restless, and on his bad days wished to return to Erin. If only there were some genuine interest in their faith to be embraced by scores of people, and not just the odd one or two! 'Odd' most certainly described a few that settled with them, who tried his patience.

Kessog, who seemed to wear patience like a garment, often instructed him, "Be persevering, my son. Continue faithful in prayer." He had watched Kessog grow grey-haired, fading away in the very obscurity and seeming irrelevancy of their island fastness. Although Kessog denied it, surely his master was concerned, deep down, for the lack of influence. Had he not noted too how Kessog had intensified his prayers of late, often keeping a nightlong vigil?

Occupied by these sullen thoughts, he became aware of a man paddling a canoe towards their island. The one-time faint speck in the distant greyness now took on a distinct definition. The canoe was piled high with wares.

"You want to trade?" called out the Pict, with the uncertain tone of a man speaking another dialect.

"Come closer, let us see what you have brought."

The Pict's face had an unwashed appearance, as though smeared with charcoal or even disfigured. As he neared the shore, swirling tattoos became clear, covering his cheeks and forehead. These had probably looked particularly fine in his youth, he thought, but with his skin growing flaccid with age, the tattoo artistry now appeared smudged.

Fillan helped the Pict haul the laden canoe partway out of the water.

"I have bear pelts, deer pelts, cow hides, sheep skins. Here, look! Good quality – no holes and well-scraped." He held a pelt to his nose, pronouncing, "No bad smell, eh." The old Pict did not smile.

"Where have you come from?" asked another monk, joining the two men. Ronan was fluent in the dialect of the Picts. This raised a smile from the old man.

"Are you a fellow Pict?" the trader asked.

"No, not really!" replied Ronan teasingly. He stretched out his arm to give the old man a friendly pat on his shoulder. The sleeve of his smock slipped back to expose part of his forearm.

"But you are tattooed like a Pict, and speak our dialect too!"

"True! In appearance, I am one of you. By birth, though, I am a Briton from Strath Clud, by inclination I lived as a Pict, and now by choice, I have become a soldier of Christ!"

This information confused the old man.

"You say you are a Briton and yet bear the emblems of the Picts! Why is that?"

"I was a trader, just like yourself, and this brought me into contact with the Fotla Picts. I made a home at Cartray for many a year, learned your tongue and ways, and liking your skill with tattoos, I decided to be decorated!"

"Oh, that is a surprise!" The old man clicked his tongue. "You Britons look down upon us, say we are uncivilised, dirty swine and all kinds of things unworthy to repeat and ought never to have been uttered."

"Well, old man, do you Picts not say that we Britons are proud, disdainful and off-hand? Do you not daub us all with the same mud?" retorted Ronan good-humouredly.

The old Pict smiled, revealing many missing teeth, with those that remained reduced to blackened stumps.

"Aye, that we do!" He grinned and, pointing his finger at Ronan, he pronounced emphatically, "But you are different."

"So, we can be friends?" asked Ronan with a tease of a smile.

"Why yes, certainly!" The old man came over to embrace Ronan with a heavy slap on his back.

"Where are you heading?" asked Fillan, this time trying as best he could to slip into the vernacular of their 'outlandish' dialect, as most Britons would deem it to be.

"Oh! You can speak like a Pict too!" The old man, bouncing with excitement, came over and pulled one of Filllan's sleeves up to inspect his forearm. "But you do not bear any Pictish emblems!" He sounded disappointed. "Have you not stayed with our people then?"

"No, I have not – at least not yet!" he replied wistfully, thinking on how he would welcome a change.

"You are young, maybe recently arrived from where you have come!"

"Not so young as you may think! My beard is maybe wispy, but I am in my mid-thirties. I have lived here for more years than I care to remember, watching Picts like yourself come paddling canoes and coracles down the loch, and others who come round the southside of the loch to trade in horses and cattle in the market of Din Brython. You return as quickly as you come, bartering your pelts for the finery of engraved glassware, wine and silver cloak clasps, prized by your warlords!"

"And do you have such finery here to barter for these pelts?" asked the old man hopefully. Ronan and Fillan laughed that they should be considered a community of wealth and sophistication.

"No, old man, we do not have anything like that," replied Ronan. "Why not join us for some food? You would be most welcome. We can then better explain what manner of people we are."

The Pict hesitated, eyeing his merchandise.

Fillan assured him, "It will be safe here."

The visitor seemed pleased by the warm welcome, shown as much by their accepting manner as by the generosity of their table. Abbot Kessog was introduced and answered the old man's enquiries, whose curiosity had been raised by this unexpected reception.

"What is your purpose here?" asked the Pict.

"We offer sanctuary; an alternative way to live that denounces violence and promotes acceptance of all men and women, irrespective of tribe, or belief, or politics."

"You mean that you are not an arm of the kings of Strath Clud!"

"No," smiled Kessog. "We serve a High King who is not of this world; one who is immortal and all-powerful."

The Pict looked puzzled to the point of being slightly suspicious. "So, what manner of men come here to join you and why do they come?"

"People are drawn out of curiosity and from need. One comes perhaps escaping a vendetta, another is driven by illness, seeking healing, or from spiritual need. Those who recognise we are passing through life all too quickly, and without power to change the tide of things, often find meaning and consolation here." The abbot seemed to pause reflectively before continuing. "But do you know what makes people remain? It is finding the One who protects."

"And you have healed people you say?"

"Not I. It is the High King. I am merely his servant."

"I am proof of that," spoke another sitting with them at the long table. "I am surprised you have not heard of our abbot's reputation."

"Come now! Whatever reputation, it comes from the Lord," mildly rebuked Kessog.

"And tell me, how do you live?" The Pict's curiosity was indeed great.

Once their meal had come to an end, Kessog assigned Fillan to show the old man around their island sanctuary.

"We are not like other communities," Fillan began with ease. "We are not blood relatives, or people of the same clan, but a community who have chosen exile from the world. Like other people, we farm, we fish. But unlike others, we keep a daily routine of prayer, study, singing psalms joyfully together and of working on illuminated manuscripts."

The old man scratched his head and looked at him with a half-opened mouth, as though he were about to speak.

"Our way of life has a familiar flow," elaborated Fillan. "A rhythm that appeals to those looking for order, away from the uncertain existence in the world. Sometimes it is this that draws people to join us and then the spiritual life begins to take on meaning."

"Oh aye, I see," the old man responded, more intrigued than comprehending.

The old Pict, looking no longer in any hurry to either barter or to leave, lingered in the scriptorium they had entered. "I am fascinated by your ways, although some things you talk about seem strange!"

Picking up a strip of vellum, the old man fingered it between his fingers. "What manner of skin is this? It is so thin and smooth."

"Ah! It is a special skill brought by us men from Erin. Let us go to the workshop that prepares these especially fine leather pages."

"I should like to see that. I have worked pelts all my life but have never come across something so smooth. And they take the dye so well."

At the place where the vellum was prepared, he was shown the implements used to scrape the skins stretched upon the frames. The process seemed familiar to the Pict and he looked perplexed how they achieved so fine a result.

"The final process involves rubbing the parchment with a pumice, then further wetting before more rubbing."

"What is pumice?"

"Here, take this."

"Oh, it is so light!" the old man exclaimed, genuinely surprised.

"More curiously, the stone floats too!"

The old man turned the stone reverently in his hand.

"In the final preparation, we use chalk or lime to treat the parchment to enable it to take inks and dyes better."

The old man smiled to learn the secret, to achieve the result he so admired. He continued to finger the pumice as though it were some magical object before trying it out. Approving the effect it had on the soft calf hide, he pronounced it to be very good. He stayed all day, even seeming to enjoy the rousing singing of the psalms.

"I am impressed by your togetherness, even though you are unrelated and come from different peoples. You even have Britons among you!"

Ronan laughed, giving the old man a friendly punch on his arm by way of feigned admonishment for the slur on his own race. He retorted, "And we even have Picts!"

The old man stood looking a bit lost and indecisive, finally saying, "I do not want to leave!"

"You do not have to," replied Fillan simply.

In the half-light of pre-dawn, Fillan again observed Kessog standing knee deep in the waters of Loch Lumon. He has been there most of the night, he exclaimed to himself, in awe of the abbot's tenacity. Kessog was seeking God's will and favour for the journey into Pictland that he and Ronan would be making with the abbot later that morning. He did not find prayer so easy, especially the vigil in the middle of the night. It was well that the monks kneeled to pray, otherwise he would fall asleep.

The hills to the east were now wreathed in the burnished light of the rising sun about to appear on the horizon. He heard Kessog conclude with a well familiar prayer, words that had been passed from Patrick to Machaloi, in what had become known as the 'Breastplate Prayer'; an entreaty uttered in times of danger. Kessog's words sounded calm but resolute over the troubled lapping of waters.

"I bind unto myself the name,
The strong name of the Trinity;
By invocation of the same,
The Three in One, and One in Three,
of whom all nature hath creation:
Eternal Father, Spirit, Word:
Praise to the Lord of my salvation,
Salvation is of Christ the Lord."

The abbot gazed up to their high peak, capped in fresh snow. It brought to Fillan's mind the illustrations their abbot often drew from this eminent mountain that formed a backdrop on all their activities. "When the summit shows clear," the abbot would say, "rising majestically into the ethereal blue, is it not like the goal of our earthly pilgrimage; distant and toilsome, but greatly to be desired?" On another occasion, Kessog would instruct, "When cloud casts a vast shadow and makes the ben seem threatening, does it not humble us mortals? Brothers, it brings awareness of our fleeting time upon the earth." Then once, in the depths of winter, he had observed, "Look for the mountain! It is lost in swirling cloud. Is it not like the lonely times when God is unseen? He is still there; it is just that the vapour of our self-interest or circumstance hides him from sight." Another time, when the clouds parted momentarily, he remarked, "Look at the resplendent top all pristine in deep snow! Note her frozen waterfalls glimmering alluringly! Is it not like the moment of divine revelation? Light pierces the long darkness of soul, to reveal what is most sublime: a lofty vision of God!"

After a hearty meal of porridge, the community came down to the shore. Fillan lifted his coracle up to see how well the pitch had remained intact, re-daubed only yesterday over the sewn seams of animal hides that covered the boat's wooden frame. He considered their journey north, an arduous trip but one he had long desired. The hills, through which they would pass, softened in the dusky blue of an early morning mist; they looked huge yet still managed to appear distant. They formed the boundary between their known world of Strath Clud and the wild region of the Fotla Picts beyond.

For much of the morning, the three pilgrims paddled up the loch, encouraged by seeing their mountain growing steadily. Streams and waterfalls came cascading down from the high crags that scarred the peak's face, giving it a vibrancy of sound and motion. Passing beyond the ben, they looked back and could no longer see Inis y Mynachon, nor the other isles that scattered the southern extent of the loch. Another large hill loomed on their left and still further, more mountains formed what seemed an impassable barrier.

His spirit was roused by the adventure that embraced the dangers of so wild an environment unknown to him, on a mission to barbarians whose reception could only be guessed and feared.

They made for shore. The sun shone with strength, hinting of summer days ahead, though when the wind blew it had the breath of snow. They stretched themselves out on the shingle of the shore, resting limbs that had been cramped all morning in their small craft.

The next stage was along a seldom-used route, where coracles had to be carried under a thick canopy of oak and birch. They soon passed a substantial waterfall whose sound filled the air, and they began the steep climb. The stream tumbled in a series of rapids and crashing cascades, with a noise accentuated by the narrow sides of the valley. They slowly ascended to the lip of the gorge. Beyond, the stream ran a much gentler course, leading them to an upland loch.

Taking to their coracles once more, they passed between the great flanks of snow-capped peaks. Fillan felt in awe of the silence of this solitude.

"Look, the birch are not showing any signs of coming into leaf up here, unlike the sprouted boughs around our isle," he remarked.

Their craft eventually ran onto the shingle at the loch's far end, from where a porterage led to another loch, one much longer and hemmed in by dense forest. A strong southwesterly wind partially helped their progress.

The rugged hilltop ridges, emerging above a dense treeline, wore an air of supreme detachment. They frequently saw deer grazing the shoreline and the solitary howl of a wolf haunted the higher hills. Late afternoon they passed through the narrows at the loch's eastern extent, in the lee of a steep hill to the south. They met a fisherman, the first man seen since leaving Loch Lumon. He had a woven wattle basket half submerged in the water, in which he kept live fish.

"Where have you come from?" the fisherman greeted as they drew near. He looked uneasy.

Ronan satisfied his curiosity. "Where do you live?"

"Down river, close to where it enters the next loch."

"What do you call this loch? It is quite a size!"

"Lengwartha. It is named so because it has been an ancient route used by cattle hustlers who sell their plunder in Strath Clud." The fisherman looked them over rather quizzically. "So, where are you bound? You do not want to linger here!" He nervously looked up at the high hillside opposite.

"We will be looking to camp soon," replied Kessog. "We are going east to Dindurn." He placed his coracle upon the ground and leaning on the paddle, Kessog questioned him. "What is it about this place that makes you feel uneasy?"

"There is an evil spirit here." The fisherman nodded in the direction of the high hillside. "Up there is the home of an unclean thing. I would not come here if it was not for the excellent fishing in this sheltered spot."

"What sort of unclean thing?"

"A ferocious thing that dwells in a cave. It is said to feed on men." He turned his eye away from the hill and looked enquiringly at Kessog. "You are not from these parts!"

"No, none of us are. I and my young companion come from Erin, across the sea."

The fisherman questioned him about the whereabouts of Erin, concluding that it was a long way indeed, but that he had heard others mention this faraway land.

"So, what made you leave your people?" queried the fisherman suspiciously.

"I am a wanderer for Christ, responding to the call to leave my country. We have a cell on Loch Lumon, where the fearful, the wondering and the sick come and find renewal."

At that moment, the fisherman flinched, scanning the hillside with visible agitation. "Did you hear that?"

The monks shook their heads.

"I think it is the fiend!" The Pict looked perturbed.

"As Christ is our protector, we need not fear," replied Kessog.

"And who is this Christ?"

"He is the Lord who became man to meet with us in our need."

"Ah, so he is one of your gods! That explains why I have not heard of him."

"Christ is not a local god. He, with his father, created everything we see. Christ cast out demons whom knew who he was. That is why we are not afraid."

The fisherman seemed to hear another sound. "That moan was louder! It is coming from over there on the hillside! Surely you heard that?"

Fillan was not surprised, for he had heard Picts and Britons talk of evil spirits, clearly oppressed.

"There! You must have heard that ferocious growl!" The fisherman quickly gathered up his things and looked at the monks incredulously for showing no signs of fleeing.

"Be still man," said Kessog. "Christ will rid you of this fiend."

"I can see him now, some loathsome thing. Do you not see? There on the far shore." He pointed with mounting consternation. "It is like he is fuming with rage."

Looking in the direction the fisherman indicated, Fillan could see nothing, although not doubting what the Pict could see.

"He is able to walk upon the water. Oh my! He is coming towards us full of malice."

"Do not go just yet," said Fillan. He then realised that the fisherman had succumbed to the power of the fiend, for he was petrified to the spot.

Stepping protectively in front of the fisherman, Kessog stretched out an arm towards the loch, to where they assumed the fiend to be approaching, and shouted across the waters.

"In the name of Christ, be gone!"

The fisherman looked up from where he had been cowering, peering from behind Kessog's back. Astonished, he was able to say, "It has obeyed you!"

"What do you see?" asked Kessog.

"The fiend just stopped dead in his tracks! Now he is running to where he came from!"

Kessog shouted across the waters, "You are banished! You have no place here!"

"The fiend appears to writhe and squirm," spoke the fisherman. "He makes a roar, like he is wounded . . . He flees quicker than it came." He traced the fiend's progress, running between copses, before disappearing over the high, treeless ridge.

"What kind of power do you have?" questioned the fisherman, astonished. "I cannot believe we are still here. It is said that no one who sees the fiend has the power to escape, and that their end is upon them! But you, you just commanded it to go and it went!"

"It is by the power of the one who made the world – no demonic power can withstand him," explained Kessog.

"And have you sent other fiends away?"

Kessog nodded. "But you know, equal to this power is the love of Christ. It encircles all who put their trust in him."

Chapter Seven

Reckonings at the Ferry

555 AD River Dee

"At least you killed a man in self-defence – or I should say, in defence of me." Oengus was trying to understand the events of the previous night. "But I killed a woman in cold blood. Both parents, killed by us!"

"It happened on the spur of the moment. At least you do not have the blood of the bairns on your hands," reasoned Taran.

"That was thanks to you. You stopped me!"

They had been talking over the scene for some time, often repeating themselves, attempting to come to terms with the brutality.

"And to think, we thought fighting would be glorious!"

"These are typical feelings after the first killing," remarked Caltram. "The first is always the worst. It is all part of coming of age."

"Better there had been no killing on your first cattle lifting!" added Nechtan emphatically.

"But what were we to do?" remonstrated Taran. "Had we not killed, we would have been killed!"

"That is true! If it was not for Taran, I would be dead," declared Oengus.

"Not all will be well," remarked Caltram, who appeared to be thinking through the likely series of events. "The Circinn of that neighbourhood will be outraged. The plight of the orphans will call for revenge."

"A vengeance that would come anyway over the plundered cattle," expanded Nechtan. "But their revenge will be more than plundering someone's herd our side of the Dee. Many will come and will not be satisfied until they have shed blood."

"If we could know their thinking, we could be prepared," said Oengus thoughtfully, keen to move on with a forward plan rather than relive the horror.

Taran broke the silence. "Maybe we could go back to the ferry – there is a cattle fair taking place this Saturday. Perhaps we can get an inkling of what the Circinn are thinking."

"That would be risky. Your faces will be recognised and arouse suspicion if you turn up so soon," objected Caltram.

"But if Taran and I were thought to be returning from our business south via the ferry . . ." Oengus looked at them with raised eyebrows. "Surely they would not suspect us?"

"No, I do not like it," remarked Nechtan.

"But would thieves go to the market just days after the incident?" replied Taran.

Once they were on their own, Caltram spoke to Oengus, "You need to seize the initiative now and prove yourself the undisputed leader."

Oengus grimaced before effusively declaring, "Cousin Taran saved my life!"

"You would have done the same for him! Taran is too soft to become warlord. I agree with you, the bairns should have been killed! It would have ended their misery as orphans and have reduced the risk of our being caught."

"I was hot-headed with the instinct to raise my sword against them. I was not thinking."

"It is not good to think too much at such times. Instincts are often best – they make survivors of us." Caltram patted his son's back, which brought no consolation to Oengus.

The cattle fair was not large, although it was the first of the season. Horse dealers came from the Fortriu tribe: one with eyes that would not engage but flashed in every direction, and the other with a scar running from his right temple across the bridge of his nose and cheek, losing itself in a red beard. No one wanted to do business with them, and they were the subject of uneasy glances and furtive remarks.

Taran and Oengus positioned themselves in the heart of the commerce, leaning against a wall as though enjoying the bustle whilst idly eating a freshly baked loaf of bread. They picked up pieces of the talk. "It was thirty head of cattle lifted – imagine thirty! . . . neighbours found the parents bodies propped against the door after hearing shouting and wailing from the bairns . . . The boy and girl are in a state of shock . . . the thieves had left a trail: a corridor of trees with clean nicks at eye level . . . tracks were followed to the pass and across the river . . . the filthy work of the Ce."

One broad shouldered Circinnian man, wrapped in a double sheepskin stitched together, made it his business to inspect every cow in the market. "Where did this one come from?"

"From my farm just upriver," came the piqued reply. "I do not deal in stolen cattle."

His blunt, accusing manner upset an older Ce couple who stayed at the ferry. "I do not like your tone! We have our own cow to sell and need to eat. Now be off with you if you are not going to buy."

"And how would you do that!" retorted the burly fellow, boldly posturing his superior bulk that rose half a head taller than anyone else in the market.

They turned their backs on him. Taran and Oengus strolled on over to look at their cow.

"Are you interested in the cow?" the couple asked. The cousins expressed enough curiosity as to be given a price, learn its age and how many calves it had had. "You are not Circinnian. You will have gathered, we people of the Ce are not popular after all this nasty business."

"And do you stay around these parts?" asked Taran.

"Aye, that is our home over there," the wife nodded in its direction. The couple asked after the cousins and appeared satisfied with their story. After the ill feeling of the Circinn, they were glad to speak with Ce folk. The couple decided to cut their losses early that day as no one was in the mood for trading and invited the cousins to take food at their home.

"Our names are Drest and Ligach," the couple said, opening their home. "Bad business, this . . . it enflames the old animosities between Ce and Circinn, who both share this village. We work at getting along together."

The couple hospitably rustled up food; drink was not in short supply. Late afternoon, the cousins were pressed to stay the night.

"That is a kind offer, but we should be on our way," excused Taran.

"Our families are expecting us home and will wonder if we do not return," added Oengus.

"I tell you what," said Taran, "we will come back another time, and yes, very soon."

The cousins returned the following market day. Finding Drest and Ligach, Taran said, "We have brought a cartload of good ash and are looking for a buyer." He pointed with his chin towards their cart.

"If it is ash, then maybe the smith will be interested to make handles for his agricultural implements. Come, I will introduce you."

The smith had worked up quite a sweat, his son the more so, who was working the bellows hard next to the intense heat of the charcoal forge.

"Keeping busy then?" remarked Drest to the blacksmith.

"Oh aye. Would you believe it: we have an order for twenty-seven swords."

"Twenty-seven! Who would be wanting that many?"

"Circinnians from way upriver. They have no local smith there."

"I have a couple of young men here who have a cartload of ash. Thought you might be interested?"

"I might be." Looking up at the cousins for the first time, he asked, "Can you supply charcoal?"

"Aye, we could," agreed Oengus. The smith poured the molten iron from a crucible into a cast. While it was cooling, he took a moment to look at the ash and beat them down to a keen price.

"We can do a low price since you promise further business with the charcoal," assented Taran.

"Come back and take some food with us," invited Drest.

"I will make a purchase first and then join you," said Taran. He rejoined them shortly, carrying four large flagons. "Ash for ale and spirit!" he remarked, looking pleased with himself.

"Why, that must have cost you!" Drest commented, a little wide-eyed. "But then, you are unmarried men without responsibilities, so you have surplus silver."

When pressed to stay the night, they did not refuse. Some of their Circinnian neighbours joined them, lingering into the evening, having got wind of a plentiful supply of beer. The drink made friends of men, smoothed over their hostilities. One Circinnian, with moustaches that grew beyond his jaw, placed his arm around Taran's shoulders and told him stories. In the manner of a drunkard, he spoke into Taran's ear in a conspiratorial manner.

"What is he saying?" asked Oengus over the loud hubbub.

"Oh, just a lot of nonsense," he replied as an aside. "Much of it is unintelligible!"

The Circinnian returned to Taran. "I do not much care for the Ce, but you are alright." He staggered and put a steadying hand on Taran's chest to stop himself from falling. He repeated his comment, now much louder for those around him to hear. Catching the eyes of his neighbours, he declared, "I want you to drink to my new friend here, Taran. He has supplied the drink tonight and that is what I call a decent thing to do!" He staggered again. A few close by raised their cups and downed their drink, nodding their appreciation in Taran's direction.

"It is time you were away home," said one of the Circinnian men. The drunk protested. The other insisted and, still being in control of his senses, had his way. Once they had left, the remaining Circinnians, aware of the change in mood, recalled that these were the people of the Ce. They were curt and sparing with their farewells.

"That was some change in atmosphere!" remarked Oengus.

Drest nodded and spoke in a hushed tone. "Not all is well, my friends. I learned that the order for the swords placed with the blacksmith are not for Circinnians way upriver, but for those from the valley where the cattle were stolen. They are mustering their neighbours for an assault."

"Who are they going to attack?"

"Us Ce, of course! But it will not be here, or through here. We have an understanding that as immediate neighbours, and for the sake of the market, we need to get along."

"Do they have any idea who took their cattle?" asked Oengus.

"Yes, they do. They know the direction that the Ce rustlers went. They do not mind whether they get the actual folk who lifted their cattle, or some innocent folk, do they? They will exact revenge and will achieve much harm, turning one Ce community against another."

"And when do you think it will be?" asked Oengus.

"You have a lot of questions! Why would you be needing to know that?" asked Drest.

The cousins shifted a little awkwardly. Taran had a ready reply. "We have recently made home upriver and are naturally wary of getting caught up and becoming the innocent victims ourselves."

"Fair enough, I suppose," declared Drest.

"We will look out for you," added Ligach, much more warmly.

On their next visit, when Taran and Oengus delivered basket loads of charcoal to the blacksmith, they sought out Drest and Ligach.

"You remind me of our own son . . ." Ligach remarked with moistened eyes and, choking with sudden emotion, was unable to continue.

"He disappeared and no one knew what became of him," explained Drest rather flatly.

They learned that the Circinn were planning to attack the Ce upriver, at the next new moon. "Blood and cattle is what they are after."

"Be certain to make yourselves scarce that night," Ligach entreated them.

Chapter Eight

The Muted One

519 AD Cartray

"You are to come home with me. We have fish aplenty and a warm place for shelter," the fisherman said, gathering up his few belongings.

"That is most kind," Kessog responded with warmth.

"Just follow me. I have trodden a path between here and home."

The monks secured their coracles upon their foreheads, using clothing as a cushion. Not long after, Fillan could smell wood smoke and then saw the huts, a sight he welcomed for he had feared the settlement was much further. They were greeted by the fisherman's wife, an adult son and his wife, along with three young children. All were busy with the usual activities of early evening, chopping wood and preparing food. A whiff of boiled turnip came to his nostrils.

"This is my wife, Benalban," the fisherman began, "and my name is Uist. You will be hungry after that journey. As for me, I am famished!" He rubbed his stomach vigorously. The pilgrims added their fish to what the fisherman had caught.

"Are you all druids?" asked the wife, observing their foreheads were shaven from ear to ear and their hair was long.

"No," replied Fillan good-humouredly. "We are like druids though!"

"Let me tell you," began Uist, suddenly animated. "These men have power and believe in one they call Christ. I saw the fiend, and if it was not for these men, I would not be here now." He described what had happened, sometimes with such excitement that he missed a word here and there.

With dusk falling fast, they renewed efforts to cook dinner, abandoned when recounting what had happened with the fiend.

"And so, what is your business at Dindurn, if you do not mind me asking?" Uist asked, stoking the fire.

"We are seeking an audience with Lord Domech," answered Kessog.

"You know Domech?" Uist's voice rose with surprise.

"No, we just know of him," clarified Kessog. "Does his rule extend here?"

"Aye. We are part of the Fotla tribe and Domech is our warlord."

"And what sort of ruler is he?" continued Kessog, seemingly sensing that Uist was happy to talk about his warlord protector.

"Well, we are quite far from Dindurn – on the edge of things, you could say. You will have noticed that there are no dwellings between here and Lumon – those are the lonely lands, haunted by spirits, where only the desperate caterans venture . . ." He paused, before adding, "And men with strange powers!" Uist stroked his bent nose. "The reach of Strath Clud is close by to the south, so we value Domech's strong rule." He took a small hand broom and carefully swept the floor to avoid raising the dust.

"Domech is building up the fortress at Dindurn," Uist continued. "Apparently, as new defences go up, more people build their huts within the expanding citadel. It is becoming quite the centre, they say, of several hundred." Uist laughed, perhaps, concluded Fillan, at the thought of so many people living together on one hill.

"Why build more defences?" enquired Kessog, who seemed keen to piece together the politics of the Fotla.

"Dindurn is strategic, as you will see, lying along a route to good farmland in the east. Dindurn will repulse an attack from the west by the Dal Riatans, who might take it into their heads to have a piece of the good lands." Uist eyed them cautiously. "They say that the influence of Dal Riata stretches across the water to Erin."

"It is true. Just a part, though, in the north."

Uist placed the broom down and, remaining in a crouched posture, looked keenly at Kessog. "You mentioned that you came from Cash or something like that?"

"Cashel," corrected Kessog. "Cashel is part of the Munster kingdom to the south and does not come under Dal Riata."

"Do you speak the same language as the Dal Riatans?" Uist proceeded, looking intently at Kessog. No doubt Uist was figuring out where their allegiances might lie, thought Fillan.

"Yes, we speak Gaelic, but we have different tribal groupings with their own kings who, at times, are at war with one another."

"Oh! That is just like us Picts!" nodded Uist. Fillan noted that he took some reassurance that their differences perhaps were not so great.

Probably aware of Uist's discomfort about their political loyalties, Kessog clarified. "We do not come as representatives of any of Erin's kingdoms or Dal Riata. Our Lord does not have an earthly kingdom, but a heavenly one. We live peaceably with all men, choosing to live in exile from our own people to share the peace of Christ. We do not force this on anyone but share our lives with those who come to us."

"Why are you going to Domech if you do not force your beliefs on anyone? He might have you killed, especially if he believes you are conniving with the Dal Riatans."

"To seek permission to start a community of Christ within your lands. There is a growing desire for our instruction in Cartray and Ucheldi Ucha – from Pictish men and women who have been visiting us on our isle. Our hope is that God's blessing might be upon you too. Think of the protection from the evil one you saw earlier! As for risking death, there is always a risk in our ventures! But men are subject to a higher authority, even warlords and kings!"

Uist appeared satisfied. The fish were gutted outside, where a couple of dogs devoured what fell. The fish were grilled over the fire then laid on a wooden communal platter, along with mashed turnip. Benalban passed a small dish of food to Uist who, taking it outside, made an offering to the Bulàch. Benalban gestured her guests to eat. The pilgrims bowed their heads, Kessog giving thanks for food and unexpected hospitality.

After the meal, the monks excused themselves to pray. Fillan went to take a firebrand from the hearth to start their own fire outside.

"You do not need to do this apart from us," protested Uist. "Please bide here that we may be instructed. What I have seen is impressive and what I have heard makes me want to hear more."

Kessog indicated Fillan to remove the scriptures from the satchel, directing him to read from a certain passage, following which Kessog made a few observations.

"Tell me," began Uist, "what do I need to do to withstand the ferocity of a fiend? What happened earlier was astonishing. Indeed, I owe my life to you."

"The power belongs to Christ. When we put our confidence in him, we have his protection. The scriptures say, *'The Lord is faithful, and he will strengthen you and protect you from the evil one.'*"

"I do choose to believe. I have seen his mercy and power with my own eyes!"

"Then you are our brother!" replied Kessog with warmth.

After more instruction, they prayed for the Lord's favour to shine upon their venture and upon Uist's household.

The next day broke grey and with a steady drizzle. As they gathered for the morning devotions, Uist and Benalban joined them.

"You mentioned baptism last night," began Uist. "What prevents us from being baptised now?"

"Nothing now that you trust," replied Kessog. Turning to Benalban, he asked, "What about you, do you believe?"

"I believe in what my husband saw and the power he witnessed when you prayed against the fiend. Why continue to be afraid of bad spirits when there is a protector?"

The baptism followed directly after breakfast and the pilgrims made ready to depart.

"God willing, we shall pass this way on our return," called out Ronan from the end coracle. "For we would share some more with our new brother and sister."

"Aye, do that," replied Uist. "We should like that very much."

"I will prepare you a good feast when you will overnight with us again," added Benalban with eagerness in her voice.

"I pray that our warlord will look favourably upon your request," Uist shouted across the water.

Fillan raised his paddle to acknowledge the greeting as they plied eastwards. The loch was short, narrowing to a point where they found an outflow that hardly moved over the flat ground, weaving before connecting with another loch. The drizzle came on heavier and became a steady rain. His wet clothing encumbered his movements and chaffed his skin.

Lining the shores of a far-reaching loch were a few huts where the forest had been cleared for meadows to graze cattle and horses. Plumes of smoke from other huts hidden from view indicated a more populated region. Beyond the loch, they greeted a group of children.

"Cartray? That is where we live! You can see it from the top of the brae," said a young lad.

"Do not follow the river," added an older girl. "It is much quicker to just walk from here."

Cartray was a sizeable community, built close to the ruins of the Roman camp that had guarded two approaches into the Highlands. Ronan acknowledged a man sharpening an axe outside his hut.

"Where are you going?" greeted the man in return.

"We are visiting Irb," replied Ronan, with the ease of a man returning to a community he knew well.

They passed a line of huts.

"Hey Ronan! We have not seen you for quite some time," a swarthy looking man called from his doorway. "Who is with you?"

"These are my fellow brothers: Kessog and Fillan."

"Come on in out of the rain," he insisted, with energetic arm motions as if herding a group of reluctant goats.

They hesitated.

"Come in, it is nearly lunch time and what is ours is yours."

The pilgrims smiled and entered the home.

"This is Forcus," Ronan introduced their host.

"Come close to the fire – you are wet through," smiled Forcus. "Dry off here and soon we will have something warm to eat. This is my wife, Beatha."

Possibly shy at having strangers suddenly fill her home, Fillan noticed that she did not look up, but continued to busy herself with chores. He observed she wore a long bracelet of bronze coiled up her wrist and it struck him as being lavish. Other than that, she was unremarkable, with thin, dark hair that looked unkempt.

Ronan seemed glad to catch up on all the local news. Fillan could feel his clothes growing warm, although still damp. His skin became itchy. As he pressed close to the hearthside, he idly watched the vapour rising from his clothes. Talk turned to the purpose of their current journey to Dindurn.

"What makes you think Domech is going to agree to you establishing a community here?" asked Forcus, turning to Kessog.

"When it comes to the will of a warlord, who can be sure!" After a lengthy pause of running his fingers through what remained of his long hair, Kessog added, "What gives more assurance is the will of heaven. He would have all the sons and daughters of the Fotla come under his protection. We pray that Lord Domech's heart will take kindly to our request."

"Domech is not someone known for a softening of heart. It is his head that rules and the strength of his sword arm. That is how he has come to power."

Fillan watched the silent Beatha adding vegetables and off-cuts of meat into a simmering cauldron. A most pleasant aroma filled the hut and made him hungry. Soon broth was being ladelled into bowls and glad thanks was given. Fillan felt his own spirits lifted.

"We have heard of this Christ to whom you pray. Irb and his wife invoke his name and not that of the Bulàch."

"We were on our way to see Irb when we met you," replied Ronan. "He is an occasional visitor to our isle."

Bread and cheese were laid before the men on a large, wooden platter.

"He speaks curious things," continued Forcus. "Tales from far off lands, of miracles and histories unheard of, and teachings to turn away from our gods. But then this lord of yours died, they say, nailed like a criminal to a tree!" Their host shook his head dismissively.

Totally unexpectedly, Beatha interjected with a note of contempt. "How can he be all-powerful if his enemies got the better of him?" She spoke with that burst of impatience, thought Fillan, of one who had held her tongue long enough.

"It was not his enemies getting the better of him. His death was intentional, a sacrificial offering to make peace between God and man," explained Kessog calmly, unperturbed by this objection.

"Poof!" The woman puffed out her cheeks. "I do not believe a word of it! Each person needs to make amends for themselves. What kind of words are these!" At this, she rose from her squatting position with a wild look flashing with much hostility towards them. She went over to the door and spat vehemently on the ground outside.

"Why would we change our ways?" she continued with clenched fists. "Our customs have served our fathers and their fathers from as long back as anyone can remember. We are the Fotla with our own gods and beliefs. Why should we change for a god of some far-off country that none of us has heard of?"

Fillan noted how flushed her cheeks had become as she paced before the group.

"Our mother goddess has made our land and everything in it, and we prosper or perish, according to how we worship her. Abandon her, and she will abandon us! The fruit of the land will wither, so why would we even consider such a thing?"

She stubbed her toes on a log. Her bosom heaved as she took in short intakes of breath through flared nostrils. Raising a hand to flick her thin hair back, the bronze armlet shone in the firelight.

"By the name of Brigantia, who is in the ascendancy now that winter has passed, I invoke her to frustrate your plans; that there will be no more talk of this Jesus in this house and in our lands, and that Domech will have nothing of it!"

Upon hearing this oath, Kessog rose to his feet; his usual calm countenance changed. He fixed her sternly with his eye. "Woman, in the name of Christ, be silent!"

To everyone's amazement, she did not retort.

"And silent you shall be, and your tongue will lose the art of talking," prophesied the abbot.

Fillan observed Beatha closely. She opened her mouth, looking as though to abuse Kessog verbally, but could say nothing. Her extreme agitation turned to anger and then to dismay. Unable to utter a single word, she stared imploringly at her husband, clutching and shaking his forearm, bidding him to do something.

"What can I do?" he replied in dismay. "I am only a man and you spoke words unworthy of a host to our guests."

He turned to Kessog. "I see that you have power!" he uttered soberly, without trace of his former dismissive tone. "Will you not reverse this curse? Please excuse my wife. As the daughter of a druid chief, she does not take kindly to others who do not follow the time-honoured ways."

Fillan had never seen anything like this, although he had read of such things in the scriptures. It was the more surprising, for Kessog was a mild-mannered man, noted for his wise dialogue and diplomacy. There were healings attributed to his prayers for he was a faithful man, but nothing sensational like making one mute or banishing a fiend! The abbot must have keenly detected her intent at the very outset of her opposition. All those nightlong vigils standing cruciform in freezing water must have made his spirit especially keen. But then, he considered, did I not detect something different about Beatha?

Beatha paced the hut, gesticulating and wringing her hands. Seeing the bread and cheese still largely untouched before her guests, she grabbed the platter, and with decisive strides made for the door. She threw the contents outside, much to the surprise of the dog, who rose and trotted out to this unexpected feast. She looked back, defiant and livid, and then threw the empty platter forcibly into a corner. She mouthed some curse.

The spoiling of the food – a desecration of blessing and human toil – explicitly breaking all taboos, made Fillan feel uneasy. He wanted to depart after such a demonstration. However, Kessog, who had been standing, unexpectedly sat down. He looked upon Beatha with a composed countenance, appearing in no hurry to respond. Why was the abbot lingering? How could he appear so unruffled after such an outburst?

Kessog took an audible intake of breath and addressed the woman. "You shall have no power of speech until we pass this way again. This will give occasion to test your own heart." Upon this pronouncement, Kessog judiciously arose, straightening out his plaid that was somewhat drier than before. "Come, let us find the home of our brother Irb and bring some encouragement to his household."

The pilgrims went out into the rain. Ronan parted with a conciliatory remark to their host, clasping Forcus about his shoulder to impart some strength, before following the others down a well-trodden and muddy way between the huts.

At Irb's home, Rowena, his wife, warmly beckoned them in. Irb lay asleep with their newborn, close to the central hearth. Coming to his senses, Irb recognised them and sat up. "Come on in, brothers – what a surprise, you are welcome. You are most welcome indeed!"

Taking an old rag, Irb wiped down the rough split boards of the floor platform about the hearth in an eager gesture to accommodate his guests. He introduced Rowena and each of his children, who were all at home in such steady rain. Questions were asked as to where they were going and for what purpose, which was all received with much interest.

"You will stay with us tonight," he urged warmly. "The rain is set in."

Fillan was glad to hear this, hoping his companions felt the same way. The matter was settled that they would remain until the next day.

Ronan spoke of the recent encounter in the previous household.

"Well, I am not surprised Beatha had that reaction!" commented Irb, before adding with a certain emphasis, "She has powers. They say that when she is in a trance, she can leave her body and travel great distances to far off places and can listen in on conversations and bring detailed report!"

"I recognised a power about her," confessed Kessog. "Once she started to speak against our purpose, the Spirit told me these were not just words." The abbot smoothed his long beard. "So that others may know that the Lord is merciful, she will regain her voice. However, I doubt she will accept this peace but will oppose all that is good."

"What will come of this?" asked Irb. "Can the Lord not do something to remove her power?"

"The Lord can do what he likes, there is no limit. But we shall not fear, for our times are in his hands and nothing will frustrate his purposes like some earthly king. Come, brothers, we rest secure in his will, knowing that we are immortal until his purposes for our lives are complete."

Kessog took the opportunity to instruct them further and concluded by singing part of a psalm. He led by singing a line which the rest repeated by way of a refrain. In this manner, Irb and his family, who did not know the words, were able to join in.

"God is our refuge and strength,
An ever-present help in trouble.
Therefore, we will not fear, though the earth give way
And the mountains fall in the heart of the sea,
Though its waters roar and foam and the mountains quake with their surging."

The children listened with evident curiosity.

"We should pray," Kessog said, "given the purpose of our quest."

"Meeting with Domech is not likely to go smoothly," Irb agreed. "He too follows the time-honoured ways, enforced by his druid advisers. He is used to having his way, and should anyone counter it, he will resort to violence."

"But Irb, know this. Who is Domech compared to the Lord? Domech is but a breath. Although he does not bow the knee to Christ, all that he has is there because of the will of him who is sovereign overall. The High King extends a hand of mercy to the people of the Fotla."

Fillan was burning to add something. "If careful explanation cannot persuade Lord Domech to allow us to establish a muintir, then the Lord will, no doubt, have other means to make him comply."

"What means do you suppose?" asked Irb.

"By whatever means," replied Kessog rather enigmatically.

Rowena, who was busy cooking, sent a couple of reluctant children into the rain to gather extra ingredients from a nearby field. Kessog asked Ronan to read. The monk took a book from his satchel, wrapped in a large piece of seal hide, well greased for waterproofing and soft and pliable for wrapping. The book, wrapped many times over, required many unfoldings. Kessog provided a reference, which the other searched for, turning the vellum pages lovingly, for it was all hand-written. He read from a page bordered by an intricately woven knot of yellow and purple, framing the finely formed black letters. The two terminals of the woven knot depicted in orange and blue, a crouching cat and an upright heron. Ronan read with care. There followed some instruction, a few questions, and they concluded with prayer.

Lunch was then served – the second one for the pilgrims.

With the rain letting up later in the afternoon, they helped Irb in his field and gathered food for the evening meal. On returning to Cartray, a change of atmosphere was palpable in the village. Folk eyed them suspiciously and some with a degree of hostility. A visitor came that evening, a thin man with pale skin and raven black hair; his forehead shaven in the style of a druid. He seemed momentarily taken aback by the visitors, which Fillan thought strange, since they were the cause of the druid's visit; then reflected that it was probably on account of their own druid-like appearance that had surprised him.

"This is Phelan," Irb introduced their visitor, adding meaningfully, "Beatha's father." Turning to Phelan, he said, "Please, will not you sit down?"

"No, I will not sit. I will come straight to the matter of what constrains me to enter this house. By what authority have you cursed my daughter?" Phelan stood stoically with his legs apart.

Kessog responded with mildness, contrasting with the druid's tone. "In Christ's name – the one who has made heaven and earth."

"We do not recognise this Christ here!" Phelan replied emphatically. "Undo your magic, or otherwise face the consequences."

"It will be undone in good time, but not for the moment."

Fillan was impressed by how calm his master remained.

"It will be at the Lord's timing, when we shall pass this way again."

"And what if you do not return from Dindurn?" The druid spoke with a menacing tone.

"Then you would better make it your business not to counter our purposes," remarked the abbot.

"Do you think Domech is just going to give in to your request to allow this strange teaching without the consent of all the wise ones? Would we risk upsetting the balance of spiritual power and order to take up with new gods?"

"Consider this. From what has been clearly demonstrated, your curses and incantations hold no effect against the soldiers of Christ! Does that not indicate that your old order is powerless?"

Phelan raised his right arm, pointing at Kessog in a threatening manner. "You have gall to come here and speak of such things. You will suffer for this!"

"I understand," Kessog replied, unruffled by the tone. "All will come well. We shall return – that much the Lord is making clear – and Beatha shall have her voice back again; not at your demand, mind you, but because Christ is compassionate."

Kessog rose unhurriedly and faintly smiled at the druid. "Consider this, Phelan – you know the power that you and your daughter wield, which this community holds in awe (and I can see that you are well respected). Despite this, though, Beatha was powerless to impose her curse upon us. Your gods could not prevent her from becoming mute. Does that not indicate the limit of the Bulàch's power? Can you not recognise a far superior power that countered the curse with a hold on her tongue? Who can withstand the power of the Lord God?"

Phelan maintained the same hostile air. He stood for a moment, as though he might say something more, before turning abruptly, leaving with a resolute step.

Two more visitors came that evening: a young couple, curious to learn more about this power, eagerly asking questions. They were prayed for before they departed. As Irb's household settled down to sleep that night, Phelan could be heard, together with a company, chanting to the spirits of the dead well into the night.

Chapter Nine

The Ambush

555 AD River Dee

The night of the new moon brought a fifty-man strong cohort of the Ce to the Dee. Leaving their horses with two men, they forded and climbed to the pass from where the Circinnian warband was due. Armed with bows, swords and spears, they concealed themselves among the rocks and shrubs on either side of the pass. Taran and Oengus went on as lookouts and found a vantage point with good cover above the pasturelands of the Circinn below.

The main warband marshalled their mental abilities for the fight ahead. The river made a silver tracery through the disturbed darkness of branches bent in the breeze; a wind that blew cool, carrying the scent of the new bracken shoots. It was too dark to make out field or wood. Overhead, an owl's call unsettled the men, waiting for what seemed an eternity.

"Upon them lads!" cried a deep, bass voice.

The battle cry was taken up immediately by a crescendo of other voices. No sooner had the shout been raised than arrows and spears began raining down to the utter dismay of the Ce. The sickening thud of pointed missiles into flesh followed by shrieks distressed the night. In the confusion of bodies falling, the Circinn hurtled down from the ridge above, ambushing their ambush! The clash of sword and cries of slaughter was brief as half of the Ce were overwhelmed, routed from one side of the valley. Their compatriots on the opposite side of the pass ran in a counter charge, reaching the place of skirmish just when what remained of their able comrades were fleeing.

Holding the upper ground, the Circinn re-grouped behind a line of shields. The Ce reinforcements paused in momentary confusion, outnumbered. A volley of arrows came raining down, picking off several of the Ce. A couple of youths, eager to prove themselves, ran upon the Circinnians.

"Come back!" bellowed Nechtan, commanding this small unit.

The youths did not turn and, reaching the Circinnian line, they both fell by spear thrusts. Many of the Ce lay dead, and the wounded, unable to rise, cried out and groaned.

Realising the hopeless position, Nechtan cried, "Lads! To the river."

The Ce ran pell-mell down the steep brae with the Circinn in hot pursuit. Three more were brought down on the desperate, headlong descent. Nechtan's party caught up with a few stragglers from the first unit, whose wounds impeded their movement.

"Run faster!" encouraged Nechtan, who caught hold of one of them by the arm. The other wounded fell prey to the swords of the Circinn.

"What is that we are hearing?" Taran spoke confused in the dark.

"It sounds like a fight. Come, let us return quickly to the pass." Oengus had already turned and started to run up the brae.

They arrived at the pass, shocked to find the bodies of their comrades.

"The rest have gone!" Oengus sounded astonished, panting heavily. "Listen, can you hear some commotion towards the river?"

Taran strained his ears and, hearing the groans of a wounded man, went over to him.

"Circinn surprised us," he spluttered. His eyelids flickered.

"Are you able to rise?" asked Taran.

"No. My chest . . . a spear." He coughed with difficulty, choked, then vomited blood.

"We will come back for you as soon as we can," Oengus tried to reassure the man. Looking at Taran, he said, "We need to be extremely cautious."

"Most definitely. Let us take a parallel route to avoid the main path."

They set off side by side, veering slightly apart as they ran downhill over broken terrain. In the darkness, Taran nearly flew into someone. Startling one another, both men slowed momentarily.

I recognise him, thought Taran, wondering which of his comrades he could be. Yet, there was something about his manner that he instinctively distrusted. The momentum of his pace and the steepness of slope carried him inexorably downhill, and uppermost in his mind was the danger of their situation with their warband routed. Although he bore a sword, as did the other man, Taran's gut instinct was not to stop and turn upon him.

He saw Oengus out in front, casting him a backwards glance. He then checked over his shoulder to the stranger he had startled, wondering if he were in pursuit. The man had struck off towards the main path. Why would he do that? Oengus rejoined him and spoke with bewilderment. "That was close!"

"I did not know who it was – he looked familiar!"

"It is that drunken Circinnian from the night at Drest and Ligach's house!"

"So that is who it was!" he thought aloud, recalling how the man had declared him to be his friend.

The cousins were now in full flight and, anxious to avoid any more Circinn, they took a direction to the west of their river crossing. They arrived at a place where the river flowed calm and deep, forcing them to swim a section. On the far bank, they hurried across the meadows and reached the road that led to the settlement that supported them on this campaign.

Taran looked at Oengus. "I wonder who is left and how it goes with our fathers?"

Oengus found Caltram awake with his knees drawn up into his chest in obvious pain.

"Oengus! So, you are alive!" Caltram said with evident relief.

"What has happened to you?"

"I took an arrow in my side. It was fired at close range and went through to my back."

"How did you get away?"

"I gritted my teeth. It was not so bad in the heat of the moment. Then once we reached the horses across the river, I just had to stay in the saddle. It was a long ride and this village could not come soon enough."

When dawn broke, a tall man with a dark fringe spoke to Caltram. "We need more payment."

"We gave you a cow!"

"That was some time ago. The situation is more dangerous for us on the borderlands."

"Another cow then."

"Two," demanded the man in a tone that was in no mood for bargaining.

Caltram nodded resignedly, rising with difficulty to his feet.

"Get the horses ready," he snapped and spat on the ground. Catching sight of Taran, he made a perceptible grimace. "Have we done a round up?"

Taran could tell from Caltram's pale complexion and bowed posture that the injury looked serious.

"There are only seventeen of us left."

Caltram swore. "That is thirty-three men lost!"

Their subdued arrival home later that evening roused the whole community. Rhynie was haunted night long with the sobs of wives and mothers.

Talorgen convened a council next morning. Caltram had to be helped to the hall; his side was wet with fresh blood and a terrible pallour covered his cheeks and forehead. His wife, Drusticc, was in constant attendance, her face narrowed with concern. Oengus was there too at his father's side. All other notables were present, including Maelchon and Gest, whose counsel from a spiritual perspective was much sought. Bereft family members drifted into the hall, anxious for some solidarity in this shared tragedy; their outbreaks of weeping filled the air with an appalling heaviness.

After the details of the main skirmish had been explained, Oengus and Taran were called to give an account of the events.

"We believed that we had good intelligence from the couple at the ferry," Taran explained, "but, of course, the outcome suggests they were accomplices of the Circinnian ambush."

How devastating this revelation felt. He and Oengus had been so keen to prove themselves and now they were having to defend their actions. Their uncle looked on, silently furious.

Caltram spoke up at this point, looking like he would not be holding on to life for much longer. "It is a tragic day to befall the Ce, not only for the many losses, but to have an informer in our midst! It is clear the Circinn had word to exact so great a defeat." Caltram looked at Taran with contempt. "Taran – you are that man!"

A murmur of shock rippled through the hall.

"What nonsense!" objected Nechtan, rising to his feet. "You speak totally without cause."

"Oh, do I, brother-in-law? It is known that on the night our two boys stayed over at the ferry, a certain Circinnian took to Taran, and he to him. Oengus says so – is that not true?"

"Father, please do not speak like this," pleaded Oengus.

"Is that not so?" Caltram insisted, raising his voice, which was faltering given his state. Shaking all over, he repeated his question a third time, glaring at his son with steely insistence.

"Well, yes, they did speak and get along," conceded Oengus. "There is no denying it. But it was the antics of a drunk and Taran was on the receiving end."

"There was some informer," proceeded Caltram menacingly. "Otherwise, how would the Circinn know about our ambush? Oengus says that Taran never spoke alone with the couple. The cousins were careful to stick together, to watch their words and mind their drink. But on the evening when the drink flowed, a friendship was made, out of earshot of Oengus . . ."

"This is all lies!" interrupted Taran.

Talorgen motioned him to be quiet, asking Caltram to continue. Perhaps recognising that Caltram did not have much time left, Taran concluded that Talorgen was allowing him his say. Uncle Caltram's reasoning were the words of one who had lost soundness of mind and therefore the council would recognise the absurdity of these claims.

"Whose idea was it that Taran and Oengus were to take up the advanced guard?" proceeded Caltram. "I will tell you: it was Taran. Knowing the attack was coming from the ridge above us, he had himself, and Oengus to avoid suspicion, lie in wait out of harm's way."

Taran shook from head to toe in total dismay. "You are mad! Why would I do such a thing? You and my people are family and comrades!"

"Be quiet!" ordered Talorgen severely.

"I will tell you why Taran behaved like this." Caltram held his head knowingly on one side, judiciously gaining the attention of the council. "He could not stomach the killing of that couple on the night of the cattle lifting. Oengus is the warrior, who would have finished off the bairns too. But no, Taran prevented him. It was plain then that Taran is no warrior. He wanted done with killing, and so left us to our fate as he waited out of harm's way."

"That is a lie and it is absurd," Nechtan shouted.

"Supposing I was like that," defended Taran, "then surely the blood of leading thirty-three of my people to their deaths would be much greater a thing to bear?"

"Quiet, quiet," Talorgen motioned, quite distraught. His reddened face accentuated the quivering of his long, white moustaches.

"And my final piece of evidence is this," continued Caltram. "When Taran was in flight, he ran into his Circinnian accomplice, the drunkard with whom he had been so friendly at the ferry. Both were armed, and Taran even had the advantage of having Oengus near him. Two against one!"

Caltram raised his chin as if to invite the audience for their prediction of such an outcome. "Taran never lifted his sword!" He paused for dramatic effect. "And nor did the Circinnian raise his sword against him."

Finding it all too painful to remain propped up on his elbow, Caltram slumped on the floor. The assembly was in a state of shock, conferring in noisy whispers. Talorgen called the meeting to a close, to reconvene again after making further investigations.

Talorgen and Conchen were sat alone when Nechtan and his wife, Domelch, joined them. Nechtan came straight to the matter. "Can you not see that Caltram's claims are the ravings of a dying man? He is the only one looking ahead, eager to promote his son, for he knows he has little time. He is not concerned about the facts. All of us, who were there from the beginning of this campaign, can vouch that these are absurd insinuations."

"Caltram offers an explanation for what has passed," Talorgen replied.

Nechtan shuffled uneasily, finding it difficult to believe Talorgen would accept so absurd a charge.

"It is plain to see," stated Domelch, wringing her hands, "that Caltram is bent on discrediting the one rival who stands in his son's way."

"The betrayal," pursued Nechtan, rubbing his neck, "arises from the complicity of the couple at the ferry. Drest and Ligach may claim to be Ce, but they are so neighbourly with the Circinn as to make them duplicit. Living at the ferry, they are bound to have divided loyalties to serve their own ends, especially when their very survival is at stake."

He presented both hands forward in a gesture to emphasise that he was stating the obvious. "They goaded Oengus and Taran to expect the Circinn to mount their counter offensive from the pass at the new moon, to draw and overwhelm us there." As an experienced tactician, Nechtan sat back, reasonably confident that his case was understood by the veteran of so many campaigns.

"So the Circinn, suspecting our ambush, set one up of their own on the ridge above, to descend upon you," said Conchen, restating his rationale. It seemed that not only did she wish to make things clear in her own head, but to make the facts obvious to Talorgen.

There was silence whilst this reasoned explanation seemed to take effect.

"But what if Taran told his Circinnian friend about our plans . . ." countered Talorgen unexpectedly. There was a sinister ring to his words.

Why had Talorgen returned to this preposterous and supposed conspiracy of his nephew? Perhaps, he reasoned, being the wily old warlord that he is, Talorgen found it incumbent to see things from all sides. Or was he really getting too old, his ability to be rational undermined by his advanced years?

"No! Why single out Taran!" interjected Domelch, now very roused. "This is madness to think Taran is a conspirator! Oengus was with him all the times they were at the ferry and has as much blame, if any blame were to be made."

"Neither Taran nor Oengus are to blame," added Nechtan emphatically.

"Then who is to blame for allowing the Circinn to strike such a blow?" demanded Talorgen, care-worn no doubt, to witness his rule descending into the abyss. He turned to

Nechtan. "Both you and Caltram, being the wise old heads and the battle-hardened campaigners that you are, have to accept some of the blame. You appear to have allowed Taran and Oengus to have made all the decisions!"

Nechtan rolled his eyes, unsuspecting a new wave of allegations. He took a deep breath. "Yes, we both gave our sons the initiative, testing their intelligence to react to developments. The purpose in the cattle lifting was to try their ability, but this was done in consultation with us. Caltram and I worked alongside our sons, giving them the benefit of our experience when required." He shook his head incredulously. "Ask yourself: what would Taran gain from being a conspirator? Why would he serve our enemies and incur the death of his own people? These ridiculous allegations are as flawed as they are absurd!"

Talorgen looked utterly withdrawn. His chin was so slumped on his chest that Nechtan wondered whether he had fallen asleep out of exhaustion, but he shortly opened his careworn eyes. "Because Taran knows he is not the equal to Oengus in this contest!"

"I do not believe I am hearing this!" Nechtan hotly remonstrated, rising to his feet then turning abruptly aside.

"And knowing he cannot win this contest," continued Talorgen in a weary monotone, "he stoops to a treacherous act, seeking the support of the Circinn to instate him as their puppet!"

"Have you gone mad?!" exclaimed Domelch, also rising to her feet.

"Just get out. Clear off, both of you!" snapped Talorgen.

Talorgen and his most trusted elders questioned Taran and Oengus individually. Their stories matched. Once again, the finger pointed at Drest and Ligach. Taran aired his dismay that a couple who had been so mild and friendly could be conspirators. When on his own, Oengus stated that he would have this couple murdered without further ado. He was no longer so quick to protest the inferred guilt of his cousin, although he was not drawn into saying a libellous word.

Talorgen sought Maelchon's council, who proposed the community join him in making offerings outside the burial cairn the following morning to confer with their ancestors. High fever kept Caltram at home. Domelch went to Caltram's home to offer her sister some practical support. "Drusticc, I am distressed to hear Caltram's accusations," she spoke in an undertone. "They are false and so damaging for Taran!"

Drusticc wrung out a cloth she had dipped into a shallow basin. She did not look up at her sister and replied almost under her breath. "No one is going to take them seriously."

"Except for Talorgen! It is his judgement afterall that counts most in this dispute!"

Alpia came to Taran's home, having looked for him at the gathering outside the cairn of the ancestors. She found him seated on a bench outside, looking deep in thought. They had not seen one another for three weeks, since Taran and Oengus rode out proud from Rhynie at the head of their warband.

"I am glad you survived," she remarked, sitting so close on the short bench that her thigh gently touched his. "I have been wondering how things were faring since the day you all left."

"That marked the start of when things went wrong." Taran's tone was flat.

"How do you mean?"

"It all began with the murder of the couple with the two young bairns!" Taran stared starkly at the ground.

"But these things sometimes happen during raids, do they not?"

They were silent for a time. The heavy overcast sky hung low, concealing the summit of the Pap of Bulàch.

"I am in deep trouble," groaned Taran. "You will wish that you were no relative of mine!"

"Sssh, do not say such things. I side with you. Talorgen is deranged but Maelchon will make him see reason." She tried to meet his eyes.

"It is not what we wished for, or expected, just a short while ago at Beltane, eh!"

"No, not what we wished for." The breeze swept some strands of hair across her face. "I will stand with you. Two are stronger than one."

Taran looked up at her and smiled faintly. He seemed taken aback by her words. She had surprised herself, but Taran had looked so bereft of hope that she recognised his need for solidarity. Besides, she did not believe in Caltram's ravings.

"I returned home with such high hopes, with a reputation to make. The whole world lay before me as I came of age, for me to lay claim to just a small piece of it."

"You will overcome this and will be the stronger for it," she assured him, stooping low again to look up into his downcast face.

"Folk seem to have trouble believing the truth." Taran spoke with difficulty, as though he was being throttled.

"What people? Your parents are with you and many others. Even Oengus, who stands to gain most, is not out to discredit you."

"The lies his father speaks, though . . . they are like poison! Talorgen seems to have already made his choice. After all, it is his opinion and the only opinion that counts!"

"The succession is not decided. Aunt Conchen is on your side – I spoke with her just earlier. She maintains your innocence and hopes to win Uncle Talorgen round."

They were silent. The weight of the world seemed upon him, and nothing that she said appeared to alleviate its burden from crushing him.

"And then there is Maelchon," she continued. "He is a man of considerable influence. Talorgen will listen to him. He can see into hidden things. Once Maelchon absolves you, as surely he must, your name will be cleared. Everyone I speak to in Rhynie maintains that it is that couple at the ferry who are to blame."

"I would not be so sure about what Maelchon will say!" Taran rolled his eyes despairingly. "These hidden things, concerning the Bulàch, are strange and uncertain." Taran bit his nail thoughtfully.

Alpia was hard pressed to know what more to say to alleviate his torment. Maybe though, if she were to reason through all the facts with her aunt, then Conchen could make a firm case to persuade Talorgen of Taran's innocence.

"It is not just the complication of what happened with the Circinn," Taran started with a new thought, "but concerns the contradictory symbols tattooed."

"What do you mean?"

"I am not supposed to talk about these symbols."

"Oh, I suspect that Maelchon, not wanting a fuss, said that so that you would not spread it all around Rhynie. But you can tell me."

"I am not so sure."

"Did you tell Oengus?"

Taran nodded.

"If you told Oengus, then you can reveal it to me. I am not going to tell others."

Taran was taciturn, which annoyed her. Eventually, he explained the symbols and their significance and concluded with a warning. "Mind you keep this to yourself, at least for the time being."

"Yes, of course I will. And do not worry, it is for Maelchon to work out the riddle."

"These past few weeks have been fraught with tensions. Oengus and Caltram seemed to work together, always seizing the initiative in making decisions, making me wonder whether I should be more assertive. Surely though, the proving of the leader, I told myself, would be in the execution of the task."

She reached out and briefly touched his hand upturned on his lap. She admired one who did not assert himself.

"Ossian's words came to mind more than once!"

"What words? You never told me you spoke with Ossian!"

"It was strange. He came seeking me out in the upland pastures soon after Beltane before disappearing the next day."

"What did he say?" Her interest was raised.

"'Be brave, be cunning, be humble!'"

"That was it?"

"He said other things that I do not well record. I have struggled with how humility would serve me, particularly when proving my worth."

She considered the bard's strange words. "They are intriguing."

"Everything is intriguing!" he complained. "Why is it that druids and bards cannot speak plainly as other men?"

"Because they deal with mystery and honour," she replied, not sharing his aversion for riddles. "You are brave, Taran, do not doubt it. As for cunning, I would say that is more Oengus' territory. As for being humble – well, I do not know – except, I see it in your nature not to advance yourself. That becomes you!"

"You speak kindly to me this day." His eyes met hers for the first time. He genuinely appeared grateful and not to misinterpret her meaning, which as an afterthought had concerned her.

"Ossian's words commend you to be cunning though." She knitted her brows.

They sat quietly, watching the lower slopes of the mountain darken under a heavy shower. When it had passed, the heather and rock came back into definition, and the trees appeared taller and closer. The sun eventually broke through, dispersing the cloud, shining brilliantly upon the peak in all its wetness.

"Let us be optimistic, for where there is hope there is a way, and where there is despair people can drown," she said, brushing some stray strands of hair from her eyes. "You have returned without injury. You are still alive, after so many have died. That is an answer to our prayers and I so wanted to know that all was well during the long wait."

"Truly?" Taran looked up. "I often thought about you . . . at least when the pressure of circumstances was off."

She laughed. "Then you cannot have thought about me that much, for the pressure must have been great!"

Taran protested.

It had only been three weeks since their heady evening together at Beltane, which had caused her to think about Taran more than she cared to. She was concerned by Taran's strong emotions for her. Feelings that could so easily flare up, she considered, could just as quickly subside. She resisted reciprocating those feelings, desiring things for once to be ordinary as they always had been, despite the boredom this produced. At least then, she could be in control.

"What can I say, Alpia? Do I have to defend myself before you as I do before others? Why do you doubt my affections?" He relaxed his clenched fists and wiped some moisture from his lips. His tone changed. "Your loveliness has comforted me all those lonely nights in the camp. Your eyes have been the first thing I saw on awakening; your tenderness towards me at Beltane, I have recalled hundreds of times. There is no other. There is nothing, no one that so competes for my attention. Yes, I admit, I have had to consciously put you out of mind at times, because I have been hard-pressed, needing my wits about me to stay alive."

She raised her eyes to meet his. Taran braved a slight smile and she permitted one in return, although an uncertain one.

"Taran, I stand with you as a friend and an ally. I believe in you and admire your character. But do not expect such outpourings from me. This is the time to stand steadfast with all your wits intact. Do not be distracted, for . . ." She was unsure whether to conclude. "For I fear for the lives of the innocent in an evil world. Mark Ossian's words, 'Be cunning' my dear cousin."

That evening Caltram passed away – three days after the skirmish. News of his death brought afresh to mind all those fiery insinuations at a time when they were deliberating towards a decision. Caltram was buried the following morning. Taran tried to offer words of comfort to Oengus but, finding it difficult to say anything good about a man who had accused him of treachery on his deathbed, his efforts fell short. Oengus would not wish to hear consolations that were not sincere.

Talorgen reconvened the court immediately after the funeral. Maelchon was to share his wisdom. Alpia sat on one side of Taran and his parents on the other. Taran noticed the cold look from Oengus on seeing their group. Oengus only had his mother there for support and she was beside herself with grief. Bad blood confounded their friendship again, he thought.

Talorgen opened the proceedings, instead of the spokesman, eager to dispense with protocol. Maelchon was invited to address the assembly. The druid seemed to make up for the lack of formalities by being especially long-winded, more than anyone would wish. He appeared troubled, putting off what needed to be said. The hall grew tense and Taran conceived of some dire outcome.

Eventually, Maelchon came to the point. "The complication has not become totally clear." The druid coughed apologetically. "This matter needs to be taken to Wroid, my druid father. It would be well that all the main parties will present themselves there at Loch Kinord."

"But that is a long day's ride to his crannog," remonstrated Talorgen, flexing his arm on the table.

"My lord – believe me, if there were another way, I would spare you the discomfort of this journey. But such discomforts are nothing compared with the gravity of the omens. The undoing of the curse that is upon us is considerable. That is why we must consult with Wroid. Just maybe, he knows of an alternative!"

"What are you talking about man? An alternative to what?" Talorgen was visibly annoyed, his whole face reddening. "Why do you persist in speaking in riddles?"

"I cannot speak plainly until I have consulted Wroid."

When Talorgen spoke, his first syllable hit an unexpected high pitch. "A curse you say! Well, it does not take a druid to deduce that!" Talorgen stared at the bare tabletop before him. He appeared to grow calmer and spoke more reflectively. "Well, if there is nothing else to be done ..." The warlord rose resolutely from his chair. "Then we will head south first thing in the morning and have this matter settled once and for all." Looking over at Oengus, who was crestfallen with his mother melting tearfully at his side, he added, "Oengus, you can prepare my chariot and I will ride with you."

Taran looked up, horrified by this public display of favouritism. Was it already decided that he was responsible for this massacre and Oengus was exonerated? What of 'the gravity of the omens' and that the 'undoing of the curse is considerable'? It seemed like a relentless nightmare taking unexpected descents to the gloomiest regions.

Alpia reached for his hand and squeezed it. Her hand was trembling.

Taran rose together with his parents, but Alpia remained rooted to the bench. Even she was abandoning him. His mother pressed in close to Taran's side, wetting his shirt with her tears. Nechtan put his arm briefly around him and they walked slowly home. His father looked exhausted as they entered their home.

Taran's mother sobbed. She lent through the window and cleared both nostrils onto the ground outside. Wiping the tears from her eyes, she sat back with some composure. "Talorgen might be short-sighted and stubborn, but it is the Bulàch who is at the heart of our distress. Maelchon is at a loss of what is to be done!"

"I am not sure he is at any loss," said Taran weightily. "He is stalling for time, seeking someone to share the responsibility with before making a grave decision."

"Caltram's death has muddied the waters for Talorgen," remarked Nechtan. "Caltram was always his preferred man for a special mission. I should have seen this coming."

Nechtan went over to a fire barely smouldering in the central hearth. He raked about the ashes with an old hatchet and blew on a charred remain that blossomed orange in the gloom. Adding kindling and breath, he brought the fire back to life. "Why did Talorgen not state from the beginning that Oengus was his choice?"

"Father! What good is such talk?" Taran said helplessly.

After a brief pause, Nechtan scattered the fire he had just brought to life. The gloom intensified within the silent hut. Just then, Alpia appeared, pausing in the doorway. Spotting Taran, she came over and sat down heavily against his thigh.

"We're drowning again!" he remarked.

No one spoke a word.

Chapter Ten

Contest at Dindurn

519 AD Dindurn

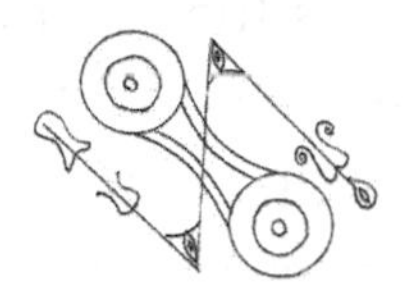 

The new day broke misty and moist, but the heaviness of rain held back. Irb and his family took part in the morning devotions and on hearing the psalms being sung, the young couple who had dropped in out of curiosity the previous night joined them. They listened to Kessog's instruction carefully.

"It is good to have you in our place," remarked Irb. "Imagine one day, if there were to be a number of us gathering to worship in Cartray."

"It is a hope that will be fulfilled sooner than you would think, I am certain of that!" uttered Kessog confidently.

"Our families and friends ridicule us for taking up these beliefs," commented Rowena. "They do not understand and do not try to either. But there are those who are curious, besides our friends here. Some have said that Christ does not seem unpredictable like the Bulàch. However, they fear what might happen should they turn from her. I have told them to look at us! Nothing bad has happened since we put our trust in Christ . . ." She looked in the direction of the couple. "Except for unkind words."

After breakfast, Irb insisted on leading them through the forest to the 'bent' loch that would direct them towards

Dindurn. Putting the open ground of Cartray behind, Fillan felt the renewing gladness of entering the spring woods sprouting into leaf. The bird song, interwoven with the sound of tumbling water, filled him with blithe hope. The rush of the thaw sweeping out of the narrow glen ahead moistened the air with particles that seemed charged with life. The narrow corridor of sky above the river focussed his view onto the steep ground, rising into shifting mist.

On reaching some small waterfalls, they put their coracles down. Half of the party relieved themselves. Fillan gently fondled a newly unfurled sycamore leaf, surprised by its delicate texture. For a few moments, the mist parted to reveal a craggy height dusted with fresh snow. He wondered how such frailty as this leaf could withstand the barbs of wintry weather. It was apparently imbued with an unseen and unimaginable resilience. He longed for a spiritual renewing that would make him flourish and leave the hard dullness of a long winter. How he longed to vault above the prosaic, everyday practice of his devotion to leap to a new level from which to behold new horizons. He recalled those distant memories of when he left Erin in the currach, wholeheartedly embracing his exile. How buoyant with expectation he had been, maybe somewhat naïve, but he believed that his coming would make a difference, that the future was pregnant with all kinds of possibilities and that here he would make profound discoveries of the Lord.

They walked on in silence until reaching a point where the current was slacker and wider than before. “This is the outlet from the loch,” Irb announced. “You can continue by coracle from here.” He went on to describe the remainder of the journey to Dindurn with the landmarks to look out for. “I wish you God’s speed. We shall be praying for his favour at Domech's court." Irb clasped each of the pilgrims warmly in turn.

They made good speed up the 'bent' loch and along sections of river beyond, until they were forced to carry their coracles for a lengthy stretch. Progress seemed laborious to Fillan. He could feel the gnawing pangs of hunger and noted the sun had reached its noontime zenith. Finally, the trees thinned before a broad expanse of loch: their long-anticipated target where they agreed to have lunch.

After a satisfying lunch of bannocks freshly baked that morning, they placed their coracles in the loch. The cloud had evaporated to reveal a couple of mighty peaks to the south, deep in snow upon which the sun shone brilliantly above the spring green fuzz of the woods. To help relieve the monotony of paddling, they sang psalms.

The pilgrims followed the loch's outflow, which ran past pastures where cattle grazed, bordered by hills. Standing isolated from a rugged ridge stood the much lower hill of Dindurn. Its craggy upper flanks were criss-crossed with fortifications, studded with huts; its summit capped with an extensive hall.

Leaving their coracles beside the river, the pilgrims walked towards the citadel. The sight was just as Irb had described: pressed into a compact mass, many huts were smouldering with smoke from cooking fires, giving the impression of an immense, reeking bonfire. Crossing a muddy stream, they climbed a steep rise to the citadel's gates. A tall sentry greeted them with a spear resting against his shoulder.

"Hello strangers – what brings you here?"

"We are from Strath Clud, seeking an audience with Lord Domech," replied Kessog.

"He is away!"

"When will he return?"

"He set out just three days ago. He will be gone a fair while."

I expect it is the spring weather that has put that idea in his mind, thought Fillan.

"Oh well, we will just sit it out then until he returns," remarked Kessog. He looked beyond the gate, up the approach road, bounded by a high wall.

"Domech is collecting tribute so he will be away many days, even weeks." The sentry studied them curiously. "So, you are druids!"

Fillan explained who they were. By now, a small crowd gathered about them, curious to understand who this Christ was of whom he spoke. He found the people of the citadel friendly, probably due to their being pilgrims who posed no threat. The sentry asked for news from Din Brython and Dal Riata, even of Erin beyond. Those who had gathered began to melt away. Following the reports of their stern warlord, who was intent on fortifying his citadel against the incursion of the peoples the pilgrims represented, he felt relieved to find the folk of Dindurn to be friendly.

They returned to their boats. Kessog said he would fish. Ronan and Fillan went in search of brushwood for their bedding and for firewood. That night they slept poorly under their coracles that they built themselves a shelter on the following day.

A routine established itself around their times of worship, attending to domestic needs like foraging for food, bartering fish and firewood for milk, cheese and bread. They became acquainted with the ordinary folk who lacked status to build within the citadel walls. The pilgrims were glad to gain their favour, a few of whom were curious to observe what the monks did during their worship. Noticing the Picts rocked their heads gently to the rhythmic cadence of the sung psalms, Kessog encouraged them to join in the singing. The abbot was patient to instruct, leading with a line for them to repeat, although singing in Latin resulted in them uttering many syllables incorrectly. Kessog made a point of praying and teaching from the scriptures in Pictish.

A week went by in this fashion without word of the warlord's return. Some new arrivals said Domech had been to this place and to that, which meant nothing to the monks, unfamiliar with their geography, until these destinations were stated in lengths of travel time from Dindurn.

As the second week passed, a dishevelled looking mother approached them. "Would you please come to see my child?" Fillan noted that her agitation had overcome an evident shyness. "My young boy has had a high fever for two days now and I am really worried. I have heard your teaching about this Lord Jesus who heals. Will he do that for my young lad?"

"Come, let us see," he replied sympathetically, rising.

The mother led them to an untidy but large hut where an older daughter was lying beside the boy.

"Come in." He noted her urgent gestures. "Please pray . . . I am afraid for his life! I lost another child under very similar circumstances."

Kessog knelt by the boy, who was breathing with shallow breaths, and placed the back of his palm on the child's forehead. "Oh! He is hot to the touch!" Turning to the mother, he said, "I am going to pray to the God who made you and me."

"I am prepared to trust," the mother replied. "I came to you because last time I went to the druid, my other son died."

Kessog looked reassuringly at the mother and then prayed. The abbot announced calmly that the fever would subside.

The mother placed her hand on her son's forehead. "He's still hot!"

"Have faith. All will be well," he said with an expansive smile.

They talked for a time, accepting a bowl of broth still warm from a pot lying in the ashes of a dying fire.

The young boy rubbed his eyes. His sister offered him a small clay bowl of water. Very soon, the lad was sitting up, taking his first food in a couple of days.

"Oh, thank you so much," said the mother.

"Do not thank us," replied the abbot, rising. "We are merely the servants. But, do thank the one who gave the healing."

"Why, of course." The mother called her daughter to her side and clutched her son. "Show me how, though."

After Kessog prayed with the mother repeating his words, they said farewell.

"No, wait," said the mother. "Is there not something I can give you?"

"There is no need, and besides you shared your broth with us," replied Kessog.

"Well maybe you could all stay under our roof. I know you were sleeping rough under your coracles at first, and the shelter you have made for yourselves does not look much more comfortable!" She glanced around her hut. "Our place is not much, but there is space for all three of you here."

"What will your husband think?"

"Oh – he will be as thankful as I am. Please do stay, it is the least we could do."

Fillan was very glad of the proper shelter and this show of special favour. As the miracle was reported around the community, they gained respect and were regarded as holy men. He even found the delay over Domech's return, which previously had felt irksome, was not felt so keenly. He enjoyed the novelty of sharing a family's household. Having only ever known adult companionship, he gave himself to play with the young children in the household, who took to him as the youngest of the three men. Keen to discover the ways of childhood he had missed out on, he surprised his fellow monks by his tree-climbing antics and running about with great abandon and howls of laughter.

He noted Ronan's impatience and the abbot's indifference over the delay. Kessog was given to much solitary prayer beyond their usual communal worship routines, often forsaking meals. He admired his master's steadfast ways, recalling that for many years, he had not embraced such austerity. Was it his age, he wondered? Why was he not like-minded? Why did these disciplines seem so difficult for him?

It felt good to be away from the hermetic isolation of Inis y Mynachon and be part of a welcoming community. It had become clear that this delay was opening the hearts of more households. In the third week, requests were made of them to pray for various ailments and for a cow that was no longer yielding much milk.

A youth called Castantin came to him distraught late one afternoon.

"Can you help me find my neighbour's axe? I have searched high and low. Now my neighbour has grown angry and is making threats!"

"Well, let us pray and maybe the Lord will reveal where the axe is located." Fillan bowed his head. After praying, he had to admit, "I do not have a word where it is."

Castantin looked at him blankly.

Why were his prayers not effective like his master's, he thought? Maybe I love my sleep too much, and I am too used to meals that going without is just too difficult. He closed his eyes with a sense of disappointment in himself and allowed his spirit to pray, not with articulated thoughts, but more allowing his frustration to be offered, along with the desire to become a more effective servant.

"Think about the last time you saw the axe," advised Ronan, "and consider what you did and where you went right after that?"

It was then that Fillan briefly saw the axe. The image flashed like distant lightning on his mind.

"I have done all of that. It is no good!" spoke Castantin, rising.

"No, wait!" interrupted Fillan. "I am not sure, but I had a glimpse of an axe just now as I was praying. It seemed to be beside a pool just below a waterfall and the axe was resting in the fork of a rowan!"

"That sounds like the place where I bathe up on the hill from time to time," spoke Castantin curiously.

"Have you been there recently, after using the axe?" asked Fillan.

The young man nodded.

"Take a look there. Maybe Fillan has a gift of seeing things!" Ronan smiled.

Castantin left them and returned that evening. "Here's the axe," he said with a big grin.

Fillan's heart swelled with thankfulness that his prayer had been answered. He felt an excitement that had not been there in his spirit for a long time.

The good will of the common people increased. Many brought small gifts of food; even those who were not in the habit of joining them during their worship times did likewise to express their appreciation and goodwill. As if to appease a troubled conscience, some noted that their druid, being in the royal retinue, was not available for these domestic needs.

News of Domech's homecoming created a gathering around the citadel's gate. Their warlord appeared amidst a band of armed warriors, advisors, tax collectors and a druid. A hearty cheer greeted their arrival. Domech cut a regal figure on the back of a pale coloured horse, draped in a blanket of embroidered finery. He was a man in his early-thirties, with a good head of dark hair swept back from his ears that grew down to his shoulders. His nose was rather hawk-like, prominent above a dark beard. He acknowledged the greetings as one accustomed to the applause that expressed respect and fear.

"If the warlord is not tired after his journey, he will have pressing matters of state to attend to," remarked Kessog. "He would not consider the business of a small band of foreign pilgrims to be of much consequence."

On the following day before noon, Kessog, Fillan and Ronan went into the citadel. They were to ask for Fergus at the inner gate. Whilst waiting in the courtyard, they looked to the top of the rock rising almost sheer and a good seventy feet above them. Ramparts intersected one another, from where archers and spearmen could take out any would be invader. The pilgrims explained their purpose to Fergus and were told to wait on a bench. The monks settled in the sunshine, enjoying its warmth and gave themselves to inner prayer. For a time, Fillan's eyes were curiously transfixed on a small depression in the ground where the grass grew more luxuriantly.

Fergus returned, expressing surprise that Domech would see them immediately. After making a body search for any concealed weapon, Fergus escorted them up a very constricted way around the base of the crag. A narrow gate led into a higher courtyard with more huts, some adorned with colourful shields emblazoned with mysterious emblems that hung beneath the thatch. From there, the length of the strath to the east could be seen; a corridor leading into the tribal heartlands, said to be the 'breadbasket' of the Fotla.

Beyond a final rampart, a narrow path rose surprisingly steep to the doorway of the great hall. The interior was windowless except for a series of small apertures, serving as lookout ports in every direction. A fire burning in the centre washed the wooden panelled walls with a warming glow. At the far end, presiding over a long table, sat Domech on a chair with a high back. A bodyguard of grim-faced warriors, armed with swords, stood about him, and sitting at the table were clerics and a druid.

"Welcome!" Domech greeted them civilly but without warmth. However, this courtesy was more than Fillan expected. "I hear that you arrived some three weeks back and have been waiting for an audience. It must be a matter of considerable importance! I hear you come from Strath Clud and that two of you even come from Erin. So, tell me, what brings you here?"

"Yes, my Lord," replied Kessog, bowing. The abbot was about to explain his purpose when Domech raised his hand.

"I also hear that you have had, let us say, an altercation with Phelan and his daughter, Beatha, of Cartray!"

"It would seem, my lord, that news travels without hindrance in your realm."

"We run an effective kingdom here," he replied drily. "Times insist that we keep vigilant watch." His tone became chastising. "Do you not know you are dealing with unseen powers, sorcery that enables Beatha to be transported great distances in a moment to whisper in my ear?" He looked at them with hostility. "Explain why you found it necessary to strike one of my subjects dumb."

"My lord, I do not belittle the powers of Beatha," began Kessog, his torso straightening. "Permit me, though, to inform you that news of her being struck dumb did not come to you by one of her shamanic flights of soul. No, it came by way of an ordinary messenger from Cartray."

Domech's face registered visible surprise. He remarked coldly, "You are something of a seer it would appear!"

Kessog went on to explain the exchange that led to the curse. Fillan noticed that the druid seated to Domech's left wanted to say something, but Domech thwarted his wishes with an abrupt raise of his hand.

"Come to the purpose, of what compelled you three to journey the lonely reaches of highland lochs, all the way to our distant court?" asked Domech with clipped tones. A glint in his eye suggested he approved of their determination and resolve. He listened with a judicial air to an account that spoke often about Christ.

"Lord, I must protest," the druid objected. The warlord gave him permission. "Our kingdom is not built by strength alone, nor by the wisdom of the elders, nor, permit me to say, by the charisma of its leader. These things certainly count for something, but they are only a part. We are where we are because of our allegiance to the Bulàch. Turn our back on her and severe consequences will follow, mark my words."

The druid spoke at length of the Bulàch's reputation, stories of what happened to leaders who did not pay due respect, indicating ones who fell in battle and others who had given up their spirits before their time.

"Tell me," Domech asked them, sounding wearied by his druid's advice that probably was all so familiar. "Can you read omens? Do you interpret dreams? Can you divine the future, as well as bring healing and harm? I have heard talk of you healing my subjects and seeing where an axe was mislaid."

"We cannot, my lord. But the One whom we serve knows all things and he chooses to impart what he will to his subjects."

Domech's face twitched impatiently. "Do not talk in riddles – be straight with me!"

"Then the answer would be that the High King does give grace to know such things as you suggest."

"Good," the warlord said peremptorily. He sat back in his chair with a self-satisfied air. "I have three tests for you to prove that you are who you say you are. The first is this. Tell me what I learned of the most importance on my recent tour. I have told no one, so tell me if you know?"

"My lord – allow me time to pray and, God willing, I will tell you what you learned of the utmost importance."

Domech agreed and dismissed the monks.

"I believe the Lord will reveal what you ask of me in just a moment. Let me seek his counsel and then I will speak of what I hear."

"Fine. Go to the far end of the hall."

The pilgrims withdrew. Fillan was surprised at how calm Kessog could be, seemingly immune to the doubts and fears that often plagued his own mind. Fillan prayed, asking that his faith might increase.

The warlord consulted with his companions about other matters, but only briefly, for Kessog announced that he would tell the warlord what he learned of the utmost importance.

"Speak up then," commanded Domech.

"You spoke with Gede, lord of the Manau, at Dumyat, where you made an alliance together. The Fotla would protect Manau from any incursion from the Goddodin in return for their aid should Dal Riata oppose you."

"You speak well, servant of Christ."

"But Lord Domech," Kessog continued, leaning slightly forward to give import to what he had to say. "I will speak more upon this, which is far more important than telling you what you already know." Kessog seemed to pause to raise suspense. "Gede has entered into an alliance with Dal Riata, in a would-be attempt to carve your kingdom between them. You are wise to be wary of the rising power of Dal Riata, for they have military ambitions. Manau, being small, aspires to extend her territory. Beware of Gede, who will send a force here on the pretext to defend Dindurn, but will in truth, turn upon you when you are most vulnerable."

"I see that you are a prophet as well as the hearer of words spoken in the secret place." He smiled thinly before proceeding to the next test.

"But lord," interrupted the druid. "We do not know if this prophecy is true. How can we trust this man?"

"His words are good. We should always be on our guard, not to trust even friends. Is that not so?" replied Domech rhetorically. "My next test is for the servant of Christ and my own discerner of mysteries. Last night I had a dream that troubled me. I would have you tell me its meaning."

The druid nodded, approving this test. Did he have a reputation for interpreting dreams, wondered Fillan. "So, tell us your dream, O lord?"

"You are to tell me what I dreamed! Then to interpret it."

"But lord, no man can do that," complained the druid.

There was an uneasy silence. Fillan could sense this was leading to trouble. Domech was looking for an excuse to have them flogged, or thrown in prison, or something worse.

Kessog spoke up. "This is your dream. You saw a vast standing stone, a huge slab, engraved with all manner of power symbols, raised up in a sacred oak grove. Many people came to the stone from far and wide with offerings and supplications, for the stone had great reputation to protect. Then you saw a man, not one of your own people, armed with a pick and shovel, digging away at the base of the slab to undermine it. The digging continued for a long time, for the slab, being so high, had been laid deep into the earth, underpinned by many boulders. The digger did not seem to weary as the hole deepened, threatening the stability of the stone. The sight of this caused you much distress. Is that not so, my lord?"

Domech nodded and raised an eyebrow. Fillan noted that Kessog's brow was sweating liberally and felt curious too at how rapidly he spoke, as if trying to keep pace, describing the things that perhaps he could see unfold before him.

"Then a sprig of mistletoe fell from the crest of the oak grove, which no doubt you saw as a good omen, for power is believed to be in the sprig and it would work some magic to reverse what seemed to be the fate of this mighty stone. These hopes were dashed, though, when the digger deliberately trampled and pulverised the mistletoe under foot and he took up his pick to finish off his work. The night passed, and a new dawn broke over the face of the earth, yet the great symbol stone remained standing. The digger, unable to abide the brightness of the light, left. As the sun came up, you looked upon the stone, which remained perfectly upright despite the depth of the hole that would seem to secure its fate. Furthermore, a new symbol, larger by far than the others, had been engraved on the reverse of the stone. That symbol was the cross of Christ!"

"This is well spoken," said the warlord, adding a nod of approval along with his thin smile. "So now, tell me what it means?"

"The dream means this. You and the Fotla are that giant incised stone, giving identity and guidance to all who come on pilgrimage there to make their offerings. The digger is the king of Dal Riata, who relentlessly goes about his work and whose outcome seems your sure defeat. The mistletoe presents a sign of hope, but it is false hope – trusting in the alliance with the Manau and in the ancient traditions from where you believe power to come. Dal Riata disdained that spiritual power and trod it underfoot.

"But the lesson is this." Kessog briefly cleared his throat. "Recourse to the old ways and powers will be to no avail. The fate of the Fotla did seem at an end until the dawn of a new era shone upon you. Salvation will come upon your people, symbolised by the marking of the cross. Who can withstand him?"

Hearing this, Domech added a sound of applause from within his throat, nodding his approval, and smiled thinly once more.

"So now to my third and final test," announced the warlord. "Water is a precious commodity upon this citadel. Every day, my subjects descend the hill to the burn at its base, to fill water skins. It is a heavy task returning with full skins that soon will need replenishing."

Turning to one of his warriors, Domech ordered two empty waterskins to be brought. Domech explained the challenge, looking first to his own druid.

"You are to invoke Brigantia to fill this empty water skin without you or the skin leaving this hall. The same goes for you, servant of Christ. To whom the full water skin belongs, his god is the true power."

Fillan felt a greater sense of impending doom, suspecting Domech of some foul trick. A sick sensation welled up from the pit of his stomach, lodging at the top of his chest. How would Kessog respond? Fillan observed how the abbot waited visibly nervous, until the druid had finally accepted that the powers he invoked were unable to fill the water skins. Fillan felt he might even vomit and urgently wanted to pray to take control of what was overcoming him.

"Lord Domech, what you ask for will not be done. Our Lord is not a magician to conjure this and that, just at some whim!"

Fillan felt appalled by Kessog's capitulation. The horror, though, was replaced by an impulse to say something. Being the junior in the party, Fillan was conscious of the impropriety to speak up on the occasion.

"Then you fail the test," pronounced Domech with a stern air, like an axe descending upon a victim.

"Permit me, lord, to speak with my master," spoke Fillan.

The warlord nodded with a degree of impatience.

"Lord," spoke Kessog, "our young brother has a word of knowledge that will serve you far greater than the miracle of filling just one skin full of water. Such knowledge will lead to an endless supply of water."

"And so, what is it that you propose?"

"To sink a well," Fillan spoke for the first time.

"Phuff!" uttered Domech with a look of disdain. "We have tried that in all kinds of places, but Dindurn is built on solid rock!"

"I do believe that it has been indicated where to sink a well," replied Fillan, surprised by the assurance of his own words.

"Then show us and we shall see!" acquiesced Domech.

"But first," Kessog interrupted, "perhaps your own druid knows of such a place? Let him speak first."

"Very well," consented Domech, looking to his druid. The druid conferred with another fellow and they spoke at length and invoked their gods.

"Come on, come on!" muttered the warlord impatiently.

"Lord, we cannot direct where. We do not believe there is any site on this rock to sink a well."

"Well spoken," responded Kessog. "Then you will concede that the Lord Christ alone directs to the site where the well is to be sunk."

Fillan felt proud of how masterful the abbot was in debate under the great strain of this confrontation. However, the sick sensation welled up again, especially now he was no longer the bystander, but his brothers' eyes were upon him, expecting him to extricate them from ill fate. He had never received a word of knowledge until the other day, when visualising where the mislaid axe was located. Despite the sense of conviction that he had another picture of knowledge, he could not stop himself from wondering: what if the site he felt drawn to was not the right place? Then what?

Kessog had more to say. "Hear this, O lord. Christ is the living water that whoever thirsts shall be satisfied. It is imperative that a well is dug without delay within the citadel, for how can you withstand a siege if your people are prevented from going outside the gates to get their daily supplies?"

"The servant of Christ speaks well." He turned to his cleric, ordering this task to be carried out without delay.

"Permit me, Lord Domech," Fillan spoke up, "to advise a dig on the north side in the lower courtyard where we were sat waiting this audience with you. I believe that I can show you the exact spot where a shaft can be sunk."

Fillan pictured the small depression in the ground his eyes had rested upon earlier in the courtyard. He could not look others in the eye and, feeling the need to regain composure, he closed his eyes. Everything now depended upon him. What if he were wrong? He refused to entertain that outcome, not that he was arrogant, but he could not afford to be distracted. Anyway, he thought, there are no alternatives; no one else has a response.

A team of men was mustered with the appropriate tools, and the digging commenced at the location indicated by Fillan. At first, the turf was soft and yielding, then they hit more resistant stuff, gravel and small stones, which although impeded the progress, did not prevent the hole from growing deeper. Domech and his officials chose to leave at this point to attend to other matters, aware that this was going to be the work of days. Everyone waited for the bedrock to be reached, and several times when it was thought that it had, a larger than usual stone was removed, and the digging continued. A team of men worked until sunset.

The next day, the digging was resumed with a relay of willing men. The shaft had to be widened and a ladder placed down one side for one man to descend to do his turn at the dig. Pails of earth were brought up on a pulley system. Two pails' worth was the measure of one man's stint at digging, unless a more resistant layer had been reached, and then a single pail was the agreed measure.

The second day concluded and the bedrock had not been reached. Feeling glad and relieved, Fillan thanked God. Day by day, the digging continued unabated, first reaching damp earth and before long, water was being drawn along with the mud from the hole. The folk in the citadel, encouraged by the progress made and the promise of having a ready source of water, grew optimistic. The monks' reputation increased, and the townsfolk, who had previously little time for them, now looked at them with deference.

Digging ceased on the fifth day when the hole filled with water as quickly as it could be removed. When Domech saw this, he summoned the three to his hall. When they entered, Domech clapped his hands and applauded with a joyful noise in his throat, nodding his approval at Fillan. His thin smile had by this time turned into a grin.

"Tell me, what is the request that brought you to Dindurn?"

"Lord Domech," began Kessog. "We have travelled along Fotla's border lands, where the Romans had once built watch towers along a hill ridge. There we have received a welcome, and now, above everything else, we desire your permission and protection to establish a muintir at Cartray and Ucheldi Ucha."

"These places, as you say, were strategic to the Romans – not that they held that line for long before our forebears forced them to retreat to their earthen wall." Domech smiled, looking less wearied by the affairs of state. "In the end, we forced them back to their stone wall far to the south. The Romans could not prevail against us." The warlord lent back in his elaborate chair, and stroking his raven black beard, remarked, "I wonder whether your religion can do better?"

"Our ways are peaceful, I assure you. We do not come to conquer! We do not force any man to believe. We offer sanctuary to those troubled in body or in soul."

"Be of good cheer, holy man. I grant your request." Domech smiled with considerable and unexpected good humour. "But you ask too little! Why should these two places alone receive your good instruction? I am also granting you a plot here, on the plain where now you reside, to establish another community. The simple peasant folk there have already taken to you. In time, we too can learn more about this High King."

Fillan's heart swelled on hearing the warlord's edict. They had come in fear and with much trembling to this despot, who had been won over through the Lord revealing things hidden to man. He felt overwhelmed with thankfulness that God had answered prayer for his own faith to be strengthened and his vision of God to be enlarged.

"Master, we thank you for your generosity. I should like to propose Fillan as the one to remain here."

Fillan could not believe his ears, unsure whether to be joyful or appalled. He looked to Domech, wondering how he would respond.

Domech smiled. "Of course! Who better than the one who sourced the water? What was it you said earlier . . . about Christ being the 'living water'?"

"That he who drinks of this water shall not thirst again," reminded Fillan.

"It is well!" Domech rose, bringing their meeting to a close and coming over to warmly shake the hands of the three pilgrims.

As they walked along the long curve of the road from the citadel, Kessog remarked, "What an outcome! But let us not be under any misapprehension as to how volatile is the favour of this young warlord!"

He took a step closer to Fillan and, putting his hand upon his shoulder, said quietly into his ear: "You have travelled far in twenty-odd years. You are no longer the youngster who set out from Erin, but have come of age and will carry on the good work started in this place. I believe Castantin shall be by your side in this work. Three weeks ago, you probably could not imagine establishing a muintir here. Nobles will come seeking your counsel from beyond the Fotla and one who the Lord has set aside for a special task will stay awhile, whom you will struggle to disciple. You are of an age with Domech and the two of you will grow old together in this place."

Chapter Eleven

Imprisoned on the Crannog

555 AD Kinord

The court in crisis arrived late evening at Wroid's crannog on the day following Caltram's burial. The visitors were ferried, one at a time, in a coracle out onto the loch to his home raised above the water. By the time Taran arrived in the last ferrying, he found the quarters very cramped as several of Wroid's extended family shared the crannog. He thought the family looked morose and poorly nourished, as though they rarely left the lake dwelling. Even the children appeared to him subdued, moving sluggishly as though sick. As the new arrivals had taken every vacant space around the central hearth, a large slate set in a clay moulding where a guttering fire burned, Taran found a corner in which to lie down. He looked up at the smoke-blackened thatch glistening like tar. Maelchon, Gest and Talorgen remained on the shore, briefing Wroid. When they arrived later that evening and had eaten, there was barely space for everyone to lie down.

In the night, the wind rose. Choppy waters, just a few feet below where Taran was lying, produced a restless sound that increased his agitation. Uncle Caltram's accusations, he suspected, still rang in everyone's ears. If Oengus were his uncle's choice, then why was the succession being prolonged? Oengus had certainly shown himself to be more ruthless and ambitious. Perhaps this current hiatus was intended by the gods for him to concede to Oengus' rule. A return to normality, cleared of suspicion and comforted by Alpia, was a most attractive prospect to him right then.

An uncomfortable spectre remained though. With Oengus elected as warlord, where would that leave him? Maybe the matter of him serving under Oengus' authority was not acceptable despite their previous agreement. What if the outrageous claims gave leverage to dispose of him? Would his uncle and Oengus stoop to that? He had been lifelong friends with his cousin, although admittedly, events since returning to Rhynie had challenged their relationship. Even so, matters were more complex. The Z-rod was the root of the curse, woven with the mysterious will of the Bulàch, which required the arbitration of the druid hierarchy. This was beyond his ken.

Alpia had journeyed with them as helpmate to Conchen. Her domestic tasks had kept her busy and they only found one occasion for a brief exchange.

"Surely the matter will be resolved very soon," she had said comfortingly, "and you will emerge stronger from this ordeal." He repeated her words through that difficult night and her empathy encouraged him. Just as dawn was breaking, Taran managed to fall asleep, a sleep that was maximised by being the last in their party to rouse in a crannog astir with domestic chores. The fire was rekindled, pots were simmering from a frame over the hearth and fresh milk, eggs and firewood were brought in a coracle by one of Wroid's nephews.

After breakfast, the druids went ashore to further deliberate, and were away so long that those abandoned in the crannog grew impatient. What revelation would they bring? Everyone else must be thinking the same, but no one can bring themselves to mention it. He looked over to Oengus several times but failed to catch his eye. Oengus appeared calm, as well he might, and even took to fishing from the side of the crannog. Finally, the coracle returned, but only with Gest and, judging by his morose look, things appeared no better.

The druid's assistant addressed Talorgen. "Maelchon and Wroid request you to join us."

"Oh, what now? What a bumbling way to conduct affairs!" Talorgen impatiently scuttled about, looking for his centurion's cloak.

They were gone a long while. The cramped confinement of the crannog and the expanse of water that separated them from land seemed to play on everyone's nerves.

Later that afternoon, Talorgen returned with the druids, all stony faced.

"What decision have you come to?" asked Conchen.

"We will explain things in due course," Talorgen replied evasively.

"I think we are owed an explanation now," demanded Nechtan.

"That would be quite inappropriate," returned Wroid with a tone of finality.

"Damn you!" uttered Nechtan, red-faced. "You hold us here like prisoners! I will remind you that we came to be part of the discussion, but you have left us out."

Maelchon unexpectedly cleared his throat. "This matter is so unprecedented that it requires careful consultation."

"Then involve us. Do we not have insight too?"

"A sacrifice will be made tomorrow at the hill of the cairns to resolve matters."

Wroid and Talorgen both glanced at Maelchon uneasily, as though he had said too much.

"What kind of sacrifice?" demanded Nechtan.

"All will be explained tomorrow," Maelchon uttered, refusing categorically to be drawn further upon the matter.

The mood was so heavy that several had no appetite to eat. Taran laid down to rest early to be alone with his thoughts. Feeling a sense of urgency, he needed to try to understand what was happening to reach a conclusion upon which to act.

Ossian's words on top of the hill came to mind: *'Make great haste when you leave, be cunning, be brave, be humble . . .'* The strange utterance seemed relevant. His growing sense of impending doom could not be eradicated by rationale. The apprehension grew as he lay there pretending to be asleep and the *'Make haste'* part of the prophecy seemed most pertinent. He also recalled Maelchon's conclusion beside the image stone at Rhynie's entrance. The salmon placed above the water beast indicated that wisdom was required to overcome the fears that lurked beneath the surface. He had to master his fears, not by surpressing, but by acting upon them.

The idea to escape came into his mind. The instinct grew out of all proportion and totally consumed him. His warrior upbringing had taught him to master fears, but what he was feeling was a deeply intuitive notion that heightened anxiety. It felt like a matter of life and death. Alpia's words came to mind. 'I fear for the lives of the innocent in an evil world. Mark Ossian's words, *'Be cunning'* my dear cousin.' What if he were the intended sacrifice? Human sacrifice had not happened in living memory but he had heard, from tales passed down, that druids on occasion had performed such rites. Could this great curse warrant so desperate a measure?

Taran decided to heed his intuition and reviewed his options. Getting to shore, where the horses were, was the first step; a big challenge given his situation. He could take his own horse and scatter the rest. His best chance was to ride into the hills west of the loch, into wild country in which to hide and bide his time. Beyond that, he had no plan.

As he lay there, Nechtan came alongside and, leaning over, kissed him on his upturned cheek. Taran did not move. The gesture was odd from a father who had last kissed him as a boy. Beyond the anger expressed, was his father feeling the same uneasiness? This lent conviction to see his escape through.

Lamps were extinguished and the last intermittent conversation died out. He waited an age. When everyone seemed fast asleep, he rose. The low flames of the fire swimming warmly over the tarry sheen of the thatch gave just enough light to show where figures were lying. He made his way carefully between the sleeping bodies to the door. Suddenly, someone grabbed his ankle firmly.

"Where are you going?" Oengus rasped through his teeth.

Taran did not appreciate the gesture, but bit his tongue, knowing he must not rouse suspicion.

"I am going out to relieve myself," he replied as naturally as he could. He felt the grip release from his heel.

Moving the sliding door ajar, he stepped onto the outer platform and pushed the door closed. Finding a wedge shape piece of wood right next to the door, he quietly forced it into the runner along which the door opened and closed. Noiselessly, he descended the ladder to where a couple of coracles were tethered to a supporting stilt of the crannog. Freeing them both and tying one to the other, he got in and paddled as quickly as he could.

Oengus raised the alarm. Taran could hear him frantically trying to prise open the jammed door. He worked the paddle furiously in a figure of eight motion, making haste whilst they remained trapped within the crannog. Coracles could not be paddled like a canoe, for they would only spin, and so progress was excruciatingly slow. The jammed door bought him precious time and on hearing it eventually freed, he glanced back and saw a couple of figures silhouetted in the doorway against the pale flicker of firelight burning within. Now a stone's throw away, Taran cast off the other coracle to make better headway. He heard an arrow whistling close by, which immediately broke the water's surface just beyond. He glanced back and saw the robust bulk of Oengus draw another arrow. His cousin was a good shot and his second arrow would probably find its target. Feeling like a sitting duck, he dived into the loch. Although he was not a great swimmer, he thrashed through the water as fast as he could towards the shore. Another arrow struck the water just in front of him.

The cold water, together with his heightened excitement, made him alert. Taking a deep breath, he submerged and swam frog-like, imitating a good swimmer he had seen recently in the Dee. Conscious of swimming in a straight line, he took powerful strokes. Feeling he had covered a lengthy distance, he came up for air. The shore still looked some distance off.

Wasting no time, he took a lung full of air and submerged before Oengus could target him. His heart pounded in his ears. His lungs started to burn but, resisting the urge to surface, he took a further ten powerful strokes, knowing his life depended upon them. At the point when he felt his chest was about to explode, he surfaced. The shore, although nearer, was still some way off. He glanced round, needing time to regulate his breathing, and was heartened to see the crannog was now some distance away.

After a third surfacing for air, his foot found the shallow bottom of the loch. Remaining wholly submerged, he lent far forward and powered himself along with his feet, digging into the mud of the loch bed and propelling his torso with his arms. On reaching the true shallows, he arose and ran swiftly to shore. He looked back and saw a figure swimming in pursuit, a good distance off.

Running over to the horses, he untied them all and, keeping hold of his own horse's halter, he spirited the remainder into a canter. He pursued on horseback, shouting like a crazed man to scatter them into the night with a pounding of hooves. Turning his horse westward, he kept to the cover of the trees whenever he could, around the northern shore of the loch. The ground was flat, and as the trees were not too dense he could move swiftly and with ease, giving him time to cast a look across to the crannog standing remote, way out in the loch. He was thankful to be making good his escape, despite Oengus' best efforts to stop him.

Rounding the thin finger of loch at the top end, he considered his next move. Whilst looking out upon this western shore from the crannog the previous day, he had noted a small glen heading up into the hills. Would that not make the perfect escape route? Leaving the flat ground around the loch, his horse slowed to a trot as they made their way into the glen. The valley soon narrowed, becoming so steep-sided that he slowed his horse to a walking pace as they double-backed in a climb out of what was becoming a ravine. Zigzagging up the steep side, he reached the cliff top that formed a line above the ravine. He stopped to listen. All was quiet except for the thud of his own heartbeat. Although still wet from the swim, he was sweating.

Taran reckoned they would not pursue until daylight. It would be difficult to find and then round up the horses he had spirited away in the dark. Without the same urgency to make haste, he still wanted to put as much distance from the crannog as he could before dawn. He experienced the huge relief of extricating himself from a very great danger and could now relax in the saddle. As his horse walked an easy passage along a broad ledge between forest and cliff, he considered what provisions he might have and started rummaging inside the pocket of the saddle blanket located rather awkwardly behind him. His horse stumbled, perhaps on a root or into a collapsed burrow, jolting them sideways towards the chasm. Alarmed by the edge, the horse had lunged in the opposite direction, pitching him. Rather than being cast to the ground, he found himself hurtling through the air over the cliff. He came crashing through the canopy of the trees below, the upper crest breaking his fall, and for a split second, he thought he would be fine. Then his arm heavily struck a thick tree limb that caused a sickening pain, before he landed on a springy forest floor, the undisturbed leaf mould of many years. He lay there stunned. He could move both legs, but his right arm, hanging limp, felt most painful.

"I have broken it," he said aloud. He sat up, angry with himself for his moment of carelessness, coinciding with the horse stumbling at the edge of the ravine. How stupid could he have been! Having executed a tremendous feat of escape, he had become preoccupied with making plans, when in hindsight, vigilance near to the ravine was clearly needed. Had his military training not spoken of the danger of lowering your guard after an imminent danger had just passed? What was he to do now?

Rising to his feet, he was glad to find that he could walk, provided he could keep his broken arm still. He gathered his bearings, an easy task due to the flow of water down the ravine. Forced to continue without his horse, he climbed upstream, keeping to the original plan of going into the vastness of the tree-covered hills of the Minamoyn Goch to evade capture. Progress was slow as the pathless way was uneven, and his broken arm was excruciatingly painful whenever it moved. He removed his plaid and, with the difficulty of only having the real use of one arm, he made it into a sling. This helped to ease the pain. Emerging beyond the ravine, he followed the stream higher into the hills. The first light of dawn paled the sky.

With the stream now small and the valley sides shallow, he struck up to reach the nearby ridge. The trees grew too dense to give a view.

He paused to consider what to do next. His pursuers would follow the horse tracks, which hopefully would wander in a different direction, giving him further time to escape. They would no doubt find his steed, and then backtrack to look for footprints descending from the horse. Not finding any, given the nature of his descent, the search would be prolonged. If the curse upon the tribe was great enough to require his sacrifice, then they would not stop their man hunt. If he were the pursuer, he would get dogs onto the trail.

His advantage, though, was hampered by his broken arm. It was only a matter of time before they would catch him. His best bet was to cross the Dee into the lands of the Circinn, confirm Talorgen's suspicions of him conniving with the enemy. That would halt their pursuit.

Once in Circinn territory, he would walk to the next stream to throw the dogs off his scent by walking back down the watercourse to the main river and cross back to the Ce side. It had to be sufficiently upriver so he would emerge a good distance from where the dogs had last picked up his scent on Ce territory. Proceeding upriver seemed the best option – too many people lived downstream who would be eager for the bounty on his head. Holding out in the higher hills beyond the river, where hardly anybody ventured, seemed the best plan.

The descent was slow and arduous with his broken arm, and the crossing of the Dee was deplorably painful as he stumbled over the boulders of the unseen riverbed. Thoughts of pursuit made him grit his teeth and the numbing effect of cold water on the fracture made moving in the river more endurable.

Much later that day, having executed his plan, he reached a huge bend in the river flowing around the bulk of an outlying hill on the Ce side. He struck up towards higher ground, making camp on a thick bed of gathered pine needles. He felt thankful, although hungry and cold as his clothes clung damp onto his body. The nights were not so cold in early June, but to one exhausted and in pain, he was shivering.

Chapter Twelve

Consolidation at Rhynie

555 AD Kinord & Rhynie

 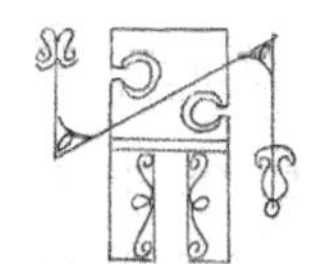

When Oengus had reached the shore, Taran had already made good his escape. Recognising the futility of looking for the freed horses in the dark, and not knowing in which direction Taran had taken, Oengus waded back out into the loch to retrieve the coracles, swimming with them back to the crannog.

"What the devil is going on?" an angry Uncle Nechtan confronted him. "Why did you shoot at Taran?"

Nechtan had forcibly stopped him from firing more than two arrows and after breaking free from his grip, he had dived into the water.

Oengus did not know how to answer and remained silent.

Talorgen spoke up. "Taran is responsible for all the setbacks we have encountered . . ."

Nechtan did not let him finish, shouting 'Nonsense!' into his face.

"Whatever your take on events," interjected Maelchon, "Taran bears a symbol that is incompatible with what Oengus bears."

"And whose fault is that?" Nechtan turned hotly on the druid. Oengus had never witnessed Uncle Nechtan losing his temper like this for he was normally a placid man.

"All was to be disclosed this morning." Maelchon's voice was calm, unperturbed by the boiling anger of Taran's father. "We were to explain the curse of the Bulàch that called for drastic measures."

"What drastic measures?" Nechtan demanded, still incensed.

The impassive Maelchon cleared his throat. "Ever since the two power symbols had been tattooed on the cousins, there has been commotion between the heavenly and earthly realms, creating a great disharmony. You must understand that giving the conflicting symbols was not the design of man. The Bulàch has chosen to confound us and shall continue until we make amends." The druid made a belch-like gesture when he pronounced the word 'amends'.

"Do get to the point," insisted Talorgen, turning to the druid.

"I am coming to it." The druid stroked his bald pate awkwardly. "The only way to break the curse of two chosen heirs was for the sacrifice of one."

There was a loud gasp from Domelch, Conchen and Alpia.

"You cannot be serious!" retorted Nechtan. Noticing how menacing Nechtan looked, Oengus placed a hand on the dagger on his own belt should things boil over.

"That was the design of the Bulàch from the first," pitched in Wroid. "To have her fill of blood and claim the male spirit of the departed for herself."

"She is also testing our commitment to her," added Maelchon.

Domelch was trembling so uncontrollably that Alpia placed an arm about her. The crannog was still for a moment. Conchen turned to Talorgen with a look of horror. "How could you consider carrying out such a plan on one of our nephews?"

"It is the sacrifice of one for the preservation of the tribe," Talorgen summarised stonily, without emotion.

"I think it is clear now why I needed to consult Wroid," spoke Maelchon, holding his head higher.

Nechtan addressed Maelchon in a tone that was insistent, as though carrying out an interrogation. "And what made you decide it was Taran to be sacrificed?"

Maelchon looked uneasily to Talorgen. Talorgen responded. "It had to be Taran. Oengus had already been chosen by the Bulàch by the symbol of governance." He now looked Nechtan straight in the eye. "Oengus was my choice, proving the more able by the tests . . ."

"How can you say that!" interrupted Nechtan with a further surge of anger. "You were not there. I was! There was nothing between the cousins in terms of intelligence and ability. If anything, Taran had the edge, as Oengus is a hothead."

"You would say that, being Taran's father. Taran is strongly suspected of conniving with the enemy. That cannot be tolerated, not even a hint of it." Talorgen stared impassively at Nechtan.

"That is nonsense!" stuttered Domelch.

Oengus almost pitied her, recognising that his own mother would say the same if the roles were reversed.

"You have lost your reason," hotly contended Nechtan, disregarding the warlord's position. "I can accept when a leader has to make an unpopular choice, but not in this matter. Your judgement is based on the allegations of a desperate and dying man with ambitions for his son." Nechtan's voice now grew hoarse. "It beggars belief that you cannot see that!"

Talorgen remained unruffled.

Nechtan then said, "But what about the Z-rod given to Taran, is that not the warlord's symbol?"

"How do you know Taran received that?" interjected Maelchon. "Taran was sworn to secrecy."

The druid was probably keen to shift the attention elsewhere, thought Oengus.

"Oh, I can tell you, he was secret enough about it! I happened to see it when he was bathing in the river. He did not know I had noticed. Anyway, talking about sworn secrecy, did you know that Oengus had told his father about the broch tattoo?"

Oengus shrugged his shoulders indifferently.

"The Z-rod is reserved for the warlord right enough," Talorgen responded. "But it is only tattooed after being inaugurated. It is invalid beforehand!"

"Then what is the meaning of the Z-rod if Taran was not to rule?" Nechtan pursued.

"Only the design of the Bulàch to claim her blood," replied Wroid.

Oengus decided to break his uncomfortable silence. "What will be the outcome, whilst the two bearers of the symbols of power continue living?"

"The curse remains," replied Wroid drily. "But maybe it will diminish once you, Oengus, become the warlord." The old druid paused before adding, "Unless some untimely end happens to Taran."

"You are talking about my son!" shouted Domelch viciously.

Nechtan came to her side and placed an arm around her. Then turning upon Oengus, he asked sternly, "Why did you shoot at Taran, since you did not know any of this?"

Everyone turned their attention upon Oengus. Domelch and Alpia looked particularly appalled. He had no answer, at least not one that was rational. Seizing Taran's ankle had been intuitive, suspecting him of something. It was that rage of having let him go that made him fire the arrows to put an end to him.

"I have seen your ambition," Nechtan continued, "fed relentlessly by your father from the time of the initiation. I had hoped that with you and Taran coming to terms with the murder, you would work well together, and so it seemed, until your father's death. This rampant desire to rule has no doubt been noted by our lord as proof that you are the man after his own heart."

Nechtan acquiesced and grew calm. Was he thinking, like him, that Taran was free and alive? For his uncle, that fact would provide hope for the bearer of the Z-rod, but as for himself, his cousin's freedom would haunt him.

After retrieving the horses, Talorgen commanded him to go with Gest and make a cursory search for Taran, to which Nechtan and Domelch strongly objected.

After Oengus and Gest had departed on horseback, Gest spoke. "I saw him riding off along the northern shore."

"Let us go that way and see if we can pick up his trail."

Following the prints of Taran's horse was a slow task and resulted in them eventually finding his riderless horse.

"It is a ruse to put us off his trail," Oengus declared.

"I would reckon Taran has made for the Circinn. Their territory is just over there." Gest pointed with his chin in the direction of the Dee valley.

Oengus clenched his fists and made a grunting noise in his frustration. "We have been searching all day! Taran will be well away from here by now."

"It will be another night at Wroid's then!" Gest looked disappointed.

"You are not keen on the idea?"

"Are you? The place is filthy and so overcrowded with us all in that ramshackled crannog!"

They turned their horses downhill towards Loch Kinord.

"We would need a good number of men to mount a proper search. As it is, we have an old man, Uncle Nechtan whose loyalties are obviously with Taran, Maelchon who is no scout and our womenfolk. Bah!" His horse lunged forward, requiring Oengus to pull on the reins. "What would you do if you were Taran?"

"As I said, make for the Circinn. That is where you and Lord Talorgen believe he has allies – your father most definitely believed that too."

Oengus stopped his horse and looked at his companion, who was of an age with himself, and pondered. Gest brought his own horse to a stop and turned it about to face him with an enquiring look. "May I know whether I have your loyalty?" Oengus asked, keen to gain an ally amidst the mounting hostilities.

"As I have been riding all day united in the same purpose as yourself – upon Taran's trail – I can say you have my loyalty."

"Good. Then I shall share this with you." He swallowed hard. "Taran has no more friends among the Circinn than I do."

Gest looked taken aback for a moment but did not convey shock, nor even mild indignation.

"But I go along with this misinformation," he continued, "that my father started and Talorgen believes, because it serves my purpose well. Do you think less of me for that?"

"No," he said simply and with sincerity. "It is clear that you are the heir chosen by the Bulàch."

Oengus believed him. "Good," he said with a note of finality. "We will leave early tomorrow for Rhynie and lay aside the futility of the search. Come, let us build a new era together: a new warlord with his favoured druid."

Gest smiled. "But Maelchon will still be chief druid – some things will not be changed."

The next day, Oengus rode between the two druids. He was keen to learn more about his destiny, but learned nothing new, although pleased to go over familiar ground that confirmed his election. Talorgen rode alone in the chariot, looking resolute, and at times wore a faint smile, which Oengus interpreted as relief to have the succession sorted. He eyed Nechtan's menacing presence with caution. Domelch rode alongside her husband, grieving the loss of their son. They were now the family in crisis! Only three days had passed since his father's death, but he regarded this was a time for being strong and resolute, to seize the moment and not be caught in a mournful attitude. It was not disrespecting his father; would Caltram not approve of him stepping up to the mark?

He noticed the lovely Alpia riding alongside Conchen. They seemed close. What was to become of her? Taran was as good as dead and surely she would soon acknowledge that. Now she was easier prey with his rival removed and dishonoured.

Upon arriving at Rhynie, Oengus used Taran's escape to his advantage, convincing many of Taran's complicity with the Circinn.

"He is not a personal enemy," Oengus maintained, hyping up the propaganda campaign. "But most regrettably has been found to be an enemy to the cause of the Ce." He concealed the truth concerning the Z-rod tattoo, lest anyone conclude that his cousin was the rightful successor. Then, on reflection, he surmised that it would be hard to conceal the truth since several people already knew of its existence. Would Uncle Nechtan not disclose it to his advantage? Well, that was not something to become anxious about. Talorgen's backing and the support of Maelchon were the only two opinions that mattered regarding the rightful succession.

"Finally, some normality has returned," Oengus said, as he stretched himself out comfortably on the thick underlay of rushes in the family home.

His mother looked at him quizzically. "How can you say that just seven days after your father's death?"

Oengus propped himself up on his elbow thoughtfully. "I suppose it is ironic to say that. What I mean by normality, though, is the absence of the acute pressure experienced over the past few days." He considered the intense struggle from which he had emerged as master and Taran had been deposed. He could not help feeling triumphant.

"It is still a pretty insensitive thing to say!" objected Derile, his sibling closest in age to himself. She had only been a small girl when he had left for his military training, and now a young woman of sixteen confronted him, transformed beyond recognition. People praised her fair looks but, being his sister, he could not see what others declared so emphatically.

"What normality have I known?" he reflected aloud. "Since returning here, how many actual days have I spent in this home? My time here in Rhynie has been so brief that no routine has established itself."

Derile cast him a hostile look.

He pulled himself up into a sitting position, believing it necessary to defend himself further. "The past three weeks have been spent on campaign on the Circinnian border! That is why being back at home is normal."

"With thirty-three dead, our father taken from us and Taran on the run – how can you even think of saying things are normal!" Her eyes looked puffy as she poked the logs on the fire.

He observed his mother busying herself with chores, choosing not to speak. She was given to lengthy silences and was not even talking with his Aunt Domelch, with whom she used to be inseparable. His other two siblings were too young and withdrawn for Oengus to consider interacting with.

"You do not understand," Oengus said, rising to his feet. "You are just a woman! What do you know of the pressures of campaigning, the tension, the intrigue, the killings . . .?"

Derile ignored him.

"I am off to see Uncle Talorgen."

"You are always off to Uncle!" retorted Derile, spoiling for a fight. "Do you not know what needs done on the farm? Do you ever think of milking . . .?"

"That is a woman's work," interrupted Oengus.

"And is it woman's work to chop and carry firewood, go hunting, to sow and weed the fields?"

Oengus made an impatient grunt as he passed her. "Being at Uncle's is my role. I have responsibilities there." He left the hut.

His uncle was pleased to see him.

"Go and fetch the Roman glassware," he ordered Alpia, who had become more permanent these days in their household due to Conchen's wishes.

"Oh, is there an occasion I am unaware of?" asked Oengus.

"What?" Talorgen looked him quizzically in the eye. "Oh, because I am calling for the fine glasses? They are there to be used and enjoyed." He chuckled slightly. "I am not going to live forever."

Alpia returned with the glasses and an amphora of wine. Oengus tried to catch her eye. He felt slightly piqued that she could ignore his presence, but it was understandable.

"It is time you learned the ways of being a leader," continued his uncle with a determined manner. "You have proved yourself to have valour . . . and, I might add, ambition. That is no bad thing in a ruler. Men need vision too, and drive to keep the momentum going. Start to lose that and your days are numbered, mark my words. Now, where was I? Yes, I was saying that you must learn how to govern."

"I am ready for that. What do you have in mind?"

"Well there is no point dilly-dallying about here with me telling you about this and that. There is nothing quite like learning your duties than by going about them. Summer is here and it is high time to do the round of our domains to gather tribute," he said brightly. "I was not feeling up to it, but I have to say, I have a new energy these days. We shall leave at next full moon on a tour of our nobles. Then all shall see you and have their opportunity to express their allegiance and to know that I have willed it."

Oengus smiled, glad to hear about a development that would take him away from Rhynie. The place had become wearisome after Derile's antagonism.

"I am concerned about settling scores with the Circinn at the ferry," he ventured tentatively. "They have killed my father and that calls for vengeance. I would like to make an example of them to show that they do not deal lightly with us, especially those who betrayed us so brazenly."

"Not for now!" Talorgen held up his hand. "First, we re-group. Besides, the Circinn will be expecting a strike from us. More to the point, your cousin has gone over to them and there is no knowing what may come of that. Shame you did not finish him off with an arrow when he was swimming from the crannog."

Oengus could not tell whether this was criticism or wishful thinking, but he felt annoyed to be reminded about this incident.

"I would have succeeded had not it been for Uncle Nechtan."

"Oh yes, your uncle," Talorgen looked up meaningfully. He fell quiet, obviously pondering some matter, which Oengus presumed were the options of how to deal with the new enemy in the camp. His uncle looked at him peculiarly. "But tell me, Oengus, why would you want to strike that couple down at the ferry if Taran was the informer?"

Realising his mistake, he allowed his agitation to show for a moment. "I do believe they had a part to play in the way things unfolded. That is to say, they were keen to goad us on."

He felt his uncle studying him before taking a good draft of wine.

Talorgen wiped his white moustaches with the back of his hand, and flattening his whiskers, he gathered the red centurion's cloak about him.

"Uncle," Oengus remarked, keen to change the subject. "Where did your cloak come from? It is particularly fine and like no other I have seen."

"It is an heirloom from the previous warlord. It is said to have once belonged to a Roman centurion. No one can corroborate that for sure, but it would explain both its excellent quality as well as its age. It is no longer as bright as when I first wore it as a young man."

Oengus picked up an edge of the cloak and inspected it closely. It was decidedly a little moth eaten and had various sewing repairs.

"We will have some music in a week's time," announced Talorgen. "We will call for the bard to sing and tell stories of feats of valour and the outworking of destinies, both great and small. There has been great tension of late and we should all be glad to put it behind us." Looking at Oengus significantly, he instructed, "It is the role of the warlord to move the community on."

His uncle looked as bright as he allowed himself to be. Not one for being jovial, Oengus was relieved by his uncle's wishes to pursue better times.

"One day," his uncle continued, slightly under his breath, leaning towards Oengus. "Songs will be made of your deeds. Be wise in all you do, so that the songs will not be an embarrassment to your ear when they are sung." The old warlord clapped his nephew on the shoulder to add emphasis.

The following week, so many came to Rhynie that many were standing outside the hall. The evening was fine, full of warm breezes and sunshine.

"What is the occasion?" asked an old man who had travelled from another community of the Ce.

"Why, have you not heard?" remarked the local man. "Oengus is the chosen one and Taran is on the run. The gods have decided on the succession – that is the occasion."

"Oengus! I know Oengus," replied the stranger. "I always said he would make the better leader. Determined he is. I mind the time when the two of them went hunting in my country, looking for wild boar. They came upon a sow suckling her piglets. Taran was all for looking for some other game, but Oengus pierced the sow through with his spear."

"That is Oengus for you – not one to hesitate, that is for sure. Mind you, the piglets would perish without their sow to suckle!"

The two old men elbowed their way through the hall to receive their food and drink. Once they had settled, they discussed the fate of the fugitive prince, Taran.

"He is gone to the Circinn they say! Made himself a byword of deviance to our people."

The traveller shook his head with disdain. "Well, if they do not kill him for his part in the cattle raid, Oengus will need to for sure. Too risky to have a wronged prince at large, influencing neighbours who will use him to their advantage."

The local took a large mouthful of pork that, for the lack of teeth, took time to chew. "What if Taran manages to talk the Circinn into open warfare to seize the lordship for himself?" asked the traveller in a quiet undertone, saying something he knew that ought not to be said, though was on people's minds.

"It has happened before, in our grandfathers' time!"

"That would bring much bloodshed." Then, as an afterthought, he added, "but it would carry the risk of much loss for the Circinn too!"

The local nodded his head sagely. He lent towards the traveller and continued in a lower voice, just loud enough to be heard over the din in the hall. "They say that Taran was tattooed with the Z-rod and that it was the druid's doing!" They looked meaningfully at one another. "But Oengus, apparently, is to be tattooed with the lordship's sign too."

"How can that be? Talorgen yet lives."

"Och, you know – new ways I suppose!"

"And when will that be?"

"At the summer solstice it is said."

"A most propitious time when the sun's at its full ascendancy."

Alpia observed that Oengus was in good spirits as she entered the hall, with the wine no doubt playing a part. He looked like one who felt fortune smiled upon him. The people appeared to be with him, along with the gods it would seem.

"Hey Alpia!" he called brightly, beckoning her to sit beside him.

She hesitated.

"Do not be bashful!" Oengus gesticulated earnestly for her to join him. He rose to his feet, pulling out the vacant chair next to his own with an exaggerated gesture.

"Come here, my dear," Conchen invited her, which would have been a fortuitous thing were it not the same seat positioned between her and Oengus.

She came over curtly smiling, aware that her cheeks were puffier than usual.

". . . then he said to me, 'How do you get three horses from two?' Then I said, 'Easy when the two are a mare and a stallion!'" Oengus threw back his head with exaggerated laughter, telling stories and riddles in fast succession.

"Do not tell me that you do not get it?" teased Oengus, his forefinger flicking the underside of a young woman's chin, who looked naively towards her smiling companions. "I can give you a lesson in private later; then you would understand!"

The girl flushed red, looking unsure of whether to leave or to smile. Her bashful hesitation seemed to amuse Oengus. Her eyes met his with suppressed amusement, before casting a look that conveyed she did not altogether mind his cheekiness.

Did Oengus not presume she had been Taran's girlfriend, she asked herself? If that was so, then Oengus was no respecter of such things and clearly, he was insensitive. Did he expect that he could just ingratiate himself with her? Did he really consider Taran well and truly out of the way?

She focussed on talking with her aunt, doing her best to ignore Oengus' attempt to lure her into his talk. How much had Oengus been in the know during the events leading up to Taran's flight? Was he just a player, like everyone else, in a game determined by Talorgen and his druids? Had Taran not spoken about the tension between them competing for the lordship? Those arrows he had fired implicated him in Taran's overthrow.

Where was Taran now? Was he as good as dead, as everyone claimed? If he were dead, then surely news would be fast in reaching their court, knowing a reward was to be had? Therefore, he must still be alive, she concluded. Could he really have gone on over to the Circinn though? That seemed like leaping out of the frying pan and into the fire. She could not find even a single grain of rationality in the lie that Taran had connived with their enemy. He had a sincere heart that led him to make noble choices. Then had not Ossian told him to be cunning, something she had encouraged him to bear in mind? Hard as she tried not to think of Taran, just to seek a moment's rest, she was unable to shift him from her mind. What could he do as the rejected one? Taran believed in his right to be warlord, conferred by being the bearer of the Z-rod.

She reprimanded herself. What is Taran to me? I am not his woman. But then, is it not right to be outraged for a noble one, who has been cast off and demonised?

"...why will you not show us your tattoo?" coaxed Eithni, leaning across the table towards Oengus, her head swaying from side to side with a broad smile.

"Maybe it is somewhere he would prefer we did not see!" suggested another woman, breaking into laughter.

Oengus needed no persuasion and quickly untied the laces on the front of his ample smock.

"Oooh!" chorused a couple of girls.

The smock, now loose and baggy, was pulled down over his right shoulder and Oengus presented his back, in a dramatic fashion, to the young women. One of them reached out and admiringly caressed the shape of the broch tattooed over the muscles.

Alpia felt frustrated ruminating over Taran's fate, which was beyond knowing. But what of her own? What did she have planned for her life? It was a question provoked by Oengus having made the succession and by Taran being at large, presumably making plans for his next steps. Just a few weeks ago, these big questions had not loomed on her horizon. Had she not too come of age along with her peers? She had become restless following the boredom that she had recently complained of, and flustered by Taran's ardent admiration, which she had not sought, but admitted to having provoked a little.

What if Taran were dead, she asked herself? The thought more than saddened her and she had to admit that it hurt to contemplate so fine a youth meeting some unfortunate end. She pictured his smiling face, could hear him pouring out his feelings for her and felt more than just flattered. She recalled again their one heady night, leaping together through the Beltane fires. That had been the start of something she had been keen to suppress. It was like a fire that combusted alarmingly quick, which needed to be dampened and controlled. Had he not awakened her heart through his appealing charisma and sincerity? She really was not to blame for that, for had she not made it clear that she regarded him nothing more than a friend and a cousin? Then she thought of him destitute and alone, striving to exist and without the comfort of knowing his feelings for her had perhaps been reciprocated.

She became aware of Nechtan staring at her, sat next to Oengus, and felt the stinging reproach in his look before he averted his gaze. He did not look her way again. She felt helpless, misunderstood, regarded as a prize for this upstart beside her to seize. She excused herself and was relieved that this did not appear to bother Oengus. Some girls were obviously intent to hook Oengus, viewing him as the most eligible catch of all young men among the Ce. Eithni's flirtatious ways, she observed, particularly seemed to be working their magic. She recalled how those two had ended up together at the Beltane celebrations, and how Eithni had afterwards confided in her about liking Oengus. Well, that would be convenient, if the two would get together and she could be left alone.

Chapter Thirteen

The Fugitive Prince

555 AD Y Minamoyn Goch

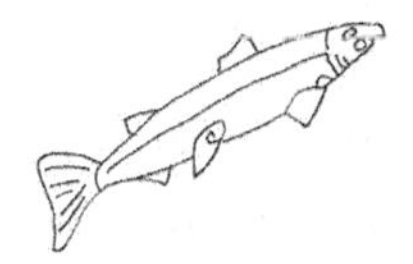

Taran awoke several times in the night, in great discomfort, aghast by his circumstances. The sheer incredulity of all that had taken place overwhelmed him. He, the innocent, had been made to run from all he knew, his people, his community, from his parents and from Alpia. He rued coming off his horse, right by the ravine of all places! Had that misfortune not happened, he would be in the mountains and not in a risky place too close to a settlement. Should the pursuit close in on him, he was no match for any man.

He tightened the sling to alleviate some of the pain. How was he going to fare if he were to head west into the mountains? It would be challenging enough without a broken arm. Going east, where it was most populated, was not an option to keep his identity concealed. West, along the Dee valley, was into unknown territory, where he presumed dwellings would be close to the river. Going northwest into the hills, where the Ce never ventured far, seemed best to evade a probable manhunt. The hills were extensive, with places to hide. His current location already bordered the wild country, and so he determined that at first light he would head that way.

The night seemed long, although darkness was short close to midsummer. At dawn, he descended into a narrow glen and drank from a stream. The far valley side rose steep, rising to a rocky ridge. Near the top, it became a scramble, reminding him constantly of how one broken arm could make the whole body infirm. From the ridge, the view was much as he expected: a series of rising hills, densely forested. If there was a place to evade capture, this was it. His eyes scanned the forest, trying to determine the lie of the land and decide on a route that would take him far from civilisation. He could just make out a clearing in the distance, perhaps where some hermit eked out a basic living. Should he risk going there? Reason told him that concealing his identity was only achievable if he were to remain alone. Pangs of hunger reminded him of how precarious his situation was, for he had found nothing to eat the previous day. He needed help if he were to survive and determined to venture to the small clearing.

Birch and pine abounded, and in places, passing through the densest growth became difficult. This was not terrain to take a horse, which offered some consolation for having lost his own. The way was easier where clusters of pines grew tall to form a canopy and prevented light from supporting much growth on the forest floor.

"Do not move another step!" came a commanding voice ahead of him.

Taran looked up. An older woman stood some forty paces off with a drawn bow.

"I come in peace," replied Taran.

The woman edged cautiously forward without taking her eyes off him. She brushed past a couple of branches then stopped, where she had an unobstructed aim. Her grey hair was streaked with white, and although elderly, Taran thought there was little doubt of her capability. She would shoot if provoked, and her aim would probably be accurate if she were used to fending for herself.

"I am not dangerous," Taran said, pointing at the makeshift sling. "I have broken my arm and am in no fit state to fight anyone. I am not even a danger to a woman."

"Who are you and where do you come from?" She was very much the master of the situation, disinclined to lower her guard.

"I am Drostan. As you can tell from my accent, I am of the Ce, such as yourself." Taran had already considered this pseudonym when lying awake in the night.

"How come you broke your arm?"

Taran explained the accident.

"So why have you not returned to your people?"

Realising that his story did not sound good, and that he needed help, he revealed part of the truth.

"I was being chased by another man whose intent is to kill me!"

"Are you not a man to stand and fight your opponent? Was there only one of them?"

"Well, yes," he began awkwardly. "I would under normal circumstances. But this man was once a friend and I had no quarrel with him, but he did with me."

"How's that?" the woman asked, keeping her bow targeted at his chest.

"Well, it was over a girl. She liked me and not him. He was jealous, wanting her badly for himself."

"You are handsome, I will give you that! But why are you coming this way? Nobody comes into these parts. What could you possibly want here?"

"After fleeing from my friend, then breaking my arm, I needed to evade him. Heading for the hills seemed best.

Last night, I slept just on the other side of the ridge behind me. I saw a clearing in the woods and thought I would make for it, to seek help whilst my arm mends." He wondered whether this sounded plausible. What more could he say to gain her trust?

"And what sort of help do you think you might get? My husband and I are old, and we live simply." She lowered her bow, but kept the arrow strung.

"I know in my present condition I will not be capable of much." He paused, thinking this would not gain favour. "That is to say, I will not be capable of doing everything at first, but I could still make myself useful. If you were to help me, I would be most thankful, and the gods would think well of your kindness to a stranger in distress. As my arm heals, I will be able to serve you and your husband with all manner of tasks about your farm. I could be very useful and then I will leave you in peace."

The wind blew the woman's hair over an eye. Her expression remained stoic, unmoved by his appeal. The birch leaves shimmered above and all around. What else could he add to gain her sympathy?

"Well, you might be of some help to us in due course, but you are going to be more of a burden than a help to begin with . . . and an extra mouth to feed, although we are coming into a season of plenty!" She shook her head vaguely. "Come and see what my husband has to say. Move slowly now . . ."

"I cannot move any other way than slowly. You have nothing to fear!"

"Walk on ahead of me and I will direct your way."

Taran walked towards her with an uncertain smile. When he was about ten paces away, she trained a taut bow on him and backed off to one side. Taran led, guided by instructions to make for the side of a copse of birch, then to a tall oak and on to a certain boulder. Eventually, they came upon a small clearing with a circular hut on one side. Its conical roof rose tall, and as Taran approached, a smaller hut appeared just behind it, with thatch reaching almost to the ground.

"You wait right here," ordered the woman. "Do not move so you can be seen from the door." She disappeared inside. Taran could hear her talking and the thin voice of an old man came in reply. They spoke at length, but he could not make out their words. The old man appeared in the doorway, wizened, with long, dishevelled hair and a grey beard that grew in a straggly manner. His clothes were dirty, in need of repair.

"And who do you say you are?" he questioned, his voice broken with age.

"Drostan."

The old man went over many of the same questions that his wife had asked earlier, keenly observing his manner as Taran responded patiently. His wife stood beside him, still armed with a bow, watching Taran fixedly.

On exhausting all his questions, the old man pronounced his verdict. "I do not believe your story, young man!"

His wife added that she was of the same opinion.

"One man would not cause you to flee your home and people over a girl." He spat copiously on the ground and walked up to Taran with the difficulty of one troubled by swollen joints. The woman also came forward, training her bow at Taran's chest. The old man reached out and squeezed Taran's broken arm.

Taran yelped, like an injured dog and staggered back a couple of steps. His body shuddered and he uttered a curse under his breath.

The woman came over to her husband and whispered something in his ear. Taran could understand their need to check his story and he now hoped they had proof that he was genuinely incapacitated.

"You have broken your arm right enough," the old man nodded with a faint smile. "Well, you have your reasons for not telling us the truth and you do genuinely seem to be in difficulty. You might be useful in time and we could do with a helping hand. The roof leaks and I cannot get up there anymore to fix it and," he nodded towards his wife, "she is not so good with roofs. She is a crack shot though, so do not go provoking her, otherwise you will be in a far worse state."

"Why would I want to harm you? You have obviously no worldly goods that would make anyone want to steal," Taran remarked.

The old man stared, unimpressed by the comment.

"You can stay. Do what you can: light fires and cook with one hand . . ." At a loss of what else to say, he added, "There will be other things to do. I am old – going the way of all flesh, so may this kindness be remembered by the gods."

"Thank you," Taran said with genuine appreciation, nodding in the direction of his wife too. "Can I ask you your names?"

"Elpin is my name and my wife is Coblaith."

"Bring the logs from over there to the chopping stump," said Coblaith unsmilingly.

The logs were in long lengths and Taran could only carry one at a time. Elpin went into the lower hut and re-emerged with an axe.

"You hold the stick and I will chop – that way we can make faster work between us." The old man soon tired. "When your arm's better, you will do the chopping."

Meanwhile Coblaith put a pot of water on the fire, and then from her field basket she took out a mountain hare shot earlier that day and went about skinning it.

Taran's attention was caught by a movement behind Elpin, which made him stand braced. "There is a wolf behind you and he is coming towards us!"

Elpin turned unperturbed and offered his hand to the wolf.

"This is Garn," said the old man. "He is a cross between a domestic dog and a wolf. He certainly has more the wolf looks of the father." The animal came over to be petted. It then proceeded to gingerly sniff Taran's hand, retracted his lips slightly and emitted a low growl of distrust.

When they had finished splitting enough logs and had brought them into the hut, they sat down beside the fire without speaking. They still seemed wary of him.

"Let me take a look at your arm, Drostan," said Coblaith, after they had finished eating lunch.

He removed it from the makeshift sling with a helping hand and pulled up his tunic sleeve over the elbow to reveal a swollen and bruised forearm. Coblaith took some water from a pot left on the ashes at the side of the fire and bathed the arm with a cloth, removing the dried blood and dirt. The warm water would have felt soothing had it not been for the pressure applied from wiping the wound.

"I am going to fix the break for you," announced Coblaith.

Taran looked at her with concern.

"No need to worry," assured Elpin. "Coblaith is skilled in these matters; an ability passed down to her by her grandmother."

"I am needing you to be brave," Coblaith said as she gently checked where the bone was fractured. "Put this between your teeth," she said, passing him a stick from the pile of firewood.

"Right, brace yourself – this is going to hurt, but it is necessary for the bone to heal straight." Coblaith pulled his wrist suddenly towards her whilst holding his elbow firm, twisting the wrist slightly in the process.

Taran flinched violently and could not help crying out in pain.

She touched the fracture. "That is it in place again. It will grow straight now, and your sword arm shall be strong once again."

"How do you know that I bear the sword?"

"I can tell from the way you speak and from your manner that you are from the warrior class. That is your business, though, if you do not choose to speak about it."

Taran chose not to talk about it.

"Elpin – can you find a straight piece of wood, the length of a forearm?"

Her husband returned with a suitable piece, which Coblaith placed alongside the broken limb, securing it with a strip of old clothing. She made and fastened a new sling from a piece of material, then taking a separate narrow strip to secure the sling arm to his chest by wrapping it right around his body and fastening the cloth at the back. It felt more comfortable moving about without the injured arm swinging in the sling.

That afternoon, he found other chores to do, keen to prove that he could help. He ground grain in the quern stone, fetched water from a nearby spring and tidied the surroundings. That evening, the couple were less wary.

"Let us be looking at your arm again," Coblaith ordered. "It is very swollen. I am going to massage it."

Taran felt uncertain.

"Believe me, it will restore your arm quicker." She looked at him reproachfully.

He sensed that Coblaith just might know what was best. That night, given an old pelt for warmth, they indicated him to bed down on the opposite side of the fire from them. The night being warm, he lay comfortably on top of the pelt.

The days passed in the simple manner of farmers: weeding, gathering what they could from the land, hunting and fetching wood and water. Garn proved his worth at hunting, retrieving what was shot. The elderly couple got used to Taran's presence and began to show signs of enjoying his company.

"We had our own son, you know," disclosed Coblaith with a longing smile. "His name was Munait – an only child. The gods did not see fit to give us more children, at least children that survived pregnancy or birth. Munait was a miracle child after we had fasted and had made blood sacrifices to Brigantia. We were already well on in years and figured this was really our final chance. Well, Munait was a gift of the gods, the treasure of our eyes. He grew to be strong and a big help on the farm."

"What happened to him?" asked Taran with much curiosity.

"One day he had gone down the glen to the Dee," explained Coblaith, "never to return. Munait and another boy had been seen, abducted by a group of Circinn from across the river."

"They were sold off as slaves presumably. We do not know if he is still alive, and if he is, where he stays," elucidated Elpin, shaking his head perceptibly.

"How long ago was that?"

"Many winters ago," Elpin paused to calculate the years. "A good twenty I should think."

"Too long to hope of seeing him again with us both well advanced in years." Coblaith shrugged her shoulders and looked forlorn. "But you know, we still hope. You have to think it, even if no news whatsoever suggests otherwise."

Many an evening was spent singing. Elpin knew many songs: love ballads, songs about battles long ago, epic ones about their history, and songs about everyday life, of hunting and sowing, about harvest thankfulness. He had even written a few himself. With a fine voice and a twinkle in his aged eyes, Taran caught a glimpse of what Elpin might have looked like as a young man. Singing animatedly made him look almost childlike in his enthusiasm. He would sometimes get so carried away that he bounced up and down on his haunches. Elpin could reach an octave lower, giving a gravelly bass drawl that lent a certain mystique to what he sang.

Taran found it compelling to join in, even when feeling tired or exhausted after working in the fields. Elpin tapped out a good rhythm on the base of pans, or by hitting one of the upright supports of the hut with a piece of firewood. Coblaith seemed used to her husband's joviality and his touches of eccentricity, although she did not join in with the same abandon. Their singing raised his spirits and made him forget his regrets for a time. Without fail, the songs sent them to sleep with a light heart.

"These are good days," Taran reflected aloud. "The summer has been hot, and the fields are looking golden like I have never noticed them before!"

"That is because you have worked them and take a pride in what you do," remarked Coblaith.

"I suppose so," he readily agreed. Looking brightly up, he asked, "Are we going to celebrate Lughnasa?"

"Of course. We always mark harvest thanksgiving, but probably not in the way you are used to. We are just two people, so it is bound to be different!"

Elpin corrected her amiably. “We are three now! We will make a grain offering and would offer milk if we had a cow. This year, we are more thankful to Brigantia, not just for the bountiful harvest, but for bringing such a helper as you at the right time.”

“The year is passing quickly.”

“Aye, it is that. So too with your arm – it has healed fast!” observed Coblaith. “Just think, some weeks ago it was useless, strapped in a sling. Now look! You can bend a bow and swing a pick!”

Taran smiled and thanked her for her good care.

Chapter Fourteen

At Odds

555 AD Rhynie & Y Broch

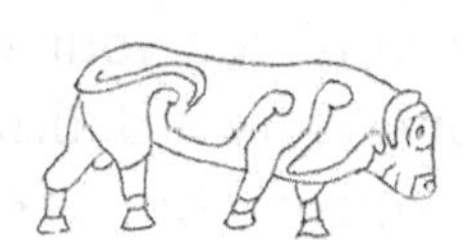

Talorgen and Oengus set off to see the extent of the lands of the Ce and meet all the note-worthies. A bard accompanied the small entourage, bringing entertainment to the halls of the nobles where they overnighted. It not only provided opportunity to make the impending succession official, and for the nobles to meet with Oengus, but enabled them to mention a handsome reward for anyone bringing news of Taran.

On reaching the sea, they travelled west by boat, as far as the mouth of the Spey – the river that defined their ancestral border with the Fortriu. The local chief in these borderlands confirmed that Galam and Brude, the Fortriu warlords, were residing at the fortress of Y Broch, just along the coast.

Y Broch stood proud on top of a jutting cliff that dropped sheer on its northern side some hundred feet. The sea enclosed the fortress on three sides; where the cliffs ceased, artificial defences of parallel earthworks topped by ramparts raised a formidable barrier. Their boat ran alongside the jetty that jutted out from the beach just below the main wall.

A guard met them as they moored their vessel. "Where are you coming from?"

"From beyond the Spey."

Despite noting their fine clothing and armour, the sentry continued to maintain the official protocol. "Tell us your business, who you are and who it is you have come to see."

"We are here to see your warlords, Galam and Brude." Talorgen stepped forward, brushing aside his own official.

"And who might you be?" asked the guard, looking Talorgen up and down.

"You do not know who I am man?" His face flushed a livid red. "I have been a visitor here for over twenty years! I am Talorgen, warlord of the Ce. Our business is a private matter, but of considerable importance to your masters, so be quick to let them know we are here."

The guard's officious manner remained unchanged, extending no courtesy.

"A messenger will be sent to the hall." The sentry spoke briefly with an orderly before the latter left.

"And is there no place for guests to wait?" Talorgen's tone was impatient.

The guard took a moment to consider the request.

"You can find a seat in the guard hut over here. It will be out of the wind."

The messenger soon returned to say an audience would be granted straight away. Oengus passed the officious guard a superior look. They were led up a way bordered by two fortified walls on either side, the one to their right being well constructed from stone, rising to the height of three men. They entered the upper citadel through a gateway where sentries peered curiously down. Oengus noticed that on either side of the gate, set above the portal, were the embossed emblems of Y Boch: the mighty bull.

These had been skilfully worked, uniform in appearance, boasting the status of this royal court. Oengus approved of their choice, representing strength, fertility and prosperity, and considered what emblem the aspiring Ce could adopt. Maybe a boar?

Led into a fine wooden hall, they were presented to the dual overlords, the outgoing Galam and his newly instated successor, Brude. They rose in a relaxed manner yet showing due deference to receive their allies.

"We have brought some gifts," Talorgen smiled and presented a couple of finely woven plaids of purple and brown. "This silver goblet is for you." He presented this to Galam. "And this," he paused as he reached down into the bag, "is a particularly fine treasure."

He presented Brude with a silver cloak pin engraved with considerable skill. Together with many fine words of allegiance and strong friendship, their arrival had been well received.

Oengus looked over the very grand hall, which far surpassed their own modest hall back in Rhynie. It gave him notions for the improvement of their own lodgings, along with the defences seen earlier from the boat, to reflect a sense of nobility and strength.

"It is good to meet you at this auspicious and historical time," spoke Talorgen, particularly addressing Galam whom he had known for many years. "I congratulate you. I heard of the succession happening here from our mutual friend, Ossian. This development gave me renewed impetus to settle our own succession of the Ce."

"Indeed, the coincided timing of the succession in our courts is remarkable," reflected Galam, "and without the bloodshed of a rebellion."

"I will be frank with you," Talorgen sidled up closer to the balding Galam and lowered his voice, which although seemed audible to Galam, caused Oengus and Brude to lean forward.

"I had two nephews to choose from, both well-trained warriors coming of age in the same year. During a series of incidents involving the Circinn, we suffered the loss of thirty-three men in a single incident with the finger of complicity falling convincingly upon my nephew, Taran."

Galam clicked his tongue several times and shook his head. "What a drastic outcome! Your own relative and one being groomed to be the warlord!"

"Exactly. Believe me, I have lost sleep and appetite over this matter, something that has disturbed me to my very bowels," confessed Talorgen, patting his abdomen. "I will come to the point. As our court was processing judgement, Taran escaped. Have you heard anything about his whereabouts?"

Galam shook his head and, turning to Brude, he did likewise.

"We strongly suspect Taran has gone over to the Circinn. He is headstrong and misguided, and now having an axe to grind, is quite frankly a threat. He will, no doubt, fight back to pursue his claim, and the Circinn might be disposed to help him against their old enemy. After all, it could be advantageous for the Circinn to place Taran at Rhynie, fashion a new alliance between them, and absolve the age-long agreement that stands between you and our peoples."

"I see . . . we cannot allow that, can we?" Galam nodded knowingly, looking across to Brude. "It is important to both our peoples that our alliance remains. The Circinn should be prevented from gaining more power and influence."

Brude agreed and for the first time spoke up. "Our relationship with the Ce is important and we will support you. If any incursion is made by the Circinn and this upstart nephew of yours, you are to call on our help." He paused and studied a sheathed dagger he was idly turning in his hands. "In return, we look for your support, if required, should Dal Riata move into our territory to the south-west. They are flexing their muscles, aspiring to have more land to grow their kingdom. We may need extra men in this likely confrontation."

"We understand one another well," Oengus spoke up, taking Brude's lead in not leaving all the diplomacy to the older men who, after all, were in the process of handing over the power. "You have our support against Dal Riata." Oengus nodded significantly to Brude.

"That is mine to grant," Talorgen spoke, looking at him sternly.

There was an awkward pause as he lent forward, staring at the floor.

"And grant it, I do," finished Talorgen with a smile. "You can count on the Ce supporting you in a war with Dal Riata, should they invade."

Brude and Galam acknowledged the oath and seemed glad.

"Come, let us take some air and stretch our legs along the ramparts." Galam gestured through a side door that led onto the highest rampart, overlooking the entire fortress.

Oengus welcomed the change of scene after a humiliating reminder that was so unnecessary, since his uncle agreed with the alliance anyway. Why did his uncle have to make a scene and shame him before his allies? Could he not see how graciously Galam allowed Brude to demonstrate his leadership?

They walked over to the battlements perched on the sheer northern side. The sound of the surf breaking upon the rocks below reached his ears, mingled with the mournful cries of the gulls. Oengus was very conscious of these unaccustomed seaside sounds.

"Let me show you something, Oengus," Galam began, putting a hand on his shoulder. He pointed with outstretched arm. "If you were to follow our coast, it leads into the narrows of a sheltered firth, beyond where we can actually see. Our fortress of Craig Padrig is over there upon a hilltop, controlling the traffic up and down the Great Glen." He added, significantly, "The Great Glen is the way to Dal Riata. Now, see that headland over there?" Galam's arm moved to the north. "That is the coast going up the way. You can make out two hills close together, quite low-lying, but distinctive."

Oengus was able to identify all the landmarks in their extensive territory.

"Those two hills stand guard, either side of a narrow that opens into a huge, sheltered basin, flanked by fine farmlands. Our coast is shaped like this," Galam placed his index fingers side by side and spread his fingertips into a V formation. "Continue north – you can just make out a dark peninsula standing out against the greyer coast behind it – that marks the entrance to a third firth."

"You have many firths," observed Oengus, interested in all that the old man had to share.

"Aye, our lands are deeply indented! Why, you should see the far west coast – the shores go in and out like the course of a snake. Travel around Fortriu is faster by far on water than by a succession of fast running horses.

"Now, can you see a pointed fin of a high peak? It is so far that you can hardly make it out. No? Then follow the coast stretching way up north, backed by a line of coastal hills."

"Yes, I see it now – it is very distant!"

"That is our boundary marker with Cait. These entire coastlands are all our territory."

"Those are only our coastal settlements that can be seen from Y Broch," elucidated Brude with a youthful swagger. "The Great Glen forms a crucial part of our domains, for it links this coast with the west coast from where merchandise comes from the south."

That evening, the two old leaders sat together getting merry for old time sake, leaving the two young warlords to converse.

"Should this errant cousin of mine come into Fortriu territory," Oengus said with a glint in his eye, "we shall handsomely reward his return, alive or dead."

"Consider that done," affirmed Brude. "The man is as good as dead should he step upon Fortriu soil."

Oengus smiled, pleased that they understood one another. Brude elaborated further on the arrangement. "I will send officials to all our nobles with news to look out for this scapegoat. They, in turn, will send information concerning him into all the byways."

"Excellent," smiled Oengus, pleased that Brude was keen to maintain favour with the Ce and ready to make agreement without consulting the old guard. Galam though, was an easier character than his own uncle, confident to leave Brude to rule.

"Give us a description of what Taran looks like, and we will convey that on," concluded Brude.

Taran's description and the amount of reward was duly given.

Buoyant with the good will of Brude and admiring Galam's readiness to stand back, Oengus broached the subject uppermost on his mind as they made the long journey back to Rhynie.

"When do you propose I take over from you?" he bluntly asked his uncle.

"Ooh, there is plenty of time. There is still lots to learn, more things to show you and much diplomacy to explain!" dismissed the old man vaguely.

This evasiveness, coupled with the humiliation at Y Broch, made him determined not to become a lackey to his uncle. He would show the old warrior his capability and intelligence and gain some respect. He came up with what he considered a flash of inspiration. "What would you say if I were to propose to give my sister, Derile, as wife to Cynbel, lord of the Circinn?"

His uncle looked at him incredulously.

Oengus quickly went on to explain. "Derile is of age and fair; a good prize for the Circinnian lord. She will be a comfort to him in his ageing years!"

"No, I will not hear of such a thing," remonstrated Talorgen, with a degree of feeling. "The Circinn are our enemies and shall remain so."

"But such an act is a peace offering! Think of it, a marriage between our people will undo whatever Taran might have succeeded in achieving with the Circinn lord."

"That is at the bottom of it: fear of your cousin! He has become nothing."

"Of course he is nothing. I think, though, that you should at least consider my idea rather than crush it outright," protested Oengus with a touch of petulance. "I tell you, I am not afraid of Taran."

"It is a foolish idea," retorted the old man, snatching the reins to the pair of horses into his hands. "And I will tell you why it is stupid," he said with passion, flicking the reins to speed up the horses. "What will Fortriu think of such an agreement? It switches long-standing allegiances and opens us to attack from a force greater than ours."

"Not if we were to bring the Fortriu into our confidence first! We can explain the reason for such an alliance," countered Oengus, not prepared to have his idea dismissed and regarded as foolish.

"It is quite out of the question. The Circinn have never been our allies for as long as anyone remembers!"

"Then maybe it is time to change things and stop the wearying border skirmishes between us."

"You are failing to see something that should be very obvious." Talorgen relaxed his hold on the reins, turning to face Oengus. "You are proposing to exchange the strongest ally from among all the tribes of the Picts for a lesser force. Where's the sense in that?"

"And by maintaining the status quo with the Fortriu," retorted Oengus, unwilling to back down, "we will always be their subordinates, paying them tribute. I mean, look at all the tithes we gathered from our own nobles! More than half of that was equal in value to that silver cloak clasp gifted to Brude! You give away, impoverishing our own state, to add to the grandness of the court of our neighbours with whom we will never be equals for as long as your policy continues. An alliance with the Circinn would be a step towards our resurgence. We can maintain the alliance with the Fortriu for as long as it seems prudent. But when the time comes, when we remove our support and have the backing of the Circinn, it might make us the force to be reckoned with."

"By the Bulàch, you have a lot to learn," pronounced Talorgen, his face looking livid against the snow whiteness of his long moustaches.

Returning to Rhynie exchanged the tension with his uncle for the morose atmosphere of his family home. He had lost his refuge in the warlord's home. If he had his own home, he could be master there. Having a wife would be the excuse to build his own place.

He thought of Alpia, the fairest of the girls in Rhynie, but the least accessible. Why was he not quite so attracted to one of the other girls, eager to be his wife? Some of them were fair, and pleasant in nature, who would become good homemakers. "But there was no chase with them," Gest had suggested when Oengus opened up to him about this matter. If they were dazzled by the prospect of becoming wife to the warlord, then why could not Alpia be just a little impressed?

Whilst frustrated in gaining her favour, he could at least find pleasure with another girl. Eithni was always pleased to see him, maintaining a playful flirtiness that he enjoyed. She knew how to play to his vanity, although he questioned her sincerity at times. But she brought the light relief he so badly craved. Was it not good to have a girl to go to, one who brought fun and rest from his stresses?

Another cause for disharmony was the proximity of his Uncle Nechtan. He remained the only eminent warrior to behave in a surly manner towards him.

He decided to be up front with him and brazenly demand some answers. "What takes you away, Uncle, for days on end?" Oengus asked without any preliminary chat.

"Why, I am looking for my son!" Nechtan replied nonchalantly.

Oengus was taken aback by his uncle's candour, seeking to aid a traitor.

"And do you know of his whereabouts?"

Nechtan was the one to look dismayed now.

"Do you think, for one moment, I would tell you?"

"So, you have found him?" responded Oengus, keen to escalate their discourse and to rile his uncle into saying something he would later regret.

Nechtan stared at him stonily then sidestepped past, making for the doorway of his hut. Oengus thought of following, but he experienced a sudden change of heart, strangely respecting that this was a father and son thing. His own father would have done the same given the reversal of their situations. Later though, as he contemplated these things on his own, Oengus came to regard it as a treasonous act, coming to believe the lie about Taran's assumed treachery, for it provided the very legitimacy to his rule.

Frustrated, he went off to visit Eithni. Unusually, no one was at home except for her. They held one another in an embrace.

"You smell of livestock," she commented, but not unkindly.

He chastised her with a faint punch on her shoulder.

"So, you did not think of freshening yourself up before coming to see me?" she chided him flirtatiously.

"Why, you could come and help me to clean up down at the stream."

She giggled. "Wait! I will get you a clean shirt and something to dry yourself with." Eithni rummaged through a chest and found what she was looking for.

"Come, let us be off before anyone returns to your house," he said, taking her by the hand and leading her briskly away into the night.

Slowing on the path, Eithni remarked, "There is a good bathing pool just over there."

"No, that is too close to the village. I know a much better place a little way upstream."

She did not protest and gamely went with him. The path was dark, their way guided only by the silvery tracery of the river. Arriving at the pool, Oengus lost no time in stripping off and entered the water, splashing himself energetically. He made lively noises, causing Eithni to laugh, as the coldness of the water washed over him. He kept up his boisterous antics, enjoying her laughter.

"Come on in! It is not that cold," enticed Oengus. "You can scrub my back."

She hesitated, before placing the garments taken from the chest over a branch. She stepped into the water and began to bathe his back slowly and thoroughly. Her hands caressed his shoulders and upper arms, wiping away the sweat and dirt and exploring his muscles, which he purposefully flexed.

"Why not take your clothes off and let me clean you?" ventured Oengus saucily.

"No, I am quite clean enough!"

"So, if you were not so clean, would you bathe then?"

"I do not know, maybe."

"Well, let us pretend that you are not so clean." He caught her low laughter. Going over to the crumbling bank, he said, "I know, we need not pretend." He stooped and scooped up soil in his hands. "I am going to make you dirty!" He was upon her in a single stride and rubbed the earth into her neck and then an arm as she protested and tried to flee.

"That was not a very nice thing of me to do!" he said teasingly. "Oh, I am sorry, truly I am. Allow me to clean you."

"No, that will not be necessary, I can do it myself."

"But it will be more fun if I give you a hand," he said, stooping down to wash the soil from his hands. When he stood upright again, Eithni had not moved. He helped her off with her dress.

Chapter Fifteen

Passing on

555 AD Y Minamoyn Goch

Taran reaped the barley and oats, threshing and winnowing the grain before laying it out to dry. Although his arm had regained its skill, it sometimes ached.

With the harvest being so good, they had surplus to trade.

"I have some necessities in mind to acquire down at the Dee before the winter," Coblaith began. Turning to Taran, she asked, "I will barter with the grain, if you can help by carrying a couple of sacks?"

"Of course."

They set off and reached near to where the woods began to thin.

"Why are you stopping here?" questioned Coblaith.

"I am sorry, I cannot go further." He looked at her meaningfully.

She seemed to understand. "This is part of your secret!"

Coblaith went on alone with one sack and some pelts to barter in the village. She shortly came back for the other sack and was away a long time. Feeling nervous, Taran withdrew some distance. Coblaith eventually reappeared, carrying a new axe. "This one is for you," she said, showing him a new knife as he emerged from cover.

Surprised at the length of their absence, Elpin was keen to see what Coblaith had brought from one of her rare trips beyond. Their meal was late that evening, but worth the wait, as Coblaith had traded some grain for a bunch of leeks, giving flavour to what would have been a tasteless soup.

"I heard some interesting news today," she began, whilst finishing her bowl.

Both men looked up with curiosity.

"They say that Talorgen announced his successor some months ago now: Oengus, a young man of great determination. Apparently, at the summer solstice, Oengus was tattooed with the prestigious Z-rod and has been accompanying his uncle on a tour of duty."

Although the news was obvious to Taran, he found his ears tingling with reports from Rhynie.

"It is also rumoured," Coblaith continued with an intrigued tone, "that there is a price on the head of a runaway prince, named Taran. Untold wealth, they say, to anyone who brings him in dead or alive! They thought he had gone over to the Circinn, but those dogs deny it."

"They would though!" chipped in Elpin, with a derogatory tone.

Coblaith shared more news in a matter of fact way, reports of people that she and Elpin knew. She was keen to remember everything she had heard.

Taran remained quiet, aware of avoiding raising any suspicion. What could he, the dispossessed, do about events against the one who held total power? Did Oengus now have Alpia too?

"Tomorrow," Taran began, changing the subject, "I will look for some fresh thatch to properly repair the roof. I saw some reeds growing by the river on our way to market earlier. You would better think of other tasks too before I leave."

"You are not thinking of going yet?" remarked Coblaith, concerned.

"Well, not just yet. But before the autumn is over, I should make my way."

"Let us not talk about that yet," Elpin said, keen to close the subject. "Drostan, you are like having a son again."

True to his word, Taran completed many things on the farm: the roof was largely rethatched, the low circular stone wall of their hut redaubed, making it draught proof for the colder season ahead. He prepared a new vegetable plot near their hut to grow onions, leeks and carrots. Breaking up the ground had been a long task without an ox and plough. These tasks were in addition to the usual daily ones, such as hunting with Garn, who had now grown attached to the new man around.

The dawns were later in breaking, and a chill wind blew down the glen, turning the birch golden. On one of his hunting forays, Taran caught sight of snow up on distant heights.

"I ought to leave," he remarked aloud. He should have done so before now, but had grown fond of the couple as they had of him, and he was keen to repay their great favour without which he would have probably perished. Tomorrow, he would make everything good for his journey and leave the day after.

On returning to the hut that evening, Elpin had been taken ill with a cough that wracked his frail frame, giving Coblaith concern. Taran decided not to mention his plan to leave just then. That night, Elpin coughed a good deal and found sleep hard, which affected the other two. At dawn, Coblaith went looking for a certain herb to brew an infusion for her husband's cough. Taran thought about the things he would need for his journey, glad of the gift of the knife, which would make an improvised spear when tied to a pole. He mended his tunic shirt and worked some grease into his leather sandals.

With the cough worsening, Elpin's breathing became more laboured despite the herbal remedy and Coblaith's care. That night, Elpin slept poorly, running a fever. Coblaith went out in search of more herbs the following morning.

Elpin gestured Taran to come on over. "I am not at all well, Drostan. I sense that my time is up!"

"Do not talk like that."

"Will you look after Coblaith? See that she is back on her feet, before you leave?"

Taran looked at the pale man, lying on the wooden slats, breathing with difficulty and in pain when he coughed. Elpin looked a little transparent, as though he had only a meagre hold on this world.

"Yes, of course I will remain to help Coblaith, until she is ready to cope . . . but you should not speak this way."

Taran remembered the questions he needed answers to for his onward journey. Elpin had been deep into the hills, as a younger man, and knew many of the ways. Waiting for his breathing to improve, Taran sought the old man's knowledge.

"There is an arduous way through our part of the Mounth, which we call the 'Minamoyn Goch'. After three days walking, you will come to a great strath on the far side, where men farm."

"Who are the people there?"

"The Fortriu."

Elpin coughed at length. After a drink of water, he continued, "You will be safe from man in the Minamoyn Goch, although there are other dangers. You go carefully,

Drostan." The old man looked up at him with a fatherly concern. "Or should I call you Taran?"

Taran smiled, feeling it unnecessary to deny his identity. He felt glad that Elpin knew, for he was like part of his closest family.

Elpin explained the way: the lie of the hills, the immense pine forests, the bears and wolves and great mountain heights. "Some are topped with duns, hill forts built by the gods, for no man ventures up there. There are large glens too, the secret ways of the gods, and twice the glens intersect one another along the route to form crossroads."

Taran went over these details repeatedly, asking the old man for clarifications, committing everything to memory.

That evening, after a long sleep during the day, Elpin asked them to sing. "Let us not be sad, but bring cheer once more to this home. We have not been singing recently, so let us sing like there is no tomorrow."

Coblaith and Taran looked at one another. Singing was the last thing on their minds, but the request had been made in earnest. Taran started with one of Elpin's favourite songs, but lacking confidence, he failed to increase the pace. Coblaith took up the melody, and the two managed to hold it together. Elpin was too congested to join in, but the music brought a smile to his face, and his eyes grew lustrous.

On the fourth day of Elpin's illness, he was only taking sips of water. The fever was consuming him and Coblaith did not leave his side that day. Learning where the herbs grew that Coblaith had gathered each day, Taran went to pick these. Once he had returned, she made a fresh brew and had difficulty persuading Elpin to drink this bitter concoction.

Too weak to talk, Taran and Coblaith assumed that Elpin would wish them to sing that evening. Unsure whether he was conscious, they continued nonetheless, knowing that if he were aware, the singing would bring him comfort.

That night, Elpin's breathing grew shallower and more intermittent. By morning, his soul had departed. They had been prepared for this, but even so, when the time had come, the finality of it shook them to the core.

After a stunned silence, followed by remarks about the final days of Elpin's suffering, Taran asked, "Where would you like him to rest?"

"Next to the vegetable plot you recently dug. I want to remember my husband, and your own kindness, together. You have done so much for us, and . . ." she paused, stemming back a wave of grief. "I wanted to add that your coming into our household in the twilight of our lives has brought much comfort and joy." Coblaith wiped away the tears from her face and managed a thin smile. Taran put an arm around her shoulders and held her a short while.

Whilst digging the grave, his own sense of loss hit him, greater than he had been prepared for. He had known Elpin for less than four months. He then considered all those he had lost as a result of being made a fugitive, and after treasuring all his memories of Alpia, for some odd reason, Talorgen came forcibly to mind. Perhaps it was because the warlord was another frail, old man? Talorgen showed a complete lack of understanding about what had happened at the ambush pass, as if he did not want to know the truth in order to have things decided sooner, whatever the cost. He did not feel guilty for the absence of love for his uncle. Harder to bear by far was a best friend's treachery, allowing ambition to denounce him. Unforgiveable, too, was the firing of those arrows. "That's how he repays me for sparing his life beside the hut of the orphans!" he uttered passionately.

A rising tide of anger and keen disappointment made him dig faster. Soon, the sweat was running liberally that he removed his smock. In this manner Coblaith found him and she immediately noted the Z-rod and viper tattooed across his back, which all these months he had successfully concealed.

"You are the runaway prince!" exclaimed Coblaith. Taran looked up quizzically, before realising why she revealed this at that moment.

"You have guessed within a day of your husband saying the same."

"We were sure it was you when we heard the news from the village."

"I will tell you all about it later. But first, let us give Elpin a fitting funeral, although I will be some while digging this grave." Taran observed how diminuitive Coblaith looked, unsure of herself, like a child facing a new experience, not knowing how to react.

"This had to come! We were both well on in years," reflected Coblaith in a detached tone. "With Elpin being weak all of last year, and continuing to deteriorate this year, I knew it would not be long. I thought I was prepared in my heart. Now it has come, I feel stricken with grief. Death is so final. I have lost my lifetime companion – my only companion."

She stopped, as her voice broke, and turned her face away to hide her tears. Taran placed a grimy hand upon her shoulder and squeezed it. Not finding words of comfort, he decided to remain quiet. She touched his hand briefly to show her appreciation.

Pulling herself together, she rose. "I will go and prepare the body, and some of his belongings, and leave you to get on with this heavy work."

"I am through the stony stuff and the soil is pure down here."

"I am glad you are here," she said, turning back. "I do not know – but I suppose I could have managed to dig a grave. I would have had to! But, having someone here is a great comfort." She turned and went towards the hut.

When the grave was ready, Taran went to the hut to find Coblaith bowed over her husband's corpse. She had combed his hair and cleaned his face. Beside his corpse was placed a large bear pelt and a few possessions. Elpin looked so withdrawn, a shadow of what he had looked just the day before, that Taran found it hard to really identify that indeed it was Elpin. Life had been taken, leaving an empty shell, robbed of its spirit and void of personality. This was in vivid contrast to his mental image of Elpin animated in song.

Between them, they raised the light corpse and rolled the bearskin under him. Elpin was so light that Taran realised he could have carried him on his own, but recognised Coblaith wanted to do her part. Each taking hold of a side of the pelt, they carried Elpin over to the freshly dug hole without it being a struggle for Coblaith. Having laid their burden beside the grave, Taran was about to descend into its depths.

"We should bury him wrapped in the bearskin," announced Coblaith assertively. "Elpin was a young man when he killed this bear – his first bear. This was the first pelt that I had prepared of this size. We were both young then, with all of life before us, and we made our home in this place."

After a suitable pause, Taran said, "I will move Elpin to the very side of the grave, so that I can easily take hold of him once I am down there. Just place his possessions to one side for now." Taran lowered himself down and took hold of the emaciated corpse without much difficulty and laid it out respectfully at his feet.

"Lay him on his side," instructed Coblaith. "It is good that you have placed his head facing west. West is to the eternal land beyond the sea." She then added wistfully, "Where youth will be regained."

She passed down his belongings: a pair of sandals, a dish containing porridge, and a water skin. Added to these were a few tools: a knife, a bow with three arrows, and the new axe that Coblaith had bartered recently at the market.

Taran looked admiringly at the axe.

"To aid him in the afterlife!" she exclaimed, reading his thoughts on giving up an unused axe. "Wrap him about with the pelt." He duly followed her instruction, and when all was set out correctly, he clambered out of the grave. Being unsure of the appropriate procedures, Taran awaited his cue to start filling the grave. Coblaith did not say anything. A sideways glance at her made it clear that there were things yet to be said. He stood with his head bowed, remembering the man who had trusted him, gave him shelter and food; the one who regarded him as a son, who had taught him most of the songs he was now glad to sing.

"O Mother Bulàch, we call upon you to receive my lord, the joy of my youth and my constant companion all the way into these our latter years," began Coblaith. "Receive him kindly into your depths, and remember not his wrongdoing, but recall his goodness, his respect, his right heart. Surround him with your blessing, that he may rise among the dead and take his place among the worthy who have gone before.

"To you Gruagach, the long-haired warrior and masterful sorcerer, we implore you to receive Elpin among your followers. Fionn, permit him to sing to your warbands, and protect him from the giants in the lands of the otherworld. May you be pleased to receive him around the hearth, on twilit evenings, to hear your stories and to learn your songs. May his songs bring you pleasure. Encircle him with your protection, from dragon and beast, and from all dark magic.

"Sluag, I implore you not to mark Elpin, that he would not be counted among the unforgiven dead. Look not on his wrongdoings, but see a man who lived with wholeness, unlike the hosts of murderers and thieves."

Coblaith fell silent and remained so a good while.

Taran was struck by the lack of guile in the way Elpin had lived. Thinking of the last prayer, whilst Elpin could not be numbered among the murderers and thieves, he could on both accounts. He shuddered.

Coblaith picked up a bowl of uncooked oatmeal and, stooping over the side, dropped it into the grave, invoking the name of the Bulàch. Taking a couple of steps back, she signalled Taran to fill in the grave.

They did not work that day but sat on the hut's threshold. Coblaith shared many reminiscences and questioned him about his life as Taran. He now felt free to tell her everything, especially the significance of sharing the last months with Elpin. It felt good not to withhold his identity with his one trusted companion. He felt no misgivings, even with the blood-price upon his head, as Coblaith was like a grandmother to him.

"It will be hard to call you Taran now," she observed.

"Better then to keep calling me Drostan – I have become accustomed to it and it is to continue to be my identity."

"And so, will you be leaving soon?"

"No. I had planned to leave a while back but you and Elpin have become family – the only family I am left with. Is that alright with you that I should stay longer?"

"Of course!" she said, wiping the tears with the back of her hand. "Do you think I relish being on my own? No. You stay as long as you want . . ." Upon reflection, she added, "But also know, that you have your own destiny to live out, which is not to remain here always as a peasant. Yours is a higher calling."

"And what calling do you suppose I have now? Oengus is the successor. Where does that leave me other than as a fugitive with a price upon my head?"

They were quiet for a time. Coblaith was the one to break the silence. "The status of warlord of the Ce is no longer yours, so that is past. Put it behind you. You are young with a whole lifetime ahead. You have been trained to be a warrior, and the gods have a purpose for the noble. They have aided you in your escape, sparing your life. These things are significant, and therefore you have a future and a purpose. You need to hold your head high and look to see what is next."

"Maybe, I can get my revenge and take the status of warlord. It will mean putting an end to Oengus just as he would have done to me."

Coblaith was silent. He found his thoughts running in a repeated cycle concerning the wrongs done to him, the misrepresentation that had cast him as traitor. Hatred grew for his cousin, for the one he had grown up with, his childhood playmate and fellow bearer of arms. Training together had formed a bond of trust, which Oengus had betrayed in a monstrous complicity with their uncle. The more he went over these reflections, the greater his resentment seethed into a great indignation crying out for vengeance. But the more he felt compelled towards exacting vengeance, the greater his own humble position became apparent. Becoming a person of little consequence, without power, placed the means of execution to pursue his claim way beyond reach.

Autumn advanced, bringing a blaze of colour to the forest, especially when the sun transformed the yellow of the birch into something truly golden, set against the evergreen of the pines. Void of any personal finery, this felt like wealth to Taran, the more precious for its transience. Even with the demise of the year and the long winter ahead, he felt hopeful. Mushrooms were gathered and a good many dried. The last of the carrots were lifted, and the cabbage was still good to be left longer in the ground. A pleasant orderliness about the farmstead that provided their own food caused him to take great pride.

The leaves fell quickly once the dawns broke frostily. The sun, hanging lower in the sky, had lost its warmth, unable to thaw the scattering of snow fallen on the lower heights. Coblaith continued to impress Taran with her fine archery skills, ensuring a plentiful supply of fresh meat. When her aim was not precise to kill a duck or a goose outright, Garn would swiftly despatch the wounded prey.

"It is thirty-two days since we buried Elpin," remarked Coblaith, who marked the days with a notch on a post to observe the necessary rituals. Tears welled up in her eyes. "I am sorry! I am only being self-centred. I remember all the good times, with the one other I had to share in the world."

The last leaves relinquished their hold upon the year and mist lingered long into the mornings. A barrenness came upon the grey woods.

A storm broke within her. He paused awkwardly, unsure of what to say. Finally, he cleared his throat and simply acknowledged, "It is natural to be sad."

They sat in silence, the cold wind moistening their eyes in sympathy with the loss felt.

"Well, we should prepare for Samhainn. It is tomorrow by my reckoning."

"I can try getting a deer – that would be a feast for the two of us," laughed Taran. "And for Garn, of course!"

"We do not need to eat all of it now. I can salt the leftovers and dry them in strips to provide during the winter." She fell quiet, watching the sagging clouds move swiftly overhead. It began to drizzle.

"You know it takes on a new meaning celebrating this festival this time round," Coblaith continued.

"How do you mean?"

"Because it is when the veil between our world, and the world of those departed, is at its thinnest. I should very much like to hear from Elpin again."

"Our druid back home spoke of Samhainn at the time I was tattooed. Unfortunately, I do not remember what was said and have not really tried to. The thing is, this Z-rod has caused me such a great undoing that I block it from my mind!"

"Perhaps the time has come to recall," gently counselled Coblaith, with a kindly smile.

With expectations buoyant, they went about the next day with thorough preparation. Taran took Garn ranging towards the upper heights, where the slopes were not so densely packed with pine. He found a vantage spot on a craggy knoll downwind from a glade. Taking cover behind a low boulder, he strung his bow as Garn settled at his feet.

The few birches stripped of leaf looked stark with their thin, mauve branches stirring in the steady breeze. The wind, blowing from the north, sounded like a rough sea in the pine crest. He tightened his tunic, tucking a section into the waistband of his trousers to eliminate a draft, and wrapped a plaid about him, keeping his arms free to draw the bow. Garn moved into a tight bundle against Taran's leg. Taran stared mesmerised by the gusts of wind ruffling the long hair around Garn's neck. The dog's eyes opened on occasion, indicating that he was merely biding his time. The cold ached deep into the mended fracture of his arm.

In this waiting game, his thoughts turned to Samhainn that evening, wondering whether Coblaith's hopes of hearing some communication from Elpin would come true. He held a sense of faith that such a thing could happen. If it were to, then what other time would it more likely occur than on this propitious occasion?

His thoughts then descended a negative spiral, rekindling all the keen animosity felt towards Oengus. The thirst for revenge, combined with his brokenness and frustration at not knowing how to pursue his cause, brought anguish. He pictured the joy known half a year back at the Beltane feast, when he had leapt through the flames with Alpia. At that moment, his world had been full of all kinds of possibilities well within his grasp. He recalled the jealous look in Oengus' eyes seeing him with the radiant Alpia. That was the turning point when ambition had got the better of his cousin, fuelling the secret whisper, 'I shall be warlord at any cost.'

Oengus had been clever to conceal how he felt, feigning appreciation, even standing up for him when Caltram had falsely accused him. He punched the ground when he considered how swiftly he had been usurped. He rued how quickly fortune changes.

In a sense of torment, he rolled onto his back, starring cold-eyed at the solid grey cloud. His eyes scanned the whole sky for the previous blue that had been so bright. It had been reduced to a tiny patch.

The dog licked his hand. On turning, Garn met his gaze with a faithful look. It brought a little consolation before the stark reminder that apart from Coblaith and this dog, he was alone.

What did he hope for, that evening at Samhainn? How very different it was now to the hopes he had verbalised to Alpia at Beltane! With his fortunes at a low ebb, he could do with some favour from the gods. Searching for anything that might bring hope, Ossian's prophecy came to mind. The strange words were so full of mystery that he had not given them thought to fathom what they could possibly mean. Life had become so fraught with schemes and dangers that he had not much considered what portent they bore. Since misfortune had taken away choice, he had felt no need for their import. Could they possibly contain insight to show the way forward? Maybe those words contained guidance on how to put his destiny back on course! Was he not, after all, the bearer of the Z-rod? Surely he was destined for something highly significant?

Then there were the words that Maelchon had uttered at the stone circle upon the hilltop, pregnant with hope of rule. Again, he was frustrated not to be able to recall much. If only he had turned these things over in his head, day by day, they would not have slipped from memory. He was angry with himself for being so preoccupied with his love for Alpia. And to what avail now, robbed of lordship and his girl? It took time for anger to subside.

He prayed to the Bulàch, that he might recall the things he had once heard, to grasp at some shreds that might piece together and make some sense of his future. The sound of the great northern wind in the crest of the pines obliterated all sound but its own. As he grappled with the desire to recall, it was as if he heard suggestions of sounds, whispers of ghosts, speaking things he needed to hear. Try as hard as he would, these sounds only remained suggestions, mere hauntings.

He was greatly dissatisfied with himself for making so light of these things at the time. And yet, he had heard the words, so surely he could recall something? Even if they were not the actual words spoken at the time, surely he could recover their gist?

Ossian had referred to direction. Yes, here was a start. South had been mentioned first, and in that direction he had to move. He was to go with something – what was it?

"With cunning and bravery and humility!" he recalled aloud. "This part I have never forgotten." Alpia had advised him to be cunning too. Had he not shown cunning already, in the ruse, pretending to head into the lands of the Circinn to throw his pursuers off his scent? Had it not taken bravery as well to flee the crannog and then to approach Coblaith's home? As for humility, well, did he not have humiliation in abundance? How would that serve him though? He thought of the state of being humbled and having humility as two things that were not necessary the same. He was bitter about his humble state. Showing humility would suggest calm acceptance of one's humble state.

"Ach! How can humility serve me to regain what is mine by rights?" But had he not learned to embrace the simplicity of a peasant's lot and feel satisfied? "Aye, maybe that is it," he spoke aloud.

Was prophecy not the foresight of things yet to come? He felt pleased that his actions and attitudes had been in accord with the prophecy, even if he had been ignorant of its words. This much had been outworked and he was living out its instruction even if it was only the very beginning part of the prophecy, of the going south part. Was that part over or yet to be entirely fulfilled? He could not recall what the prophecy had said concerning what would happen there in the south. He was still to cross the Minamoyn Goch, but that was not so much south, more the necessary passage beyond which he could head south. The rest of the prophecy was vital to recall.

West, north and east had been mentioned too – definitely, every point of direction – and it had been in that order, but what purpose did this serve? Beyond recalling the relevance of those bearings, he could recollect forewarnings of a long struggle ahead, underlined by changes of direction, frustration and suffering. Well, he knew plenty about that already. But in the end, he would win through! Was that not what the prophecy claimed?

Comforted by recalling that much, he wondered whether more of what had been said would come to mind if he searched for the utterances with all his soul.

What of Maelchon's words spoken at the stone circle? Surely these were easier to recall, having anticipated hearing things concerning his destiny, rather than hearing the sudden and unexpected volley of Ossian's words?

The druid had said that he was perplexed. Yes, 'perplexed' had been the very word he had used. The Z-rod was the symbol exclusively set aside for the warlord and that Maelchon had felt most uncomfortable to confer this tattoo whilst Talorgen was still ruling.

"But I am not the warlord – I have been made a fugitive!" Taran complained aloud. "But come on, think. Recall what else was said?" he goaded himself on. The

Z-rod symbolised power from on high, like a lightning bolt, a connection between the god of the sky and the earth of the Bulàch. This was a most propitious sign. Surely it meant that he would become the warlord, but that his time was not yet.

"It seems I have much wandering to do first – maybe gathering together support, a band of men to help overthrow Oengus." This thought brought some relief to the torment. He had petitioned the Bulàch to recall some of the things spoken, and now acknowledged that help in a simple prayer, bringing him a degree of hope. He determined to cultivate his worship of her.

He had gleaned two significant truths, distilled from all the traffic of his thoughts and recollections. Firstly, that there is no greater way to grow spiritually than to be aware of your dependence in a place of humility; secondly, success was not all about self-effort to make things happen, although the will to succeed is a good foundation upon which destiny could be allowed to outwork its designs. These utterances instilled a sense of hope, encouraging him to continue in prayer. By the end of his prayer, he was aware of how very cold he had become; even Garn pressed closer to him. The oppressive hopelessness felt earlier, though, was not as pressing.

Aware of a movement in the forest below, he peered cautiously over the rock and saw a grazing fawn. Reaching for his bow, he fixed an arrow and drew it.

"Oh Bulàch – I implore you to permit me to take one of your cattle. Grant me favour and turn about my fortunes."

The arrow hit the fawn in its side, bringing it to the ground with a groan and a thrashing of legs. Garn was instantly speeding down the brae to seize the fawn by the throat, hastening its end. It was dead by the time Taran arrived. He thanked the Bulàch as he went about gutting the animal. The beast was not big, but its meat would supply current and future needs. Fastening a rope about the fawn's torso with a slipknot that tightened behind the hind legs, he dragged it downhill through the woods with a lightness in his heart.

That evening, they roasted a leg of deer on a spit over the open fire. Coblaith baked some flat bread on a heated stone, which went well with the turnip broth. The soup was flavoured with herbs gathered in the summer, dried from a beam in their smoky hut. She left an offering of food and drink outside and they ate heartily. The roasted meat, accompanied by fermented drink, brought gladness to their hearts.

"Better not drink too much if we are to have our wits about us on this Samhainn evening," chuckled Coblaith.

Taran was in a talkative mood, sharing all he could recall of what Maelchon and Ossian had spoken.

"Why have not you talked about these things before? It has been weeks since I have known your true identity!" Her tone expressed no reproach, only genuine curiosity.

"In all truth, I have not thought of these things much until today. Recent months have passed in a daze – I have been in a state of great shock. All the calamities brought such a swift change to my fortunes. I had to take on a new identity, forget being the prince that I am and humble myself to a peasant's life. This has kept me subdued. I have been dismayed, overrun by misfortune." Pausing and looking into the old woman's face, he added warmly, "But, I have had the very great fortune to have been led to your household!"

The flames were burning low, leaving a pulsing ruby heart of many embers. Both felt content with bellies full from the fortune of the hunt. Now was time to mark the rites. Taran considered himself more the willing observer than a partaker, curious to note the supplications Coblaith made to the Bulàch. She appeared used to this role from previous experience. Not wishing to hear from any particular departed one – except for Elpin, and that was for Coblaith's sake – he still hoped to learn something that would give him direction.

Coblaith went through the routine of chanting and reciting, remembered snatches passed down from forebears appropriate for such occasions. She became more focussed, less self-aware, taken up by a spiritual fervour that increased the speed of her voice. Her old and tired features became animated, washed in an ethereal light from the fire. She rose to her feet with raised arms, imploring to hear from Elpin's spirit. Then she was quiet. Taran observed her lips moving with an agitation.

"O spirit speak – I know there is one here with a message to speak!" Coblaith's body grew taut and she held herself noble. She was quiet, seemingly listening. Then she spoke – her part in a conversation. "Identify yourself to us!" she paused and listened. "How goes it with you my beloved Elpin? . . . It gladdens me so much to hear from you. Tell me, do you have a message for us? . . . Do you have any idea where . . . where he might be living? And do you have any message for Taran? . . . And what things might those be? . . . Is that all I need to tell him? . . . Then farewell my beloved – I will not be long in joining you."

She stood a short while, opening her eyes like one emerging from a deep sleep, loosening limbs that had grown taut.

"Well," said Taran, unable to contain himself any longer. "What did Elpin have to say?"

"Yes, it was Elpin," she replied in a flat voice. "He said that I should know that it was him and not to doubt. 'Your recently departed, beloved one' were the words he used. He went on to say that he was not in torment, but felt lonely without me. He added that his suffering was over.

"Then he said, 'I have been searching and asking for our Munait and am convinced that he is not among the dead.' Then I asked where our son might be – well you would have heard my part, any way. He said that he was no more among the Picts, but with a people of a different tongue – across the sea it would seem. He did not state exactly where, for he did not know for sure."

"And what else did he have to say?" asked Taran, as Coblaith seemed to think she had come to the end. "You spoke about me, and that there was a message."

"Oh, yes. I was just lost in thought about where my son could be. Elpin mentioned that you have been trying to recall things, things spoken with grave importance that you should remember."

"How surprising that he should say the very things I have been thinking about earlier!" responded Taran.

"That you should not have such little consideration for prophecies!"

"Well, that is true, and do I not know it! So, what else did he say – did he mention anything about Ossian's prophetic utterances?"

"Elpin did not say anymore. I am sorry, it is not very helpful."

"Are you certain there was not anything else?"

"Only to tell you to look out for our son."

Later that night, as Taran was lying awake, he felt disappointed that Elpin had not been more helpful. Elpin had even seemed indifferent, chastising him for treating prophecies with poor regard. He appeared unlike the man he had been when alive – although Coblaith had been comforted. He shifted uncomfortably about this communication with the dead.

Looking on the embers glowing in the hearth, he considered what a gift of the gods was this elemental fire, providing warmth, light and security; even giving life itself, for who would survive the winter without its warmth? He felt blessed by recollecting part of Ossian's prophecy, understanding that the forgotten utterances were there within his mind and he needed to dig deeper into its recesses to locate the remainder. Blowing gently, the top layer of ash was removed from the embers, revealing their ruby heart. He was mesmerised by the pulsing manner of their glowing mass. Lost in a dreamy sense of wonder, and yet aware of seeking to probe further into his memory, a sudden and brief image flashed upon his mind. He had glimpsed himself running with a flaming firebrand, a picture fading as swiftly as it had come.

"Bearing fire to the north!" he uttered strangely, as though speaking involuntarily. What does this mean? Going to the north was the climax of Ossian's prophecy, for 'the fulfilment and the anticipation of the learned ones'.

"Yes, that was it! Were those not Ossian's very words!" he exclaimed. "I know for sure, as day is day, that was what Ossian had said. But 'bearing fire to the north' did not seem the bard's words, more a fresh revelation that appeared connected with the learned ones awaiting his coming in the north."

He felt animated, delighted to have found a key missing piece.

Chapter Sixteen

The Waiting

555 AD Rhynie

"How much longer do you think I have to wait until Talorgen passes the leadership on to me?" Oengus complained to Gest. Their friendship had strengthened since his return from the tour of duty. Of similar age, from noble backgrounds, both were becoming fully fledged in their respective roles.

"Has Talorgen not indicated when exactly?"

"No, he is evasive," scowled Oengus. "It seems the more I try to prove I am ready, the more he takes exception to the idea of handing over control. I had imagined that I would have taken over after the mid-summer solstice when the Z-rod was tattooed upon me!"

They were sitting on a bench outside Gest's hut, which set apart from the main community upon the hill, provided a peaceful retreat for Oengus, away from the sullen mood of his own home. The stream flowed close by, made cloudy by the heavy August rainfalls.

"It is like my uncle has been re-energised after the succession was settled. Have you not noticed a lot more life in the old man these days? But tell me something, what do you make of the Z-rod that Taran received?"

"Nothing more to add to what you already know." Gest shrugged his shoulders. "You should ask Maelchon – he was the one to whom the Bulàch communicated."

"Maelchon!" Oengus' voice sounded a note of protest. "That would be like trying to get water from a stone to ask him! How do you manage to work under him?"

"He has a lot of knowledge," defended Gest with a good-natured smile.

"But generally, about Z-rods, what can be said?" pursued Oengus, ruffling his curly red hair.

"The Z-rod represents the fertility principle. The lightning bolt is sent by the sky-god to impregnate the earth goddess; the union between male and female deities. The warlord bears the Z-rod as the representative of his people and as the custodian of the land who honours the fertility principle."

"So, why confer this upon Taran – what could it possibly convey, do you suppose?"

"Ordinarily, that he is the warlord."

"And should that still bother me, since I now bear the Z-rod too?" puzzled Oengus.

Gest considered before replying. "It works on two levels: the work of the gods and that of man. Your election also came through Talorgen and the consent of the council."

"Yes, because Taran proved to be a traitor!"

"Come, you are believing the lie!" Gest looked reproachfully from under his brows.

Oengus smiled sarcastically and with a degree of irritation.

Gest continued to speak with ease, giving clarity to the complexity of the situation. "Both you and I know that Taran is no traitor. You had more ambition, can be ruthless, are more focussed than Taran – attributes that Talorgen values. And you did not have any smear of conniving with the enemy in the unfolding of events, and so you were chosen. That is the outworking on the human level."

"But what about the heavenly level?" persisted Oengus, visibly bothered by the uncertainty.

"The broch symbol is a strong indicator of your status – convenor over the council. That is the exclusive role of the warlord, is it not? A clear statement and unambiguous."

"Except when received at the same time as Taran's Z-rod," returned Oengus more impatiently.

"Well, if he is dead, then that is the end of the matter!" Gest replied simply, gesturing with his hands turned out, palms up.

"And how can we be sure he is dead?"

There was a long pause. Oengus looked across the stream to the holy mountain, whose top was under a pall of cloud.

"Well, I have a suggestion," Gest said slowly, stroking his thin wispy beard. "Let us consult with the deer priestesses of the Bulàch. There is a woman among them, known as Maevis, renowned for her ability to shape-shift. She is able to travel great distances in a short time, seeking answers to people's queries. We can ask her to look for Taran."

One evening soon after, Gest led Oengus to an oak wood, a good horse ride from Rhynie. A bonfire was burning in a glade with a group of figures encircling the fire. As the two men approached, Oengus stopped in his tracks. The figures were half human and half deer.

"What weird trick of magic is this?" he said, looking to Gest for an explanation.

"As priestesses of the Bulàch, they have a deer like appearance, for deer are her honoured cattle."

"But they walk upright on human legs!"

"Come closer," Gest smiled easily. "It is not as strange as it appears in this fire light," the young druid assured.

On nearing the group, he saw that their deer part was a costume pulled over the upper body. The garb included sleeves – the forelegs of a deer – from which emerged human hands. The deer head was a poor imitation, not so life-like on closer inspection, with holes for the eyes to help the wearer to see. Startling, though, was the nakedness of the women from the waist down; their identities concealed by the deer costume. He had never seen such a sight, and felt uneasy and yet fascinated.

One of the deer priestesses came over. "Oh, it is you, Gest! What brings you here?" The voice sounded slightly muffled coming from within the head of the deer mask.

"We have come to consult Maevis," spoke Gest. "Oengus has a question of importance for Maevis. Would you lead us to her?"

"She is just over there – come with me." The woman led them around the circle of the deer priestesses. In the light from the fire, he made out a crescent moon intersected with a V-rod tattooed across her right buttock.

Maevis sat upon a chair, wearing a simple long grey dress that reached her ankles. Upon her head, the top half of a real deer's skull was secured by a cord fastened under her chin. She wore her dark hair long and loose, with a fringe cut high on her forehead accentuating the length of her pale face.

Maevis turned to them with eyes looking a little distant, even enchanted. "What is it that you seek?" she asked rather lifelessly, with a hint of not welcoming their intrusion.

"I need to know whether Taran is still alive!" he made his request simply.

"I am to search for Taran and tell you whether he still lives?" Maevis clarified, without looking in their direction.

"And if he is alive, tell me where he is," he boldly added.

Maevis half turned her head towards him but made no reply. She then looked down into her lap, presenting the deer skull staring back at them.

They were gestured to wait at the edge of the glade. "You will be summoned once Maevis has returned," explained the priestess.

"Who are these women?" he asked incredulously once they were alone. "I mean, do you know them?"

"Oh yes, I know them. I have even tattooed several of them."

He could just make out the white of Gest's teeth.

"They are all fertile mothers, living in a community on the far side of this hill. Some have ended up there, jilted by lovers."

"And do they always meet here, every night, dressed like this and naked too?" Oengus eyes were repeatedly drawn towards their exotic display. They were voluptuous and he knew the allurement was inappropriate given the gravity of his enquiry. He shifted uncomfortably on his feet.

"They meet upon various stages of the moon to carry out their rituals. Men come too at certain seasons, to dance with them in a petition to Brigantia, for the fertility of the herd and for abundance of the crop. They bring gifts and leave their seed too with the priestesses, if you know what I mean."

"You mean in a kind of prostitution?" he could feel his mouth gaping.

"No. That is to put far too crude a definition upon it. These are acts of veneration and supplication, combining human coupling with the desired fruitful union between the sky god and Brigantia. I am surprised you do not know about such things?"

"How could I! I was a mere boy when I was sent from Rhynie. My foster father was all about military training and did not have time for such things. He was not a religious man."

The circling of the fire continued without much animation, in a kind of measured pacing, usually in step with one another, and sometimes with the slow lifting of arms to shoulder height. Maevis remained slumped in her seat, looking to his eye, as though she had fallen asleep. He caught sight of the quarter moon beyond the oak crest. No sound reached his ears except the distant crackling of the bonfire. He wondered how much of the night they were to wait, and again found himself enthralled by the deer women. Intrigued by the ritual played out in the swimming firelight, he caught sight of the moon periodically, noting its gradual progress above the crest of the oak wood. Feeling cold, they moved closer to the fire.

Eventually one of the deer priestesses came over, her identity unknown, but he thought her voice sounded familiar. Perhaps she was the same woman who had first approached them? Noting the crescent moon tattooed on her buttock, he convinced himself that this was so. As she led them over to Maevis, they passed closer to the procession where he observed that the other priestesses bore this symbol also upon their right buttock.

Holding her head erect, Maevis looked more present.

"Taran lives," she informed, before they had time to question.

He waited, expecting her to continue, but she did not. "Do you know where he lives?"

"In the forest!"

He shifted a little impatiently. "The forest is an extensive place. Can you be more specific?"

"Not so very far from here."

"Well, would you know whether it is in the territory of the Circinn?"

"I went on fleet, deer feet that rarely touch the ground."

"Well, did you cross a big river with mountains rising on the far side?"

"No," returned the priestess. "I cannot tell you anymore except that he stays with an elderly couple." Maevis conveyed their audience was over.

Oengus spent much time considering what to do with this information. If Taran was alive, and had not gone over to the Circinn, then maybe Uncle Nechtan could lead him to his whereabouts. A few days later, he learned from his mother that Nechtan was to make one of his frequent trips away for a couple of nights. Here is my opportunity, he smiled to himself.

He followed Nechtan at a discreet distance along the road travelled to Wroid's crannog. This heightened his suspicions that Taran was in the vicinity. He carried his bow, intending to finish his cousin off with a well-aimed shot. He would have had Taran before if Nechtan had not meddled. They walked all day, detouring from the track that led to the crannog to follow a much fainter path heading to the hills and the great forest that covered them. This fitted with Maevis' description from her spirit flight, but then, he acquiesced, so did many places in their region. The fact that it was Nechtan leading gave him hope of discovering his cousin's hideout. Furthermore, the area was close to where they had recovered Taran's horse after his escape.

Nechtan seemed in no hurry and passed the time of day gathering a great many mushrooms, which he meticulously cleaned with a knife. As the sun set behind the rising hills, Nechtan pitched camp near a stream. Oengus concealed himself some distance off behind a boulder. He saw his uncle gather firewood then start a fire, which he enviously looked upon as his uncle warmed himself. He felt the damp from the forest floor rising through his knees. He shifted position. Now Nechtan was cooking the mushrooms and a gust of wind teased him with their delicious earthy smell. Oengus disconsolately watched him eat with a certain relish, recalling that he only had some stale bread and cheese to dine on. It was going to be a long night without a fire. Nechtan then prepared a bed from a stash of dense juniper boughs lopped off from the lower trunks. He laid them out close to the fire and eventually settled down to rest. Oengus could not afford making any noise by lopping off branches and could only gather a pile of pine needles to settle on.

For much of the night, Oengus laid awake, vigilant and unable to sleep due to the cold and damp. His plaid was drenched with dew. Near morning, exhausted, he dozed off.

When he awoke, Nechtan had gone. He went over to the campfire, now quite burnt out, looking for traces of passage his uncle had taken. As he fanned out from the remains of the campfire, he looked for any disturbance of the thick needles that littered the forest floor. It was not easy discerning what could be the markings of a man, but he detected traces of recent passage and hoped to be on Nechtan's trail. Coming over a rise, he came upon his uncle just ahead of him, so close that he had to drop to the ground. Had he been spotted? Clutching his sword, he slowly withdrew it, keen to avoid the shaft from making a noise on the metal lined lip of the scabbard. He arched his back and peered over the top of the rise. Nechtan was walking on, seemingly oblivious to his presence.

Keeping a good distance, their route meandered through woods where the trees grew sparser. Nechtan settled for a while in a clearing. He too had a bow, which he now strung. Oengus did likewise. They waited a long while. His uncle shot a rabbit. Retrieving it, he gutted the animal and put it in a bag.

They wandered on without any deliberation, moving, he thought, in an arc. The change in direction was confirmed by observing the northerly side of the tree trunks where the mosses and lichens grew more abundantly. Their way passed through endless forest without path or trace of human habitation. Oengus had to drop back further to prevent his footfall from being heard on the debris of the forest floor. Streams were crossed and lochs were passed. All day they continued tramping under the forest crest, never gaining a view. Judging by where the sun was setting, they were no longer heading north but more returning east, coming back on where they had come from.

Nechtan pitched camp and soon had a fire kindled, upon which he roasted the rabbit. Oengus imagined the tasty meat as he ate his own stale bread and cheese. He could fancy that he smelt the roast meat, but he was too distant to pick up the scent. Two days now had passed on the trail, seemingly wandering aimlessly. Perhaps Nechtan did not know where Taran was hiding? Or maybe his uncle had spotted him, but not letting on, continued in this aimless fashion just to frustrate him.

He decided not to keep watch that night, but to give in to sleep, hoping to wake before dawn to resume his watch. He fell asleep whilst Nechtan sang a song in a low voice beside his campfire, whittling away at a tree limb with a long knife.

Waking before dawn, Oengus made out the smouldering remains of the campfire and a figure lying next to it, huddled in a plaid. He had a long wait whilst Nechtan seemingly slept soundly. Eventually, his uncle rose and was on his way again. The day was overcast and showers of rain blew in on a fresh breeze. It was hard to make out where the sun was, but gauging by the moss on the tree trunks, Oengus was sure they were heading back east, confirmed when coming out of the hills into regions that were familiar, not so far from Rhynie. By midday, Nechtan had reached the village, completing what appeared to Oengus a purposeless trip. What was he about? He did not rouse suspicion by returning directly home, but called on Gest at the other end of the village and confided in his friend, who was none the wiser.

After sundown, he returned home and, about to go in the door, he heard Nechtan's voice remark. "Took your time coming back!"

"I am just back from Piccardy, where I had some business to attend."

"You are as bad a liar as you are a scout," stated Nechtan. "What were you doing following me?" Nechtan came on over from his threshold to confront him.

Not having a ready answer, he said the only thing that came into his head. "Well, what is that to you?"

"Thought you would follow me so that I would lead you to Taran, eh?" continued his uncle in a threatening tone, now standing close enough to take a swipe with a fist.

Oengus did not have anything to say. What was the use of words when his cover had been exposed? He felt roused by his uncle's taunts.

"Getting to your head, is it?" Nechtan chided. "Taran is alive! Taran the clever one, who outwitted you at the crannog, making good his escape. Taran who evaded your arrows, who outswam you. Taran, the first to bear the Z-rod, waiting for his moment to pounce and have done with you, a vile and treacherous serpent." He took a half step forward at a proximity people do not stand to talk. "And you have the audacity to make out my son as the traitor!" he rasped through clenched teeth. "I tell you, your end is nigh!"

Oengus felt his uncle's breath and a small drop of spittle land upon his face.

"Leave him alone!" screamed Drusticc, realising what was going on. She stepped out of the hut and pushed herself between them.

"It is alright Mother, I can look after myself," he replied, stepping aside to face his uncle defiantly.

"Well said," said Nechtan, clapping his hands slowly three times. "You know how to look after yourself! Dispense with truth, never mind honour . . ."

"Stop it, I say," interjected Drusticc, again placing herself between them. She pushed Oengus behind her and, facing her brother in law, said, "Do you not think we have had enough misery upon our household? How can you taunt us like this? Have you no respect for Caltram? Are you going to mock a poor widow and pick a fight with her son? What has come over you, brother? Have some decency!"

The commotion brought Domelch from her hut. "Come in please," she gently said to her husband. Placing her arm firmly but without force through his, she turned Nechtan about and led him back to their door.

Oengus kicked the ground hard, causing his foot to throb. His mother tried to lead him inside, as her sister had done with Nechtan, but Oengus cast her arm off and strode away.

"Where are you going?"

He did not bother to reply.

She asked the same question again.

"That is my business."

Needing to sooth his nerves, he visited Eithni. She knew how to calm him. He had been seeing a lot of Eithni, arranging clandestine meetings in the woods to satisfy an appetite with a woman who had been compromised. She looked proud of her power to attract, even to enthral, and being so willing, he felt no qualms of guilt.

"Oengus – when can we announce we are together and no longer have to make these secret meetings?" she asked, her head resting on his chest.

"Sometime soon!" he answered evasively.

"When exactly?"

"Why the hurry?"

She hesitated and bit her lip. "It has been two months since I had my monthly bleeding and I have been feeling sick in the morning, too. I think I am with child!"

Oengus felt dismayed. "I had thought we could be married when I am finally instated as warlord and my uncle steps down. That would have been the time to announce our union. But now, with this news . . ."

"Can you not persuade Talorgen to handover sooner? Would it not be good to part no more and to share a life under the same roof?" she asked wistfully, looking up into his eyes.

He nodded and smiled.

"And where would we live exactly? Will you build us our own house?"

"Well, of course I will," he said, entertaining her wishes. "We can build a house close to the meeting hall as befitting my status."

"We will not have to move in to Talorgen's home then?"

"Of course not. My uncle still needs a place to live."

"Good, as I do not much care for his place. It is small and quite old. When can you start to build our home? It will take quite a while . . . better to start sooner, so that when the time comes to be publicly declared a couple, we will not lose time in moving in."

"You have it all sorted it would seem!" he replied humoured. "I will speak with my uncle about where we can site our home."

"We will have a ceremony, will we not, with a feast and lots of guests to come to celebrate our union?"

"Of course. We will invite all our relatives and friends. We will have musicians and bards and there will be dancing through to the breaking of dawn."

They were silent awhile enjoying the long embrace. Eithni was the first to break the silence. "When exactly will you speak with your uncle?"

He did not reply. He was recovering from the shock that Eithni was with child and how this suddenly put pressure on him to spur things forward.

"You did say we would be married when you are finally instated."

He broke free from her embrace and rose to take a step away.

"What is wrong, my love?" Eithni said, rising to meet him. "I did not mean to anger you!"

"I do not know when Uncle will hand over power!" he spoke with a degree of desperation.

They were silent. Oengus stood looking out into the night with folded arms. Eithni clung on to him from behind and felt like a burden upon his back.

"If we do not know when that will be," ventured Eithni rather cautiously, "then do we really need to wait for that to happen before we are married?"

"Just leave it!" Oengus said, flushed with annoyance. "Can you not see that I want that day to happen sooner rather than later?"

"When we will be married?" she asked by way of clarification.

"Marriage! Marriage! That is all you think about. That is not going to happen before my uncle steps down."

"I am sorry," she said, sidling up to his chest. He breathed heavily, encumbered by her person. Concern for her feelings, though, made him put up with her need to cling. Eventually he put an arm around her. They found a sense of togetherness and reconciliation without need for further words.

Some weeks later, with the fall of the last remaining leaves and the onset of winter, Oengus walked resolutely to Eithni's home.

"Uncle shows no inclination of relinquishing his grip on the warlordship!" he blurted out to her like a crossed child. "He just deliberately cuts me short whenever I broach the subject of handover."

"Then let us forget waiting until you become sole warlord," insisted Eithni. "What is really stopping us from marrying now? We have a child on the way."

He said nothing. He did not even look up at her.

"Why will you not consider it?" she continued with mounting frustration evident in her voice.

He looked onto the grey bare head of the woods down in the glen beneath their settlement. He felt detached from what she had to say, having heard the usual line of argument many times.

"Why do you not talk to me? Ugh, you are becoming impossible!" She stamped her foot and turned away.

Oengus whistled a tune low on his breath but audible for Eithni to be roused.

"You are a good for nothing!" she snapped, about to launch off into a tirade.

He cut across her. "I have had enough!" He began to walk away.

"What? You are leaving or finishing with me?" she exclaimed, enflamed.

"Finishing!" he pronounced with finality. He stopped, turned around and added very coldly, "You did not really think it was going to last?"

His words seemed to take time to register with her and he regretted having said his final statement. However, he wanted to be clear things were over between them.

"How could you?" Her voice was cold as she mastered the situation. "What about the life we talked about together!"

"That was back then," he returned indifferently.

"That was only a few weeks ago," she corrected.

"Anyway, I am leaving you now," he said quietly, turning again to leave.

"Why?"

"There is no point in talking about it. It is best dealt with bluntly."

"For you it might be!" Her eyes flashed at him. "And what is to become of me?"

He stopped for a moment, looking at her thoughtfully. "If your family throw you out, you could join the priestesses of the Bulàch. They are glad to take in fertile women."

She walked over briskly and slapped him across the face. He raised a hand, but thinking better of it, walked away. He felt relieved to have made a clean break. The nastiness of parting was over and he could breathe freer. Now he could make his own decisions without deferring to anyone, at least in this matter.

Some time after his breaking up with Eithni, Uncle Talorgen remarked to him, “I think it would be good, young man, if you were to marry! It helps settle a young man, gives some stability and a home of your own!”

“Well, the idea is not a bad one!”

“Well, do you have someone in mind?” Talorgen asked, scrutinising his face.

He paused, hesitant, a little uncomfortable. Deciding that it did not much matter what his uncle thought anyway, he might as well just say the girl’s name. “Alpia.”

“Alpia!” Talorgen looked up, having been occupied in tightening the binding about the scabbard to his dagger. “A good choice, but a surprising one. I had heard that you are intimate with her friend – what is her name?” Talorgen made a circular gesture with his hand.

“Eithni,” he informed drily. “That is over now.”

“Why Alpia? She and Taran were together?”

“Not because of that.” Now it was out in the open, maybe he could use it to his advantage. “She is close to Aunt Conchen and understands the ways of court . . .”

“Quite right!” Talorgen interrupted, nodding his head with approval. “Has she returned any favour?”

“Well no, at least not yet. She is still holding out for Taran, I believe.”

“Bah! The man is as good as dead. Leave it to me, I will have a word with her.”

He thought it better to leave his uncle thinking Taran was dead than to reveal what he had learned from Maevis.

Later that day, Alpia was attending to Conchen as she did every day. She did not consider it a duty, for she was genuinely fond of her aunt. Both had been similarly outraged by what had happened at the crannog, giving them a shared understanding of events. Conchen had confided that Taran had been her favourite, disapproving of her husband's choice in selecting Oengus, yet understanding that Oengus' sheer force of ambition was a quality that would have appealed to him.

Alpia grew conscious that her uncle had his eyes fixed on her as she busied herself about their hut.

"You would make a good wife for a warlord," he remarked approvingly.

Alpia looked up, irritated, but made no reply.

"You are familiar with the ways of court," continued Talorgen, "and are of age to marry. What do you think?"

He knows no subtlety, she thought, blunt as always in matters with that manner of being used to having his own way. She felt her stomach tightening.

"Oh, leave the poor girl alone," remonstrated Conchen, without any humour.

"I would like to hear what she has to say on the matter," persisted Talorgen, keeping his eyes fixed on Alpia.

"Well lord, if you are thinking of me and Oengus, then it is quite out of the question!"

"Who else would I be thinking of?" Talorgen replied prickily. "You know Taran is dead."

"I do not believe it," she contradicted with a degree of conviction.

"Bah, nonsense girl!" he uttered with a good deal of vehemence. He swallowed audibly. "If he is not physically dead, he is as good as dead! You cannot go holding out for one who is ousted from the court and spurned by the gods. His existence, should he still live, is of no consequence."

"Talorgen, must you have this conversation with Alpia?" Conchen protested.

"Why? I have her best interests at heart," he defended with an innocent air.

Conchen laughed sarcastically.

"My lord, you presume wrongly that I am holding out for Taran." His presumptions angered her. With a man like her uncle, as with many men, the idea of just a friendship between a man and a woman was inconceivable, and that annoyed her, for it belittled her noble affections for her missing friend.

"You have feelings for Taran. It was clear to all seeing the two of you together."

She could feel her face flush. How dare he judge her in such matters?

Talorgen continued in an unexpected softer tone, "I can understand those feelings might still be difficult to overcome, but you need to face up to reality. What, is it already four or five months since he disappeared without trace or word? Following your heart is only going to put your life on hold and cause unnecessary grief."

"You presume wrongly, my lord," she said with difficulty to contain her passion. "Taran is a friend, nothing more. And even if he were dead, and may the Bulàch not permit that, he would be of infinitely greater worth than Oengus alive." Her declaration surprised her. Her uncle had so riled her with his earthy presumptions and disregard for anything truly noble that she had been roused to defend her defamed friend.

"Many a maiden would think him a good catch," he continued, ignoring her words. "He could give you status and security here, your own home and, if the gods are willing, a family." He tried to speak convincingly.

"Have you no sensibilities, Talorgen!" hotly objected Conchen. "Oengus was the one who shot at her friend!"

"Nonsense! Taran's a traitor, the cause of many deaths through his conniving with the enemy! Those are the plain facts, woman." Talorgen looked dismissively at the two women and turned abruptly away.

That night, Talorgen suddenly fell sick. By morning, he was dead.

"His spirit has departed," announced Maelchon, looking up at Conchen stooping over her husband's body. She looked numb. Turning away, she sat down on some bedding in the corner of the hut.

Alpia came to sit beside her. "You should try to rest awhile now, for you have been caring for him for much of the night." She placed an arm about her aunt's shoulders.

"Oh, I do feel tired, very tired!" She yawned at length. "And I also feel very old!"

Alpia patted her hand comfortingly.

Maelchon lent towards the two women and said gravely, "I will leave you just now. I will tell the news of our lord's passing to those who need to know."

"Do what needs to be done," Conchen said with a vague, dismissive gesture. "Wait a moment," she added, as the druid had already turned to go. "Can I leave you to make all the necessary arrangements?"

"You can depend upon me," he returned with a slight bow.

Conchen looked dry eyed at the day's brightness upon the threshold. Her breathing had grown shallow.

"Come! You must rest." Alpia rearranged the bedding.

"I suppose I should. A couple of nights' good rest would do me good." She sighed wearily.

"Do sleep; you will feel stronger then to face things."

Alpia wanted to ask how Talorgen had so quickly gone downhill, when just yesterday he had seemed his usual robust self. She searched for a tactful way to bring the matter up. "Did Maelchon mention anything about the cause of uncle's death?"

"It was his age! He has lived to a good age and been fortunate to keep in reasonable health all this time."

"It was very sudden! One day he is active and making decisions, then in the night falls into a state of rapid decline."

"But that is the nature of death with some. It is not always a long debilitating illness that takes everyone away." She glanced up at her niece before reverting her gaze to the doorway. "He complained of severe chest pains, a tightening grip that seemed to be squeezing his very life. His skin turned pale and was clammy to touch. He went downhill fast after that and was especially anxious. The gods have spared him from suffering interminably."

Alpia was surprised at how calm a widow could talk about her husband's death. Why were there no tears or outbursts of grief? For a moment, she considered if her aunt had brought on Talorgen's death. He had been a difficult man to live with and maybe she was out of her mind by his high-handed manner.

Knowing her aunt's kind nature, foul play seemed inconceivable. If there was something untoward, it would more likely be Oengus. His impatience to rule was known within the household. She would not be alone in thinking that either. Eithni had revealed to her not long ago about a certain potion that could cause the heart to stop.

Chapter Seventeen

Beneath the Duns of the Gods

556 AD Y Minamoyn Goch

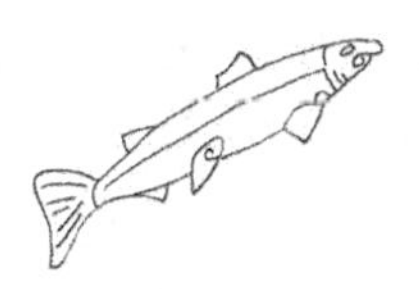  

The winter had been long, especially the nights, twice the length of daytime. The winter solstice passed without ceremony for Coblaith and Taran, but noted nonetheless as a great turning point, when darkness would decrease and daylight would have the ascendancy. This was a crucial stopping of the huge reversal that had begun since summer had waned. Frost now seized the ground like iron, and it seemed nothing fruitful could ever emerge from so solid a ground. The winds blew bitterly cold, filled with sleet and hail, rain and flurries of snow that kept one inside for lengthy periods. The cycle had reached the lowest ebb of decay and inertia.

Despite the turning point, the cold grew more intense and snow fell abundantly, even though the sun began to peep once more over the near high ridge tops. Coblaith and Taran were glad of a plentiful supply of firewood, of a goodly store of oats and rarely were short of something to hunt. Despite such blessings, the winter grimness with its subdued light leaking through the heavy overcast skies still maintained an interminable hold upon earth and man.

"We should sing!" suggested Taran one evening, sitting with Coblaith around the crackling fire.

"That would be good – like the old days, eh!" Coblaith's expression brightened for a moment, perhaps visualising her husband's face animated in song. Then it was like the skies darkened over her, leaving her fighting back the tears.

"I am sorry. I should not have suggested we sing. After all, I do not have a voice like Elpin's."

"No, do not say that – you have a fine voice. And yes, it would be good to sing again – ignore my tears." She dried her eyes, and raising her face with a brave smile, said, "I do not know why we have not sung before now!"

Encouraged, he struck up a familiar melody, a little hesitant at first. Coblaith started to sing more robustly, aware that without Elpin's voice a greater effort was required. It gave Taran renewed confidence. She brightened as good memories came to mind. They were grinning properly, probably for the first time since they had buried Elpin; smiles of gladness to honour his memory. A pattern of singing each evening was reestablished, just as it had been back in the day.

Celandine appeared first as the harbinger of spring, soon joined by the wood anemone. Primroses followed as the purple saxifrage appeared on the hills, bringing a joy to the heart. The unstoppable resurgence of new life sprung with unabated vigour, taking captive the once unyielding mass of frozen ground.

The inevitable matter of Taran's departure had been avoided. He had not the heart to bring it up, though he had thought long and hard about the long hike over the Minamoyn Goch. It was Coblaith who unexpectedly raised the subject one morning, as they were finishing their breakfast.

"You will need to start equipping yourself for the journey. Mind what Elpin said: you were not to delay, but to make haste once the spring is upon us."

She went over to a basket hanging from the side of the hut. "I have been sorting through things that would be useful to take with you. Here are a couple of traps; I still have two more for myself, so I do not want to hear any protest. I have two bows, so you are to have the larger one since I am finding it increasingly difficult to draw it properly these days. The arrows in this quiver are yours. Oh, and here's a knife – you will need one." Coblaith was remarkably matter of fact about all this.

"But I have a knife – a fine double-edged one, remember? You bought it when we went to the River Dee last autumn."

She smiled, no doubt being reminded of the barter, and removed her own knife from the basket.

"You will need this bear pelt, for the nights are raw in the mountains."

He protested.

"It is yours anyway. You have been using it all this time. Take it; I do not want any protest. You will be doing my heart good, knowing that you are well-prepared." She fixed him with an intent gaze. "Besides, you will bring more joy if you receive my gifts without protest."

They agreed that his departure should be the day after tomorrow.

Coblaith went to the village to get some necessary provisions, and whilst she was away, Taran prepared as much as he could about the farm. He put things in order and grew the size of the woodpile to gargantuan proportions.

The departure was weighing heavily upon him. It was not so much the hostility of the surroundings that lay ahead, but the thought of leaving Coblaith on her own genuinely disturbed him. Knowing that Coblaith's healing had been aided by having him around, how would she fare entirely on her own for the first time in decades? Without doubt she would cope practically, but the loneliness in that isolated farmstead would perhaps be too much.

Coblaith returned from the village with half a cheese and some twine. She also brought news. “Talorgen is no more – he has gone to be with his ancestors. Apparently, he passed away without any illness. Some think it strange that he was healthy one day and then dead the next. Still, these things happen, I suppose.”

Taran was not surprised about his uncle dying under dubious circumstances with Oengus ready to benefit from his demise. He felt no sadness, only resentment, remembering how Talorgen had been the agent that demanded his life as a sacrifice.

He pondered gloomily awhile before considering Coblaith’s situation. “What about you – how are you going to fare once I am gone?”

“Oh, you are not to bother about me!” she responded dismissively. “I know folk in the village, so I can go there when I am lonely; maybe even move there if the farm becomes too much.”

The morning of departure came. A good deal of rain was on the wind, making him instinctively feel like remaining around the hearth. But he was not going to delay a decision which had been difficult to reach. His things were ready, a hearty breakfast had been eaten and food provisions were in his bag.

“Let me petition Brigantia to allow you safe passage through the wilds of the Minamoyn Goch,” began Coblaith, looking braver than he would have expected. She began her invocation, standing over him, whilst he remained seated beside the hearthstone. A way into her prayer, her tone changed from saying the expected things.

"May Taran be enabled to recall all of Elpin's instructions as to the right route through the mountains. Bring to mind too, the prophetic utterances that Maelchon and Ossian had communicated, that this shall guide and give strength through all kinds of trials."

Taran was relieved to have salvaged much prophecy, although exactly how much remained uncertain. To aid retention, he repeated prophecies and instructions to himself, providing a mental map of where he was to go and for what he was destined.

"I see an immense boulder," Coblaith continued in prayer, her tone changing from one in which petitions are made to one of inspiration. "A great slab lies fallen from a high cliff. It rests on top of lesser ones, forming a colossal roof. I see a low gap giving access to a hollow space underneath, capable of sheltering several men. This refuge lies at the head of a glen, above a loch, ringed with immense crags."

She stopped, and taking him by the hand, seemed intent to impart some interpretation.

"What I saw might have some symbolic meaning, but I think it describes a place you are to find. It is a significant stage of a journey, a vital part of your onward progress, in fact, so important, I feel, towards fulfilling your destiny. Going to that stone refuge will both strengthen and guide you. I cannot say more without it becoming my own thoughts."

He verified what he heard and in the process helped commit it to memory. Acutely aware of his humble state, having no power, he aspired to be wise, strong in faith in the Bulàch who could reverse fortunes.

They now had to say farewell, neither wanting this moment and feeling its great awkwardness. Coblaith physically gave him a push over the threshold. Garn rose all excited, anticipating an adventure ahead.

"You are to stay here!" Taran commanded the dog.

Garn looked crestfallen and sat down reluctantly.

"No, Garn should go with you," remonstrated Coblaith.

Taran protested vigorously.

"You are his new master since Elpin has passed away. He could prove very useful on your precarious journey."

"But you will benefit from Garn's ability to finish off and retrieve the kill for you. Besides, he will be company for you when I am gone and a protection with you being alone on the farmstead."

Neither of them had anticipated what to do with Garn. The dog sat there, looking intelligently from one to the other, as though partly understanding their dilemma.

"You are Garn's new master; he belongs to you. Besides, I can always get a puppy from the village. Then it would be my dog," she acquiesced aloud. "Aye, that I will do."

Taran understood that Garn's help, and even protection, could make the difference of survival in the wilds. However, he knew Coblaith's strong will; once her mind was made up, she was impossible to counter.

"If I am to have Garn, I want you to have this." He removed from his belt the dagger gifted him by Talorgen on his coming of age.

Coblaith reached for it hesitantly, looking confused. Instinctively, she drew the dagger from its sheath. "It's beautiful," she gasped, looking at the ornate swirls along its blade. "but I cannot possibly accept. This is too fine and belongs to the noble."

"I want you to have it, for it belongs to a life that has passed, which brings painful memories. Besides, it is the gift from the one who believed lies and demanded my sacrifice.

I do not want such a gift! Anyway, as you say, it belongs to the noble – and there is no one nobler in spirit than you."

"I shall treasure it then," she pronounced, decisively pushing the dagger back into its sheath. "And I choose not to recall the original giver, but shall remember a generous-hearted one who is like a son to me, who gave me this exquisite keepsake."

"It rightly belongs to you. Your kindness gave me new life, for truly without you, I would have soon perished with a useless arm."

Parting took steel to sever a bond, strengthened by shared struggles and grief. He could not bring himself to look back at first, but at the end of the field he had dug last autumn, at the side of which lay Elpin's mortal remains, he stopped and turned. Coblaith was there upon the threshold. She waved once, then promptly withdrew indoors.

He walked on among the birch showing tips of green, ready to burst into leaf at the next sunny day. He turned again, knowing this was the last view of the roundhouse that had restored his life, half-hoping that he might take one final look upon a special lady, but she was gone.

Garn stepped with a jaunty gait, relishing the adventure that hung like a cloud over his master.

The first part of the journey was reassuringly easy, being known territory. He was to follow the river upstream into the main glen. Without a proper track, he took the ways trodden by deer, wolves and bear, keeping close to the river. The pinewoods were dense, but in the boggy places, bay willow shrubs grew abundantly, opening the views.

It rained all day. Although the bearskin, still containing the natural lanolin, did repel the water, the wind ensured moisture to penetrate through any gap, however small. His morale was challenged, adding to the heaviness of leaving

Coblaith. Picking his way around the worst parts of the swampy ground made for a circuitous course. He stumbled over sphagnum moss that had deceptively looked firmer, and sank sometimes knee-deep into the waterlogged mire. Sighting a loch beyond the bog was uplifting, for Elpin had suggested resting there for the first night.

He felt strong enough to continue further but decided it would be best to use the remainder of the daylight to prepare camp. A wolf crying in the distance roused Garn's curiosity. A reply came from another. Taran felt concerned for Garn, for if the pack got a whiff of his presence, they would be upon the lone Garn mercilessly.

"We will erect a platform up in a tree – eh, what do you think of that, Garn?"

The dog's eyes glanced up at him momentarily, conveying what seemed to him an uncertain look. After inspecting some pine trees, he found one with two sturdy limbs growing at the same height and fanning out into a V-shape. He then chopped straight branches from other trees and, laying these across the limbs, the platform began to take shape. Taking a stick to expose the roots of an aspen, he unearthed a long one; cutting it near to the tree, he pulled out a lengthy section. Using the pliable but strong length, he threaded this up and then under each cut bough of the platform, securing these to the two tree limbs. Taran inspected his work with a degree of satisfaction.

"It will be good to sleep off the ground!" he remarked to Garn, as he kneaded his feet into the saturated ground.

The rain let up early evening. Having noticed a trout swimming in the shallows, Taran went in search of a straight branch. Finding one, he sized it to the length of a spear shaft and fastened his double-bladed knife to it with twine. Armed with a harpoon, he had not long to wait before seeing a small trout emerge from the weed. He thought his aim and dexterity would have been enough to spear it, but the trout darted off unharmed. He was not lucky with the next trout either and had a long wait before another appeared, which this time he succeeded in piercing.

"Oh no!" he exclaimed, disheartened to find that all the moss, lichen and bracken stashed away in his satchel for kindling was soaked through. Gutting and filleting the fish finely, he ate the flesh raw, setting aside a piece for Garn. With all the moisture, his bread was disintegrating, but he did not waste these precious rations.

"Well Garn, if we had managed a fire, the smell of cooking fish might have attracted the wolves!"

Garn looked back at his master with a cocked head, as though semi-understanding what he was talking about.

"Well, I suppose it is time to sleep!" Taran said, rising from his crouched posture.

The platform, being twice his height off the ground, was easily accessible for him but impossible for Garn. He placed a sturdy branch against the tree's trunk to act like a ramp. With Garn's weight and bulk, it took several attempts before successfully delivering a rather reluctant dog onto the platform.

"I will keep my knife fastened to this shaft, just in case." He lay the makeshift spear carefully beside and tried to make the platform comfortable. The rain returned. He was so wet that the water ran off his hair and eyebrows, trickling into his eyes. It was miserable for morale just lying there, taking whatever the weather unleashed. The rain was not as bad as the cold though. It might have been spring, but the nights still felt freezing.

"I wish I had some canopy to erect over us!"

The exposure to the elements was harsh. Drawing Garn to him, he folded himself compactly about the dog. After a while, he began to sense the dog's body warmth. It was not much, but at least it was something. Sleep was difficult, fraught with the noises of the wild that kept both man and dog alert.

He mentally went over the route for the next day, encouraged to recall Elpin's directions, wondering if he would find the way as he envisaged it. He considered too Coblaith's vision, recognising his need of every help with the odds so stacked against him. Which stage of this journey would he see the rock refuge? Maybe it would be on a future trip? The stone certainly had not featured in Elpin's instructions. He longed for dawn, to be on their way again. Recalling instructions started to become annoying for their compulsive nature. Exhaustion finally got the better of him.

A noise awoke him. He could hear something grunting and the sound of vegetation being disturbed. Peering through the darkness, he saw a bear silhouetted against the paler colour of the loch, foraging where he had gutted the trout. After standing upright, nosing the air, the bear lumbered towards them, not mindful of the shrubbery lying in its way.

The hairs on the back of his neck stood on end.

Stopping to sniff the air again, the bear advanced with deliberation, lured to their tree. Garn peered over the side of the platform, and with retracted lips, emitted a low growl. Taking hold of his spear, he took up a crouching posture, steadying himself with a hand firmly clasping the tree trunk.

The bear stood erect at the foot of the tree, its head not far from the level of the platform. Knowing height offered no protection, he shouted at the beast and Garn growled much louder in a menacing manner. The bear hesitated, before taking hold of the trunk. Taran lashed out with his knife spear and grazed the bear's foreleg. It growled and withdrew to ground level, licking its wound. The taste of its own blood seemed to insense the bear. It bellowed purposefully with a kind of war cry that chilled the blood. Its huge, dark bulk, ready to unleash a tremendous fury, was petrifying to look upon. Taran was furious with himself for ineffectually combatting so intimidating an adversary in what could be his one and only chance. He broke into a cold sweat.

The second assault was far less tentative. The bear launched itself in a single movement to confront its prey. Taran could not afford to be wild this time with his spear. Fixing its attention upon Taran, the bear did not anticipate Garn launching an attack, biting into its foreleg with such ferocity and with a tearing motion. The bear roared with a sound rumbling from deep within, full of pain and anger that rattled its lips. Its vile breath filled Taran's nostrils. Quickly retracting its arm with Garn attached, the bear flung the dog through the air.

Taran had just the one lunge before the bear would take hold of him, and now quite on his own, he knew this strike could not be ill-conceived. He drove his spear at the bear's head, its point ripping open a part of its nose and muzzle. Making a short yelp, the bear withdrew at once, slithering ungainly down the trunk. Garn immediately launched himself onto their injured assailant that, although pierced, was still capable of instant murder. In the heat of the moment, Taran instinctively followed Garn's example and jumped down, bellowing at the top of his voice. He drove his spear into the bear's rump, who not expecting such an assault from two directions, swiftly retreated with a limp.

Both breathed heavily and Taran trembled uncontrollably. Garn hobbled towards him, brushing up against his master's leg. Petting him, he looked him over for wounds, thankful to find no grievous injury. He remained crouched, soothing himself as much as the dog by repeatedly running his hand down Garn's back.

"Are you alright? That was a close to death thing!"

Having regained some composure, he realised it was safer, whilst it was still dark, to be back up in the tree. It took several attempts again to raise Garn on to the platform, who did not take kindly to being manhandled. Prepared to fight to their deaths, it took an age to calm down. Sleep was impossible.

The new day broke overcast, the rain falling as a dense drizzle in a continually passing mist. Taran's limbs were stiff from lying on a platform where every knot and lump had become apparent.

"Hey Garn, there will be no fire again. Everything is soaked!" He took a small handful of oats, now a mulch, and chewed them without appetite.

They followed the loch shore, reaching the far end sooner than expected. A gentle rise led to a low pass from where he looked back on the scene of a traumatic night.

"You gods! Thank you," he muttered.

Beyond the pass, the small mountain stream grew, fed by several tributaries flowing down from mist wreathed heights. Further on, a glen ran west, narrow and steep, with a large body of water flowing fast. He had expected a 'crossroads, where four glens met', as Elpin had described it. Unsure of the way, he kept to the main river course. Shortly, he came to what possibly could be a small glen opening to his right, hidden in the profusion of the forest. To be sure this was the fourth valley forming the crossroads, he followed a stream up through the trees. The forest grew so dense as to be impenetrable.

"Damn it!" He stepped into the stream and proceeded up its bed.

A short climb brought them to a boggy place, where the pine ceased to grow. He cursed again to be wading through thick bog. At the far end, a lip forming a low pass provided a view of a broad valley falling away to the east.

"This is the fourth glen," he said with conviction, confirming Elpin's crossroads description.

He returned to the other glen, where the vigorous mountain torrent flowed, and set off westwards, up through a narrow. From a rocky knoll rising above the trees, he viewed an extensive glen passing deep into the heart of the lofty Minamoyn Goch. The rain had stopped and with a good breeze blowing, his clothing felt less burdensome as it started to dry. He ate more soggy oats and watched Garn give chase to a hare that eventually eluded him. The dog returned limping and lay panting a long while.

"You are a sorrowful sight!" Taran petted him. "What a splendid dog you are, though."

He strung his bow, fixed an arrow and waited to see what might provide a meal for his faithful hound. Five ducks eventually flew low overhead, alighting on the calm of a river pool just below. They were so close that it was not hard to hit one with a single arrow.

"Go on Garn, there is your breakfast!"

The dog limped down to the pool, gathered the dead bird and brought it back. Taran plucked some of the feathers from around the duck's breast and tossed it before the dog.

Elpin's instruction was to continue at great length up this glen, holding fast to the main river, ignoring the many tributaries and smaller glens. He felt a little agitated about the extent of this glen, a journey, which Elpin had not been able to recall so clearly, made way back in his youth.

"Well, we have both eaten, so what is keeping us, eh?" Garn rose with his master as they set off westwards into the heart of the wilds.

The glen was narrow with steep sides rising to distant heights veiled in the thinning mist. The river carved undeterred, eating away at the feet of the mountains, leaving level areas opposite its erosive course. There, the ground, too boggy for trees, made for easier walking with open views. Later that morning, as the last of the mist dissolved from the great heights, he noticed what looked like ancient duns, still largely intact, crowning several summits.

Who would build up there, he thought? These cannot be the work of man! Elpin had mentioned these, a detail Taran regarded as an aside that had not seemed significant at the time. 'The duns of the gods themselves', Elpin had referred to them, which at the time had seemed a fanciful comment.

"Who am I to look upon these?" he muttered, feeling disturbed. What right had a mere mortal to wander through the domain of the immortals? This was a rare place, the likes of which he had never seen before. Far-reaching eyes were felt to peer down from their lookout posts. Only the audacious and foolish, or the desperate like himself, would venture into such inhospitable glens. The thought so unnerved him that he determined not to look up and incur the wrath of the gods. Who would ever come this way? Well, Elpin had, but he was a rare one indeed. Maybe Elpin had not wished to unnerve him more by elaborating on how he had felt when passing below the duns of the gods.

A broad marsh made him take to the raised ground above the bog, where pine and birch provided some cover from the watchful eyes above. This was difficult ground though, undulating, at an angle that challenged balance, with heather growing densely in places, restricting his stride. Garn led the way, trotting but with a limp, making much easier work of the terrain than his master. He stopped periodically to look back and wait for Taran to catch up. Tired, Taran found himself choosing his route too meticulously, rather than just intuitively, making it even more time consuming and frustrating.

A series of long rock slabs brought a welcome change of pace, though he felt exposed again before the lofty duns. He pushed on with some urgency, until he was halted. Two adders, basking in the warm spring sun, were intertwined in an amorous embrace on the warm rock. At first, they seemed oblivious to his presence, but then noticing him, one disengaged, coiling into a striking posture. Taran gave them a wide berth, hurrying on, worried whether Garn had been bitten. His fears proved unfounded as Garn kept up his usual pace.

Some way on, they rested. Whilst it would be good to get beyond this glen at the earliest possibility, he reasoned, more vigilance was required. Taking the bracken and lichen kindling from his bag, he festooned these over the branches of a pine, and gathered more lichen and a large sprig of dead heather, bleached a light grey, broken off some time ago by a heavy animal.

He considered the two adders. Were they not good omens? Certainly, they featured much on their standing stones, especially incorporated with the Z-rod, just like the tattoo on his back. For half the year, the adders were not to be seen, seemingly dead with the winter, vanished from the land of the living. Then, miraculously they re-emerge, resurrected the coming spring, renewing as they cast off their old skin. Were they not rather like the Bulàch: the old hag of winter transforming herself as the youthful Brigantia come the spring? No wonder man revered them, expressing new beginnings beyond death. They presented a very potent image, one of both mortality from their bite and immortality from their annual resurrection.

Could their appearance be a sign to give him hope for the future? And two of them – a double blessing! Their act of procreating was surely a great omen. Was this journey not one of moving beyond the winter of his misfortunes? Was the fugitive prince not on his way back up, resurgent?

A fresh shower of rain sent him gathering his kindling that had almost dried. Stashing it away in a very damp satchel made him doubt whether it could be kindled later. The thought of being without a fire again, to dry and warm himself as well as to cook, gnawed away at his morale.

He, the unwelcome intruder, again felt the watchful presence from the crumbling duns on high. Maybe the gods had sent the bear for trespassing on the edge of the immortals' territory?

The light dimmed as solid cloud once more filled the sky from end to end. The rain fell so copiously that he no longer bothered to wipe the excess moisture from his face. He noted that about on every fifth step, a drip fell from the end of his nose, helping him to mark his pace and progress. He pressed on across another far-reaching bog, alongside the river, devoid of trees; keen to put this haunted glen behind him by nightfall. He did not look for cover anymore, reasoning that gods being gods would know of his presence and therefore it was futile to think he could evade their gaze.

The glen just went on. The going was not too bad, traversing the frequent floodplains with some dexterity. Later that day, he noted the river flowing faster. Ahead rose higher ground, over which the river tumbled in a series of cascades.

"Maybe I am nearing the upper reaches!"

The ground became firmer, ascending the slope, under the wind whispering pines. Emerging over a rise, a great and stark basin, void of trees, opened out before them.

They reached a marshy confluence of rivers and followed the greater of the two into an extensive bog. The difficult terrain was filled with peat hags and a litter of random boulders. In the centre of this desolation, he turned about full circle, noting the other 'crossroad' he had been anticipating – another rare meeting of four glens. The way ahead rose into an enclosed place, mounted by great heights and rocky crags.

"Elpin's words were to continue west from the crossroads," he recalled aloud, "until I reach a loch. Above that would be the pass to the north, leading towards the great strath on the far side."

Mounting the rise, the loch lay before them; a steely grey sheet of water, shadowed by sheer brooding crags at the far end and a sky full of racing dark clouds. Above the steep crags rose vast horizons covered in deep snow, sweeping upwards into the cloud. It felt a forbidding place. Cold blasts of wind raised small waves, which broke, with a plaintive sound, on a pebbly shore. How few men could have looked upon these waters! Certainly, the only footprints in the gravel were those of deer and wolf. He could plainly make out the pass he was to make for, a lower dip between two vast heights. In such a desolate place, where man did not belong, he was keen to push beyond.

Climbing towards the pass, the wind picked up. Taran paused to adjust his clothing. He looked down to the far end of the loch hemmed in by an austere ring of vast cliffs that rose dramatically. These corries had evidently been the scenes of many avalanches, scattering the landscape with enormous boulders and great shoots of grey scree.

"What a place of upheavals!" he exclaimed.

Garn whined, eager to reach the pass and the glen beyond, where there would be shelter from the raw wind.

The scene so impressed, though, that Taran lingered to take his fill. Soon frozen stiff, he started swiftly towards the pass, hoping to find a kinder land on the other side. The prospect of shelter, knowing that the main trek through the Minamoyn Goch would be behind, was enticing. But something nagged within, causing him to pause without understanding why. He tried to brush it off, and continued with the ascent to the pass, but the unrest could not be dismissed. The trouble seemed to increase the further he climbed. Now close to the pass, he felt inexplicably bothered that he had to stop. It annoyed him greatly, having nearly reached his goal.

"Why, of course!" he exclaimed. "Coblaith's vision of the fallen boulders from the cliffs!"

It was not a welcome revelation, because the thought of backtracking over ground that had been difficult to gain was demoralising. His energy was largely spent. The prospect too of making camp down by the hostile shore of the loch beneath the looming cliffs was a most unpleasant one. All his natural inclinations urged him to reach for the safety on the far side of the pass.

Coblaith had said that the stone of refuge was so significant that she used a phrase to emphasise its importance. How did she put it? 'So important towards fulfilling your destiny.'

Ignore it at his peril! On his own, without a single follower to assist his cause, what chance did he have? His one hope was to muster strength inwardly, to heed prophecies and signs. Had these not been given to guide him to a place of strength and breakthrough?

He made his way back down the hill just climbed, all the distance to the lochside, fighting all the while his reluctance. The water foamed white with an agitated murmur. The route along the loch shore proved to be much more uneven and boggy than it had looked from above. In the upper reaches, the loch shore was littered with large boulders, difficult to negotiate a course through. The debris at the foot of the great corrie was truly immense, some slabs matching the description in Coblaith's vision.

The rain, turning to a soggy sleet, flew in large, wet blobs.

They crossed a stream fed from the corrie. Above, two cascades flowed over great slabs set at a steep angle, forming a V-shape before becoming one stream. The V-shape was such a significant symbol upon their standing stones that Taran could not fail to make the association with either an arrow broken or a sword bent, purposefully rendered useless by a warrior as a votive offering. He was familiar with this yielding of the best from quiver or armoury as a sacrifice, imploring victory in a forthcoming battle. He scooped up a handful of water and drank it as one would a potion that would make one strong again. His spirit felt invigorated, convincing himself that fortune would turn about and he would not remain the fugitive forever.

Making their way up the brae towards the great tumbled debris fallen from the heights, they came to a great slab with an overhang, offering some protection from the rain. He wondered whether this was the place Coblaith had seen. With the area littered with other such large debris, he went on to explore other possibilities and came to another huge slab that had fallen in such a way as to present more of an open cave. The huge entrance did not fit the vision's description of a small place, into which it was just large enough to scramble. He continued among more immense boulders, passing through a narrow passage where one huge slab lay close to others. Rounding this, a low gap appeared beneath the slab on his right: a small aperture at ground level, perhaps large enough to just crawl through. Stooping down, he peered within, his eyes took time to adjust to the twilight. He began to make out a sizeable cavern and that was only the part that could be seen from this entrance. The vast rock had fallen over a natural hollow in the ground, of such a size for the slab to form a vault above. It looked bone dry within, a welcome sight given their saturated state.

"Come on Garn, let us go in!"

Garn was not keen to venture into the mystery of a dark chamber and could not be persuaded.

"Maybe there is a bear or wolf inside," thought Taran. He decided to walk around the perimeter of the slab, checking for another opening. Garn was glad to follow. Part way round, they found a small aperture, too small to crawl through, for it was more a window into the cavern. He made a loud bellow and only heard the echo of his voice reverberate within; a sound that unnerved Garn the more. As nothing ran out, he felt confident no beast was sheltering within. Returning to the low entrance, he sat in its cramped confinement, and turning sideways, sidled down, squeezing through into the hollow. It opened, high enough to walk in a stooped manner just a pace or two within. The space grew low towards its extremities. He coaxed Garn to follow, who as soon as he was properly within the cavern, started to growl low, looking intently into a darkened corner of the cave.

A pile of firewood came into view. Only a person could have placed it there, he thought as he stepped cautiously forward. He suddenly froze. With horror, Taran made out a body lying there. It was not clear whether the person was alive or not.

"Welcome Taran!" spoke a voice from the shadows.

The hairs rose on the back of his neck. Garn growled more menacingly.

"Who are you? How do you know my name?"

Chapter Eighteen

Called to Account

555 AD Rhynie

After Talorgen's funeral – a simple affair expressing respect more than any shows of grief – Oengus was re-energised. He made a trip to Y Broch to formalise an understanding with Brude. The matter concerned the sensitive topic of his proposed alliance with the Circinn, through marrying his sister to Cynbel, their ageing warlord. An oath of allegiance to Brude was required from Oengus, along with a payment of tribute. Oengus returned to Rhynie, losing no time in sending two representatives to the Circinn, who returned within the week with an agreement to the marriage. Oengus was feeling pleased with how swiftly his new initiatives were being accepted as he set his own mark in ushering in a new era.

"Do I not get a say in who I marry?" protested Derile, her head pressed down into her shoulders.

"It is an honour for you to be wed to a warlord." Oengus cast her an engaging smile.

"But he is old!"

"Then you will probably not have to put up with him for that long!" Oengus exclaimed with a hollow sounding laugh. "You will be provided for life this way."

"I want to stay here where I belong," she said, more heated. "I do not have ambitions to marry a man of power!"

"Do you think this is not all a bit hasty?" interjected their mother. "Why the hurry?"

"This is not some spur of the moment decision, you know!" Oengus felt piqued by his mother trying to exert control as if he were still a boy. "This has been something I have considered ever since I became Uncle's heir. It is not some dreamt up notion. I do know what I am about."

"And what did he have to say on the matter? He could never stand the Circinn," persisted his mother.

"It does not matter what Uncle thought! He could be very stubborn at times, foolishly so, which perpetuated many heedless skirmishes. I am the new ruler and I am decreeing a time for change, to bring an end to the long-standing animosities that impoverish both sides. This is not a matter for discussion, as if there was a choice for Derile. Things have been decided and set in motion."

"You are just selling me off like some article." Derile spoke with spirit, her eyes flashing lividly at her brother.

"Why are you being so negative?!" Oengus rose to his feet and started to pace in front of the fire. "Consider this – you will be at the centre of the Circinn court, and that is an immense rise for a sixteen-year-old girl, and so very different to your obscure life here. With you being in the direct royal line of our grandmother, a future ruler will be reckoned through your marriage union. A future Circinnian warlord may trace their legitimacy to the royal line of the Ce. We and they may become one people in time."

He stopped before her, trying to catch her eye. "You will lack nothing, will never go hungry. You will wear the best clothes; have a maid to wait upon you. And you are not going to be far away either," he continued with a conciliatory tone. "You will be able to return, and mother can go and visit you there."

"It is easy for you to say this – you do not have to marry an old man! It is not what I want. I do not share these ambitions. All I want is to stay here and marry someone my own age." Tears now brimmed in her eyes and her quivering mouth closed as she swallowed heavily. She clasped her hands about her knees, refusing to look him in the face despite his efforts to make eye contact.

"It is not a matter of what you want," returned Oengus, now feeling impatient. Overcome with frustration, he was lost for words.

"You cannot just ride rough shod over people's lives and not care for how they feel!" Derile looked up. "You are my brother! You are acting like some stranger who has no concern for how I feel."

"Feelings do not come into it," Oengus replied dispassionately. "We all have to put up with things we had rather not have to bear."

"You should be looking out for Derile's interests," Drusticc spoke, wringing her hands.

"I am looking after her interests!" Oengus replied despairingly.

"More like your own interests," replied Derile hotly. "You just do as you please, grab whatever you want. Look at Eithni!" She turned to look boldly at him. "You win her affections to use her and when you have grown tired, you just cast her off!"

"That is not your business!" Oengus felt his face flush hot.

"You are callous. A hothead who just does as he pleases."

"You will not speak to me like that."

"No one else is going to speak to you like that now that Talorgen is no more, except . . ." She did not finish her sentence.

"Except who?" contested Oengus.

She looked defiantly at him. "Except Uncle Nechtan!"

"Be quiet. How dare you speak like that?" His head spun with emotion, outraged at the perceived ingratitude of a little sister. He took a deep breath and mastered himself. "I have tried to be kind to you, but you are just stupid and ungrateful. You have no choice in the matter – you will wed Cynbel and I will make sure there is no delay about it." At this, he stormed out of the hut, heedless of his mother's protests.

Oengus was true to his word. Within the month, just before Samhainn, Derile was taken to Dinottar on the Circinn coast, close to the border with the lands of the Ce, and was wed to the elderly Cynbel. It was a first in living memory, the peoples of the Ce and Circinn gathered for a friendly purpose. The mood was joyous except for the hapless sixteen-year-old bride. The encounter achieved what Oengus had hoped: a breaking of the age-old animosity, paving a new start for inter-tribal relations.

Once the wedding party had returned to Rhynie, Oengus accompanied Gest on the eve of Samhainn to consult with the high priestess of the Bulàch who, along with her fellow priestesses, was observing annual rites in the oak grove. The trees were almost stripped of leaves and what remained had turned a dull brown. The ground lay thick with fallen foliage, crisped by frost, and felt slightly springy to the step. An age-old wisdom from the earth seeped upwards from its dark, mysterious vaults in the form of a pungent odour of humus.

Colder than on their previous visit, the fire seemed bigger; a burning presence that drew people in not only for warmth but by inciting man, with its mesmerising flames flicking upwards, to challenge the darkness of the night.

The bonfire pulsed with an energy, making noises like some living thing, wheezing for one moment and then hissing steam, until without warning it made sudden explosive noises. Small projectiles were lividly spat out; glowing sparks burst upwards to expire without trace. The night held tight to its secrets, quick to suppress any illumination that challenged its current supremacy.

"What is it that you seek?" asked Maevis. She looked much more engaging, compared to their previous consultation, perhaps due to their arriving early.

"I seek the favour of the Bulàch," replied Oengus simply. Maevis looked inquisitively, expecting him to elaborate.

"Is there one with whom you wish to consult beyond the vale of death?"

Oengus considered briefly. Was there someone to petition for help? No one came to mind. He had not really thought things through that thoroughly. "I am aware that I need the favour of the Bulàch, for on my own, hopes of my plans succeeding are more difficult."

"You are not wanting me to venture far this time on a spirit flight?" Her tone sounded slightly mocking, lacking, to Oengus' mind, a certain respect for his status. However, he did not check this, mindful of his need for her assistance.

"I assumed that Samhainn's eve was an appropriate time to declare my dependence upon the Bulàch and to commit myself in venerating her." He ruffled his hair in his awkward agitation. "I do need her blessing!"

Maevis coldly looked him over. Oengus started to feel uneasy under the intensity of her scrutiny.

"If you are to truly venerate the Bulàch, then be mindful that you are being called to account," Maevis replied enigmatically, increasing the tension.

"What?" He smarted under her rebuke. Swallowing his pride, he reasoned aloud. "The Bulàch sees the thoughts and actions of us mortals – I am aware of that!"

His discomfort deepened considerably. What was the high priestess withholding? His pride precluded confessing any fault. Anyway, was her position not subservient to his own? Her function was to serve the needs of the community, especially eminent persons such as himself. The irony, though, was that he, as warlord, needed to acknowledge her mediatorial role with the spiritual realm. This was essential for the prospering of his plans. Maevis had to be respected if she were to be compliant with his wishes.

"You seem displeased with me on some account!" Oengus tentatively continued. "Tell me what offends?"

Maevis gave him an icy, searching look, seemingly not feeling in the least awkward with the tension. She pushed back the deer skull from her brow, allowing the firelight to play over the vague sheen across her serene and aloof brow.

"You believe as ruler that you can do as you please with whoever. You expect the Bulàch to just approve your actions because you come to her high priestess seeking her blessing?"

Oengus was taken aback by this reprimand. He wanted to hit back but managed to acquiesce. What wrongdoing did she have in mind? His mouth felt dry. Moistening his lips, he asked with some difficulty, "What specifically offends?"

Maevis appeared in no hurry to respond. Did she recognise the superiority of her position as he sought the Bulàch's blessing? Would Maevis call him to account? Several people came to mind whom he had perhaps wronged. With each one, though, he felt his response justified; the actions of a strong man, required of his position.

"I could cite the circumstances of Talorgen's death!" she began calculatingly.

Did she stall deliberately with her insinuation?

Gest looked askance at him, a quick sidelong glance, before reverting his attention to the high priestess. She proceeded to address the young warlord with total composure.

"But it is not your uncle's death that protests most." Maevis looked at him unblinkingly and masterfully. "He received retribution for the way he dealt with others. But you, you hold family of little account: a cousin with whom you used to be close, ousted; a young sister unwillingly wed to an ancient man; your widowed mother spurned! If such is your regard for your own kind, then it is little wonder that you despise the one you used to love."

"Speak clearly now," he said, feeling the blood rush to his cheeks, preparing himself to weather the storm.

"Eithni, who is with your child, has taken refuge with our sisterhood!"

"What is that to you? Surely that benefits your cause!" Although he felt pangs of guilt, he refused to show remorse.

Seemingly unflustered by his callous remark, Maevis continued to hold him steadily under an unrelenting gaze. She bore the composure of a judge calling a criminal to account. "You consider yourself a law unto yourself when you regard there is no one to stop you. But you also recognise you are answerable to a far higher authority. That inconsistency will be your undoing!"

Oengus looked away, regretting that he had sought this audience. His attention was drawn towards the hind priestesses rotating around the fire. Was Eithni among them? It was impossible to tell, given that their heads and torsos were covered to the waist by the deer costumes. It struck him forcibly how absurd his position was, seeking mediation for the Bulàch's blessing from a company where he was perceived to have wronged one of its members.

"Come on Gest, we have no further business here!" He abruptly left without looking at Maevis.

Oengus visited Aunt Conchen the following day. She was a calm and steadying presence in a community where he hardly had friends, in an environment where he had to strive against those who would defy him. Seeing Alpia was undoubtedly another motive. Even though she tended to ignore him, he hoped his frequent visits might eventually accustom her to accepting his presence and help overcome her aversion. In time, she might learn to appreciate him. He aspired to be a better man before her, keen to prove that he could be worthy of at least her attention, if not her affection.

"You do not look well," observed Conchen as he came over to kiss her on her cheek.

"No, my spirit is downcast."

"Why, what is the problem? Are you sickening from something?" She seemed to ask with genuine concern. "Come, sit beside me." She gestured him to sit upon the deer hide.

"No, I am well . . ." He slumped down beside her. "Well, in body, that is!"

"What troubles you?" The gentle tone diminished, making way for the practical manner of a trusted confidant, mindful of his situation. She placed her elderly wrinkled hand briefly on his and withdrew it almost immediately; a gesture intended to convey that she could be trusted, that he had her full attention.

He felt at a loss of where to begin.

"Alpia," Conchen caught her niece's attention as she swept the far side of the hut. "Would you mind fetching some water as we are low? If you can pick some marjoram growing down by the river, then perhaps we can have a hot drink, that is if the frost has not already got it."

Alpia lent the broom against the wall and quietly withdrew good-naturedly with a couple of empty water skins. It was some distance down to the river and she would be gone awhile.

"I feel as though I am blundering forwards," he blurted out, "trying to consolidate my position. I am not making friends and I wonder whether I have the respect of the people!"

Conchen was quiet but gave him her full attention.

"How did Uncle start out when he became warlord?"

"He blundered too, do not doubt it!" She paused, biting her lower lip. "Truth be said, he blundered all through his life, imposing his will, irrespective of the feelings of others. That was his style, showing a strong hand and an unswerving will. That was his idea of how a leader should be! But you know there are other ways too . . ." She left her thought unfinished.

"I felt that I should be like Uncle. After all, he is the model I have of how a warlord should behave." He picked at a scab on his wrist that was not ready for removing.

"I know," Conchen began with a degree of understanding in her tone. "You have had to prove yourself to Uncle with a show of strength and supremacy. That was the way to gain his respect and made you his choice as successor." Again, she patted his hand briefly. "Now, you have a choice to make. Either you continue to be like Uncle, imposing your will and ruthlessly crushing any dissent, or you cast that style aside and aim to inspire people and, earning their respect, they will follow you."

The simplistic setting out of these two leadership models, displaying her homely wisdom, appealed to Oengus. How refreshing this was to hear amidst the disapproval and opposition.

"So, you do not think I should take Uncle's lead?"

"No, I do not," she replied emphatically. "He was so stubborn at times, overbearing and hard to get along with!"

"But you remained together all those years?" he replied with a certain incredulity.

"A wife is called to be loyal to her man!" She sighed heavily. "There were times when he relented with me, when I could persuade him to take a different line, or at least to soften his approach. Being able to influence, even if only a little, gave me hope to persevere. At least I could be a moderating influence sometimes, which probably helped to prolong his rule. But it was not easy."

This was all something of a revelation. Taking Talorgen's lead no longer appeared the only way. "I have not made the best of starts, have I?" confessed Oengus.

Conchen looked compassionately upon him and gave a faint smile.

"Some things are too late to undo, like with Derile; although the old age of her husband will surely release her soon. But what will you do about the things you can change?" She paused judiciously, proceeding with sensitivity. "Like with Eithni?"

The offence of his actions smarted once again. Last night, when Maevis had broached the matter, there was only cold judgement, forcing him against a wall with nowhere to go. The pangs of guilt had been felt then. His own sister had accused him of just 'discarding' Eithni, having satisfied his appetite. He now felt pity for the destitution he had caused a girl who once brought him a certain happiness unknown before. The distastefulness of his actions turned to a keen disgust that he found particularly nauseating. Had he turned into a megalomaniac like his uncle? From the time he started to accompany the old warlord, had he not increasingly felt an aversion towards his despotic ways?

He had arrived at a cliff edge, brought to his senses before he too would blindly follow, plunging to the same depths.

"Do you have any feelings for Eithni?" challenged his aunt.

"Feelings?" Oengus questioned. He thoughtfully examined himself. "Feelings of guilt and of pity, yes!"

"And what about love?"

"I do not know. I did once love her, of sorts, I suppose." He spoke into his upturned hands.

"What do you think is the right thing to do?" continued Conchen.

With his pride totally deflated, acknowledging the error of his ways, he was keen to make restitution. He could now see things clearer concerning the right action. "I should bring her back here."

"Back to her family or what?" pursued Conchen, not unkindly.

"I have fathered a child, so I should be responsible." He felt a flicker of warmth rising from the pit of his stomach. "No, more than just feeling responsible, I should be glad to nurture that child."

"That is good. You know, in time, you might come to love Eithni. Love has different expressions." Conchen paused, perceptibly shaking her head. "Do not think I do not know that! I have experienced every stage of love. When you are young, you only think of passionate love as the true love. It is like a grass fire after a prolonged drought, flaring up with intense heat, consuming everything in reach. But that type of love does not last. Love matures and becomes more a matter of commitment that develops an appreciation and friendship. At times, that act of willing to love another takes a determined grittiness to remain steadfast, to make the best of things, to put the best interpretation on the actions and words of others. That is the heart of love, choosing to love when all the odds are stacked against you. I can tell you, that commitment can produce rewards." She smiled more broadly at her nephew. "And it certainly produces character."

The two of them were quiet for a time, comfortable in one another's presence. The morning grew brighter outside, intensifying in the threshold where the shadows were shortening.

"When we are young, we struggle to comprehend well," his aunt continued. "Especially with you men! You feel the need to prove yourselves, to earn the respect or fear of others. But now I have grown old, I realise it is better not to hurry. Patiently biding your time is the way to grow wise. As a ruler, you need to be wise, just as much as proving yourself to be strong."

Conchen sucked air through a gap in her teeth and ran her hand through her thin grey hair. "Would that we could all have our time again, then we would not make so many blunders." She sighed with what seemed genuine regret. "But you know, if I can pass on a little wisdom in my old age to the likes of you, Oengus, then I feel that I am still doing some good, that my life is not just passing in vain."

"You are doing good! You speak from experience, with knowledge and a concern for me, and I am truly thankful!"

"Well, thank the Bulàch that you have come to your senses. It is not always too late to repair damage done. And I am glad that I still have a role to play with my nephew."

Oengus spent the day reviewing everything, particularly examining his thoughts and feelings stirred by Maevis and his aunt. He felt it right to take Eithni back, but was wary of acting on impulse. He wanted to think things through on his own, unpressured by others and the circumstance of the moment. The more he considered everything, the clearer the course of action became.

A new day brought an even greater conviction. Without wasting further time, he rode to the community of the priestesses of the Bulàch, where he enquired after Eithni's whereabouts from a woman washing clothes down by the stream.

"She stays over in that hut with an older woman. You should find her there."

Oengus approached the hut, tethering his horse to a nearby tree. The door had been moved to one side, but the interior was too dark to see into. He cleared his throat noisily to announce his presence. Eithni appeared in the doorway. She looked tired and somewhat dishevelled. She showed no emotion on seeing him.

"Eithni! What can I say?" Although he had rehearsed the main import of what he wanted to communicate, he had not thought through the preliminaries to overcome the awkwardness of what he now felt. Eithni regarded him rather blankly. The morning light brought out the auburn touch to her hair, which looked particularly fine against the pallour of her skin. She did look destitute, however, washed up in a strange place, toiling for her keep in a stranger's home. This was quite a contrast to what had drawn him to her in the early days when she was vivacious and flirty. He knew he was to blame for that change.

"I am so sorry for what I did. I have come to bring you back to Rhynie, to be with me!"

She looked surprised, even disbelieving.

"Who is that you are talking to?" came the voice of her much older companion. A note of irritation was detectable in her tone.

"Just give me a moment," Eithni replied, turning her head back into the hut. "I will be back presently. I will take the water skins to be filled." She left Oengus aside the threshold, whilst she retrieved the water containers from within. Things had not got off to such a good start. He had imagined her to show emotion, at least anger at his reappearance, or perhaps even gladness. But this muted manner was impossible to read. It did not alter his resolve.

Eithni appeared again, and without looking at him or pausing in her stride, she made towards the stream. Oengus followed.

"I know it is quite unexpected me turning up like this. I suppose it is quite a surprise. I have been a fool and have wronged you! I want to make amends."

She stopped and looked him in the eye. "You think that you can just take me back like that?" She strode off with a determined pace.

"I have come to my senses!" he said, catching her up and hoping that she would stop.

She ignored him, making for the stream where she placed the containers down.

"Eithni! I understand that you are angry with me, but honestly I can tell you that I regret . . ." He scrambled about for the right words to define why his regret was so keen, and finding nothing suitable, blurted out, "Throwing you off!" There was no point in eloquence over such a despicable action.

She made no reply. She steadied a foot on a smooth, rounded stone out in the stream, and squatting low, submerged the skin under the water. It bubbled greedily from its mouth. It took what seemed an age to fill. Eventually, she rose with the skin full and looked at the other container close to where Oengus was standing.

"Pass me the other skin," she said flatly.

Oengus brought it over. They exchanged skins.

"Will you not consider coming back with me now? What is there here for you? We can make a new start together." The irony struck him that he as warlord was finding his will difficult to be taken seriously.

"I have made a new start here."

"It is not much of a life though."

"You took choice away and left me only with this!" she said, embittered.

"I know, I know!" He felt repentant.

"And what awaits me back in Rhynie? The anger of my people, the disapproval of the community. I have lost everything!"

"That was how things stood when you left." Oengus wiped his moustaches clear from his mouth. "But I am not asking you to come back as it was before. I am asking you to be my wife."

Having filled the second container, she straightened herself and stumbled slightly. Putting a foot into the water to regain her balance, she pulled herself up straight. She looked almost regal for a moment, in control of her destiny. She smoothed her smock, revealing the growing bulge of her belly, before skipping nimbly back on to the bank.

What more did he have to say to regain her confidence? Seeing her condition brought home the enormity of what it must have been for Eithni back in Rhynie, to feel her position no longer tenable and forced to come to this community of exile. It had been he who had callously suggested that she could find refuge here.

"Eithni, we once felt such a gladness together. Do you think that we could both work at getting that back again?"

"You surprise me," she looked at him for the first time with any sense of engagement. "This is a strange proposal of marriage! Young women dream of it being much different."

Oengus bit his lip, feeling like a swimmer going against a strong current, wondering whether he was making any headway. At least she was talking to him now; surely, that was progress.

"True. I know it should be different, that we should not have had this breakup resulting in you leaving."

"Spurned by you as well as by my own family!" she added with feeling.

Oengus slumped his shoulders forward. He was out of his depth, groping for some consolation to offer. He spoke up finally. "Does the course of love relationships ever run smoothly?" he said, clutching at anything to make some defence.

She stood silent, looking down at the pebbly bank, her arm hanging limp with the weight of the full water skin.

"That was more than a mere lover's tiff! I was rejected, driven out." She breathed heavily.

"I am not expressing myself well. Again, I can only say how very sorry I am for the pain I have caused you!"

"It will not be easy to go back and show my face."

Here was the first indication that she was considering his proposal, and he was encouraged. "No, it would be very difficult to go back on your own! But if you are alongside me, well, that is going to be different. I am here for you now, as your husband, as a father to our child."

"You do not mention anything about love! Do you love me anymore?"

"Yes, of course I do!" he remonstrated. "That is why I am here!" He felt the lie in his declaration, until he considered his aunt's words. Had she not said that love had many different expressions? He no longer felt any of that passionate love for Eithni, but maybe that would return if they had the opportunity for a fresh start. What he was feeling at that moment was the gritty love that Conchen had spoken about, the determination to commit, to see a difficulty through.

He reached a hand out to her. She took his hand and smiled faintly. Sidling up to her, he put a protective arm around her. They both dropped the waterskins, which spilled out and turned the grey dusty pebbles into shiny colours of green, like a distant forest, and grey, like the sky at dusk. Some of the stones were striped with veins of white quartz or a rust red. They remained in that silence that reconciliation and togetherness bring.

Eithni broke the silence. "I'd better go and gather together my things!"

Oengus smiled. "And I will draw the water afresh and bring it over."

"No. Let us together draw the water afresh."

On their return to Rhynie, Maelchon blessed their union and a feast was held to formalise their marriage. The massive reversal in Eithni's fortunes was the talk of the town, some of it uncharitable, but mostly she was well received. She could have held her head high, having achieved what she and many of her peers had aspired to: becoming the wife of the warlord. Eithni, though, only expressed relief to return without the reproach of her community.

"I am proud of you," remarked Conchen, the day following the wedding celebrations, when Oengus went to visit her. "This marriage will help to stabilise your position. You have been seen to do the right thing. You did not have to take her back, but you showed a generous spirit and a compassionate heart; qualities to be admired."

"Well, it is in no small part thanks to you!" he smiled.

"And where are you intending to live? Are you planning to remain in your mother's house for long?"

"She is keen that we remain. She says my bringing Eithni to live with her has been the first joyous occasion for a long while."

"So, you are all reconciled?"

"It seems so."

"But you know what I think," she said after a pause. "You should build your own place."

"Oh yes, I will, eventually."

"I mean, you should make your own place straight away. Do not delay."

"Why the haste?"

"It is not easy for a young bride to live under her mother-in-law's roof," she said knowingly. "But more than that, it is time to establish your own household, close to the meeting hall where a leader is expected to live."

"Eithni and I talked about that back in the summer."

"I know just the very place."

"Now that winter's here, there are many idle hands to help built it quickly."

"And how is Eithni feeling?"

"She still has lots of energy, even with a growing belly!" he laughed under his breath. "Well, I had better be on my way and organise a group to help me build."

"Come back this evening to tell me how things are progressing." He kissed her, and just before he turned to go, she added, "You know, Alpia is pleased that Eithni is back."

He turned and went outside. He thought it strange that his aunt should refer to Alpia's approval. His marriage had just added the final barrier, adding to the many that stood between them. Without delusion, he could not help thinking that if Alpia were his wife, how buoyant would be his mood. How infinitely greater that would be than the satisfaction of knowing he had just done the right thing.

Even if Taran's death could be proved, she would hold him responsible. He admonished himself for these idle thoughts, although he was secretly glad, in an absurd way, that Alpia approved of his actions. He reminded himself that he was married to Eithni and must make the best of things as they stood.

Chapter Nineteen

The Stone of Refuge

556 AD Y Minamoyn Goch

 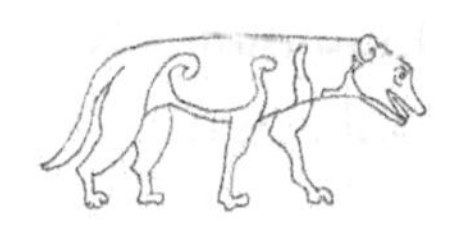

"Come closer," spoke a kindly voice, that of an older man, sounding vaguely familiar. "Then you will surely recognise me."

Very warily, Taran moved forward, clutching his spear. The man's head was in silhouette against the low aperture bright with daylight. Where had he heard that voice before? He wondered, for it was not someone who he knew well. Garn held his ground, emitting an intermittent growl. This shelter rock was such an inconceivable place to meet another human that Taran wondered whether this presence was perhaps a spirit.

Edging another step toward the dark form, he peered cautiously through the gloom at the recumbent figure, who had darkest shadow for a face.

"I will come no further until you reveal yourself," said Taran, ready to lunge with his spear.

A good-natured laugh greeted him, resonating around the low cavern.

"Why Taran, it is me, Ossian!"

Taran laughed nervously. "Ossian, is it really you?" he said with relief and incredulous joy. "Wha' . . . what are you doing here?"

"To meet you," the ancient bard replied warmly.

"How did you know I would be here? Wait! That does not make sense – I did not know I would be here myself, so how could you?"

"Indeed, it will surely be a mystery to you – a very great mystery," he said, finishing with a sigh to imply something beyond mortal ken. Taran removed his satchel and traps that had been slung over his shoulder.

"I think we should hunt something for supper," suggested Ossian.

"My kindling is too wet to start a fire. What rain! I am wet through to the bone."

The bard unwrapped a waxed hide from a metal box and presented dry kindling.

They exited the cavern. The snow flurry had passed, leaving a fine, transparent layer of sleet upon the ground.

"Look, here are the tracks of a hare!" observed Taran. "Let us get under cover behind the big boulder there."

Taran asked the question foremost on his mind. "What brings you here to meet me?"

"To help you on your way," he returned, in a tone that was stating the obvious. "To offer you counsel, so that your outcomes may in time prosper. But all in due course . . . there is no hurry – we have all night."

"Tell me, at least, how you knew to meet me here?"

Ossian smiled, enjoying his perplexity. "It was not communicated to me by ordinary means. I am, what you might say, something of a wizard! We delve into investigating the hidden things . . ." Ossian winked at him.

"A wizard, a bard, a storyteller and a prophet," he remarked, shaking his head with a vague sense of incredulity, although forced to believe on account of the evidence.

"Did I not foresee trouble when we last met?" The old man cocked his head to one side. "I saw your cousin's determination, fed by his father's ambitions that respected no bounds. You were seen to have won the girl you were both after. Robbed in love, they say, makes one ambitious for power. That seized Oengus and was very clear to see, not requiring any wizardry to divine as much. It is easier to gain your own will once you are at the top. And now he is warlord, he has a wife."

"Uh! Do you know who?"

"Not exactly sure – a girl of his own age from Rhynie."

"If I say her name, then maybe you would recall. Did he marry Alpia?"

"Alpia? I am not sure – could be!" Ossian tried to sound convincing.

"I would rather you were sure," insisted Taran.

"I cannot say. Taran," the wizard spoke his name unexpectedly harshly, "do not get distracted like last time, you know what it cost you!"

"Have you seen them?" he persisted, unable to allow the question to drop.

"No, I have not set foot on the lands of the Ce since I parted from you at Beltane, a year ago. This kind of news travels fast, including the other marriage – Oengus' sister wed to the warlord of the Circinn. He is a wily one, that cousin of yours, determined to rule with guile and might."

Taran was fuming with resentment and asked the question now preoccupying his mind. "Is there any hope for me to win back the lordship of the Ce?"

"Why do you ask? It did not seem that important to you last year! Your ambition is not that of Oengus'."

"That was back then." He felt piqued, having to confess as much. "He has betrayed me, proved himself treacherous and would have killed me had the gods not intervened!

And now to add grave insult to injury, he has probably taken my girl."

"Well, that was all decreed – such things cannot be changed."

Just then, a hare came into view, ambling towards the corridor between the boulders. Taran fired an arrow but somehow missed, even though the animal was not that far away.

"You will have one next time, I would think," spoke Ossian, rising to his feet. "I am going back to the cavern to get a fire going."

Taran also rose to retrieve the arrow. He inspected the flights and found part of the feather had come away from the shaft. Putting it to one side, he drew a fresh arrow and took up position once more behind the boulder. The wind was rising and, having been stationary for quite a while, he felt cold. He adjusted his damp plaid, wrapping a part around his neck. He had a long wait. The loch was now quite ruffled, showing breaking crests. A leadened gloom subdued the land as the mist gathered on the upper heights in a thick, boiling mass.

Had Oengus taken Alpia as his wife? Such an action felt a deliberate injury to spite him in his exile. Well, Oengus was succeeding in all that he set his heart on achieving. He felt an ache gnawing at the back of his throat and despised his cousin.

"Oh Alpia," he said aloud. What hopes he had for them together, but then he had to leave Rhynie all too soon before she could love him in return. His hopes were dashed to smithereens and a deep resentment grew.

A movement on the slope to his right attracted his attention. Emerging from the mist rolling down from the heights was a small herd of deer, looking to graze on the grass growing to the side of the screes. He would have preferred a hare or two, for a deer was far too much for their needs! But he was perishing cold and they needed to eat. He trained his bow and waited for them to come closer. The wind blew down the loch, between him and the herd.

"Just sta-a-ay!" he murmured under his breath to Garn, who had become agitated with the sight of the herd. "Forgive me Bulàch for taking one of your cattle. I would not, but you know we have need, great need." A fawn had come close.

The arrow pierced its chest and it collapsed without struggle as the rest of the herd evaporated.

Taran dragged the carcass by one of its legs near to the stone of refuge, where he butchered a part for their evening meal. Garn was given part of the liver. He arranged the remainder of the liver, heart and kidneys on a clean stone slab and with a hind leg re-entered the cave to a fire that was already crackling.

"You got a deer!" the bard said with surprise.

"I know. I feel bad, for it is wrong to take something so large, but there was nothing else!"

Taran laid down the small stone slab of the choicest parts and prepared these into slithers to roast.

"Can you tell me anything about the future? My future? Will I be able to overcome Oengus?"

"Wanting the lordship now more than ever?" Ossian observed, in no hurry to answer his question. "The balance has swung and now it is you who has been robbed of the one you loved, and some might say cheated through deceit from becoming the warlord."

The wizard left his statement hanging in the air. Just when Taran thought Ossian would not speak, the old man continued in an approving tone. "You are proving yourself able! Fending in the wilds, overcoming misfortune and all kinds of hardships."

"Sir, you are not answering me in a straightforward manner – will I be able to rule over the Ce one day?"

"Well, yes, you will," the bard conceded matter-of-factly, and after scratching his grey beard he added mischievously, "and no you will not!"

"What is that supposed to mean! More riddles, just like the symbols tattooed on Oengus and I on the day of our initiation! Why does everything have to be veiled in mystery and be so contradictory in my life?"

"That is a very good question."

With that, the bard mused thoughtfully, re-arranging a part of the fire.

Taran removed some of his wet clothing and draped these over sticks he had upended for that purpose close to the fire. The cavern was still cold and he shivered.

"Do you know the proverb, *'Cunning is more powerful than strength'*?"

Taran gave a perceptible nod. "When in a position of weakness, you need to be wise and cunning . . . if you are to overcome the odds."

"Correct," pronounced the wizard, pausing to feed a couple of thicker sticks into the fire. "You will have to be patient, very patient, to persevere and not lose hope. Your journey is not an easy one, but the process of getting to your goal will be the means to make you potentially great." Ossian paused, looking up from beneath his wiry eyebrows. "There will be times when, through despair and seeming futility, you will want to finish it all. How you respond to hardship and disappointment will make the difference between success or failure. Are you beginning to understand your destiny? It is quite apart from the role of ordinary men."

"I would wish I were destined for a more ordinary life!"

"For a life of obscurity?" the wizard raised his brows. "Tut-tut, come now! Where is that ambition you subscribed to a moment ago?"

"What is the harm in wishing for a quiet life? I have been farming, and though it is hard, it is rewarding work and purposeful. To stand back at the end of the day and see a vegetable patch freshly dug, or to look upon a new repair to the thatch that fixed a leaking roof – that is satisfying. But from what you are saying, I am to work hard and not see results for a long time, if at all."

"If you seek to inspire men to follow you," Ossian spoke in measured tones, "the right attitude needs to be cultivated. That does not just come to us. To be a man of influence who inspires others to follow, a man to whom people come to seek counsel, you have first to prove you have become master of yourself." His eyes fixed him with a steady gaze. "If you are tossed about by every small wave, uncertain of your course, where is the inspiration in that? What kind of example would you be setting! Do not despise discipline."

After a pause, he added sagely, "As fire to the cauldron produces a meal, as water on parched ground nourishes and produces oats, so does adversity create a man of resolve."

Both looked thoughtfully at the fire, now giving off a good heat. The firelight danced over the walls and roof of their cavern and swam over their faces, giving them a strange aura.

"Do you mind the prophetic words I spoke to you upon the ridge above your home?" Ossian looked at him searchingly.

"I have to admit that I do not remember all – and that is to my shame and it is not for want of trying to recall."

He blushed with this admission of handling things of importance lightly that did not seem so relevant at the time. Quickly, he continued before the bard could chastise him. "But this much I do recall: that I was to make great haste, to be cunning, to be brave, to be humble. I am to head south, and then something about going west to the isles. But the end goal would be in the north, where I would bear fire for 'the fulfilment and the anticipation of the learned ones'."

"Well, I have to say that you remember more than what I expected! And now, I will remind you of the rest of what was revealed upon the ridge, at least words to that effect. Going to the south will bring about your surrender, your transformation will happen in the isles of the west. Bind those words to your heart."

Ossian looked for assent that he would take care of this prophecy, which he readily gave.

"You are correct about what will happen in the north, although you have added a bit: 'bearing fire'!"

"That part came to me in a vision and seemed to tie in with the prophecy."

"Remember too," Ossian went on gravely, "that heartache and anguish await you – they will be your lot and portion for a time – that many journeys lie ahead, involving many turnings, of seemingly going back, leading to confusion. But if you persevere, you will do great deeds and mighty acts, and that the road walked in achieving these, will be the making of the man.

"But . . ." The bard paused and wagged his finger. "There is mystery, even to me, that I cannot yet fathom, for it has not been revealed. The prophecy ended with an utterance that is mysterious. Do you remember what I said? Well, I will not embarrass you by your admitting that you have forgotten. Mark these words well this time, for they are not mine, but come from heaven. Commit them to memory, hide them as you would place treasure in a safe place to which you will return from time to time. You are to take heart: 'through one you will overcome the world'. Those are the closing words of the prophecy. I sense this is of huge importance, not only for you, but for our people."

"Oh, so much mystery!" Taran sighed. "Would that I could have had a sure and certain road like Oengus has taken. His way is clear!"

"To look on the success of another always seems sweet! But it is rarely so for that man," remarked the older man.

Taran reversed the long slice of meat on the point of his spear. The cavern was beginning to be filled with the enticing smell of cooking meat. Ossian seemed as much lost in thought than he was himself.

"I want to ask about the addition I received in a vision, of my 'bearing fire' to the learned ones in the north. Is it correct to assume that it is tied in with this prophecy?"

Ossian pondered. "Hmm – fire is significant; it is an elemental thing, gift from the gods . . . a bringer of light. These prophecies certainly do not contradict, but rather add emphasis to your mission. Something as elemental and of huge importance as fire will be a gift well received, especially if it be anticipated by learned ones for an age, banishing the dark and cold of their world."

He closed his eyes momentarily before continuing. "Whilst the full significance of these words is not for us to know at this moment, you can be sure that they remain wrapped up in your mysterious destiny. What that fire is will become apparent, of that I am certain. Meanwhile, be encouraged, especially when you are down and all seems lost, that there is purpose to your striving. There will be a good outcome to your heartache. You are not to give up, but to push on, to fulfil that destiny."

"What is the reason why I bear this Z-rod?"

"That is another perplexing thing," smiled the bard. "Maybe there is a connection between it and the bearing fire. Let us see. The Z-rod represents lightning – power from the heavens – and sometimes where it strikes, fire occurs, the gift of the gods. We shall have to delve further into such things with supplications and patiently await the unfolding of the revelation over time and the passing of events."

"You do not think that the Z-rod implies that I am to rule my people?"

"Oh, I think you will rule! But when, and in what manner, that is not so straightforward," the wizard spoke mysteriously.

Taran inspected the meat and, finding it cooked, offered it to Ossian.

"I have a piece cooking!"

"Take this, I insist."

Ossian took it with thanks. Taran placed another long, thin piece on the tip. The fire was now giving off an intense heat and cooked the meat quickly.

"Tomorrow," began Ossian, "we will climb the pass together and then part company. You are to go south, as you already know, in accordance with the prophecy. The influence of the Fortriu extends to the strath that you will come out onto. A price hangs on your head there, and a description of your identity has been made known. Do not tarry, but push south over the Gaick Pass of the Mounth. In the south, men will not be concerned by a fugitive prince from the Ce." After a pause, he added, "I would choose another name!"

"I have already done. I am Drostan."

"Drostan, eh? Good," chuckled the old man, before returning to his instructions. "You will arrive in the lands of the Fotla who have established their seat of power at Dindurn. Make for there, but be wary of its ruler. On the plain below Dindurn's fortress, you will find a man called Fillan – one who calls himself a 'Soldier of Christ'. He will receive you well and give you refuge among the community that is thriving there."

"What is a 'Soldier of Christ'?" he asked curiously.

"This Fillan is like a druid. He possesses great spiritual insight. His ability does not come from the Bulàch, for he follows the Christ, the foreign god – the one they say who saves. Remember, I spoke about this religion when I came to Rhynie?"

Ossian watched him tasting his first piece of meat, whilst grilling another morsel. "They are men of peace in whom there is no guile. Even though they are men of influence, they do not wield it as our druids would, but are mild in manner. Their influence is taking some hold in the south, although most would still worship the Bulàch."

"Surely, what good can come from those who teach us to turn away from the Bulàch? She holds the power for the Picts. Turn from her at our peril."

"I was of the same mind," Ossian replied with understanding. "That was until a while ago. It would seem that those who become 'Soldiers of Christ' are immune to the wrathful vengeance of the Bulàch!" Ossian raised a bushy eyebrow. "She seems powerless to touch them, or to stop the influence of their teachings."

Taran observed the wizard, who appeared to be turning over something in his mind, wondering whether to share it. Ossian ate a morsel from his knife, and when he had finished chewing it, shared this recollection. "Once, I cursed Fillan due to the number of Picts he had turned from the Bulàch! I invoked that he would be diseased and perish; that his teachings would likewise fail. I cursed him to his face. Instead of growing angry or afraid, he smiled with such calm! He stretched out an arm, and placing his hand gently upon my shoulder, he blessed me. I had no words to say!" Ossian shook his head incredulously.

Taran was surprised to hear that the wizard's power lacked potency.

Ossian was keen to continue. "I felt ashamed, unworthy to be in his presence. Fillan does not act like a man. His ways are foreign, and by that I do not just mean that he comes from Erin. It is an extraordinary differentness. He lives by another rule, following an unknown god, whose power protects, whose influence infiltrates and persuades men to follow. Like it or not, your future, Taran, is somehow bound up with Fillan and his people – I am sure of it."

"But . . ." protested Taran.

The old man held up his hand. "I have been searching long about how you should proceed from this current low ebb, to realise your destiny. It is always Fillan who comes to mind. He is your 'surrender' in the south. He will prepare you and set you off west in accordance with the prophecy."

Ossian had a far-reaching look in his eye. "Times are changing, Taran – the old order is under stress and losing its efficacy, and this Christ is in his ascendancy."

"I do not like what I hear. Why should I flee so far? Why should I appeal for help from a people who are not Picts? Must I trust a foreigner and adopt his ways? Is this the way to reclaim my lost inheritance?" Taran felt annoyed by advice that went contrary to the way he thought. "It would make better sense if you counselled me to speak to the warlord of the Fotla, one of our own, who could perhaps muster a force to overthrow Oengus?"

"You speak of the way of the world!" admonished Ossian unexpectedly. Smoothing his eyebrows, he spoke with conviction. "Put such thoughts of armed aggression out of your head – they are doomed to fail if you seek to overthrow in your own strength."

He felt immense confusion, though he recognised Ossian's wisdom, the knowledge gleaned from rubbing shoulders with all kinds of people.

Ossian continued to air his thoughts. "You will hold power, but only by following an unworldly path. You are to be the bearer of the celestial power of fire, befitting the force of the Z-rod, which is not mustered as one would a warband. As the saying goes, 'do not play with fire', for though we can harness it, it has the tendency to get out of hand, and rather than aid, it will burn us. If you are to be the bearer of a gift that cannot be fully owned, then you have to prove yourself worthy of being the chosen recipient."

The howls of several wolves heard in the distance reminded Taran of their remoteness. "Anyway, enough of all this talk. I think we have exhausted what can be said about such things. I only counsel you, not to be closed to things that might appear alien to you. Be open-minded, be wise to receive the teaching of others, if you desire to rise above your present predicament. Know this: we Picts do not hold all the wisdom and power of this mysterious world."

Ossian started to sing about some Pictish champions who joined forces with a neighbouring tribe and ousted pirates who controlled their shore. It was the stuff of valour, a story of fine horses, of skilfully crafted swords and finely wrought armour. It contained a lament for a fallen hero, and praised the prowess of men who won the day, slaying the pirates all to a man. The song ended with the joyful return of the hardy remnant.

They roasted more meat, soon finishing off the heart, kidneys and what remained of the liver before they made a start on the leg. Garn had his fill too. The fire was kept stacked from the great pile Ossian had gathered before Taran had arrived, and wet clothes were drying. Cries from the wolf pack sounded much closer than before, but neither was unsettled as they heartily sang. Thanks to Elpin, Taran joined in many of the songs, bringing good cheer to his heart.

Chapter Twenty

The Spirit of Garn

556 AD Y Minamoyn Goch

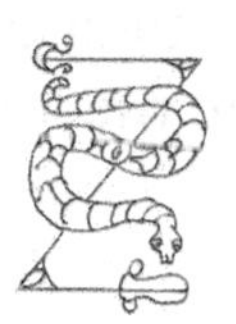

A commotion outside made them abruptly stop mid-song. Garn was on his feet, growling. Taran took hold of the scruff of his neck, restraining him from venturing out from the cavern. Ossian went to the refuge's entrance.

"Wolves are fighting over the hind's carcass!" reported Ossian. "Taran – go to the other opening at the far end of the cave. There is a wall there. Ensure it is high enough to prevent wolves from entering."

The ferocity of the wolf skirmish was intense. They snarled so viciously as they tore at the remains of the deer carcass that it seemed they were ripping one another apart.

Taran found the gap insufficient between the stone wall and the very low height of the roof slab at far end, which he had not reached earlier when inspecting outside the refuge. He busily started filling the low gap with large stones. A low snarl made him peer into the darkness, and though he could not make out its form, the unmistakeable wolf sound curdled his blood. Not having his spear to hand, he hurled a stone. The wolf yelped with pain and withdrew. Taran doubled-up under the low roof and moved like a spider scurrying across the floor. Taking his spear, he returned to find the wolf had entered the cavern. Garn was onto it with fury. Being adept at fighting, the wolf had seized Garn by the leg and before it could render further injury, Taran ran it through with his spear. Ossian appeared just as three more wolves were squeezing between the unfinished barrier and the roof slab. The smell of blood and the sight of their dead one seemed to enrage them.

"What about the main entrance – should not you be there?" shouted Taran, keeping the wolves at bay with his spear for the moment whilst holding Garn back.

"The door is taken care of. I will bring fire!" Ossian moved crab-like under the low roof and returned with a couple of flaming brands. Taran had killed another wolf and the fire forced the other two to retreat beyond the barrier. Noticing Ossian was streaming with sweat, he became aware of being hot himself.

"Let us drag these dead ones over to close the gap," spoke Ossian. Between them they dragged the corpses, raising them awkwardly to wedge between the stone barrier and the low roof of the slab.

"Come outside to give me cover with the firebrands, and I will get the few rocks needed to finish closing this opening."

They squeezed through the gap.

"Garn! Stay there!" Taran ordered.

"Be quick. Just toss them inside the cave," Ossian spoke urgently.

The menacing appearance of several sets of wolf eyes glowered. Perhaps the sight of the dead ones from their pack made them reconsider their attack, yet they continued to snarl with deadly threats.

"That will be enough to close the gap," said Taran.

"No, throw in a few more," ordered the wizard, keeping the wolves at bay with the flaming brands. Taran thought of objecting, but the tone was emphatic.

"Stay – come no closer!" Ossian commanded the wolves who, now overcoming their indecisiveness, edged nearer with evil intent. Dropping one of the firebrands that had expired, Taran noticed Ossian holding his staff horizontally.

"Metris obdey!" spoke Ossian, full of the mystery of an incantation. Taran saw the wolves unwillingly halted in their tracks, their legs trying to move yet seeming fixed to the ground.

"Get inside!" ordered Ossian.

Taran slithered back into the cavern with Ossian right behind.

"Build this wall fast. The wolves will not be immobilised for long."

An effective barrier was soon completed. True to Taran's estimation, they did not require all the stones Ossian had ordered him to throw into the cavern.

The wizard remarked, "Let us seal off the main entrance."

"I thought you said it had been taken care of!" Taran replied with alarm. "But come to think of it, how could you, in the time you had?" He sidled over to the small orifice, astounded to find it barred only by two lengthy pieces of firewood wedged into the rocky opening. Two wolves pressed in on the other side, desperate to enter but restricted by the narrow confines and the spars.

Ossian came forward with a heavy stone. "I think we will sleep better if there is a sturdier physical defence between them and us!"

So that was what all the extra stone was for, he thought.

Garn's wound was deep and bleeding. "You are in a pitiful state," remarked Taran, inspecting the wound. He sang his dog's praises to Ossian, relating the bear incident.

Ossian recited, "There will come much strife, like a blight threatening to consume. Heartache and anguish lie before you. Many a journey awaits, full of ordeals that you consider will be your undoing, though these are in truth, rites of passage for your own preparation. You will be the doer of mighty deeds and the acts will be the making of the man."

Taran shuddered inwardly.

With the cavern secure, they stoked the fire and lay down for the night. Garn was pressed against his master. The commotion outside evaporated as the wolf pack withdrew.

They dismantled the barricade in the morning. A forlorn Garn hobbled out very stiff, sniffing at the slaughter from the previous night. The wind blew cold down from the corrie, ruffling his thick mane.

"Come on Garn – back to the pass," Taran encouraged him. He followed slowly, having difficulties negotiating the bouldery sections where high craggy outcrops pressed in close to the loch. Sometimes Taran lifted him over the obstructions. They struck up toward the pass, where the way was clear, making haste with Garn soldiering behind. By the time they reached the snow-covered pass, rain and snow had wet them through.

"At least it was good to set off in dry clothes," remarked Taran.

They descended into a long glen, flanked by steep hills rising into grey cloud. Entering the forest forced them to be mindful of both low branches above and broken ground beneath, making progress laboriously slow. Then they reached the mountain stream, which from times of spate had scoured out a narrow floor, cleared of trees. It made for good progress. Garn, though, was unable to keep pace. Several times they waited and once they emerged into more open country, leaving behind the main mountainous massif, they relaxed their pace and Garn walked alongside.

"Oh, what a relief to be beyond the Minamoyn Goch!" remarked Taran, weary from the ordeals of the past couple of days.

"This is where we part," announced Ossian. "My way follows the river, and yours is across the ford here. Pass along the foot of these hills until you come to a narrow glen with a green loch. There, follow the stream flowing out the far end until you reach a larger loch. You will see a trail leading down into the strath. Do not take it – it would not do to be questioned by the many folk who live in those parts. Walk rough, keeping the high hills close on your left. Eventually, you will reach the trail south over the Mounth and will be clear of the lands of the Fortriu. The way south is obvious, trodden by the feet of many a traveller. Beyond the Gaick Pass, you will enter the kinder country of the Fotla. Just ask for the way to Dindurn; most travellers in those parts will know. You still have quite a journey ahead, another three days."

"So, I am only halfway!" Taran sounded disconsolate.

"Aye, but the worst half by far is behind you."

"And where are you bound?"

"Brude's court at Craig Padrig. His star is rising. He will become the overlord of more tribes, mark my words. I go to entertain with story and song – a good cover to observe and gain the favour of the court."

Looking as though he were going to bid farewell, Ossian spoke in a lower voice. "A word before we part. Say nothing about me being a wizard. It serves me well to be regarded as nothing more than a travelling bard. I conceal my powers, using them only when absolutely necessary." He tapped his brow with his forefinger. "Well, recall, night and day, all that you have been told, particularly the prophetic utterances. Respect the learned saint, Fillan of Dindurn."

"Shall we meet again?" he asked, reluctant to lose Ossian's guidance and companionship.

"I am sure we will," Ossian replied with a smile. His jaw moved, as though he were chewing on something. "I very much wish to see the outcome of all of this. Be assured that you do not go alone and that I will do what I can to help you during your adventures ahead."

They clasped one another. Ossian resolutely broke the embrace, and without further word, set off downstream. Taran stopped frequently to watch Ossian's progress. The latter never looked back. He felt his arm had been strengthened by this mysteriously contrived meeting under the stone of refuge.

He followed the line of hills and entered a narrow glen leading to the green lochan. It shone alluringly through the pine forest, nestled at the foot of a steep crag.

"Come and arise, O fairest of the fair; come and dry your hair in the sun. Come my lovelies and keep poor Gwid company. Sing me the songs that are my joy."

The sing-song drawl came from a squat man, moving along the shoreline with a bouncy step that almost verged on becoming a dance. He appeared to address the waters of the green lochan, as Taran could not see anyone there. Taran quietly called Garn to heel.

"O bonnie maidens of the deep, will you not come out and play with lonely old Gwid? Will you not bring gladness to the glen and sweetness into the heart of all living creatures? Gwid awaits, long has he waited, longing for just a glimpse. Surely your clothes are dry now – they have been long hanging in the trees. The wind has caressed them all day long, as lovesick with these as I am with you. They rustle with the sound of dryness, clothes that are beautifully green to befit comely bodies such as yours. The emerald of your attire is so fetching against your golden red locks . . ."

The little man did a skip before reeling about, like one who was drunk.

Taran moved forward.

"Await! Who comes here? Has Gwid a visitor? I think we have visitors. Oh yes, we do, we do." He looked expectantly through the trees, with a smile that had that mixture of joy and melancholy, rather like his dance.

"It is I, Drostan, with his dog."

The little fellow looked disappointed; the smile vanishing from his face.

"What do you want?" asked Gwid, sullenly.

"I want nothing – I am just passing by and will leave you alone."

"Why, you do not want to know who I am, or know what manner of loch is this? Are you not intrigued to behold the beautiful things who inhabit its waters? Oh, to see the fair ones will take away all other plans. Their beauty is breathtaking, quite captivating, yes captivating it is to see them bathing naked in these waters. I assure you; one look and you will not want to go further. Who would? Why should you pass by?"

"Have you lived here long?"

"Have I lived here long!" He laughed with delight and clapped his hands. "Have I lived here long?" he repeated, dancing on the spot before crouching down on his haunches. "Old Gwid has lived here many summers, too many to count. I was a young man when I first came. Hunting for deer I was. Then I saw the fair maidens of the loch bathing, washing their clothes and hanging them in the trees over there. I have never left, making my home here. It is an enchanting place."

"Aye, it sounds it," replied Taran knowingly. "You should leave this place."

"No," he snapped petulantly. "The faery folk are delightful to behold. Captivating, quite captivating they are – who would want to leave? You would be mad to! But here, what is this that walks with you – a wolf! What foul fiend is he? And fiend that he is, what might you be?"

The old man looked appalled and continued with his ranting. "The foul wolf might spirit the faery folk away. You cannot stay, no, you must not, must they?"

"We are moving on this very moment," assured Taran, starting off. He recognised that Gwid's lust for the maidens of the loch had grown so powerful an addiction that he was totally consumed.

"I see the wolf bleeds," Gwid said curiously.

"He is not a wolf, though he has some likeness." Taran did not wish to tarry another moment, sensing Gwid's malevolence. "We are on our way."

"Oh so soon! What is the hurry? Bide here awhile. You might see the fair maids break the surface of the water with their milk white skin and golden red hair, winnowing through the green waters."

"We are not staying. Remember, you wanted us to leave quickly because of my dog."

"What dog?" Gwid looked surprised. His brief innocence changed to one who was deeply disturbed. "That is no dog," he rasped. "It is a foul fiend, dripping its horrible blood on this hallowed ground where the faery folk roam. What evil footprints might he leave? What badness will he drip? He could undo the charm of this place."

Ignoring him, Taran quickened his pace along the loch shore, calling Garn to heel.

"Look to the waters – here they appear!" enticed the little old man. But Taran would not look, whether they be real or not. Should they be truly breaking the surface, he had no wish to be enchanted to either become like this pitiful Gwid or fall into this would-be enchanter's powers.

Gwid followed with bouncy steps, singing snippets of song. Taran broke into a trot, urging Garn to keep pace, which he did at first, until his master broke into a run. They passed a ramshackled place, relieved to no longer hear the pursuing steps of the enchanted one. Taran looked back, pausing for his faithful hound to catch up. Garn suddenly fell to the ground with a loud whine and began to kick pathetically on his side.

"What has happened?" he cried. Whilst running back, he glimpsed a movement in the trees beyond and caught sight of Gwid, running in the opposite direction, bow in hand.

Taran fell to his knees, stroking his dog's head, inspecting where an arrow lay embedded in his side. Gripping the arrow, and holding Garn firmly with his other hand, he eased the shaft slightly. The arrowhead was not barbed. After quickly pulling the shaft free, the wound began to bleed copiously. He staunched the flow with his plaid.

Garn began to shiver and pant shallowly. Blood trickled from his open mouth, but when he coughed, which he did more frequently, blood spouted on to the grass.

"O Garn, stay with me yet," Taran entreated, leaning his face close to Garn's head.

The dog's eyes fixed a pathetic look upon his master, powerless to even lift his head. Placing a hand under Garn's neck, he caressed his head. Garn did not remove his gaze, and now looked almost apologetic. Breathing less frantically, he fought reason to half-hope his companion was overcoming the wound. Garn's breathing grew shallower though, like one drowning, unable to tread water longer. Taran's other hand, placed over the wound, grew sticky with the blood that was clotting. He felt helpless.

"I wonder if the arrow had been poisoned, or perhaps even enchanted!" His eyes moistened. As Garn's lifeblood seeped through his fingers, Taran felt a murderous intent to despatch Gwid.

"My dear, dear companion! You and I have shared so much these past months." He looked up to see if Gwid were about. All was still, except for the gentle fluttering of the birch leaves. He attuned himself to his surroundings, alert to the slightest sound. Freeing his hands, he strung his bow and fixed an arrow to its string. He lay down, face to face with his dog.

"Garn – loyal friend and great protector. You rescued us from the bear, and last night gave me time to take on the wolves by attacking one."

He caressed the fur that grew long about his neck, gently taking hold of the thick folds of loose skin, knowing Garn found it comforting to be massaged there. Perhaps Garn could recall a distant time, when his mother's mouth would have picked him up by the nape of his neck, to carry him off to a secure place.

"You have enjoyed a new lease of life, to roam far from home on hunts with me. You had a second youth, and to show your appreciation, you acknowledged me as your new master. As for me, you became my companion, faithful and true, at a time when I have been stripped of everything."

Garn's eyes looked dull and unseeing, like his spirit had already gone. Taran wept before Garn's last breath.

A great anger rose from his bowels, welling up into his chest. Standing up and breathing heavily, he felt intoxicated. Swaying slightly, he uttered murderous threats to despatch the half-crazed man who had cruelly robbed him of his one companion on this terrible adventure. He picked up his spear purposefully and carried his bow in the other hand.

"Why did Garn have to die?" He consciously put his grief aside for a moment. "You crazed man – you will die for this life you have taken!" He strode off towards the enchanted lochan, warrior-like, every sense bristling, anticipating the skirmish.

Stopping suddenly in his deadly tracks, a contrary thought came. "I will not take his life. Killing Gwid would be too good for him. Better to leave him here, haunted, perishing for the rest of his days."

He trotted back and picked up his few possessions. He lifted Garn across his shoulders, wanting to go a long way from the enchanted loch. Every so often, he looked back, checking if he were being followed. Garn was heavy. He shifted the dead weight onto his left shoulder, keeping Garn secure by holding his hind legs. His right hand clasped an arrow shaft, secured to the bowstring; as he strode along, the bow occasionally brushed the taller heather. He reckoned that he could fire an arrow quickly by releasing Garn and grasping the bow shaft with his freed hand.

He suffered Garn's heaviness a long while. He could bury him anywhere, as he had gone a safe distance, but chose to deliberately bear Garn further, as some funereal rite to honour the deceased.

"I have no one in this world now!" he kept repeating.

The more he ached to bear this burden, he believed, the greater the tribute rendered. The sweat ran liberally from his brow, smarting his already grieving eyes.

"You should have remained with Coblaith," he lamented. "You would have had more useful years there to serve your mistress, finishing off what she struck with her bow and retrieving the catch. You would have been great companions, to banish hundreds of lonely evenings. Instead, you have been uselessly slain by a crazed man!"

He bit his lip in remorse. "Oh, it is all so pointless!"

Reaching a glade beside an old river course, he placed Garn into a hollow.

"Your life has gone!" He said over the corpse. "A mere carcass remains."

Recognising Garn's identity was no longer in this lifeless form, he reflected that his own identity had changed since leaving Rhynie. Was there meaning in these transformations? Garn had had a second life through Taran, fresh opportunities that previously had appeared beyond reach. Rhynie was left behind, but he still legitimately bore the Z-rod. Probably it pointed to a different destiny to what had been believed. Could it be greater than being the warlord of his people?

He ran his fingers through the thick, shaggy mane about Garn's neck one final time. Taking the rocks from the old riverbed, he piled these over Garn and raised a fitting cairn.

"It has not been for nothing, Garn. You have taught me whatever the injury, to never give up. That persevering spirit is what I need most. May your spirit go with me, to help fulfil the quest that I have had the misfortune . . . or perhaps my fortune, to be chosen for."

Taran moved off, wounded but not down, feeling indomitable.

Chapter Twenty-One

Fillan's Muintir

556 AD Dindurn

Fillan stood in the waters of a loch in the place that he had considered home these past thirty-seven springs. The shadow of pre-dawn was paling over a land held in sublime stillness, revealing pine forests making for the high ridges. Down in the valley, the hardwoods looked downy as they came into leaf, peering into the waters where snow-capped peaks were mirrored.

> "God, kindle Thou in my heart within
> A flame of love to my neighbour,
> To my foe, to my friend, to my kindred all,
> To the brave, to the knave, to the slave,
> O son of loveliest Mary,
> From the lowliest thing that liveth
> To the name that is highest of all."

Fillan lowered his arms, wearied from being outstretched in their cruciform stance, and waded with some difficulty back to shore. His ashen pale face, almost merging with the shade of his grey hair, gave him an otherworldly aura. His frozen limbs remained largely unresponsive, so his attempt to quicken his pace once on dry ground proved futile. This recent practice of an occasional nightlong vigil in the loch was in deliberate imitation of Father Kessog. He questioned, though, whether this practice was of help to him, especially having reached seventy-four years of age. However, being unsettled of late, he had resorted to this austere discipline to be open to revelation. He felt that restlessness that had characterised his youth, bringing a sense of impatience and mild dissatisfaction over the lack of change and progress.

He walked the plain towards the mighty rock of Dindurn, to where his once single cell had now been multiplied by those who worshipped the God of the Gael from across the sea. The muintir had grown considerably, but he wondered whether it had stagnated and contemplated what more he could do before he went to be with his Lord.

He entered the oratory at their morning hour of worship, still feeling chilled, perceiving a shadow of sickness to hover over him. The usual routine was observed that brought a comfort to his soul through its familiarity. But after their devotions were concluded, he approached Castantin, the only one remaining alive from among his first disciples. He had a special affection for him because the losing of the borrowed axe had brought to light his sometime gift of second sight.

"Castantin, I am feeling somewhat feverish, so I am taking to my bed!"

"Oh?" Castantin uttered, surprised.

"I know – I am just not myself today!"

"Perhaps you should avoid these vigils in the loch – at least for a time."

The abbot nodded. "Come for me before midday. Wake me if I have not stirred by then."

Castantin bowed his head with consent and respect, then left him.

It was not long before Fillan was asleep. He had unsettled dreams, most of which were beyond recall, but they left the impression of commotion and frustration. He sat up to drink some water. Still feeling weak, he lay down once again and prayed.

"O High King of Heaven, grant me renewed vision that our purpose may not become as sluggish as this frail body of mine. May my life not end with a whimper as all faculties diminish and fade into nothingness. Prevent my final time from becoming futile, staled by custom, but quicken my spirit, I pray, that I may be alert to serve your great purposes . . ." His prayers continued with that same anxiety until sleep gathered him up in its current.

He dreamed of further commotion and conflict driven by vain ambition. It concerned one from his own muintir whom he did not recognise, a young man with as noble a bearing as Kessog had in his early years. The dream was disjointed and full of seeming contradictions. He awoke troubled and perplexed, wanting to dismiss the dream but feeling strangely unsettled by it. He prayed, seeking peace with the one who had been his lifelong anam cara. In a subconcious pause, he saw the image of a young man arriving exhausted. His face seemed familiar, not that he had seen him in life, but he had the appearance of the noble one in his dream.

"Ah, Castantin!" he greeted his companion who had come to wake him up. "If I am not mistaken, there is a young man arriving very soon, maybe even today, at the end of an arduous journey, so make the guest cell ready. Once that is prepared, go to the east road beyond Dindurn and await his approach. Make sure he comes directly here and not up to the citadel."

Castantin withdrew.

Fillan felt odd. Others may have visions and dreams but his own were usually unintelligible. However, this one felt significant. He had dreamed when his spirit was seeking fresh direction and therefore it felt especially pertinent, so he could not dismiss it as he normally would.

He busied himself with the remaining routines of the day, looking out for Castantin, but he did not come until after sunset. Castantin reported that no one had come who fitted the description of an exhausted young traveller.

The following morning, Fillan sent Castantin out on to the road again to wait this arrival. "He will have the bearing of a noble Pict," he had added, to help identify the man.

The same happened again – no one had come matching that description.

On the third day, undiminished in his certitude that the young noble would come, he sent Castantin to wait beyond Dindurn's rock on the road coming from the east. Fillan waited impatiently all day, finding it difficult to focus on his tasks. Probably he will arrive this evening, he thought, thinking there was significance in this being the third day and that three had a sense of fullness. He was disappointed when Castantin returned at the day's close, alone.

Undeterred, he sent Castantin back to the designated meeting place on the fourth day. His fellow monk looked somewhat downhearted but obeyed the abbot's order. "I will give it a week for this young man to arrive and if he does not, then I admit my vision was only a meaningless dream."

Fillan recalled something Father Kessog had once said to him. What was it now? Something about a noble who would be hard to disciple, whom the Lord had chosen. He had hoped that prophecy referred to Domech, but the wily warlord appeared fixed in his intransigence.

Taran was walking the final stretch of road towards Dindurn with a limp in his step, when he was greeted by an old man with a druid-like appearance. "Have you come to meet with Fillan?"

He was taken by surprise by this question, which came without preamble and had knowledge of his purpose. "Yes, I have! But what is that to you?"

"I am Castantin – a soldier of Christ. I will lead you to our muintir to meet with our abbot." Unsure how to proceed, the monk asked what was obvious: "Have you had a very long journey?"

"I have been walking nearly a week on the trail!"

The old monk looked him over briefly. "Are you injured?" he asked with some concern.

"No, just exhausted. Why do you ask?"

"There is a fair amount of what looks like dried blood on your plaid!"

"Oh, that! That was a big injury!"

The old man looked at him bemused.

"Some mad man killed my faithful dog. I tried to save its life and I became bloodied."

Seeming to be satisfied with his answer, he enquired in a friendly manner, "What is your name and who is your tribe?"

"I am Drostan of the Ce. You are a Gael, are you not?"

"No! I am a Pict like yourself. Why do you say that?"

Taran hesitated. "Because you do not behave like a Pict!"

Castantin smiled curiously then beckoned to the road. "Come – the muintir is only a short distance away."

"Why were you waiting as though you were expecting me?"

"Fillan, our abbot, had a premonition that you would be coming. He is a holy man, given to strenuous prayer vigils, and he sometimes sees things uncommon to others." The old man related Fillan's knowledge about where the well shaft should be sunk on the rock.

"But tell me," asked Taran, slowing in the road. "Why do you receive total strangers, not knowing who they might be? They could cause you harm."

Castantin smiled, seemingly used to such questions. "Christ can come in all sorts of guises, so we are welcoming and hospitable as if receiving the Lord himself. *'Whenever you did this for one of the least important of these brothers of mine, you did it for me'* are the words he spoke about receiving strangers. We are taught to regard what others might regard common and ordinary as possibly divine."

How odd these people think, he thought.

"Do not worry – what seems strange now, will become clearer in time."

Passing the huge shadow of the rock, they crossed the fields below, entering a gap in the vallum that encircled many cells clustered about the wooden oratory. An old man emerged doubled-up from the low entrance of a simple hut, then straightening himself to full stature, he looked more youthful than his long, grey hair suggested. Taran was struck by his benevolent, wise-looking eyes that greeted him before they diminished in the laughter of a hundred lines. They reminded him of an owl's.

"This is Fillan," said Castantin, who disappeared after a brief exchange.

"Welcome, welcome to our community." Fillan gestured Taran towards a larger hut. On entering, they sat on two wooden benches that formed a V-shape in the corner.

"It is our tradition here," began Fillan, "to welcome all, wherever they are from, and whatever the circumstances that brings people here. Do you come seeking refuge?"

Taran shifted uneasily on the bench.

"Drostan, you are free to talk. Whatever you divulge will be just between you and me. No retribution, just acceptance. We deal with what needs to be confessed before the High King."

"Ossian advised me to come here," began Taran, explaining their recent meeting, adding also some of the circumstances of his leaving the Ce. Fillan listened sagely, occasionally nodding to indicate he was following the narrative, and all the time his owl-like eyes examined him, penetrating through to his core.

They sat in quietness for longer than he felt comfortable with and, not wishing to elaborate further, Fillan broke the silence. "As I said, you are welcome, Drostan. You are safe with us." Then he added meaningfully from under his brows, "And you can be who you want to be."

Taran resisted the urge to shift uncomfortably on the bench.

"Today you are to rest," continued Fillan. "You will stay in the guest house and eat your meals with the *muintir* – it is a concept of family – the foundation upon which our community is built. I will assign you a brother to show you around and explain things. After three days, if you are comfortable to remain, you will join in all our activities, waking early for prayer and meditation, going to the fields, caring for livestock. You will enter into our rhythm, punctuated with worship and study. It is an orderly cycle, reassuring, although it will appear strange at first."

He looked at Taran with slightly knitted brows. "I do not suppose you can read or write?"

"No."

"We will teach you," Fillan responded, with a brightness that made his wrinkled face look young. "Open your heart and mind to learn new things . . ." He paused, before adding emphatically, "Many new things. In time, you will decide whether to leave the old life behind and follow the King. Through repentance comes renewal; a time when you will start seeing the goodness of God in all things."

"And what happens to those who do not adapt?" queried Taran, folding his arms.

"They are free to go! No one is forced, against their will, to remain. Naturally there will be challenges." Fillan looked at him compassionately. "Come, let me assign you a companion – I know just the man, similar in age to yourself."

They emerged from the roundhouse and went to a communal kitchen busy with the preparations for their evening meal.

"Aniel, this is Drostan, newly arrived from the Ce tribe. You are to be his companion and instruct him in our ways."

Aniel looked up with a friendly greeting. "You look hungry," he observed. He stepped aside to a cupboard and, cutting some cheese, he added a piece of bread on a platter. "Here, eat. It will help as the next meal is still some time off."

"Well, I shall leave you two together. Show him to the guest room when he has finished eating."

"And who shall be assigned to be his anam cara?" asked Aniel.

"I will fulfil that role," replied Fillan. Taran noted that the young monk seemed surprised.

The days, and even the nights, were strictly ordered. He felt relieved to put behind him the gruelling treks and the dangers of the wilds, thankful to receive shelter and food after the precarious nature of the past week. He was not destitute and vulnerable like after his escape from the crannog, living in obscurity.

On the third day, Taran had a short interview with Fillan in which it was decided he would remain. Aniel was instructed to take a razor to Taran's hair and make him look like a soldier of Christ. Taran watched his long and wavy forelocks fall to the ground as Aniel scraped the razor across the front of his scalp, in a line from one ear to the other. It felt drastic for a young man who had once prized his dashing appearance, but he surrendered to their ways as the prophecy said would happen in the south. He recognised this was a necessary transition, giving up those feelings of impotency as a powerless prince by taking on a new and strange identity.

Better fortune perhaps awaited him, making a new start by embracing a system that had drive and purpose. Despite the austerity of the ways of the muintir, and the sheer frugality of their meals, which barely nourished, he approved of the disciplined commitment, even though the goal of knowing their God remained something of an enigma.

"You know, learning to be a monk is rather like preparing to be a warrior!" he remarked to Aniel as they were weeding a field.

"How do you mean?"

"Well, soldiers of Christ have a strong discipline to work and to learn and to worship. There is a time and place for everything, except idleness. Even sleep is interrupted by attending prayers in the middle of the night! In my youth, I was forced to conform to a strict regime under my foster father, learning every form of martial combat, how to campaign, how to forage in the wilds and to undergo rigorous physical training."

"It is a discipline to be worthy soldiers of Christ."

Taran considered his friend's reply and nodded with approval. He would apply the same attitude here in Dindurn, to conform and be disciplined, as he had done for his military training. He had no alternative option and he respected Ossian's choice that this was a necessary stage to progress him forward. The farm labouring was already familiar, and he enjoyed the simplicity of honest, hard work. He also embraced the psalm singing, which although very different from the songs Elpin had taught him, brought that sense of togetherness when people sang. He valued being in community after the months of living with Elpin and Coblaith.

The strange quietness about the brotherhood, on the other hand, was hard to adjust to, especially the reverential stillness when listening to the reading of scripture or hearing the lengthy prayer routines. He understood none of this at first, with it mostly being in Latin. Then he came to view it as a thing of sublime mystery, necessary in worshipping a foreign God. It felt as strange as Maelchon's supplications when he slipped into the ancient tongue. Even when not engaging in acts of devotion, their lives were uncommonly disciplined, characterised by a sobriety he had not encountered before and was unsure of whether he could be like-minded. He missed the cheer of jovial comrades, the wise cracks of teasing friends.

"It is strange," continued Taran, airing aloud his feelings, "even the chores we do – digging, fetching water, chopping wood – you perform like acts of veneration!"

Aniel smiled with understanding. "I know, brother. When you see it as a task that just needs to be done, it can become irksome and you can feel frustrated by the tedium. But when you think that the simple task is 'as though serving the king himself,' it takes on a new significance.

Greater care and pride are taken. It becomes an act of devotion, a glad offering of skill and strength."

Taran shook his head with a little incredulity, understanding the concept but not sharing the outlook.

"Drostan – why did you turn your back on being a warrior?"

"Uh, killing is something that bothers me."

"Have you killed anyone?" asked Aniel with curiosity.

"Just one person." He paused, uncomfortable with this disclosure. "I should say two, for I had intent to murder another, and had almost carried it out, when I was constrained. Maybe it was Christ who stopped my hand from slaying a wretch who killed my dog!" In his mind, he added Oengus as a third person he would kill. Am I truly uncomfortable, then, about murdering?

"And what about you?"

"Me? No, I was never a warrior, just an ordinary peasant who turned to Christ."

"I know that! But have you never struck another in anger?"

"I have. I was not always gentle before, especially when I had had a drink!" His face clouded with the recollection.

"Come in, Drostan – take a seat," invited Fillan, some months into his time in the muintir. "Tell me, how do things fare with you?"

"I remain thankful to have found this safe haven. Truly, it is a place of peace from the enmity of the world," remarked Taran. He then added to himself: and beyond the eye and pursuit of my enemies.

Fillan looked at him searchingly. It was not an unkindly look. Taran felt a little uncomfortable. Do I have to be more guarded even with my thoughts?

"What enmity do you have in mind?"

"Oh, just the jostling for position, the making of a living – that kind of thing." His hand made a dismissive gesture.

The abbot stared without expression. Perhaps aware of this penetrative gaze, he seemed to make the effort to smile, a broadening and peaceful smile.

"How is your understanding of Latin?"

"I believe I am making progress. When I first arrived, I did not have a single word!"

"It takes time and a good deal of diligence," Fillan encouraged. "All monks try to master the tongue of the Romans. I have seen that your writing skills are developing . . . it shows you are persevering. As the scriptures say, *perseverance produces character, and character, hope*!"

The abbot produced a book, and passing it to Taran, indicated from where to read. He listened with patience, sometimes even pleasure, at the stuttering effort that was far from fluent, yet remained intelligible.

"Do you understand what you read?"

"Just some words, here and there. The general sense is still hidden from me."

Fillan went over a section, carefully explaining the meaning in Pictish, concluding with some spiritual instruction.

"I have noticed that you like labouring in the fields and caring for the herds. It surprises me, for you are of noble birth."

That came as no surprise to him for Coblaith had guessed that immediately.

"There is something in your manner that reminds me of Kessog, one-time prince of Cashel and my anam cara."

"As you rightly observe, I was not brought up to farm – but it does satisfy me." He elaborated on what he enjoyed about caring for the land and herd.

"And how are you getting along with your brothers?"

"Without discord I would say."

"Aniel seems to be close?"

"Yes, we have got on well from the beginning. There is no guile in him!"

"That is a strange thing to say! Hopefully, you will not find guile within the muintir . . . although I am under no illusions as to it being the perfect community." Fillan looked out of the tiny window in their cell and spoke without turning to Taran. "What would you say, is the thing that challenges you most, besides Latin?"

Taran thought for a minute. "Perhaps feeling hungry all the time!" He laughed nervously, although he was in earnest.

"It is a discipline, is it not! We practise austerity, to conquer every appetite . . ." The abbot took the opportunity to teach about their various spiritual practices, which Taran listened to carefully, answering questions when asked, but not offering any contrary opinion; for although there were natural objections, he understood and respected the need for discipline to become a useful soldier of Christ.

"And now let me pray for you," Fillan indicated, concluding a familiar routine. The prayer was lengthy and unworthy of note until its conclusion. "May your hand, heavenly Father, shape Drostan, a warrior of a man, to be like Kessog. Make him a spiritual prince, serving your kingdom. Train his mouth to speak heavenly words, with the same proud skill his warrior hand can wield a sword. Raise his courage, to storm the ranks of the enemy, even if he should be the only man left standing in the assault."

Fillan paused long enough for Taran to glance up. The abbot proceeded in a slightly higher pitch and more animated.

"I believe you have a special task for Drostan, a series of assignments to acquire seven graces to become the warrior who still stands after all the powers of this world and hell itself has been unleashed. Drostan," Fillan addressed him, making him look up only to find the abbot was still praying.

"May these be acquired:
mercy to confound the foe,
and to bind up the injured;
humility and perseverance as characteristics
to be known by and be outstanding in.
Render your sword in surrender
so that obedience to the King will be complete
and thereby, to be rid of all pride so as to love totally.
May valour, to champion the oppressed, be for
your renown;
and peace abundant when considering apparent failure;
hope to prove firm in the face of despair;
and faithfulness to lead to the very ends of the earth.
Where there is loss, may gain be known;
with ill repute, the High King's approval;
where there is disgust, the favour of the Almighty;
and when in poverty to perceive the riches of the
Everlasting's glory.
And so be it – Amen."

A quietness enveloped the cell, like water that has plummeted over a cascade grows calm in a deep pool. It felt like he was immersed and held in buoyant suspension. He straightened himself, emerging almost as if from an awakening, a homecoming to the ordinary, to all as it should be, in the tingling stillness of the cell.

"Arise, Lord Drostan, your destiny calls; a glorious one, although fraught with dangers and immense challenges. But for now, you still have much preparation and the testing of a great trial."

What did he mean? He felt Fillan observing him, looking on with compassion. He blinked, his eyes adjusting to the light. Partially unfocussed, he was drawn to the slow, gentle flow of the sunlit particles of dust, lazily drifting the room.

"Although much lies ahead, your pilgrimage has already begun. There are seven graces to acquire – the biblical number of completeness – and a further two graces can be added to make nine, the sacred number for us Celts. I think you will know more than I about how this is so."

Fillan looked at him kindly, perhaps with an understanding recalled from his own youthful pilgrimage from Erin that Fillan occasionally referred to when considering the adjustment to a strange place.

"Your character has been shaped through perseverance – the first of the graces and one that as a warrior, you will prize, as I have learned from the life example of dear Kessog from his former days as prince. And the second, humility, I would suspect has been something of an unfolding enigma for you."

Although this talk probed his life, his past and future, Taran did not feel uncomfortable to be the focus this time, recognising the undeniable character of the prophetic. In the heady confusion of what all of this meant, he remembered recent feelings of total impotency when forced to take on the alias of Drostan and throw his lot in with Coblaith. That utter powerlessness to change the big course of events had disarmed him of any guile. It had opened him to petition, once to the Bulàch and now to Christ. Vision and prophecy counted when bereft of influence. It forced one to pass through a portal, away from the chicaneries of this world, into the sunlit stillness of another realm, bigger, that enveloped and impacted the kingdom of men. Although ignorant of what his future role would take, he knew that his progress would be proportionate to his ability to recall and to follow, to dare and not to shrink back from the spectres that shadowed his path. For a moment, the heroic nature of this call enthralled, and in the next moment appalled. It was like stepping out on to a knife-like ridge with profound drops on either side. Somehow it was possible to traverse, but the odds looked stacked against his succeeding.

"Humility is the attitude required to learn; to receive heavenly enabling. But this is not a first, is it, Drostan?"

Fillan leant forward, fixing him with that penetrating gaze of a holy man to read the soul of another.

"The humility which constrained you as a prince to become a peasant, is the manner to progress as a monk. My son, you are here for just a wee while, so learn well whilst you have others to instruct you. In a short time, your destiny will lead you to the west if you do not stand in the way of it."

Excerpt from Part Two of the Z-Rod

Taran became aware of a shadowy form following them. He looked back and saw a large bulk of a person running towards them.

"It is Aniel with another coracle," enlightened the abbot. "Go! Run, for you are quicker than me, and wait for me at the edge of the woods on the southern corner of the loch."

Taran ran briskly. A three-quarter moon emerged from behind a cloud, illuminating the meadow. Taran made towards a dark shadowy line of tall trees along the edge of the pasture. Looking back, he noted the far off muintir gathered in darkness. A strong breeze blowing down the strath turned back the leaves and made the branches clatter vigorously. Shadows stirred fleetingly and imagining Domech's men closing in on him, he ran in earnest. He reached the woods above the loch and waited. His laboured breathing began to subside. Aniel then arrived, followed not that long after by Fillan.

"Take both coracles close to the water but wait concealed among the shrubs," the abbot instructed. Aniel left.

"Here is a satchel full of provisions for your journey, complete with knife, tinder, flint, food and clothes from your cell." The abbot passed him the leather bag. "I have been concerned for your salvation, even before you confessed to worshipping the Bulàch. I have often wondered what the outcome would be and have been confused by the premonition about your coming, suggesting you would be a great soldier of Christ."

Fillan fixed him earnestly with his gentle eyes. "I still choose to believe this will become true. But, you need to rid yourself of this destructive revenge and give up all hope of regaining your lost kingdom. You are an intelligent man, although I do not fully understand how you could have been taken in by Domech!"

"I was flattered and therefore duped. Domech made it sound plausible, with him being in effect, master over the Circinn . . ."

The old saint interrupted. "Domech is no master over the Circinn!"

"But he told me of a great victory won when the Circinnian nobles were in chains and Domech could have had them all decapitated."

"No such thing happened. The Circinnian power is at least equal to that of the Fotla, if not greater. You were told what you wanted to hear and were gullible enough to believe. Anyway, no time for recriminations now. Relinquish all thought about becoming warlord over the Ce. It is not to be – do you hear me? Yours is a higher calling!"

"What could be a higher calling?" he stated.

"That will become clear once you have seen the King in all his glory. Such a vision will strip away all worldly ambition and give you a heart for greater things.

"Listen carefully, we have so little time and you must be away!" Fillan's tone was clipped, making it the more surprising when the abbot added, "But first, I will pray for you." He did not pray for long and his prayer showed as much concern for Taran's spiritual salvation as for his physical safety.

"I have an instruction for you," added Fillan, placing a hand upon Taran's shoulder. "You are to take the course of white martyrdom."

"What is that?" he asked dubiously, fearing adventures involving tribulation were about to recommence.

"White martyrdom is what I undertook along with Kessog. It is a leaving of home, of all that is familiar, forsaking all security, in an abandonment to the will of the High King. At its heart is a pursuit to know him profoundly. Your white martyrdom will take you west to Dal Riata. Make for Dunadd and present this note to the king."

He took a small roll of parchment from the abbot.

"He will assist you in your quest. At the earliest opportunity, take a boat north along the coast, to territories beyond Dal Riata, to a Pictish place of pilgrimage. In a picture, I saw a conical shaped peak rising from a whale back of a hill that forms an island. The conical peak is distinctive, looking like its top has been sliced at an angle by a giant sword. Make for the peak which, I hope, is to become the place of your renewal."

Taran listened with incredulity, marking all his words, keen not to forget any detail.

"The purpose of your pilgrimage is different from that of the Picts. This is your opportunity to know the King and to pursue your destiny. That destiny has something about . . ." He paused. A puzzled expression came across his face as he pronounced, "something about 'bearing fire to the north'."

The hairs on the back of Taran's neck stood on end, making him suddenly declare. "I do not dismiss any of what you are saying." He stopped involuntarily, choked by emotion. "I have been slow to learn, unwilling to walk the path of obedience. Please forgive me!"

"Seek the forgiveness of the King who has a significant purpose for you to fulfil. Now make all haste – you will reach Cartray tomorrow where Ronan will help send you on your way with fresh provisions. Aniel knows the way west, a journey that goes by a hamlet of believers near the great Loch Lengwartha. They too will supply your needs for your journey westward beyond Lengwartha to Loch Lumon and over the narrow neck of land that will lead to the sea. There, take a boat bound for Dal Riata. Do not overnight in any of these places because Domech will have his men on your trail and will guess this course."

"Is there no alternative route?"

"There is, but it is wild and we do not have friends to help you that way. But remember however far the journey may be that *'two people shorten the road'* and an unseen third will make it safe. Go with all haste and you will outrun Domech's men – they will not pursue beyond their own territory because you do not mean that great a deal to Domech other than acquiring silver and gaining the favour of the Circinn and the Ce."

Glossary

With many of the original Brittonic/Pictish place names forgotten, educated guesses have been made using the Brittonic (Old Welsh) equivalent of current Gaelic names. Although little is currently known about Pictish language, it did have its linguistic variations from the rest of ancient Britain, and these differences, when known, have been used. The pronunciation has been phonetically transliterated (at the expense of correct spellings that are complicated to pronounce for non-Welsh speakers) to help with the flow and enjoyment of the drama. Besides, as the Picts were largely an illiterate people, they would not have had approved spellings.

Alt Clud – Brittonic for 'rock on the Clyde' which is how the inhabitants of the rock referred to Din Brython; modern day Dumbarton.

Candida Casa – monastery, founded by Ninian, in modern day Whithorn, Galloway.

Cartray – 'the town of the fort' in recognition of the Roman garrison at modern day Callander that lay in ruins at the time of our story. Callander is an anglicisation derived from Gaelic, Calasraid, with different possible meanings.

Craig Padrig – Craig Phadrig in Gaelic, stronghold of the Fortriu at the top of the Great Glen, above modern-day Inverness.

Dal Riata – Scots kingdom in modern-day Argyll.

Din Brython – Literally 'Fort of the Britons', capital of Strath Clud (Strathclyde), also known as Alt Clud; modern day Dumbarton.

Dindurn – hillfort of the Fotla Picts, near St Fillans, Perthshire.

Din Eidyn – Edinburgh, hillfort and centre of power for the Britons of Goddodin.

Dinottar – Dunottar fort, a Pictish stronghold upon the cliffs near modern day Stonehaven.

Druim Alba – mountainous country separating Dal Riata from the Picts.

Dunadd – hillfort capital of Dal Riata, near modern day Kilmartin.

Erin – (Ireland) divided into sub kingdoms, e.g. Munster – Connacht – Leinster etc.

Goddodin – Northern Briton kingdom in current SE Scotland.

Loch Gunalon – Loch Earn, derived from the Gaelic: Eireann, simplified as 'Erin' (Ireland). I have used the Welsh for 'Loch of the Irish', referring possibly to the Irish monks who passed up this water to approach Dindurn, hillfort of the Fotla Picts.

Loch Lengwartha – Loch Katrine, literally meaning loch of the cattle hustlers.

Loch Lumon – Loch Lomond.

Manau or Maetae – a one-time eminent people group in Roman times, confined in 6th century AD to the environs of modern-day Stirling, with their fort at Dumyat.

Minamoyn Goch – The Cairngorm Mountains, which are otherwise much lesser known by their Gaelic name:

Am Monadh Ruadh, 'the red hills'. 'Minamoyn Goch' is a Brittonic rendering of 'the red hills'.

Mounth – Grampian Mountains, dividing northern and southern Picts.

Nendrum – early monastic settlement on an island on Strangford Lough, in modern day Northern Ireland.

Rheged – Kingdom of Britons south of Strath Clud.

Rhynie – seat of the Ce warlords.

Strath Clud – Strathclyde.

Ucheldi Ucha – a Brittonic rendering of 'Upper Highland', the meaning of Auchterarder.

Y Broch – major seat of power for the Fortriu Picts, now modern-day Burghead.

Definition of other words

Anam Cara – soul mate, denoting a mentor.

Angle – Saxon – Jute – Germanic tribes who established themselves in current day England.

Bairns – children.

Bannock – a round, flat bread baked on a sandstone slab in the early historical period.

Beli Mawr – Celtic sun god.

Beltane – early summer pagan festival.

Brae – a slope.

Brigantia – the transformation of the Bulàch (mother earth goddess) from the old hag into the young maiden at springtime, known as 'Bride' to the Gaels.

Briton – the indigenous Celtic peoples of Britain before the arrivals of Angles, Saxons and Jutes.

Broch – an Iron-age tower with double walls, two to three storeys in height, occupied by high status people for domestic and defensive purposes.

Bulàch – probably Brittonic/Pictish for 'old hag' or 'witch', the mother earth goddess known by the Gaels as the Cailleach, and in 20th century Scotland, as 'Beira'. The Bulàch transforms herself into the youthful goddess 'Brigantia' come spring, when the Bulàch drinks from the well of eternal youth.

Coracle – a light craft for one person made of stitched and pitched animal hides stretched over a wooden frame.

Currach – a leather craft, larger than the coracle, powered by rowers and a sail.

Din – dun, an Iron-age hillfort.

Gael – refers to a speaker of Gaelic, the language of the Irish and of Dal Riata.

Lughnasa – the harvest festival.

Muintir – Christian community – colony of heaven, also known as a monastery, a term avoided as it gives an unhelpful impression of a medieval equivalent far removed from the basic building structure used in this early time.

Oratory – the simple chapel in the centre of the monastic community.

Ostara – the spring equinox festival.

Pict – the indigenous peoples north of the Forth-Clyde divide.

Pictish Tribes (7): **Fortriu – Fotla – Fib – Fidach – Cait – Ce – Circinn** [see map]

Saint – an early biblical term for a Christian pilgrim, not referring to the special holy status conferred on an individual by papal decree.

Samhainn – Halloween festival.

Scriptorium – a dedicated place where illuminated scripts were prepared.

Strath – a long, wide valley.

Torc – a neck ring adornment worn by high-status warriors.

Vallum – an earth mound about a settlement.

Vellum – parchment.

Yule – end of year pagan festival.

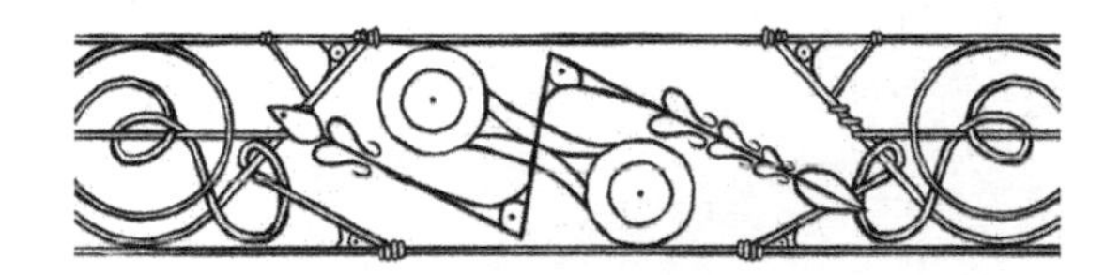

Pictish Tribes (7): Fortriu – Fotla – Fib – Fidach – Cait – Ce – Circinn [see map]

Saint – in early [illegible] a term for a Christian pilgrim, not referring to [illegible] status [illegible] individual [illegible]

Samhain – Halloween festival

scriptorium – a dedicated place where illuminated scripts were produced

Strath – a long, wide valley

torc – neck ring adornment worn by high-status warriors

[illegible] about a settlement

Vellum – parchment

Yule – end of year pagan festival